Edward Ellis Morris

A Memoir of George Higinbotham

An Australian Politician and Chief Justice of Victoria

Edward Ellis Morris

A Memoir of George Higinbotham
An Australian Politician and Chief Justice of Victoria

ISBN/EAN: 9783337134006

Printed in Europe, USA, Canada, Australia, Japan

Cover: Foto ©Raphael Reischuk / pixelio.de

More available books at **www.hansebooks.com**

A MEMOIR

OF

EORGE HIGINBOTHAM

AN AUSTRALIAN POLITICIAN
AND CHIEF JUSTICE OF VICTORIA

BY

EDWARD E. MORRIS

London
MACMILLAN AND CO.
AND NEW YORK
1895

RICHARD CLAY AND SONS, LIMITED,
LONDON AND BUNGAY.

PREFACE

My picture is finished, and I can add no more little touches to it. No longer can I paint out this bit nor paint in that, nor can I add brighter colours to the background to make the central figure clearer. Probably every painter, when he reaches this point, recognises in himself a mixed feeling,—pleasure that his work is completed, and doubt whether it expresses all that he wished it to express. With me the doubt is the stronger feeling. I know that I have not accomplished what I wished and that I shall not satisfy friends and admirers; but yet I trust that the portrait is like and that the surroundings are made clear. I have done what I could.

I wish heartily to thank the many friends who have helped in my work. The names of some are given at various points in the book; the names of others are withheld at their own request. Without this help, which was readily given, I could not have done as much as I have. I thank all who have helped me with sympathy, with advice, with information.

The following letter, which was not addressed to me but to another, from the veteran Sir George Grey of New Zealand, will be read with interest :—

I entertained a great admiration for the late Chief Justice Higinbotham. On one occasion when a difficulty had arisen with the Maoris, at my suggestion he was invited by the Government to come to New Zealand to act as arbitrator, and at great inconvenience to himself he had consented to come. Political changes unfortunately put an end to the proposal. But it is my belief that, if that good man had come to New Zealand, much bloodshed would have been avoided, so highly was he respected by all parties.

It is a matter of regret to me to add that I have not been able to discover the date or any details of this matter.

The two likenesses in this book—one of Mr. Higinbotham as Attorney-General, the other as Chief Justice—are reproduced from photographs by Messrs. Johnstone O'Shannessy and Company, Limited, of Collins Street, Melbourne.

EDWARD E. MORRIS.

January 15, 1895.

TABLE OF CONTENTS

INTRODUCTION

It has long been an object of my ambition to write the life of George Higinbotham. It was my good fortune to know him intimately during the last fourteen years of his life, and with perfect freedom to discuss with him political, social and literary topics as they arose. Though I have been told that he hesitated to discuss religious questions with the same freedom lest he should hurt my feelings, I never noticed this hesitation, and I am inclined to claim that I knew his whole mind better than any one who is now alive. Yet, I never ventured to mention my project to him, for there was not a little reason to fear that he would have forbidden it. He was a very modest man, and could not be brought to believe that others were interested in him or in his views. He was shocked at the indiscreet revelations in some modern biographies, and left behind him a memorandum dated April, 1874, requesting that all his manuscript books and accounts should be destroyed without being read or examined by any one but his wife. Ten years later the request was renewed in another memorandum :—" All my MS. books and old diaries," " all political and professional remains and papers," " without delay," were " to be burnt." These are strong words, and the wish expressed in them was religiously carried out. With the wish to write the life strong within me, I assisted in the burning, knowing that I was destroying material which would have been of priceless value to a biographer.

Then came the question whether, under such circumstances, it was right for me to undertake a biography at all, and this question caused me great searching of heart. It was quite certain that a life or lives would appear. More than one was planned, and in three cases I was consulted, in two application was made to me for assistance. By several, I might almost say by many, friends, I was urged to undertake the work, because, as they said, I was the most fit from my knowledge of Mr. Higinbotham's life and views to perform it. As his son-in-law, I had to consider whether it was better that the life should be written by a member of the family or one not connected with it. After due reflection, I decided to accept the office at the same time painful and pleasant, and to do my utmost to give to the world a true picture of one who was much misunderstood, who was often praised on wrong grounds and blamed on wrong grounds, but whose name and memory have a fascination for many Australians.

One very able and enthusiastic notice of George Higinbotham's life that appeared immediately after he was taken from us was headed "The Greatest of Australia's Dead." Without any comparison with other eminent Australians, the mere fact that this view is widely entertained makes it right to face the question whether the natural modesty of a great man, even if it had expressed itself in a wish that his life should not be written, is a sufficient reason for obedience to that wish. In Mr. Higinbotham's case no such wish was ever expressed, and perhaps for the sufficient reason that the idea never occurred to him as likely; but if it had been, ought it to command obedience? Thackeray one day in disgust at a biography which was all adulation and undeserved praise, tapped the book, and said to his daughter: "When I am gone, I hope nothing like this will be written about me."

That daughter is a singularly capable writer, and has written delightfully of others, gracefully and with due reticence, but love-loyal to her father's least wish she has refrained from writing his life. Unauthorised biographies have of course appeared, but through that remark of the novelist English Literature is the poorer. It would not be right that biographies should only be written of those who were not modest and retiring. Mr. Higinbotham had much to do with the early days of constitutional government in the Australian colonies. He was connected with more than one important controversy as to political principles, and as to the relations between the mother-country and the colonies. These controversies are important as history, and, as according to the proverb, history repeats itself, they may some day be important again in politics. His work in consolidation of the statute law on two separate occasions, once when he was Attorney-General, once when he was Chief Justice, deserves to be duly recorded, as well as his views on the further subject of codification. But the influence and character of the man were more important than acts or views, and it seems to me a solemn duty to strive as far as in me lies to set these forth for the admiration of those who did not know him as I did, and for the coming generations.

I asked one of his sons, now in Dublin, what he thought about my undertaking this memoir, and his answer runs : " I am quite certain that to suppose it would be against my father's wishes to write and publish his life is quite erroneous, and arises from not understanding him. If he could be asked, my father would say : 'If the people of Victoria wish it, I do not withhold my consent.'"

The University, Melbourne, *October*, 1893.

MEMOIR OF GEORGE HIGINBOTHAM

CHAPTER I

FAMILY HISTORY

The name Higinbotham—Of Dutch Origin—Ancestor at the Battle of
the Boyne—Quartermaster Thomas Higinbotham—His Estate—
Andrew—Henry—Miss Verner—The Father, Henry Higinbotham
—The Mother, Sarah Wilson, and her Father, Joseph Wilson,
a Friend of George Washington.

THROUGHOUT Australia the name of Higinbotham has been
so long well known, and those who have borne it so highly
respected, that it does not excite in Australian minds the
same feeling of oddity that the name produces in the minds
of others when they hear it first. Though not spelt and not
pronounced exactly in the same way, it is practically the same
name as that which the authors of the *Rejected Addresses*
bestowed on the dauntless fireman, and to which they found
so quaint a rhyme. It is one of the names that in his first
Essay in Criticism the fastidious Mr. Matthew Arnold
mentions as showing, on the part of our English stock, an
"original shortcoming in the more delicate spiritual percep-
tions." The origin of the name is not absolutely certain, but
it is probably a popular corruption of a Dutch name. English
soldiers in India made the peculiarly English-looking Hobson-
Jobson out of the native cries Hosein, Hassan. In the same
way the Irish of the Pale made a name which assumed something of an English look out of the patronymic of a Dutchman, who came to Ireland in the army of William III. The
Dutch name corrupted is probably Hoogenboom, which would

mean "lofty tree," though there are some who hold that the Dutch word is Eikenboom, answering to the German Eichenbaum, an oak-tree.[1]

Readers of Motley's histories, or those who from other sources know the qualities by which the Dutch won their independence, will recognise the same qualities in George Higinbotham, whose grandfather's grandfather was a Dutchman.

This Dutch ancestor came over to Ireland with William of Orange—William the Liberator, as some prefer to call him —and was present at the Battle of the Boyne. Information comes from a relative that the "spot is still shown on the banks of the river where he, with two others of his comrades, drew Schomberg out of the water." A monument has been erected where Schomberg fell.

Macaulay, in his famous account of the battle, tells us that " Schomberg gave the word. Solmes's Blues "—a regiment of Dutch infantry—"were the first to move. They marched gallantly, with drums beating, to the brink of the Boyne. Then the drums stopped ; and the men, ten abreast, descended into the water." A little later Macaulay tells us that " Schomberg, who had remained on the northern bank, and who had thence watched the progress of his troops with the eye of a general, now thought that the emergency required from him the personal exertion of a soldier. Those who stood about him besought him in vain to put on his cuirass. Without defensive armour he rode through the river." This must be the occasion referred to in the family tradition, but it is a little difficult to understand how the three soldiers helped the general out of the water if he was still on horseback. The incident occurred but a short time—only a few minutes indeed—before the gallant Schomberg was killed.

[1] The member of the family who has studied the subject most closely holds that other families, spelling the name with double g, though settled in Ireland, were of English and further back of German origin. In 1665, five years after the Restoration, the will was proved of a certain Hiknebotham "trooper in Captain Staples' regiment." According to this theory there are two names of distinct families, somewhat attracted to each other, and the change is thus indicated :—

Old German. Ickenbaum. Hiknebotham. Higginbotham.
Dutch . . Hoogenboom. Hogenboham. Higinbotham.

In the earlier documents the name is frequently spelt Higinbothom.

The family tradition speaks of three brothers who came over with William of Orange, and declares that one of them settled in Co. Cavan, one in Dublin, and one in Cork. It is not however possible to verify all the details of the tradition, which moreover is confused and divided as to the capacity in which any of the three brothers served in William's army. A diligent search amongst the wills in the Dublin Record Office gives us "Thomas Higinbotham, Quartermaster." The quartermaster is an officer in the army whose duty it is to look after the *quartering* of the troops, the supply of their provisions and similar matters; but the exact rank does not stand clear from the title. In the present day the quartermaster-general is an officer of high rank. It is not however known whether "Quartermaster Thomas Higinbotham "—the title is thus used of him in official records—held that office at the Boyne, nor indeed whether he was actually the warrior of the Boyne or his son. The will of Thomas Higinbotham was proved in 1737, the year in which Gibbon was born, George II. having been ten years on the throne. Between the date of the battle and the death of Thomas there is an interval of nearly fifty years, and in the interval lie all Marlborough's campaigns. It is tantalising to be unable to fill such gaps in history. If Thomas be the Dutchman, the probability is that in the memorable battle he was either a junior officer, or that he fought in the ranks, and that later in life he was promoted to this half civil, half military appointment of quartermaster. The right to a coat of arms attached to his will seems to prove that he was a man of some family position, at least of gentle birth. He is the brother who settled in County Cavan, where he held an estate called Tullymaglowny or Tanamaghlounan, the meaning of which Erse or Keltic name was the shorter English Nutfield. The five-syllabled name is spelt in various ways, and by the middle of the century it had been superseded by the English equivalent. The present importance was not attached to spelling in earlier times, even in the case of proper names, the best instance being the variety of shapes given to the name Shakspeare. No estate was granted to Thomas Higinbotham after the Williamite confiscations, nor does his name stand upon the list of purchasers of confiscated estates, which had been sold by 1702—1703. Nutfield was first leased and then bought by the family. The estate, which is situated in the parish of Drung, Co. Cavan, was about sixty acres in extent, together with four acres of bog-land. No house now exists; only a single arch shows where once the house stood.

Thomas Higinbotham of Tanamaghlounan was the great-great-grandfather of George Higinbotham. The quarter-master had five sons and three daughters. He must have been well off, for each of his sons has house and lands, and in his will he leaves Nutfield to his youngest son Andrew, since the others were already provided for. Andrew Higin-botham is described as "of Nutfield, Co. Cavan, gent."; and his will was proved in 1765, the year in which the Stamp Act for the American colonies was passed. Henry, the second son of Andrew, settled in Dublin, where he lived in Linen Hall Street. His will is dated and was proved in 1789, the date of the beginning of the French Revolution. This Henry married a young widow lady named Dobbs, whose maiden name was Jane Verner. Married to Mr. Dobbs in the last week of January 1773, she was a widow by the end of June. Miss Verner's maternal grandfather was a captain of cavalry at the battle of the Boyne. She was an aunt of Sir William Verner, a lieutenant-colonel under Wellington in the later battles of the Peninsular War, and severely wounded at Waterloo, who did not die until 1871 at the ripe age of eighty-nine, having for his political services to the Conservative party been made a baronet in 1845. His place of residence was Church Hill, Armagh, where this lady, George Higinbotham's paternal grandmother, was brought up, but she was married a dozen years before her nephew was born. Mr. Henry Higinbotham had three sons and three daughters. Two of the sons were employed at Dublin Castle, one, if not both of them, in the Secretaryship. The youngest son, Henry Higinbotham, was for many years a merchant of the City of Dublin. His town residence was at 4, Mountjoy Square, then the fashionable part of Dublin. In his political views and sympathies Mr. Henry Higinbotham belonged to the old-fashioned Conservative school: he was a strong loyalist of the Church and State type. One who knew him well describes him as possessing the same charm of manner and sweetness of character that distinguished his son. He had six sons and two daughters; and the youngest of his eight children is the subject of the present memoir, born in Dublin on April 19, 1826.

Heredity, however, must not be traced only on one side. George Higinbotham's mother's maiden name was Sarah Wilson. The Wilsons were of Scotch origin and mostly "children of the manse." They moved into Ireland with the wave of Presbyterian emigration from Scotland, and belong rather to Ulster than to any more southern part of Ireland. Towards the end of the last century, about the time of the French Revolution or a little before, Mr. Joseph Wilson married a Miss Rose Anne Moore, a great beauty known in her day as the "belle of the north." This Mr. Joseph Wilson had travelled far, and had resided in Philadelphia for some years. There he was acquainted with George Washington, with whose political aspirations he was in strong sympathy. After the War of Independence he became an American citizen, and when afterwards he returned to live in Dublin, he was for some years the American Consul in Dublin, and when he died his son succeeded to the position. According to the doctrine that a mother's qualities pass to the sons and a father's to the daughters, George Higinbotham inherited much from his maternal grandfather. Mr. Joseph Wilson is described as a man of strong common sense and fine judgment. His religious sympathies were Unitarian, and his political principles strongly Liberal at a time when, owing to the violent recoil caused by the French Revolution, Liberalism was most unpopular. So recently had he been hostile to Great Britain that his sympathies are said to have been with the Irish Rebellion of the end of the last century. Of course as an American Consul he could not do more than give his sympathy to the defeated cause. On this latter point, however, it is advisable to add a caution. His grandson's views on the Irish Rebellion are not reported, but his views upon the present struggle with respect to the government of Ireland were clear and distinct. A warm friend to Ireland, he was strongly in favour of the Union, and opposed to Home Rule, especially feeling the strongest disapproval of the means adopted by the followers of Mr. Parnell.

Mr. Joseph Wilson died in 1809, and two years later his only daughter married Mr. Henry Higinbotham.

Mr. Wilson's family possess a portrait of George Washington, and the family tradition runs that Washington stood for the picture to please his friend. Washington is represented standing in a blue coat with brass buttons, wearing a sort of military headgear. In his hand he holds the scroll of American independence, whilst the British flag lies prostrate, if not exactly at, yet near his feet.[1] As Mrs. Henry Higinbotham was the only daughter of this American Consul, it is natural to think that she called her youngest son after the great American, " first in war, first in peace, and first in the hearts of his countrymen." This, however, is only surmise, and not based on evidence.

[1] I regret to find that no mention is made of this picture in the careful account of Washington portraits at the end of Justin Winsor's *History of America*, vol. vii.

CHAPTER II

Royal School of Dungannon—Its History—The Headmaster, Rev. J. R. Darley—His Farewell Speech—Testimony of Sir F. Darley—Thrashing of a Bully—Queen's Scholarship—Trinity College, Dublin—Higinbotham's Record—It Lacks its Crown—Mrs. Brougham—Reminiscences of Dean of Lismore.

ENVIRONMENT and education are factors in the production of a man as important as heredity. We have now to consider the formal parts of the education of George Higinbotham. Having received a very careful early training at home, he went to school at Dungannon and then to college at Trinity, Dublin.

The Royal School of Dungannon was founded on April 20th, 1614. This is claimed on the prospectus of the school; but characteristically enough it was not founded at Dungannon, but at another place, Mountjoy, on the shores of Lough Neagh. It seems that at the Plantation of Ulster in the reign of King James I., when the greater part of six counties was parcelled out amongst English and Scottish settlers, some of the confiscated estates which had escheated to the Crown in that province were conveyed to the Archbishop of Armagh in trust to maintain grammar schools for the education of youth in learning and religion. Four schools were founded, ever afterwards known as the Royal Schools, all situated in Ulster and all exclusively Protestant. The school at Mountjoy continued there for over a century, and was transplanted to Dungannon, in 1720. The present school buildings were erected about 1790. There have been considerable additions to them of late years, bringing the school up to the level of modern requirements, but the principal parts of the buildings were the same during the first half of the present century as they are now.

One of the modern requirements of a school with any pretension to be a public school, is the keeping of records; but apparently in those days it was not thought to be important. No record of admissions has been preserved, but from a private source it has been ascertained that his years were between thirteen and fourteen when George Higinbotham entered the Dungannon School. In December, 1841, his name occurs in a prize list as having obtained "10 Premiums," but unfortunately the exact meaning of a "premium" is not recorded. At an English public school ten would be considered a large number of prizes, but as many as nine boys in the Dungannon list obtained more than ten, amongst whom is "Douse, 15." In spite of the variation in spelling this schoolfellow was afterwards the humorous M.P., and later Chief Baron Dowse. From the order of names in the list it would appear as if Higinbotham, then aged 15½, was drawing nigh to the head of the school, for only five names are printed before his.

The headmaster of the Royal School, Dungannon, from the beginning of 1831 for a period of nearly twenty years, was the Rev. John Richard Darley,[1] himself a pupil of the school. Mr. Darley after giving up the school was a parish clergyman for nearly a quarter of a century, and then he was elected Bishop of Kilmore, being the second Irish bishop elected after the Disestablishment of the Irish Church. Under Mr. Darley the Royal School of Dungannon, sometimes incorrectly called Dungannon College, held a very high reputation, and was considered to be the first of all Irish schools. He was evidently a good schoolmaster of an old-fashioned type, and published works on the Grecian drama and on Homer. On the present prospectus of the school, beneath a coat of arms bearing a castle gate, there hangs a laurel-crowned bundle of books, which are labelled respectively Horace, Geometry, Xenophon, and English Literature. The last is certainly a modern addition to the bundle. In the two decades when Mr. Darley was headmaster the curriculum

---

[1] Born 1799, and died 1884.

consisted chiefly of the classics, tempered by a little mathe
matics. Education was in the pre-Arnoldian era, though the
hero of this memoir was sixteen when Arnold died. It was
not until after Arnold's death that the new influence spread
to other schools than Rugby, and it was naturally some time
before it crossed St. George's Channel. It is not attaching
blame to Mr. Darley to say that he was of his own period.
The following quotation from the speech which he made to
the boys when he left Dungannon conveys an image of the
man he was:

For twenty-four years, four at Dundalk and twenty at Dungannon,
the Lord has prospered my work. My school has been uniformly
successful. The greatest love and affection have existed between my
pupils and myself. Never have they done anything intentionally in
word or deed to give me the slightest pain or annoyance. Their
conduct has been most exemplary, their success in college most
distinguished. Many are now distinguished members of the church,
of the bar, of the army. Many have fallen asleep in the Lord and
are now happy members of the church above in glory. And to what
do I attribute this great success? Not to any peculiar talents or
acquirements of my own, but simply to this, that I have ever based
education on the Word of God, that I have made the circulation of
Gospel truth of paramount importance and that I have daily instructed
my dear pupils in the Holy Scriptures.

It is natural that when a man is abandoning a work in
which he has spent many happy years, his heart should be
open, and that he should perhaps exaggerate a little. A well-
known English schoolmaster on a similar occasion said, that
recently with one pen he had signed 500 reports, and not one
that was not good: whereupon the comment rises—then they
could not all have been true. The doctrine of the corruption
of human nature held by both these clergymen, or even the
law of average requires that there should be some naughty
boys.

Sir Frederick Darley, the Chief Justice of New South
Wales, was under his uncle at the Royal School, Dungannon,
and being asked for his memories of the school at the time
when his brother Chief Justice was there, kindly wrote:

I was at Dungannon College with the late Chief Justice, but for a
short time only. I regret to say that my recollection of that time, over
fifty-two years ago, is rather dim. When I went to Dungannon in
October, 1840, the Chief Justice had been there for some time, and had

acquired a good position and obtained much influence in the school. I recollect I entertained for him the most profound respect, and although there were older boys there he then appeared to me to stand head and shoulders over all others in every good and manly quality. He was a great favourite, particularly with the younger boys. School life in those days was a rough one, and I well recollect the Chief Justice on more than one occasion interfering for the protection of little boys when bullied. I was then a little fellow about ten years of age, and I know he frequently befriended me.

There is one story which can, I believe, be authenticated. A little boy appeared in the school in a garment of which he was very proud, because it was remarkable for a great display of buttons. It occurred to a big boy that it would be humorous to remove the buttons, and much to the little boy's distress he carried out his joke, whereupon George Higinbotham intervened like one of Homer's avenging deities, and thrashed the big boy. It is said that in after years all three of the persons of this little drama were in Australia, but they did not meet to renew their memories of it. Having heard the story, I told it to my father-in-law; but he would not acknowledge it, and put it aside with a laugh.

At the Examination for Queen's Scholarships, recently held in the University, Mr. GEORGE HIGINBOTHAM, a Pupil of *Dungannon School*, was awarded *first* place among the Candidates from all the Royal Schools, to which such Scholarships are attached.

The following *Pupils of Dungannon School* obtained—

Mr. Higinbotham—A Queen's Scholarship of £50 per annum for five years.
Mr. MacSorley—A Queen's Scholarship of £30 per annum for five years.
Mr. Armstrong—A Queen's Scholarship of £30 per annum for two years.

The above is an extract from an old advertisement, dated 27th December, 1843. It will be observed that "the University" means Trinity College, Dublin; there was then no other in Ireland, and the English Universities were out of the question. A copy of a letter from the headmaster is preserved, in which he congratulates the winner of the scholarship, and adds, "By beating the three who gained first places at July, October, and November (Examinations), you have brought me more credit than any boy ever yet did." It seems, however, that there was some little difficulty about the award of the scholarship, on the ground that the winner had not gone up direct from school to the examination. The regulations of the Board of Education required that there should be no interval. In this case there was an interval of nine months, during which the candidate had been reading privately or coaching in Dublin with a view to improving his prospects of success.

"It was found, however," wrote the Secretary of the Board or some member whose letter has been preserved, "that the regulation has not been always enforced with perfect regularity, and it was a sincere gratification to me, and I believe to every member present at a well-attended meeting yesterday, that upon that ground we could admit to the enjoyment of a scholarship one whose answering had been so distinguished as that of your young friend was reported to have been by his examiners at the late examination."

This was a brilliant commencement to a university career, the technical particulars of which are subjoined in a list compiled from official sources in Trinity College, Dublin.

1844. As a Junior Freshman.

In Literis Humanioribus.

First Rank.

Hilary Term . . .	Second Place.
Trinity Term . .	Third Place.
Michaelmas Term .	Second Place.

1845. As a Senior Freshman.

In Literis Humanioribus.

First Rank.

Hilary Term	First Place.
Trinity Term	Fourth Place.
Michaelmas Term . . .	Second Place.

In the examination for admission to the Rank of Sophister which is called the "Little go" and is a general examination.

Fifth Place.

1846. As Junior Sophister.

In Literis Humanioribus.

First Rank.

Hilary Term .   Second Place.

In the two later terms he was evidently preparing for the approaching Scholarship, which he obtained.

1847. As a Senior Sophister.

In Literis Humanioribus.

First Rank.

Hilary Term .   .   --
Trinity Term .   .   The only Honour man.

Probably all the rest were working for degree.
1848. B.A. degree at the first commencement of Michaelmas Term.
      1st Grade.   Respondent.   3rd Place.

Each university has its own phraseology, and there are
several of these university expressions which will not be
familiar even to men of other universities.   The term
" respondent " means a pass-man who does exceptionally well,
and answers to the " honorary fourth " of contemporary
Oxford.   This much seems clear from the record, that this is
a good university career, though not of exceptional brilliance,
but that it did not receive its crown and finish.   In the
mind of every one who understands the record would rise
the expectation that it would end in Senior Moderatorship,
that is, a First Class in Honours in the Degree Examination,
and possibly in a Fellowship.   What is the reason for this
seeming failure at the close ?   To this inquiry a near relative
of his own time makes answer : " After the achievement of
the above collegiate successes ' a change came o'er the spirit of
his dream.' "   A train of providential events during the middle
of the forties, 1843–1847, brought about the turning-point in
George's life of prosperity.   That " tide in the affairs of men,
which taken at the flood leads on to fortune," had come for
him.   He was one of the comparatively few who, whether
consciously or otherwise " take it at the flood," and in the end

realise the prediction. With a characteristic energy of mind which loves to translate itself into action he resolved to exchange the lettered ease of a University career for one which should bear at once more immediately and practically upon the profession for which he was destined.

Amongst George Higinbotham's books are two prizes gained at Trinity College—Müller's *History of Grecian Literature*, and Butler's *Analogy and Sermons*. The latter is much marked, and evidently has been closely studied. The subjects for which the prizes were given are not recorded in them.

The Historical Society is the great debating society of Trinity College. It is rightly famous, as nearly every Irishman of note has had some connection with it. George Higinbotham not only belonged to it and took part in the debates, but he served on the General Committee for a year. It was in this society that he first won his spurs as a debater. A contemporary testifies that his speeches were "very much to the point."

A mere record of success in university examinations after all gives but little insight into a student's life at the university. The regular work of a university, what may be called its legitimate business, is, in the case of hard-working students, such as George Higinbotham certainly was, a very important element in their mental history, but it is almost more important to know about companionship and similar influences at that seminal period of life. It is in a sense characteristic of George Higinbotham that his most important friendship was with a lady some twenty years older than himself, who influenced him greatly. Mrs. Brougham was the widow of a clergyman, and the daughter of Sir John Macartney, Bart., a member of the old Irish House of Commons before the Act of Union. Left a widow very young with two sons, she had settled in Dublin for the benefit of their education, to which she devoted herself with complete singleness of purpose. Education at schools did not in those days cover so wide an extent as at present, and this lady tried to supplement the teaching of her sons by introducing them to the beauties of English literature. As the boys grew up, she cultivated friendships for them, and her brother, that venerable man the Dean of Melbourne, has told me that amongst the young men of her acquaintance she picked out Robert and George Higinbotham as the two with whom she was most pleased to see her sons intimate. The elder of these sons, the Dean of Lismore, was George Higinbotham's chief friend amongst his college contemporaries. In the following letter the Dean has kindly written his reminiscences of the old days. His letter includes one written in the last six months of the Chief Justice's life, containing a warm appreciation of the late Mrs. Brougham, who passed away but shortly before him. It may be well here to state that he was not given to exaggeration in the use of language. When he wrote he wrote calmly, and language which from the lips of some might appear extreme expressed his deliberate feelings. Even if he had not written the words himself, all who knew him intimately knew that Mrs. Brougham was "the oldest, the most steadfast and the most revered" of his friends. She was a woman of singular liberality of thought, openness of mind and greatness of character.

DEANERY, LISMORE.
March 22nd, 1893.

MY DEAR MR. HIGINBOTHAM,—

I cannot now remember whether I first met your father when we were reading for entrance in T.C.D. in 1843, or for the Hilary Term Examination in 1844. We entered on the same day and got fifth and sixth places out of 105 candidates. After this, we read together for nearly three years, at first with Mr. Rutledge, who was afterwards a Fellow, and subsequently by ourselves.

Your father had been educated at Dungannon, and got a Royal Exhibition soon after he entered college. He got first Honours in Classics at every examination in his Freshman years, and then an University Scholarship. So far, he and I had run side by side, but, in the beginning of our Senior Sophister year, just when we were beginning to think that it was time for us to see about our Classical Gold Medals, he was unexpectedly obliged to go to London and prevented from going on with his College work, so that he did not take his degree for some time after.

He and I read together for some examinations, without a "grinder" (as the equivalent to an Oxford "coach," is called in T.C.D.) Fluent translation was then thought a great deal of, and we used to translate aloud to each other for hours together, and I well remember your father translating page after page of Greek and Latin historians, poets, orators, and dramatists steadily and literally, without pause or hesitation, just as if he was reading an English author.

He took a great interest in the "Historical Society," and often took part in the debates, and in the private business which followed them. Games and athletics were not much in vogue in the "forties," but we had a good deal of boating, and though your father never rowed a race, he often came down to the Rowing Club, and pulled his oar sturdily, with the same determination that he showed in everything he undertook.

Some of my College friends used to come once a week to spend the evening at my mother's house. Amongst them were—J. Y. Rutledge, afterwards a F.T.C.D., H. Fleming, now Dean of Cloyne, and his brother Becher, W. St. J. Clerke, a mathematical Gold Medal man,—your father, and his brother Robert, a Gold Medallist in Logics and Ethics. Amongst other things, we used to write papers in prose or verse, with fictitious signatures, which my mother used to read aloud, and then they were discussed and criticized. I have two of your father's papers still, and I send them to you as they are probably some of his earliest attempts at English composition. He was a great admirer of Dickens, and I think you will see some traces of that author's style, in the paper on "The Historical Society."

I also send you a couple of " Honour papers on Homer and Aristophanes," which were given at the first and third examinations he and I went in for, as they will show you the class of questions which were given to Freshmen half a century since.

After our university course was ended, your father went to London, and I went to a country parish, where they thought—perhaps rightly —that a gold medal for a yearling shorthorn at the spring show was a far higher distinction than one awarded by the university.

I did not hear directly from your father for many many years, but he and my mother used regularly to correspond, so that we often heard of each other indirectly.

My mother was the Dean of Melbourne's only sister, and when she died in January, 1892, at the age of eighty-seven, I wrote to tell your father, and received the following answer :

"July 17, 1892.

" My dear Henry,—

"I lately received your kind letter of May 17th. I had previously learned from my sister-in-law and by newspaper the death of your mother. She was the oldest and the most steadfast and the most revered friend I had the unmerited happiness to possess in this world. Neither time, nor long separation, nor the known diversity of our thoughts and interests appeared to change her kind disposition to me, from the time I first had the privilege to know her more than forty-five years ago. Her memory will be precious to me as to you for the rest of my life. Her thoughtfulness at the supreme moment was very characteristic. I do not remember giving her a ring, but I shall be glad to receive it back with her last message, and to keep it, with many tokens she has sent to me from time to time.

" There are some Trinity men, not many, in Victoria, and they have been interested in the Tercentenary Celebration in Dublin. Our action, I fear, will be justly thought ignominious, if, unhappily, it be noticed at all. The times are so bad that only about £150 could be raised. That was our misfortune, not our fault. But the majority decided that this sum, instead of being given to Trinity to help to erect the new hall there, should be applied to found prizes in our own University of Melbourne! The Venerable Dean of Melbourne, with whom I was proud to find myself in company on this point, said that our sympathy with Alma Mater could only be described in Goldsmith's lines :—

> " ' Her generosity was such
>   It almost seemed divine,—
> She fed the hungry every day
>   When—she sat down to dine.'

" Please give, &c., &c.

> " I remain,
> " Your old friend,
> " GEORGE HIGINBOTHAM."

This was the last communication I received from him, and like our earliest, it referred to " old Trinity."

> I remain,
> Yours very faithfully,
> HENRY BROUGHAM.

Of the documents which the Dean transmits, it is perhaps not necessary to print examination papers in Homer and Aristophanes. Those who have dealt much with examination papers know the remarkable family likeness in those necessary, but not interesting, products of human ingenuity. Nearly fifty years ago they were not very different from what they are to-day. Of the two essays one is on the Historical Society and the other on the theme, " Is a strong sense of the ridiculous a desirable quality, or not?" The essayist answers the question in the negative, and chiefly on moral grounds. Ridicule " never conferred a single benefit, averted a single ill, dried a single tear, or imparted one single atom of real and permanent pleasure."

The Tercentenary of Trinity College, to which allusion is made in this letter, took place in 1892. Delegates from other universities far and near attended at Dublin, the two Australian universities of Sydney and Melbourne being represented. Many honorary degrees were conferred on visitors, and some *in absentia* on distinguished sons of Trinity. It was a matter of regret that the university did not offer the compliment to the Chief Justice of Victoria, who had brought honour to his Alma Mater. It is not certain that he who refused knighthood from his sovereign would have accepted the offer, but it is certain on account of the love that he bore towards his university he would have highly appreciated the compliment.

CHAPTER III

JOURNALIST IN LONDON

In 1847, at about the time when he came of age, George
Higinbotham went to London. It was a natural thing to do.
For many years Ireland, like Scotland, has produced more
men of brains and education than were needed to fill the
positions open to them at home, and they naturally swarmed
into England, India, and the Colonies. The two years 1845
and 1846 were the years of the Irish Famine that followed
on the failure of the potato crop. The famine was followed
by wholesale emigration from Ireland, so that the population
of that country was reduced from eight millions to five.

Young men with brains seeking to make their way in the
world are attracted to London. Higinbotham's plan was to
support himself by journalism until he could be called to
the bar, and then to practise as a barrister. Shortly after
his arrival in London he joined the staff of the *Morning
Chronicle*, at first as a general reporter, and after he had
learnt shorthand he became a parliamentary reporter. Throughout life he always found the knowledge of shorthand of great
value to him, though of late years his system (an earlier form of
Pitman's) was looked upon as old-fashioned, for in forty years
great improvements were of course introduced into the art.
On the margin of books he wrote shorthand notes; of an

important letter he made a shorthand draft; his judgments on the bench were composed in shorthand. If old-fashioned, his shorthand was neat and accurate, and he could always read his own notes.

In February, 1848, the *Morning Chronicle* passed into the hands of a new proprietary, and was placed under a new editor. It is not possible to ascertain whether Mr. Higinbotham was working for the paper during the few months that immediately preceded the transfer. The paper was then nearly eighty years old, and had certainly a brilliant history. It was first established in 1769, about half-way between the Seven Years' War and the American War, in the very year in which the first of the Letters of Junius was published. Its first editor and in part proprietor was William Woodfall, a man of importance in the history of the press. To force of will and literary ability he added a wonderful memory, which enabled him to report debates in Parliament without taking a note. His favourite attitude in the Visitors' Gallery is described as leaning on a stick with his eyes closed, and this position he only varied when a new speaker addressed the house. Woodfall's time was just about the close of the long struggle between Parliament and the Press, and though Woodfall was permitted as a stranger to hear the debates, he would not have been allowed to take notes.

Twenty years later, in 1789, the year famous for the beginning of the French Revolution, Mr. James Perry became editor of the paper in Woodfall's place, and after a while a half-proprietor. He possessed a genius for newspaper editing, and during his long reign of over thirty years the *Morning Chronicle* became the leading English newspaper.

In 1850 Mr. Knight Hunt published a book on the history of newspapers under the title *The Fourth Estate.* His account of the *Morning Chronicle* closes with words here repeated on Byron's principle that " bright names do hallow song."

The *Morning Chronicle* must not be dismissed without remembering that Sheridan speaks of it in his *Critic*; that Canning linked it into one of his poems; that Byron honoured it with a " Familiar Epistle " ; that Hazlitt wrote for its columns some of the finest criticisms in our or any other language: and that for it also were the first " Sketches by Boz " prepared.

This list of the distinctions of the paper might have been made much longer. Charles James Fox was intimate with Mr. Perry, the editor. Samuel Taylor Coleridge, just before enlisting in the cavalry under the name of Silas Titus Comberbatch, sent a poem to the editor, soliciting "the loan of a guinea for a distressed author"—himself. Mr. John Campbell, afterwards Lord Campbell, wrote for it the remarkable criticism of *Romeo and Juliet*: "It is too long for these days; and we would recommend the author, before he puts it again on the stage, to cut it down." Another and more poetic Campbell, Thomas Campbell, the poet, tried journalism in the *Morning Chronicle*, but not being successful therein settled down to the *Poets' Corner*, to which he contributed as many as twenty poems in a year. Porson, who was Perry's brother-in-law, probably wrote for him. Sir James Mackintosh also assisted Perry with contributions. Mr. James Grant, a later newspaper historian, is right in saying—"It is due to the memory of Mr. Perry to state that he raised the moral, social, and intellectual character of the *Morning Chronicle* to an elevation to which no newspaper, whether English or foreign, had ever before attained." Mr. Perry died in 1821.

The third editor of the *Chronicle*, Mr. John Black, was also a remarkable man. Scotch of the Scotch, a lover of metaphysics, addicted to elaborate essays rather than sparkling leaders, he was a man of capacity and rare judgment. James Mill was an intimate friend and trusted ally of Black, of whom his son, John Stuart Mill, speaks with strong praise in his *Autobiography*. The most characteristic story about Black is told in the *Gentleman's Magazine* for 1855 (p. 213). He was calling on Lord Melbourne, who in his abrupt way said, "Mr. Black, you are the only person who comes to see me who forgets who I am. You forget that I am Prime Minister." Black was stammering out an apology, when Lord Melbourne continued, "You never ask me for anything, and I wish you would." "I am truly obliged to you," answered Black, "but I don't want anything. I am editor of the *Morning Chronicle*, I like my business, and I live happily on my income." "Then, by God, I envy you," exclaimed the Premier, "and you are the only man I ever did."

Black is said to have prided himself on being a judge of men, and he certainly secured the assistance of able contributors, amongst whom the most important was Charles Dickens. In 1835 and 1836 Dickens was reporting for the *Morning Chronicle* in the gallery of the House of Commons. The statement made by Mr. Knight Hunt about the first "Sketches by Boz" is not strictly correct. Some of the later sketches were published in the *Evening Chronicle*, which was not a separate paper but a later edition of the *Morning Chronicle*, with later news and livelier articles. Dickens had a great regard for Black, and in common with other friends was indignant and distressed when a new proprietor dismissed the experienced editor from his post to make room for a son-in-law.

For a space of seventy-four years, from 1769 to 1843, the *Morning Chronicle* had only had three editors, all able men, of whom as a journalist Perry was the greatest. The paper lived for nineteen years more; but for the most part it was like a vessel in chopping seas. The defection of Dickens was more important than would at first appear, for it led to the establishment of a formidable rival. Dickens was angry that the new editor, on the score of expense, refused an offer of certain articles to be written as travel-pictures of Italy. On his return from Italy he conferred with his publishers and others, and the result was the *Daily News*. Of the new paper Dickens was the first editor—a racehorse between shafts—but in less than three weeks he discovered his own complete unfitness for the post, and retired in time to prevent the utter ruin of the paper. The *Daily News* represented advanced Liberalism, whilst the *Chronicle* still continued Whig, or very moderate Liberal, but its days of Whiggism were nearly over. In February, 1848, the paper was bought by the Peelites. Four names are mentioned amongst the new proprietors, the Duke of Newcastle, the Earl of Lincoln, Sidney Herbert, and Mr. W. E. Gladstone.

Sir Robert Peel, whose devoted followers these were, had been out of office about twenty months. In the middle of 1846 the Repeal of the Corn Laws had been carried. But on the very day that the third reading was passed in the House of Lords, a bill for the better government of Ireland was thrown out in the Commons, and in consequence of that defeat Sir Robert Peel resigned. In the teeth of many of his former followers Peel had succeeded in repealing the Corn Laws through the assistance of the Opposition, but the members of the Opposition did not feel bound to support him on any other matter than Free Trade. They thought his Irish measure too stringent and voted against him. Lord John Russell succeeded Peel as Prime Minister, with Lord Palmerston as Foreign Secretary, the latter being the special favourite of the *Morning Chronicle*. The Ministry was at first in an actual minority in the House of Commons, but received the support of Peel and his immediate followers the Peelites. On leaving office Peel was in an extraordinary political position. Sitting on the Opposition benches, he had more real influence than the ministers themselves. To a man of smaller moral worth such power might have been dangerous, but Peel had won the esteem of the great body of his countrymen by his candid and manly confession that he was wrong about Protection, and in or out of office he was the most influential man in the country, except the Duke of Wellington.

After the Repeal of the Corn Laws, the Conservatives hardly dared to avow themselves as Protectionist, but many of the party felt so bitterly against those who had brought about the change, that the Peelites gradually drew more and more away from them, until at length they were absorbed into the Liberal party.

Mr. Grant says that "the *Morning Chronicle*, under its new proprietors and editorship, became the organ of the Peel party in politics, and of the Puseyite party in the Church." The latter clause is of course an unfriendly criticism. The nickname "Puseyite" is only used by those who are hostile : a friend would have said "high church." From 1848 to 1854 the paper remained in the hands of its new proprietors, and then it was sold, because the separate existence of the party was almost at an end, but partly also because the paper was being conducted at a serious loss, estimated at £10,000 a year. In an obituary notice of Chief Justice Higinbotham in the London *Graphic* we are told that he was "one of that clever and accomplished band of literary men who then formed the Parliamentary staff of the *Morning Chronicle*—a journal that was, in the days of Mr. Beresford Hope's managing proprietorship, Mr. John Douglas Cook's editorship, and Mr. Philip Harwood's assistant editorship, the most perfect 'daily,' in points of literary form and style, and never yet surpassed." Higinbotham's connection with the paper was nearly coincident with the period thus described. He may have joined it a little earlier; he certainly left it a little before its close.

Let us briefly run through the events of that time. The year was one of revolution in many countries of Europe. The Smith O'Brien trouble in Ireland and the Chartist Movement in England were milder forms of the same agitation. In 1850 a fall from a horse removed the great Sir Robert Peel from the scene. In 1851 came the Great Exhibition of All Nations in Hyde Park, together with a general expectation of universal peace. In December of the same year took place the *Coup d'Etat* in France, by which Louis Napoleon, President of the Republic since 1848, made himself Emperor of the French, an event which affected English political history. Lord Palmerston felt a strong sympathy for the Emperor, and wrote despatches compromising the Ministry which had determined to be neutral. Lord Palmerston was therefore dismissed from the Foreign Office, and a little later took his revenge by voting against the militia bill of his former leader. In February, 1852, therefore, a Conservative ministry came into office under the Earl of Derby, with Mr. Disraeli as Chancellor of the Exchequer. During the year the Duke of Wellington died; and the new Houses of Parliament were opened. In December the Earl of Aberdeen came into power, and in his Cabinet many Peelites found place, Mr. Gladstone being Chancellor of the Exchequer. It was this ministry which a little later "drifted" into the Crimean War. It was not, however, until March, 1854, that war was declared, and by that time the subject of this memoir was either in Australia or drawing near to its shores. In that year the *Morning Chronicle*, with an average daily circulation of only 2,500, was sold once more.

Thenceforward, until its death in 1862, the paper dragged on a miserable existence, quite unworthy of its former history. It may almost be said that it ignobly ended as a vassal slave of France, for the new proprietor accepted a subsidy from the Emperor of the French to make the *Morning Chronicle* his organ in the English press, and actually sued the French Government in the French law-courts for non-payment of a part of his hire. Meanwhile Mr. Beresford Hope established the *Saturday Review*, and appointed Mr. Cook the first editor, while many of the brilliant writers of the *Morning Chronicle's* penultimate period helped to make the early years of the *Saturday Review* famous. The *Saturday Review* may be said to have sprung from the ashes of the Peelite *Morning Chronicle*.

The managers of the *Morning Chronicle* during its Peelite period were anxious not to confine their attention to politics, but to give the paper weight on social questions of the day. The Great Exhibition furnished an admirable opening, and no paper took such elaborate pains to describe every part of the great show and draw from it all conceivable lessons. A series of exhibition supplements appeared, which were deservedly admired, but they did not lead to a permanent improvement in the circulation. Articles also appeared on the condition of the poor in town and country, of which the most important were contributed by Mr. Henry Mayhew, and formed the basis of the well-known book *London Labour and the London Poor*. It is not known whether Higinbotham was engaged in any of these articles. Indeed, but few stories of his journalistic work are preserved. On the day of the Duke of Wellington's funeral he was on duty as a reporter in Piccadilly. It was a melancholy duty, for Higinbotham was a warm admirer of his countryman the Iron Duke, who had the same qualities that he had—prompt decision and resolute will. A story is repeated that as a young man he was told off to report a Waterloo dinner, but that when the Duke rose to speak, the spirit of hero-worship was so strong upon the young pressman that, gazing with admiration on the Duke's face and drinking in his words, he forgot his duty as a reporter, and took no notes of the speech. The report of the speech in the *Morning Chronicle* had to be furnished by the kindness of a less ardent reporter belonging to some other paper. As illustrating hero-worship, the story is *ben trovato*; but the Duke never spoke at any length, and the interest in his words would probably have helped out even a memory that was perhaps never very good. A very similar story Higinbotham used to tell himself about a speech by Mr. Gladstone, which it was his duty to report from the gallery in the House. The interest which the reporter felt in the speech was so intense that his short-hand notes became confused, and ultimately were so incomplete as to be worthless.

Some writers for the press, perhaps not many, keep copies of the articles that they write, neatly pasted into a book. When Mr. Walter Besant came to prepare the life of Professor Palmer, the Orientalist, who fell a victim to Arab ferocity, he found his journalistic activity represented by several volumes of extracts. The only copy of the *Morning Chronicle* that Mr. Higinbotham left behind him is that for November 30, 1850. On it is written in a hand, something like his, " Reviews of the *Keepsake* and *Court Album*." As they are probably his, a couple of short extracts may be given. The *Keepsake* was edited by Miss Power, a niece of " the late Lady Blessington," and contained contributions by Sir E. B. Lytton, A. Tennyson, Walter Savage Landor, R. Monckton Milnes, besides other writers of less permanent repute. There is a full account of certain stories from the *Keepsake*, and then a short comment on Tennyson, who had been appointed Poet Laureate eleven days before the review appeared. No allusion whatever is made to the fact, and it is possible the review was written before the appointment was made. *The Princess* had been published three years before, and *In Memoriam* that very year.

The poetry of the present volume of the *Keepsake* is, on the whole, scarcely equal in merit to the prose contributions. Yet here are three stanzas by Tennyson, which, if we mistake not, will be welcome as flowers in spring to all who can find in the abrupt irregular verse of " The Two Voices " a deep current of great thoughts and the massive elements of a noble faith, enveloped though they be in speculative doubt and an intellectual darkness " that may be felt."

> " What time I wasted youthful hours,
>   One of the shining wingèd powers
>   Showed me vast cliffs, with crowns of towers.
>
> " As towards that gracious light I bowed,
>   They seemed high palaces and proud,
>   Hid now and then with sliding cloud.
>
> " He said, ' The labour is not small ;
>   Yet winds the pathway free to all—
>   Take care thou dost not fear to fall ! ' "

The *Court Album* contained a series of fourteen ladies' portraits. The review is written in a courtly tone of admiration. Two sentences only shall be quoted, which will show

that the author's style was formed before Macaulay and short
sentences came in.

Nor are we forgetful of the dictum of Lord Bacon (*sic*), " that that
is the best part of beauty which a picture cannot express," and we fear
that in addition to having our judgment " disabled," which since the
days of Paris, has always been the result of any expression of opinion on
the claims of rival beauties, we should lay ourselves open to the charge
of presumption in venturing to come to any conclusion at all on so
momentous a subject from the necessarily inadequate and imperfect
testimony of an engraving.

We cordially recommend this volume to those who wish to possess
themselves of really good specimens of the engraver's *burin*, and still
more to all who have the higher wish of implanting in their hearts and
memories the bright glances and sunny smiles of those whose presence
is the fairest ornament of an Englishman's home, and whose remembered image constitutes, in their absence, one of the best and purest of
his pleasures.

This high and chivalrous appreciation of women was always
a note of George Higinbotham's mind.

It remains to be said that the *lustrum* during which
George Higinbotham was reporting in London, chiefly in the
gallery of the House of Commons, was a famous time in
literature. Among the new books then appearing that were
likely to help in forming a young man's mind, were many
which are counted among the permanent treasures of English
literature.

Dickens, whose newspaper enterprises have been mentioned
in this chapter, began his work young, and had already published seven of his most famous novels. *David Copperfield* is
his only novel of the time. Thackeray, who was tempted to
write occasionally for the *Morning Chronicle*, made his reputation as a novelist by *Vanity Fair*, in 1847, which he followed
quickly by *Pendennis, Esmond*, and the *English Humourists*.
Vanity Fair, and Charlotte Brontë's *Jane Eyre*, are the
greatest novels of 1847, but in that year Disraeli's *Tancred*
also appeared. Charles Kingsley was dabbling in deep waters
with *Alton Locke* and that strange book *Yeast*. Lord Lytton
published, in two consecutive years, *The Caxtons* and *Harold*.
Tennyson was not the only poet before the public, though he
was probably the most read. A. H. Clough and Matthew
Arnold each gave forth a volume of poems in 1848. Hood's
Poems of Wit and Humour belong to the previous year.

whilst in the following, Robert Browning's *Poems*, and in the year after *Easter Eve and Christmas Day* found audience fit though few, probably very few, and his wife's *Sonnets from the Portuguese* showed how poets can love.   Amongst writers of prose other than fiction Carlyle, whose influence was strongest, is represented by the *Latter-Day Pamphlets*, and the *Life of Sterling.* The first two volumes of Macaulay's *History of England*, really the history of the English Revolution and its results, appeared in the year when all countries, other than England, seemed to be in the throes of revolution. In the same year Mill's *Political Economy* found ready acceptance; whilst John Ruskin, who in after life often girded on his armour to attack what is known as the orthodox Political Economy, that is, the teaching of Mill and his followers, is only represented by the *Seven Lamps of Architecture* and the first volume of the *Stones of Venice.* His friends and allies rather than followers were in 1850 issuing *The Germ*, a small magazine, the organ of Pre-Raphaelitism.

In all these books there were many influences at work, thought was fermenting in many minds, and no generous young man can altogether escape the inspiration of his time.

CHAPTER IV

CALL TO THE BAR AND EMIGRATION

FORTY years ago a change was made in the method of admission to the learned profession of barrister. Since that change
some knowledge of the law has been regarded as a condition
precedent, but in the earlier period, to which George Higinbotham's call belongs, it was not thought necessary that future
lawyers should be taught law. On April 20th, 1848, George
Higinbotham, having then been about a year in London,
entered himself as a student-at-law at Lincoln's Inn. No
one required of a student-at-law that he should study. If
he so desired, he studied.

A friend, whose call at Lincoln's Inn was a little earlier,
writes :—

In my time the only requirement before call was the ridiculous
one of having eaten so many dinners in so many terms, and the having
presented yourself before the senior barrister at the Bar table, and
having read one or two lines of a mock opinion prepared, as I believe,
by the butler, which would run somewhat as follows :—" I am of
opinion that the widow was entitled to dower out of Blackacre," at
which point the senior barrister would bow, and the candidate
walked away, thinking what a farce the whole thing was. I forget

the technical name given to the farce, but it was admittedly done for
the purpose of presenting every candidate for call before his Inn, so
that the Bar of the Inn could inspect him and see whether he was fit
to be called. Well, we were all called. Then we were supposed to
have wine and dessert in a room, I think, underneath the hall, where
we invited those Benchers who dined on that day at the Hall to par-
take of our feast. The rascals came in numbers, because we were
required to present every Bencher, who honoured us thus, with two
bottles of Madeira and three bags of "comfits" to take home with
them, the latter being notoriously looked after by the Benchers'
children, who kept their fathers up to the mark on call-day with a
view to the lollies.

The use of this last word proves that the friend was
resident in Australia.

There was at that time no examination; but in February,
1852, a scheme was promulgated to provide for lectures and
examinations. The first lecturers were appointed in January,
1853; and on June 6th of that year George Higinbotham was
called to the Bar. It is easy to imagine with what feelings
he went through the farce above described, and how warmly
he welcomed the prospect of reform.

When a man is called to the Bar, unless he has interest
amongst solicitors, an interval ensues before briefs come to
him. Of course, if he has private means sufficient to keep
him, he can wait until an opportunity may offer. The delay,
if not too long, will do no hurt; the young barrister will
continue to read law; he will frequent the courts and become
acquainted with their practice. Some day a barrister will be
absent, and a solicitor will turn to the briefless one, or a judge
will assign counsel to an undefended prisoner; then he has
his opening. The higher branch of the law is still a profession in which

> A few by wit or fortune led
> May beat a pathway out to wealth and fame.

The number of nominal barristers in England is very large,
much larger than present or prospective litigation needs.
Many who are called never mean to practise. Their *rôle* in life
is different—perhaps to be country gentlemen; and the future
justice of the peace qualifies for his work by being called to the
Bar. Even when all these nominal barristers are deducted, the

number is too large. Earl Stanhope tells that once in conversation Macaulay illustrated this excess by pointing out to him that "the ancient device of the Templars had been two knights upon one horse, to indicate the original poverty of their order; and he observed that the same device might be as aptly applied to the modern members of the Temple—two barristers at least to one cause!" If the newly-called barrister has no private means and has to work at once for daily bread, there is no doubt that the chance of an opportunity offering itself is greatly diminished. The law is a jealous mistress, and if a man takes to teaching or to journalism, he may not be at hand when wanted. He is in the position of one trying to combine incongruous things. The solicitor at any rate will fancy that he is not whole-hearted in his legal work. Even to be known as a cricketer has before now damaged a young barrister's chances. To the man without family connections amongst solicitors, who happens to be what the song describes as "an impecunious party," the Bar of all professions offers the worst outlook.

George Higinbotham having been called to the Bar, on looking round him saw little reason to hope for advancement in his profession, or even for any work at all in it.

> What is that which I should turn to, lighting upon days like these ?
> Every door is barr'd with gold, and opens but to golden keys.
> Every gate is throng'd with suitors, all the markets overflow.

It may be that thoughts like these ran through his mind : it may be that they were expressed in these very words, for *Locksley Hall* had been published eleven years, and the volume that contained the poem was in its eighth edition, and was the favourite reading of young men. If gold was the metal that barred the door and gold the metal that would open it, another and apparently shorter way to obtain the key was being everywhere spoken about. Two years previously gold had been discovered in Australia, and the bold and venturesome were hurrying to Australia to dig for it. For no special qualifications were required, no training as a miner. These diggings were alluvial, and any man who had strength to dig might, if he were fortunate, find in a few weeks enough to make him rich for life. The principal outfit needed was a stout heart, and there is no doubt that George Higinbotham was equipped with that. Once in later years I asked him why he came out to Australia, and he said: "I was in despair about making my way at home."

To those who in after years knew the dignified judge there seems something almost humorous in the idea of his digging, rocking the cradle, eagerly panning out, and mixing in all the rough-and-ready life of the gold-fields. To those who knew his indifference to gain, willingness to give rather than receive, and strong aversion to speculation, there seems something incongruous that he should care to seek gold at all. But the difference of age must be remembered. At twenty-seven the need was borne in upon him that something must be done, a path chosen and entered upon, and the spirit of venture was strong within him. As a matter of fact he never did dig. A friend in London gave him the wise counsel to pack his wig and gown, and take them with him, as there would be need of lawyers in Melbourne quite as much as of diggers on Ballarat. Almost from the moment of reaching Victoria, work in journalism and at the Bar offered itself in abundance. The attraction of digging for gold was not strong enough to draw him from the work in town thus immediately present, and very soon all idea of digging was abandoned. There is reason to believe that Mr. Higinbotham never regretted his resolution to come to Australia. He did once say to me that if he had his life over again he would choose country pursuits in preference to a town life; but it is difficult to determine whether this was a deep-seated feeling in his mind, or a passing fancy.

Whether it be true or not that, as the ancient poet says, gold is best unfound and left in the earth, there is no doubt that the discovery of gold made an enormous difference in the history of Australia. A writer in 1854 told how an admiral whom he had known had said to him that he was a midshipman serving in the Channel Fleet when the first ships carrying convicts to New South Wales passed down the Channel, that his captain put a hand upon his shoulder and said, "Mark those ships, youngster; they are going forth to found a new empire." Erasmus Darwin, grandfather of Charles Darwin, a year or two later was writing verses that prophesied the future greatness of Sydney. In one of his latest poems Campbell wrote of Australia :—

> As in a cradled Hercules we trace
> The lines of empire on thy infant face.

It seemed, however, as if the infant were growing but slowly. In 1850, sixty-two years, or nearly two generations, after the arrival of Governor Phillip and his ships at Botany, in spite of transportation and immigration, the whole white population of Australia did not reach a quarter of a million. In 1891 it was over three millions. Very soon after the middle of the century gold was discovered, and the discovery acted as a magnet to population. The question whether it was better for Australia that its development should be thus hastened by the discovery of gold need not here be considered, nor the question whether population is in any way an index to prosperity. About the importance of the discovery no two opinions can be held. It changed the face of society in Australia. Hitherto flocks and herds were the chief, and almost the only, source of wealth. Of agriculture there was comparatively little. There were a few merchants, and a few professional men. But the former were engaged in the exportation of wool, and the supplying of necessaries to squatters ; the latter may be said similarly to have depended on the staple product of the country. The price of wool regulated the welfare of the community. Gold brought population, created variety of industries, and gave work to many more to furnish supplies necessary for this larger population.

In 1850 the law passed the Imperial Parliament creating the Colony of Victoria, by separating the district of Port Phillip from New South Wales. On the 1st of July, 1851, it came into force. In that very month it was announced that gold had been discovered in Victoria. Scientific men had held that there must be gold in Australia ; shepherds had here and there found lumps of the precious metal. Officials, apprehensive of the consequences, had tried to conceal such discoveries, and had actually concealed them for a while. But the discovery of gold in the neighbourhood of Bathurst, made the people, in what was soon to be called Victoria, during all the winter of 1851 anxious to discover gold in their own district. A Gold Committee was appointed, and during July gold was reported in various parts of the colony. At Clunes it was discovered by a strange coincidence on the very day on which the colony began its separate existence. The rich gold-field of Ballarat was discovered in August. There had been a rush to Bathurst, and there was now a rush to the various gold-fields of Victoria. This rush was for about a year confined to people in the colonies, but within the colonies it was for a time almost universal. Men left their ordinary occupations, and went to dig for gold. The least desirable of the new arrivals in the colony came from Van Diemen's Land, and an outbreak of crime and lawlessness was the result.

Meanwhile the news of the discovery reached Europe. It is certainly surprising to find how slowly the news must have travelled, for it was not until September, 1852, that the first detachment from Great Britain arrived. Those who were near at hand had thus at least a year's start. There was no telegraph, no steamer even; but the letters and papers that told of the new El Dorado were conveyed by sailing ship round the Horn. The would-be diggers had then to come out in a sailing ship, and it was not at all uncommon for a voyage to take four months. This calculation leaves about four months for the making up of minds. Probably the first accounts were only partially believed, and men waited until the gold-ships arrived in England with large cargoes of the precious metal. Then the story spread and began to influence imaginations. Then came ship after ship crowded with passengers, from Liverpool, from London, from Southampton, from Glasgow. It is stated that nearly 150,000, mostly men, came to Victoria within twenty months. To this extent it is possible to be more precise. On March 2nd, 1851, a census was taken, and the population amounted to 77,345. On April 26th, 1854, the population was enumerated at 236,798.

No doubt many of these immigrants, like Mr. Higinbotham, never went to the gold-fields at all.

This sudden influx of population upset all existing arrangements. Almost all of the new-comers went to Melbourne; but that was only a small town, and in a very short space of time its population was doubled, and trebled. There were not houses enough to receive all the new-comers, wherefore

Canvas Town sprang up. A large piece of ground, about two miles by one, lying to the south of the river Yarra, was entirely covered with tents. Emphasis has often been laid on the lawlessness of the diggers. There is rather room for surprise at their law-abiding character. The danger of simple lawlessness and crime was greatest at first, the danger of rebellion at a later time, but the latter might have been entirely avoided by a little tact on the part of the authorities. Amongst the first attracted to the gold-fields were many convicts from neighbouring colonies. Their number has indeed been estimated at 10,000, but it was probably not so large. Some of these men were only too pleased to mix with the general people, and took great care not to come again within the clutches of the law. Many were guilty of outrage and violence, of which the robbery of the gold-ship, *Nelson*, was the worst example. It is probable that nothing was known of many deeds of violence wrought in lonely gullies far from the eyes of fellow-men.

The character of the later immigrants, from Europe, was very different. As a rule perfectly law-abiding, they were strong, self-reliant, and courageous men, and most of them made admirable colonists.

The ship *Briseis* 1,141 tons, Captain J. R. Brown, left Liverpool on December 1st, 1853. This classical name was afterwards given to a famous racehorse in Melbourne, and was pronounced in very strange ways. The wonder rises whether the ship's name involved any allusion to the colour of the sails—usually more white in pictures than in reality. It was with her snow-white hue [1] that the captive maiden took the fancy of Achilles. Mr. Higinbotham might easily have found a larger ship, as many larger ships were then making the voyage to Melbourne. The vessel, described as belonging to the Eagle Line of Packets, brought out ten cabin passengers and thirty-nine in the second cabin. [2] Some of the passengers had been transferred from the ship *Sapphire*, which was wrecked a few weeks before, soon after

[1] Serva Briseis niveo colore
    Movit Achillem.
[2] The names of the ten were thus given in the papers on arrival in Hobson's Bay : " Mr. and Mrs. Robinson, Mr. and Mrs. Robertson,

commencing the voyage to Melbourne. The *Briseis* through-out her passage had very light winds : only one day did she make over 300 miles, and the whole voyage from Liverpool to Hobson's Bay lasted 100 days. Even forty years ago that was a long passage ; in the present day so swift and convenient are steamers that the time then taken on the single voyage would be sufficient for a trip to Australia and back, including a sojourn of more than a month. The passenger by the *Briseis* best known to fame, according to the testimony of a fellow-passenger, was " greatly respected by all on board for his uniform courtesy to each." He brought with him a quadrant, and taught himself how to take the sun so as to ascertain the ship's position. It is said that the captain had no sympathy with this thirst for knowledge on the part of a landsman, and looked on the passenger's conduct as an intrusion on his own province. Mr. Higinbotham studied astronomy on the voyage, and of course kept a diary. In later life he sometimes commented on Bacon's shrewd remark " that in sea-voyages, where there is nothing to be seen but sky and sea, men should make diaries ; but in land-travel, wherein so much is to be observed, for the most part they omit it, as if chance were fitter to be registered than observation."

The account of the *Briseis* and her voyage furnished to the two Melbourne morning papers winds up with the following eulogy :—" When her cargo is discharged, we understand her lines will bear comparison with the finest clippers, and the neatness and order on board does credit to her commander." The ship was heavily laden, her cargo amounting to 1,600 tons—nearly half as much again as her register. The cargo may well be described as miscellaneous. The heavy articles included 400 tons of coal, 8,000 bricks, and a good deal of iron ; but the list also includes large quantities of food, such as butter and cheese, of beer, and, most characteristic of all, 324 cases of champagne, the favourite drink of the lucky digger. When, in 1878, a building was being erected in a suburb not far to the south of Melbourne, the builders reported to me that a little below the surface the soil seemed to consist of sardine tins and broken champagne bottles.

Misses Redmond (2), Messrs. Graham, Higginbotham. Clayton, and Kidston." The name Redmond should have been Redmayne.

It was on the 10th of March, 1854, that the *Briseis* cast anchor in Hobson's Bay. On the 27th of the same month Mr. George Higinbotham, barrister of Lincoln's Inn, was admitted to the Victorian Bar. The fact is not recorded in the daily papers, but it will be found on " Y.ᵉ Rolle of Y.ᵉ Utter Barristers in yᵉ Supreme Court of Victoria," preserved in the library of the Law Courts. Mr. Higinbotham's name stands forty-ninth. It is unfortunate that the record was not written up at the time ; it is still in pencil, and is inaccurate as to the date of the Lincoln's Inn call, but the Victorian admission is in all probability correctly dated. It was pretty quick after landing. The intervening time must have been rather an exciting fortnight in a new and wild place such as was the Melbourne of that day. The friend who advised the bringing of the wig and gown was right. Legal work in Court came almost at once after the admission to the Victorian Bar, for barristers were wanted. The first brief was in the County Court, and was for the plaintiff in an action brought to recover money due upon a promissory note. The action was undefended, and the new barrister was ignorant of the procedure. He used to tell with a smile how relieved he felt when the judge, a kindly middle-aged man, who spoke with a lisp, said, " I think, Misther Higinbotham, if you will justh put in the note, that will do."

An intimate friend says that either before or after this brief there came an interval of something very like despair, when all funds were exhausted and no work came in. The interval must have been short, and suddenly the tide turned, and the particular turn of tide is characteristic of the state of the colony. One court day a barrister in large practice was drunk and incapable of work. Five of his briefs were brought in a hurry to Higinbotham, who acquitted himself well with them, and never afterwards lacked work.

CHAPTER V

Canvas Town Marriage— Emerald Hill, now South Melbourne—
Exercise—Higinbotham a volunteer—Story of camp—Testimony
of Rev. R. B. Dickinson—Arrival of Thomas Higinbotham—News
of death of Rev. Robert Higinbotham— A short notice of his life
—Bishop Alexander's lines.

On his first arrival in the colony Mr. Higinbotham lived for
a short time in Canvas Town. A lady now living in
Melbourne vividly remembers his helpfulness as a neighbour ;
but he could not have remained very long in tents, for he
afterwards lived at a boarding-house in Fitzroy long enough
to form lifelong friendships. On the 30th of September,
1854, within seven months of his arrival in the colony, he
was married. At Christ Church, St. Kilda, by the Rev.
David Seddon, George Higinbotham, native of Dublin, was
married to Miss Margaret Foreman, spinster, native of Kent.
It was to a cottage on Emerald Hill that he took his bride
home. This house, which was his residence for seven years
until he moved to Brighton, is situated in Montague Street,
about fifty yards south from Banks Street. In appearance this
cottage with its roof of shingles was most unpretending, but
it was more comfortable than its appearance promised.

An engagement with the *Argus*, of which more is said later,
began in August, 1856. Up to that month Mr. Higinbotham's
time was occupied with work at the Bar, and it is said that he
wrote occasionally for the *Morning Herald*, a paper which then
disputed with the *Argus* the position of leading journal of
the colony. The house in Emerald Hill was conveniently
situated for his *Argus* work, which often detained the editor

until a late hour, when he usually rode home. It is a little difficult to conceive, but I have it on the authority of an entirely credible witness who had every opportunity of knowing, that Mr. Higinbotham continued his work at the Bar during a greater part of the time that he was editor of the *Argus*.

At first the journalistic work occupied all his time and energies. Then he began to fear he was losing touch with his legal work, and it is said that Mr. Ireland especially urged him not to abandon the law altogether. From that time he was regularly in chambers or in court at ten o'clock in the morning. His doctor protested that he was burning the candle at both ends. But a naturally strong constitution, and plenty of exercise, enabled him to disregard the doctor's protests. Rowing and riding were the favourite forms of exercise. Two or three times a week Mr. Higinbotham would go on the ·Yarra, generally sculling. But he was especially fond of riding, and loved to handle a spirited, or even what many would think a refractory, horse. There is no doubt that he was an excellent rider, preferring though short himself a tall horse. In later life gymnastic exercises on the Ling or Swedish system, took the place of the rowing. Mr. Higinbotham always maintained that regular systematic exercises with the dumb-bells taken with the body *in the proper position*, were more conducive to health than a much longer time devoted to unsystematic exercise, such as walking or lawn-tennis.

Emerald Hill was the first municipality established under a Local Self-Government Act, introduced by Captain (now Sir Andrew) Clarke. Mr. Higinbotham was never a candidate for municipal honours ; but Mr. Service, who was afterwards twice Premier of Victoria, and in 1880 appointed Mr. Higinbotham a judge, remembers that when he himself was a candidate for a seat in the local municipal council, Mr. Higinbotham was his nominator. Emerald Hill is now called South Melbourne, being one of the many places in Australasia dissatisfied with its original name. It is not unkind to say that the reason for the change of the distinctive name was the desire to float a loan upon more favourable terms. It was thought that the capitalist at a distance, who had perhaps never heard of Emerald Hill, would more readily know South Melbourne. For similar reasons, and at about the same time, Port Melbourne and North Melbourne took their new names. But it must be remembered that the hill was no hill at all, except to dwellers on the plains, and then on the principle that "amongst the blind the one-eyed is king." Moreover, if ever the hill was green, that colour has long vanished from its aspect. The early inhabitants were very fond of the place, and always spoke of themselves as living "on the hill."

In 1854, when the 40th infantry went to New Zealand, volunteers were enrolled in Melbourne, and Mr. Higinbotham thought it to be his duty to join the ranks. He was sworn in in February, 1855, upon the same day as Mr. James Service and other citizens afterwards more or less prominent. There are many who still remember Mr. Higinbotham as a volunteer, how he took his place with others on guard at Government House or at the Treasury, pacing to and fro for two hours at a time on "sentry-go," like any paid soldier.

When later he left Emerald Hill he was transferred to the Brighton corps, which was afterwards converted into Coast Artillery. It cannot be said that any special taste for the military life impelled him to this service, for he never cared to be more than a full private. His name was kept on the books of the Brighton Artillery Corps until its disbandment on the 30th of June, 1877, but he does not appear to have attended any parade after the end of December, 1870. The following scene has been described to me, to show the thoroughness with which he performed his duties :—

Scene—The Werribee camp. Time—half past four in the morning. Company paraded ; and the officer commanding the company announces that the two men whose names are first on the roster are to fetch the meat from the butcher's, the next four to fetch wood, and so on. "Orderly sergeant, call the names." "George Higinbotham, Richard Hale Budd." A sort of shudder passed through the ranks when it was seen to whom the most unpleasant duty had fallen—a graduate of Dublin a leading barrister, and a graduate of Cambridge the Secretary to the Education Department. The orderly sergeant asked the officer if he might be permitted to find volunteers to take this work off their hands, adding that he could easily find forty. A young bricklayer and a young labourer came readily forward, but they could not persuade. "Budd, they want to relieve us of this work because it is disagreeable. What do you say?" A resolute "No" was the answer. And the best-educated men in the company marched to the butcher's, waited for the meat, and brought it back skewered on their ramrods. The officer who then commanded the company, when telling the story finished with the words: "He was the very best soldier that I ever had in the ranks."

By the side of this military testimony may be placed the following brief sketch of early days by the Rev. R. B. Dickinson, incumbent of St. Luke's Church:—

Mr. George Higinbotham was a Trustee of St. Luke's for some years, from 1857 onwards. He was conspicuous for his regular attendance at church, and the conscientious discharge of all the duties appertaining to his office. He contributed liberally to the erection and maintenance of the church; and whenever there was any deficiency in the funds, supplied it himself. He was always the same—modest, unobtrusive, and painstaking. Of course parochial affairs afforded very little scope for his fine intellect and philosophical turn of mind. But in many private conversations with him, I found how deeply settled his faith was, so far—and so far only—as it could be reconciled with reason. Not that he was so shallow as to suppose that faith did not often—and infinitely—transcend reason; but he felt, and felt truly, that it must never contradict it, or any of those great moral verities which the collective mind of Christianised humanity has accepted as real and right. This, necessarily, led him to reject many of the so-called orthodox views of the Gospel; but I am sure that, in those days at least, he never rejected that Gospel itself.

As a private friend he was a model of considerateness and courtesy, and to spend an evening with him, and with his equally friendly and generous brother Thomas, was, on a small scale, a kind of symposium —a social and intellectual treat that could rarely be enjoyed in colonial life.

If it is not out of place, I should like to be allowed to add my tribute of respectful affection for his most gentle and Christian wife. As one of our district-visitors, and as a most sympathetic helper of the poor in all their troubles, I have never known her superior, and rarely her equal.

The presence and assistance of these kind friends supported and cheered me, as a young clergyman, amidst the stress and strain of the pioneer work of those days; and their worth will never be forgotten by me.

In October, 1857, Mr. Higinbotham was joined by his brother Thomas, afterwards very well known as the Engineer-in-Chief of Victorian Railways, an office which he held for eighteen years uninterruptedly. In the Minutes of Proceedings of the Institution of Civil Engineers,[1] vol. lxiii., being the volume for the session of 1880–81, there is an obituary notice of Mr. Thomas Higinbotham, who died in September, 1880. It is from the pen of his brother George, and may be quoted as an example of restrained biography. The early part is given here :—

Mr. Thomas Higinbotham was born in Dublin, in the year 1819. He was the third son of Mr. Henry Higinbotham, a merchant of that city. He received a sound general education at Castle Dawson school, near Blackrock, and he afterwards attended the drawing and mathematical classes and lectures at the Royal Dublin Society House, Kildare Street, Dublin, where he acquired the rudiments of his professional education. About the year 1840 he left Ireland, and entered the office, in London, of Sir William Cubitt, Past-President Inst. C.E., then in the front rank as a civil engineer. Shortly afterwards, the railway mania reached its height ; Sir William Cubitt's office was full to overflowing of work of all kinds, and Mr. Higinbotham had opportunities, of which he diligently availed himself, of gaining complete and accurate knowledge of the theory and of the indoor practice of railway construction, and of the proceedings before railway committees of the House of Commons. He was subsequently appointed assistant-engineer on the Ashford and Canterbury branch of the South-Eastern Railway ; and he again filled a similar position on another branch line in Lancashire. Having won the approval and confidence of his superiors in these works of construction, he was next promoted to the office of resident engineer on the Huntingdon section of the Great Northern Railway, of which Sir William Cubitt was the consulting engineer. After the completion of this line Mr. Higinbotham practised in London for two or three years, and at the end of the year 1857 he emigrated to Victoria. Shortly after arriving in Melbourne he was invited by the Government to accept the office of Chief Engineer of Roads and Bridges of the colony. Three years afterwards he was appointed Engineer-in-Chief of Victorian Railways.

With the exception of eighteen months, during which Mr. Thomas Higinbotham was absent from the colony on a tour of inspection of railway systems in other lands, the two brothers lived together for a period of twenty-three years. The relations between them can only be described as ideal. During part of the time the colony was distracted by the fiercest party feeling on political questions, and the sympathies of the two brothers were enlisted on opposite sides. That fact

[1] Elected a member, February 7th, 1854.

never made the least difference between them, never caused the slightest ruffle in their friendship. It is not creditable to human nature that we are compelled to add that such true affection and wise toleration of difference are very rare.

Not many months after the arrival of this brother came the saddening news of the death of another, the Rev. Robert Higinbotham, the youngest, except George, of the family of eight. There was just one year and a half difference between the two brothers. Not only was Robert the nearest to George of all his brothers in point of age, but they had been a good deal together in their bringing up, and were closely connected by the ties of affection. They were fellow-students of Trinity College, Dublin, the elder brother being in university standing only one year senior to the younger; but from the end of their college days their different careers in life divided them. Whilst the younger of the two went, first to London, then to Melbourne, the elder was ordained, and after a short time spent in a country curacy in the north of Ireland, became curate to the Cathedral in Derry. After seven years of useful work in that city he was carried off by " a typhus fever contracted in the discharge of his duty, in the thirty-third year of his age and the tenth of his ministry of sympathy and consolation." These words are taken from the preface contributed by the Rev. William Alexander, now Bishop of Derry, to a small volume of sermons by the Rev. Robert Higinbotham, published in Dublin in 1859.[1] A portrait prefixed to the little book shows a face with a strong family likeness to his brother George, a face which seems to justify the few words of the same preface about " the gentle reserve and unpretending simplicity which were the characteristics of its beloved author." Shortly after his death there appeared in the *Sentinel*, a Derry paper, a careful and sympathetic sketch of his character, of which a part may well be copied in these pages. It is manifestly written by one who knew Mr. Higinbotham well.

The work of a parochial clergyman, in a city like our own, rarely appeals, in any considerable degree, to general interest. It has few romantic aspects. Its dates and eras are not those of the world. Its

[1] Dublin : Hodges, Smith, and Co., 104 Grafton Street, booksellers to the university.

influences are noiseless, like the beneficent agencies of nature, which are forgotten because they are unobtrusive, and remind us of their utility most eloquently when they are suspended. To our departed friend Providence had assigned the faculties of reflection rather than those of observation. He was a beautiful and judicious thinker rather than an accomplished rhetorician. In his collegiate career he had achieved the highest university distinction in the moral sciences. The influence of these earlier studies had coloured the whole complexion of his mind. We do not mean that his sermons were those of an " ape of Epictetus," as the moral essayists of the pulpit in the last century have been severely designated. They were purely and truly evangelical. His ethics were baptised in the " fountain opened for sin and for unclean- ness." The moral strokes which he delighted to draw were copied from the lineaments of crucified love, as they are exhibited in the pages of the inspired evangelists, who held the pencil of the Holy Ghost. His favourite sermons in his favourite Bishop Butler, were those on the love of God. Hence his pulpit discourses were, perhaps, of too pensive and refined a cast for general appreciation. The feathered fall of his Christian ethical teachings might not often startle or surprise ; but we know that they found audience " fit," if " few." They awakened echoes in congenial spirits ; while no attentive listener could fail to perceive that the preacher had steeped his thoughts in his heart - -that he spoke because he believed. Such of his sermons or lectures as have occasionally appeared in our columns, were character- ised by chastened and thoughtful brevity, lucid arrangement, and much delicacy of illustration. An aged clergyman of this diocese, distinguished for the extent of his scholarship and the acuteness of his judgment, pronounced Mr. Higinbotham's lecture on the Greek Revo- lution to be a performance of the highest order.

But his ministry found the peculiar field for its richest developments beside the bed of sickness, and in the house of mourning. There was a sympathy, there was a refinement of tenderness in his manner, on such occasions, learned in heavenly meditation and in communion with Him who " can be touched with the feeling of our infirmities." To use a favourite expression of his own, " the human sympathies of the Redeemer " had touched the sympathies of · his heart into life and music. His disposition was naturally pensive ; he had what the great poet calls " the quiet heart " ; yet he brought with him into every society a noble and tender gaiety, which made religion beautiful in the eyes of the youngest and most thoughtless. His conversation had nothing forced or conventional. It was like a sweet and natural air that winds into itself many threads of harmony ; but it always revolved round two kindred notes—the character of Christ, and the bliss of Heaven.

He was eminently formed for friendship. No cloud of envy or jealousy ever seemed to dwell upon the serenity of his renewed nature.

Within two years preceding his death Mr. Higinbotham had been married to Josephine, daughter of Colonel Jones, of the 12th Regiment, and great sympathy was felt with his young widow. Mrs. Robert Higinbotham, who lived for many years of her life at Bournemouth, wrote a memoir of her sister, Miss Agnes Jones, who had made a name for herself in connection with nursing, especially in workhouse hospitals. To this book an article by Miss Florence Nightingale is prefixed as an introduction, and the book has been translated into many European languages.[1]

Bishop Alexander wrote several poems upon the death of his friend. The best known of these is the epitaph graven on a mural tablet on the walls of Derry Cathedral :—

> Down through our crowded lanes, and closer air,
> O friend, how beautiful thy footsteps were :
> When through the fever's waves of fire they trod,
> A form was with thee like the Son of God.
> 'Twas but one step for those victorious feet
> From their day's walk unto the golden street ;
> And they who watch'd that walk, so bright and brief,
> Have mark'd this marble with their hope and grief.[2]

A scrap from a relative's letter, dated December, 1862, offers a comment on the lines :—

I have received word from a clergyman to-day that in the late summer visit paid by the Bishop of Oxford (Wilberforce) to Derry, on the occasion of his accompanying the Bishop of Derry to see the cathedral, he said, after reading Mr. Alexander's *in memoriam* lines on darling Robert's mural tablet, "I would willingly give my Oxford mitre to have been the composer of those lines."

[1] London : Strahan and Co. 1869.
[2] *St. Augustine's Holiday, and Other Poems*, by William Alexander, Bishop of Derry and Raphoe. London : Kegan Paul, Trench, and Co. 1886.

CHAPTER VI

THE EDITOR OF THE "ARGUS"

"I am in the place where I am demanded of conscience to speak the truth, and therefore the truth I speak, impugn it whoso list."

Earlier history of the *Argus*—Established June 2nd, 1842—Mr. Edward Wilson buys it—Absorption of other papers—Some account of Mr. Wilson—His views of the policy of the paper—Mr. Wilson needs rest, and, appointing Mr. Higinbotham as editor, leaves the colony—On his return leaves the editor undisturbed—Relations between owner and editor—Mr. James Smith's reminiscences of his former editor—One personal reference, Mr. Higinbotham's appointment as J.P.—Was the editor over-careful? Letter to Mr. Hugh George.

WHEN Mr. Higinbotham became editor of the *Argus*, that newspaper was a little over fourteen years old, for it came into being on the 2nd of June, 1842. In the old world fourteen years may not seem long in the life of a newspaper: yet in London many papers have earned fame, and have disappeared within a smaller span. There is no analogy between the life of an individual and the existence of a paper, which need not have a childhood: and there is no reason why a paper should not, especially in a young country, "flash into fiery life from nothing," and establish influence before it is a month old. As compared with its later self, the *Argus* may be said to have had a childhood and a period of adolescence. Its childhood was in the days when the whole community was not only young, but small. In 1842 the estimated population of the colony was (to use the accurate figures of Mr. Hayter) 23,799. In the census of 1857 the enumeration was 410,766.

In 1847 the *Argus* was bought by Mr. Edward Wilson, who shortly afterwards also bought, in order to absorb it, the *Patriot*, the newspaper belonging to Mr. John Pascoe Fawkner, often called the "Father of Victoria," because of the expedition that he organised in Tasmania, which, however, on arrival, found John Batman in possession. Fawkner was a public-spirited citizen, and certainly established the first paper in the settlement, of which the *Port Phillip Patriot* may fairly be considered the legitimate descendant. In 1852, after the gold-fever had begun, another rival paper, or in a sense two rival papers, were incorporated with the *Argus*, for Mr. Wilson bought the *Daily News*, which had previously absorbed the *Times*. Even the owners of these last two papers would hardly have claimed for them the importance that their names suggest.

The gold-fever must have been a terrible time for the managers of a newspaper. Tidings would come of a "rush." Writers, reporters, and printers, would start off for the diggings on the shortest notice. In Port Jackson and Port Phillip there were frequently ships without sailors. The bishop and the governor groomed their own horses, as they were without servants. All heads were turned, and for a while Melbourne was almost deserted, yet subscribers wanted their daily paper, and the *Argus* never disappointed them. The man at the head of the affairs at the *Argus* office, part owner, editor, manager, and chief writer, energetically pushing his own business, vigorously fighting for the public good, was Edward Wilson, who was not a trained journalist, but one who had almost by chance stumbled upon this, his true vocation.

Edward Wilson was born at Hampstead, almost within the sound of Bow Bells, in 1814, the year before the Battle of Waterloo. He was educated at a private school in Hampstead, and amongst his schoolfellows were several whom he met again in Victoria. Amongst others is mentioned Mr. William Clark Haines, first Premier of Victoria; but Haines must have been a big boy when Wilson was a small boy, for he was seven years older. Commerce was at first intended to be Wilson's line in life, and he entered a house of business in London, but the high stool and the desk were utterly distasteful to him; he longed for a more adventurous life, wherefore he determined to emigrate to Australia. His destination was Sydney, but the ship, on which he was, put into Port Phillip, and he was so pleased with all he heard about the infant settlement and its future prospects, that he promptly determined to cast in his lot with it. This was in the year 1842, the very year in which the *Argus* was established, but five years before Wilson had anything to do with it. Sheep and cattle, or some occupation subsidiary to the rearing and shearing of sheep and the raising of cattle, engrossed the attention of every one connected with Port Phillip, except the few officials ; and Mr. Wilson bought a cattle station near Dandenong, but the young man (he was twenty-eight when he arrived) took a great interest in public affairs. Like the Irishman of the story he was "agin the government." Some letters violently criticising the actions of Mr. C. J. Latrobe, the superintendent of Port Phillip, appeared in the *Argus* signed "Iota." They were from Wilson's pen, and these letters may be said to have revealed Wilson to himself : his thoughts were turned towards journalism. Then came the purchase of the *Argus* in 1847, and though partners were admitted later, Mr. Wilson remained all his life the chief proprietor of the *Argus*, and through ten eventful, crowded, vigorous years, he was editor and the life and soul of the paper. In these ten years there came in quick succession—first, separation from New South Wales, or the beginning of the colony of Victoria : secondly, the discovery of gold, and consequent influx of population ; and, thirdly, the establishment of responsible government. The *Argus* under Wilson was keenly in favour of the first and third : was hostile to the unwise administration that led to the conflicts with the diggers ; resisted the influx to the diggings of convicts from across the Straits ; and was strongly opposed to the continuance of transportation to Australia. As long as he was editor, Mr. Wilson was always on the popular side. Squatter though he had been, he desired to settle the people on the land ; and the policy connected with the phrase "Unlock the lands" was the policy of the *Argus*; indeed it is said[1] that it was Wilson who formulated the demand contained in that famous watchword.

The nine years of arduous labour at length affected Wilson's

[1] Blair's *Cyclopædia of Australasia*.

health, and especially his eyesight. His fortune was made, and he desired rest, which his doctors also recommended that he should take. Therefore he determined to revisit England, which he had left, aged twenty-eight, to seek his fortune. Fifteen years had passed and he was returning a wealthy man. With the full consent of his partners Mr. Wilson selected Mr. Higinbotham to take the editorial chair. It is true the new editor was only thirty, but young men were filling many of the important positions in the colony. The London *Times* has had a younger editor, and Mr. Wilson himself was only three years older when he began the same work.

Mr. Wilson left Melbourne for England in the middle of April, 1857, by the P. and O. steamer that carried the mail. An account of his voyage appeared in a little book which he published some two years later, called *Rambles at the Antipodes*. So familiar is the voyage now that it is no longer permissible to describe it, but the difference between the facilities of the present day and the time of Mr. Wilson's voyage is made clear, when we notice that he was in Ceylon, praising the neighbourhood of Point de Galle as a very paradise, a few days after the outbreak of the Indian Mutiny, having no conception how near he was to a volcano in full eruption, and that there was a risk even of his paradise being lost. Mr. Wilson's intention was, when he returned to Victoria, to resume work at the *Argus* office, but either he was so well satisfied with his substitute, or the leisure that he had hardly earned was so pleasant to him, that he never again occupied the editor's chair. After twelve months' absence he returned to Victoria, and then travelled in other Australasian colonies, in New Zealand, which is the tourists' land of the south, and in Queensland, which was separated from New South Wales at the end of 1859. These travels formed the bulk of Mr. Wilson's little volume already mentioned, the contents of which first appeared as letters in the *Argus*. In 1861 the Victorian Acclimatisation Society was founded, Mr. Wilson being one of its chief founders and its first president. If it be true that the society introduced the sparrow, and unfortunately the house-sparrow rather than the hedge-sparrow, there is a set-off in the number of British song-birds introduced and in the admirable Zoological Gardens in the Royal Park, Melbourne, which in many respects need not fear comparison with the London Gardens in the Regent's Park. Friends of the society may claim that it did not import the rabbit, nor the hare, nor the fox, nor the Hanover rat, nor the Cape weed, nor the Scotch thistle. In 1864 Mr. Wilson returned to England and finding that his eyes were better there, settled at Hayes, in Kent. His affection for the colony remained undiminished, as well as his interest in all colonial matters. By his will he left his property for kind and philanthropic objects, to give life pensions to ladies who were relatives or friends, and the revenue of the remainder to charities in Victoria, the money to be divided year by year as his trustees should determine. He further directed that his body should be brought out to the colony for interment. His useful life came to a close on January 10th, 1878, the day after a well-remembered date in Victorian history, usually known as Black Wednesday.

Long before Mr. Wilson's second voyage to England the editor of the *Argus* had resigned. Mr. Higinbotham would brook no interference in his work as editor. His theory of an editor's position was clear, logical, and definite; it was that the proprietors of a paper should choose a man whom they could trust, and then trust him completely and implicitly. If at any time they saw reason to withdraw their confidence, they should tell him frankly. But an editor in his own province and so long as he was editor should be absolute. He would have no council to guide or control him. Mr. Wilson, though a proprietor, was to be as one of the public in his dealings with the editor. If he wrote a letter, it should be inserted and criticised—neglected, supported, or answered, just as if the writer had no property in the paper: and to Mr. Wilson's honour it must be said that he submitted, even cheerfully, to the application of this doctrine. But a change was coming over Mr. Wilson's views; they were undergoing a not unnatural change in the direction of Conservatism. If in April, 1857, he saw eye to eye with his editor, two years later he no longer did; and Mr. Higinbotham one day found out, to his great surprise, that there were fundamental differences between the two of them on Victorian politics. At once he submitted his resignation, which with the usual polite expressions of regret was accepted.

In his later life Mr. Higinbotham frequently spoke to me

of the strong feeling of respect he entertained for Mr. Edward Wilson. One point deserves special mention. Mr. Wilson strongly advised him, as editor, not to go "into society," in order that he might avoid even the appearance of belonging to any particular *côterie*. The advice was in itself palatable, as its recipient was of the opinion of John Stuart Mill, that much of our modern social intercourse was a sheer waste of time. From that time forward Mr. Higinbotham never went into society. Having formed the rule and appreciated its advantages he did not find any difficulty in adhering to it afterwards; and he told me he found the habit of utmost value during his political life.

Mr. James Smith, one of Mr. Higinbotham's friends and fellow-workers on the *Argus*—himself now, after thirty-seven years' connection with that journal, the *doyen* of Melbourne journalists—has written the following interesting account of his former editor :—

My recollections of Mr. Higinbotham as an editor are exceeding pleasant ones, and are not darkened by the shadow of a single cloud, however transitory. His colleagues felt that they were associated with a gentleman who was eminently capable, inflexibly just, uniformly courteous and considerate, and animated by a dignity and delicacy of feeling which were exhibited no less towards the contributors whom he made his personal friends, than towards the messengers and office boys who fetched and carried proofs. He inspired a sentiment of affectionate loyalty in the minds of those who worked with him, and his own example of assiduity and devotion in the service of the *Argus* called forth an emulation of zeal and ability on the part of those who constituted what may be called his staff officers. He knew how to stimulate their efforts by a few words of judicious praise, and he introduced a system of remunerating his leader-writers according to his own estimate of the quality of their work—the maximum *honorarium* being fifty per cent. above the minimum— which had the effect of calling forth all their best powers in whatever they were engaged upon.

His own position was a thoroughly independent one ; so much so, that I have known views put forward by one of the principal proprietors of the paper, in the shape of a letter addressed to the editor, criticised and controverted in the leading columns of the same or a subsequent issue. But while Mr. Higinbotham was resolute and unyielding in the assertion and defence of his own opinions on the political and social questions of the day, he scrupulously respected the opinions of his colleagues. He never expected these to be modified, much less changed so as to bring them into harmony with his own. And herein, it should be added, he was faithful to the conduct and policy of every editor of the *Argus*, from Mr. Edward Wilson downwards. When Mr. Higinbotham discussed with a contributor some topic of the day which seemed to call for immediate comment, if that contributor differed from his chief upon any essential point, the subject was passed on to another writer whose views might happen to be more thoroughly in accordance with those of the editor.

In general, he was remarkable for the grave suavity of his manner and the amenity of his disposition. The expression of his countenance was naturally serious, but when it broke into a smile, it was like a ray of sunshine playing over his face. A tale of wrong stirred him to the quick, a narrative of injustice roused a fierce feeling of indignation within him ; and when his sympathies were excited, he displayed an almost womanly tenderness of emotion ; for, as it seems to me, he combined a masculine vigour of intellect with a feminine warmth and goodness of heart.

At the time of which I write, when my opportunities of studying so remarkable a personality were of daily occurrence, and when our relations were of a peculiarly intimate and confidential character, it struck me that his views of human life and of mankind taken in the mass, were somewhat optimistic, and not such as are generally entertained by older thinkers,

"Full of sad experience moving toward the stillness of their rest."

For, just as many men are in the habit of projecting a gigantic shadow of themselves upon a Brocken mist, and misnaming it God ; so I think he saw in " the people " a multiplication of his own image, an aggregation of beings as intelligent, as honest, as disinterested, as enlightened, as affectionate, and as incorruptible as himself. And a commonwealth composed of Higinbothams would render it comparatively easy to realise the dreams of a Plato, a More, a Campanella, or a Charles Renouvier. But men, being what they are, have to be reasoned with and instructed through the columns of a newspaper, with a constant regard to the hard facts of human nature, and with a due allowance for the large element of stupidity, ignorance, prejudice and selfishness to be met with in all communities. And herein lay the weak point, as I take it, of Mr. Higinbotham as a journalist. He addressed himself to an ideal public,—a public which, as I have said, was a multiplied reflection of himself. He gave it credit for an amount of intellectual capacity, a moral elevation of purpose, a purity of motive, and a nobility of patriotism, which it certainly did not possess ; while the absence of these qualities in the average newspaper reader, caused a good deal that was addressed to him to fall upon his eyes and ears either unregarded or uncomprehended. In a word, Mr. Higinbotham was a solitary thinker, and not a man of affairs ; and I think that, catching the infection of his influence and example, some of us occasionally talked over the heads of our audience.

Mill's Essay *On Liberty* was first published during his editorship of the *Argus*, and it devolved upon myself to write a series of articles expository of the principles laid down in that book ; and I well remember the enthusiasm they inspired in his own mind, and the echo which the words of the philosopher supplied to his own thoughts. But in our conversations on the subject, I noticed that the idealist always predominated over the practical politician when discussing it. He seemed loth to admit that that beautiful abstraction which stood for "the people" in his own mind, would be liable to abuse unlimited freedom, or that the despotism of a multitude might become even more odious and intolerable than the arbitrary power of a single tyrant. And being enamoured of liberty, Mr. Higinbotham was, of course, an ardent upholder of the theory and practice of free trade, which no one at that time dreamt of assailing ; for almost every adult Victorian had emigrated from the mother country, and we had all too vivid a recollection of the evils and miseries which had been inflicted upon it by protection, to contemplate the possibility of the hydra-headed monster lifting up its head in a British colony.

I had many opportunities, both at the period I speak of, and in later years, of conversing with Mr. Higinbotham on religious and psychological questions. In the absence of any more rigorous definition, I should be disposed to regard him, at that time, as a Christian theist, entertaining a profound belief in the Unity of the Godhead, and an equally profound admiration and veneration for the life and work of the Son of Man. Like most original and independent thinkers, he was not orthodox, and his ideas with respect to the hereafter seemed to me to present a remarkable similitude to those which find expression in *In Memoriam ;* as if he had been conducted by a train of reflection and reasoning, personal to himself, to the same conclusions as those arrived at by the poet. The key to, and the explanation of, his own religious faith and practice were to be found, as it appears to me, in his reverent appreciation of the words, "If a man love not his brother whom he hath seen, how can he love God whom he hath not seen ?" and in his acute perception of the fact that the second of the "two great commandments" comprehends the first. And his religious belief was no barren assent of the understanding to certain theological propositions, but flowered out in deeds of practical and unostentatious benevolence, inspired by motives of tender sympathy and humane compassion, and performed, whenever practicable, in such a way as that they might not be observed and praised of men ; for no one felt more strongly than himself that "the best portion of a good man's life" is made up of

> "His little, nameless, unremembered acts
> Of kindness and of love."

Only once was reference made in the paper to any matter personal to the editor. On June 14th, 1857, Mr. Higinbotham's appointment as Justice of the Peace appeared in the *Government Gazette.* As it was known that he was editor of the *Argus,* suspicions were at once entertained that the appointment was made by the Ministry to placate the *Argus.*

Some two months later the editor inserted the following brief explanation :—

Early in the year 1856 the present editor of this journal was a resident of Emerald Hill, following professional pursuits and wholly unconnected with the colonial Press. At that time he had the honour to receive an invitation, unsolicited on his part, that he would allow his name to be placed in the commission, the want being in the district in which he resided and the selection falling on him. Whilst appreciating the compliment, though not anxious to enter upon the discharge of new duties, he intimated his willingness to accept the proposal. This was in the month of March, 1856. Subsequently some delay took place in gazetting the new appointments to the magistracy, and it was explained that the arrival of Sir Henry Barkly was waited for. Thus matters stood until the month of August, when the first engagements with this journal were entered into. . . . . At the commencement of the year his Excellency landed,[1] and the editor of the *Argus* deeming it probable that the commission would be now issued, and feeling that the new relations upon which he had entered would in the state of political feeling in the colony render his acceptance of proposals made under different circumstances liable to misconception, wrote to the Attorney-General (the present Chief Justice),[2] requesting that his name might be withdrawn from the list of proposed Justices of the Peace. His letter was dated and forwarded on the 16th of January. It was written without any thought of any circumstances ever calling for its publication.

The following are its *ipsissima verba*, omitting only the superscription and the signature :

The Editor of the " Argus " to the Attorney-General.

" *Argus* Office, January 16th, 1857.

" My dear Sir,— You informed me some time ago, in conversation, that the offer which I had the honour of receiving from the late Acting Governor, in the early part of last year, of appointment to a Justiceship of the Peace would not be fulfilled until the arrival of Sir Henry Barkly, when my name, and those of others who had accepted a similar offer, would be gazetted.

" Since my interview with you I have accepted the editorship of the *Argus* newspaper. Considering the relations which are supposed to exist between the Government and this journal, I fear that my appointment would give rise to rumours injurious as well to the Government as to the *Argus*, and no explanation would wholly counteract their effect.

" I have, therefore, come to the determination— though I own it is with some regret—not to ask for a fulfilment of the promise made to

---

[1] As a matter of fact it was December 26th, 1856.
[2] Sir William Stawell.

me by the late Acting Governor; and I now address you, as the first Law Officer, for the purpose of requesting that you will have my name removed from the list of intended magistrates.

"I have also to request that you will be so good as to write to me, to state that it is at my own request the appointment will not be made."

The editor regrets that in this instance he has found it necessary to depart from the rule by which the conduct of the *Argus* is ordinarily guided. But it appeared to him proper to publish this statement in order to vindicate the political independence of this journal,—an independence the great mass of the public will give it credit for having sustained until now, and which whilst it remains in the hands of its present conductor shall not be compromised.

The following criticism is taken from an obituary notice in an English paper [1]:—

Alike as journalist, barrister, and judge, he was exceedingly conscientious. When he was editor of the *Melbourne Argus* he so carefully corrected the proofs, and so strenuously insisted on reading and verifying everything that went into type, that sometimes the paper did not come out until six and even seven in the morning, with the result that early trains were missed, much to the disgust of up-country subscribers.

It is no doubt true that the editor was conscientious, and even fastidious, nor was he ever a quick writer; but close inquiry on the spot elicits no memories of such a mischief-working conscience. The delay mentioned was due to badness of machinery and perhaps to the trouble in the printing department of the paper, alluded to in the letter here given, written by Mr. Higinbotham about Mr. Hugh George, in which the former bears testimony to the good work done by the latter at the *Argus* office.

I think it was in the year 1856 that Mr. George and I first became acquainted. It was about that time that Mr. George came out from the London *Times* office to take charge of the mechanical arrangements of the *Argus* newspaper, of which I was then the editor. Prior to his arrival, there was considerable discontent and trouble in the printing department of the paper, which involved much anxiety and additional and longer labour in the editor's branch. I well remember the extraordinary and instantaneous effect produced by Mr. George. Thoroughly acquainted with his business, he at once ascertained the causes of discontent. He readily yielded to those demands of the

---

[1] The *Pall Mall Budget*, January 5th, 1893.

printers which he found to be just ; and by mingled firmness and moderation, guided by consummate discretion, he at once restored discipline, order, and contentment, which were never afterwards disturbed during the time I was connected with the paper. In a few days after his arrival, some of us in the editor's department were enabled through his aid to go home from our work at one o'clock, or two o'clock, or three o'clock in the morning, instead of at four o'clock, or five o'clock, or six o'clock, or even as late as seven o'clock, the hours we had kept for some short time previously. My first feelings, therefore, towards Mr. George were those of high respect, and a sense of official and personal obligation. They became stronger as daily intercourse made us better acquainted, and I have always had a lively pleasure in believing that our friendship was not even interrupted for a moment, when long afterwards it became my painful duty to have Mr. George committed to the custody of the Sergeant-at-Arms for a contempt of the Legislative Assembly, committed by him as the publisher of the *Argus*. I should not omit to state that the *Argus* under Mr. George was the first Victorian newspaper to acquire the appearance and arrangement of matter that distinguish a first-class London newspaper.

CHAPTER VII

EDITORIAL VIEWS

Short History of Period, three years from August, 1856—Burke and
Wills Expedition—A Possible War with France—State Aid to
Religion—Education—Women—Capital Punishment—Aborigines
—Unemployed—Land Policy—Labour—Vote by Ballot—Demo-
cracy—Party Government—Leaders of Democracy.

THE period during which Mr. Higinbotham was editor of
the *Argus* lasted for rather less than three years, beginning
in August, 1856. Responsible government had been introduced in Victoria in November, 1855, and the new system
was therefore less than nine months old, when he began his
work. Whilst he sat in the editor's chair there were no
fewer than three changes of ministry: universal suffrage and
vote by ballot became the law of the land. Sir Henry
Barkly arrived to be Governor of the colony and Sir William
Stawell was appointed Chief Justice. They were stirring
times, but there is little to chronicle with respect to them.
Population was increasing rapidly by immigration: most of
the immigrants were adventurous and energetic: and, as is
evident from the newspaper, life was rough, whilst a certain
degree of lawlessness prevailed.

One of the most important incidents during the period was
the offer made through the *Argus*, by an anonymous correspondent, of the sum of £1,000 towards the promotion of a
judicious scheme of exploration in the interior. "With a
modesty and unobtrusiveness which doubly enhanced the
value of his munificent offer, he desired that his name should
remain unknown." The editor of the *Argus* religiously kept
the secret, until Mr. Ambrose Kyte allowed his name to be

revealed. It was this offer that led to the famous Burke and Wills expedition.

Many subjects were discussed in the columns of the *Argus*. It is known that the editor wrote a great deal himself. Of course he was responsible for everything in the paper, and a few passages selected almost at random may serve to show the sentiments that found favour with the editor.

In August, 1858, there seemed some probability of a war with France.

Honour and duty should impel us to remain staunch and loyal to the mother-country in her hour of trial. [August 30th, 1858.]

The relations of the State to religion and to education find frequent treatment. From an article in favour of State Aid the following is extracted :—

Looked at from the general and social and not from the individual point of view we apprehend that all forms of religious belief which acknowledge and enforce the rules of moral duty are " equally useful " to society. [June 2nd, 1857.]

Ultimate withdrawal of State Aid is expected, when the churches should be ready to run alone.

But that the State Aid should be withdrawn immediately is what few even of the conscientious objectors to the present system can actually desire. [July 27th, 1859.]
Meanwhile complete equality of all the churches is advocated. [November 9th, 1858.]
The connection of Church and State in educational matters cannot last much longer. . . . The school must no longer be a mere adjunct of the church. [September 27, 1858.]

The position of women is discussed, and the paper is in favour of changes in the law, which have been since made, as well as of a degree of freedom hardly yet reached by the sex. Here is one excerpt :—

A model woman according to a very prevalent conception of the character is little better than an amiable idiot ; and any woman who evinces strength of mind and vigour of intellect becomes an object of derision and a butt for the feeble sarcasm of the mentally destitute of the other sex. [June 25th, 1858.]

The editor's strong feeling of humanity is revealed in the following :—

The treatment of the Aborigines has from the commencement of the settlement of the continent been a standing reproach against colonists. [February 3rd, 1859.]

Here follows a statement of a view, which later experience caused Mr. Higinbotham to change :—

We are convinced that the abolition of capital punishment should at least be tried, were it only for a time. It would be easy to revert to barbarism should amelioration appear to be premature. [December 10th, 1858.]

The " Unemployed " difficulty was felt early in the colony's history. Its solution is found in settlement upon the land.

In the meantime, pending the preparation and adoption of legislative measures for encouraging the settlement of population on the soil, and for converting idle consumers into active producers, the painful fact of the present existence of much actual and severe destitution must be dealt with and cannot brook delay. For the sake of humanity, for the credit of the colony, and out of regard to the interests of society, the Government must not suffer such an anomaly and reproach to continue. It is not with alms that we would supply these homeless and destitute men.   We would neither destroy their self-respect nor recognise pauperism as one of the normal conditions of any industrious section of the community. [December 7th, 1858.]

Here is a Land Policy well nigh in a nutshell :-

It lies in a general tax on alienated land, whether cultivated or not cultivated.   The man who lives upon the produce of his land can afford to pay a small annual charge upon it, whilst the man who merely occupies, and whose occupation actually constitutes a barrier against cultivation, deserves to pay it. [August 21st, 1858.]

The editor writes strongly upon the just rights of honest labour, including the right of combination to raise wages :—

We have an anxious desire to see a high rate of wages prevailing here, and we regard the prosperity of the great mass of the people as more important than almost any other consideration.   But we neither feel, nor are prepared to simulate, the smallest sympathy for the loud drones who try to discourage others from honest work, in order that they may be able to live on the wages of agitation, without honest work. [September 8th, 1857.]

In the early days of the country's politics it is natural that the suffrage, the true principles of representation, and the

ballot should be frequently discussed, as they are from the
point of view of the mother-country as well as of Victoria
It was on such subjects that controversy arose, honourable to
both, between Mr. Edward Wilson, the proprietor, and Mr.
Higinbotham, the editor.   The ballot is defended against
the charge of cowardice :—

These men, in their country's crisis, would act nobly, we doubt
not, as their ancestors did.   The mistake of the *Times* is to assume
that the country is always in a crisis of a nature to develop ordinary
men into heroes.   [August 18th, 1858.]

But the ballot, electoral districts, and the incidence of the
suffrage are more or less matters of machinery.   Democracy
is the principle that underlies them all.   Longer extracts are
given to set forth the teaching of the *Argus* "leaders."   The
influence of M. de Tocqueville is strongly marked in them :—

The form of government to which the condition of a new and
progressive society such as ours naturally gives rise is essentially democratic. . . . We may therefore accept democracy as a fact which, with
whatever feelings we may regard it, we can neither resist nor neglect.
Like all the forces of Nature it is an enormous power either for good
or for evil.   It comes upon us with the overwhelming might of a
physical law, and it brings with it the tremendous sanctions with
which such laws are invested.   If we be content merely to direct its
action, it is able to render us good service : but if we resist it, it will
destroy us : the stone which the skilful builder makes the support of his
whole fabric will crush to powder the rash or the unwary, who provoke
and withstand its fall.   [February 13th, 1858.]
We hold that the great end of all electoral systems is as far as
possible to secure justice and good government to every individual :
that no amount of wealth gives any one an extra claim as to these
matters : that a community is not a commercial company, in which a
man should have a voice potential to the number of shares he is able to
buy : that the claim to be well governed rests upon something quite
apart from one's power of paying the expenses of government ; that
Lazarus has as much right to be considered in legislation as Dives : and
that all men who live in a country have as large an interest in its good
government, and as equal a stake in it, that their mere pecuniary possessions are but as dust in the balance. . . . What Carlyle calls the "mere
counting of heads" is no doubt at all times a most fallible method of
arriving at the truth, but in some form it is an essential of all electoral
systems, nay, it is the electoral system itself, and defective as it is, human
intelligence has as yet devised no better mode of picking out mankind's
proper governors. . . . We cannot, so long as the electoral system
endures, avoid the evil of subordinating the will of some men to that
of some others.   If there is a contest one side must be beaten in order

that there may be a conclusion. In other words the minority must give way to the majority, and this evil is imposed upon the former unavoidably and in the very nature of things. . . . Extension of the suffrage to its utmost conceivable limits could mean nothing more liberal than adequate representation of the majority, and how to secure justice to the minority may even already have become the more critical question. [May 18th, 1857.]

The following is on Party Government.

In fact one of the strongest arguments which can be employed against government by party in all the colonial possessions of Great Britain is this— that it leads to the constant exclusion from the executive of a portion of the very few men who are peculiarly qualified for public life, and renders impossible the formation of a Cabinet which shall include all those who are eminent for their administrative capacity. . . . Under the existing state of things, not only is such a combination of the counsels and efforts of the best men for the service of the State effectually precluded, but they are arrayed in hostility towards each other, the grounds of difference being more frequently personal than political, and half the time and all the zeal of the disputants are expended in a conflict utterly barren of advantage to the country, rarely productive of honour to the disputants, and frequently offering the most injurious impediments to the necessary transaction of public business. [April 14th, 1859.]

Matthew Arnold admires in Edmund Burke the detachment which enabled him to see the second side of a question. Here, from the pen of one who had imbibed much from Burke's teaching, is a statement of the true corrective of Democracy which he accepts as the will of God. It is the last quotation from the *Argus* articles that need be reproduced.

We recently called the attention of those who are alarmed at our career of political change to the fact that these changes inevitably result from our social condition and that the question of their completion is merely one of a little longer or a little shorter time. In such circumstances resistance becomes folly, if not worse. It is therefore incumbent on all enlightened men who love their country and desire to aid its real progress, to consider well what part they are henceforward to take in political life. The path of duty is distinct and broad : the educated classes, so far from shrinking from public affairs, must now beyond all times be found at their posts. Their influence is as legitimate and its foundations are as deeply laid as those of Democracy itself. [Here follows a quotation from Edmund Burke on natural aristocracy.] Every society must contain the element of Conservatism and the element of progress. In our case the development of the latter element is unusually rapid. If the growth of the Conservative element do not bear some proportion to this rapid development, if the relation between the two elements be destroyed, that development will become morbid, and the symmetry of the entire social body will be destroyed. . . . The people must have leaders: it is from the very nature of things impossible that they should continue without some guidance. If then their natural leaders desert them, to whom are they to look? Who will fill the vacant places which the natural aristocracy have abdicated? The answer to the question is plain. Then will be the time for the political quack, for the trader in sedition, for all that obscure brood that, too idle and too worthless to live by honest industry, fatten upon popular ignorance and credulity; such men rejoice in civil commotions and in the divisions of society. These divisions are to them not merely a source of profit, but the actual condition of their existence. These are the men who by their senseless clamour would gladly scare from public life all men of cleaner hands and nobler aspirations. These and these only are the men who, amid the great detriment of the public, would derive an advantage from that dereliction of duty, against which we raise our warning voice. Let, then, our independent men look to it. The question for their consideration is whether they will be the leaders of the people or whether they will resign that position to the most unfit and the most dangerous hands. On their conduct more than on that of any other class the future welfare of the colony depends. [February 17th. 1858.]

> "So spake the prophet centuries ago.
> Is not his prophecy a history now?"

Are not his words trumpet-tongued to stir the educated to their duty in politics

CHAPTER VIII

M. L. A.

Elected for Brighton without opposition, May, 1861 —The Hon. C. H.
Ebden his Predecessor— Views in Speech for Universal Suffrage ;
against Party Government ; on the Land Question ; on Education ;
on State Aid to Religion ; on Payment of Members, and on Protection—Short Time in the House Supports Heales' Government —It
is defeated General Election Too independent and therefore
defeated, August 2nd— Re-elected April 8th, 1862 Rising into
prominence in the House— Defeat of O'Shanassy *cum* Haines
Government.

MR. HIGINBOTHAM'S political career began in 1861. In the
April of that year he was thirty-five, and many members of
the Legislative Assembly were younger. He was a barrister
in good practice and much respected by his neighbours : and
it was not unnatural that, when a vacancy occurred in the
representation of Brighton, where he and his brother had
recently come to reside, a considerable number of the electors
should have invited him to come forward for that constituency.
The vacancy was caused by the resignation of the Hon.
Charles Hotson Ebden. Thirty years previously Mr. Ebden
had emigrated to New South Wales, and had engaged in
squatting pursuits on the Murray, and afterwards in that
part of the colony which became Victoria. For many years
he had taken a prominent part in politics. In 1843 he had
been elected one of the first four members who represented
the Port Phillip district in the Legislative Council of New
South Wales. When the five years for which he had been
elected elapsed, he declined to be nominated a second time.
He told the electors that "he could not any longer lend
himself to the perpetration of what was only a farce. Port

Phillip was not, in fact, represented ; she was misrepresented."
It was on that occasion, and in order forcibly to arrest
attention in England, that Earl Grey was elected member for
Melbourne.   This whimsical proceeding had the desired effect
and the separation of the colony followed.   When Victoria
was made into a separate colony, Mr. Ebden was appointed
Auditor-General ; but after holding that office for a little over
a year he resigned.   At a little later date he was Treasurer
of the colony under responsible government, being a member
of the third administration formed.   Mr. Ebden resigned his
seat in May, 1861, and went to England.   He is perhaps best
remembered now for his own remark that he was growing
"disgustingly rich."

On 7th May, 1861, the Speaker announced that he had
received a letter from Mr. Ebden resigning his seat for
Brighton.   Four days later Mr. Higinbotham addressed the
electors.   It is evident that considerable interest was excited
in his candidature, for the *Argus* gave a verbatim report of
this speech.   In it the candidate's views are stated freely and
without reserve, and the subjects treated are the following :
universal suffrage, party government, the land question,
education, and State aid to religion.   The candidate was
questioned as to his views on protection and payment of
members.   After a few opening remarks Mr. Higinbotham
answered those who contended that universal suffrage was the
cause of all the woes of the colony.

From the time that I was able or that I attempted to form an
opinion on political matters, I accepted with hearty satisfaction, and I
have since always retained a belief in, the sound constitutional doctrine
—or at least a doctrine which has been adopted by the soundest constitutional writers—that every individual in a free country who contri-
butes to the taxes of the State ought to enjoy a vote in the selection of
those who legislate for the State ; and except where a strong political
necessity interferes—a necessity which modifies abstract opinions as
well as controls events—that that suffrage, that right of voting, ought
to be withheld from none.   Now, I admit that, under certain circumstances and in certain countries this necessity may exist at the present
time.   I believe it does exist in England.

The ground for this necessity was then set forth—the
pauperism that is to be found in England.

I think there might be very great danger in extending the suffrage
indiscriminately in a country where so large a pauper class exists.   I

admit it may be a considerable time before universal suffrage can be restored to England. I say " restored," because I believe there is sound historical and constitutional authority for believing that universal suffrage existed in England before a property qualification was heard of.

The speaker then set forth "another ground founded on necessity which, I think, would justify a limitation of the franchise," total ignorance. " But," he added, " I think it would be a very great disgrace to a free country if that ground of disqualification were long permitted to exist." The State should see that such ignorance was removed. A proper system of registration of voters should require that no man should be registered as a voter who could not write his own name.

Universal suffrage may be regarded as the foundation-stone of democracy : and the inspection of the foundations was thus put into the first place in the speech, which then passed on to the duties of a member, and the question of party government. Mr. Higinbotham's views on this are of greater importance and interest than on all the questions of the day put together.

He was always a vigorous advocate for strong government, and held that frequent changes of ministry weakened government itself. Afterwards he became a member of the strongest ministry that ever held the reins of office in Victoria, strongest in talent and strongest in the support that it received from the people. It was also the ministry that enjoyed the longest political life. It is interesting to hear Mr. Higinbotham's views at the beginning of his political life, and they may be compared with similar sentiments that he expressed towards the close.

During the last half-century of English political history, the power of the representatives in the House of Commons over the government of the day has been steadily increasing, and the interference of representatives in Parliament with the government of the day has been more frequently exercised. During the fifty years that preceded the passing of the first Reform Bill there were ten changes of government in England. Each government lasted, on an average, five years, and every change was produced by a cause totally unconnected with the action of the House of Commons. During the thirty years that have elapsed since the passing of the Reform Bill, there have been eight or nine changes of government in England, and every one of those changes, with one exception, was produced by the action and direct vote of the House of Commons. And when we come to our own colony we find that, during the six years which have elapsed since the passing of the Constitution, there have been six changes of government, each government lasting, on an average, one year, and that every one of those changes, with the exception of the first, has been produced by the action and the direct interference of the Legislative Assembly. Now this, I think, is a very significant fact. It shows that the power of the representatives in Parliament over the government of the day is steadily increasing, and I am afraid that the direct power of the constituencies over members of Parliament has not increased in the same proportion. I wish that it did. If constituencies were more frequently to ask themselves and their representatives, for what reason, for what motives, from what impulses they seek to overthrow governments one after another—were the attention of constituencies directed to the conduct of their representatives in that way—I think the changes of government in this colony would be less frequent. I believe there is a general tendency of public opinion to this point—that these frequent changes of government are a source of unmixed injury to the public interest. Almost every successive government that has gone into office during the last six years has been weaker in every respect than its predecessor—weaker in point of Parliamentary influence; weaker in the confidence of the majority in Parliament; weaker, if it be not invidious to refer to it, in the personal composition of its members—until it has come to this, that government often exists, not so much through the confidence of Parliament as through the contempt of a Parliamentary majority. There is another serious evil. These frequent changes practically have the effect of placing the government of this colony in the hands of persons who are not responsible to Parliament. When a Minister who has not been in office previously enters office he is necessarily unacquainted with the duties and details of his department, and so long as he remains ignorant of these duties and details he is necessarily the pupil of the chief clerk of his department. Well, what is the result? A gentleman is installed in office. He is supposed by Parliament and the country to be responsible for the affairs of his department. In point of fact it is not so. After he has been in office a few months, and has begun to discharge the duties of his office and to manage his department efficiently, some fresh Parliamentary cabal ripens against the government, and he gives place to another as ignorant as he formerly was of the duties of his office, and destined, in all probability, to become also the pupil of a subordinate. Now, I think you will agree with me, that it is both mischievous and deplorable for the government to be vested in the hands of persons who, whatever their capacity may be, are not responsible to Parliament or the country. But, if these changes have been injurious to government, both in composition and action. I think they have proved no less injurious to Parliament itself. The Parliament of Victoria, since the inauguration of the Constitution, has passed a large number of acts—some 120, I believe, in six years. But if you examine them, you will find that the importance of them bears a very small proportion to the number, and even their number bears no proportion at all to the length of public time occupied in discussing them. If we were to ask ourselves what are the most important subjects which ought to occupy the earliest attention of the Parliament of a new country, I think we should be inclined to say that the education or instruction of the youth of the country and the settlement of the question relating to the public lands are the two subjects which claim the first and second places on the statute-book. Now, of these two questions, one has been only partially disposed of by the Legislature, and, although various attempts have been made to settle it, not a single act has been passed on the subject of the other. And while this neglect of the most important subjects of legislation has been taking place, we find that the frequent changes of government have so exasperated the minds of members of Parliament against one another, and so distracted their attention from the business of legislation, that legislation in the House of Assembly, as admitted by most persons, is, in fact, at the present time at a stand-still. And all this results from a system, defended by some persons, very mistakably I think, on the ground of English precedents—the system of government by party. I have heard this system defended on the ground of necessity—that legislation can be carried on only by means of a party government. If I felt myself compelled to come to that conclusion, I should entertain the most gloomy prospects as to the operation of representative institutions in this country. But I do not believe it is necessary; nay, more, I do not believe it will long be found to be even possible. It is perfectly true that there have been occasions in English history, within the memory of most of us, when government by party was necessary. There have been occasions when the public mind of England has been agitated on some great question—a question the discussion of which has lasted for many years, dividing the whole country into two adverse parties. When it was a question whether the Roman Catholics should be admitted into Parliament or kept out —when it was a question whether the first Reform Bill should be passed into law or not—when it was a question whether the tax on foreign corn should be retained or not, not merely was a Parliamentary party formed, but the whole nation was divided into two parties. I recollect the last of those events sufficiently to know that private friendships were sometimes formed, and private friendships were even sometimes sundered, by agreement or difference, as the case might be, on the absorbing topic of the day: and of course it follows, as a necessary consequence, that when a whole people is divided on one particular subject, and when that disagreement forms a question which is debated and agitated for many years, Parliament must be divided into two parties, differing in opinion, according to the people whom they represent. Differences of opinion of that kind do not exist here. They do not even now exist at home. If a person were to take any one of the questions discussed here, I think he would not say it was of such a nature that two men of similar character and personally friendly to one another might not fairly and honestly arrive at different conclusions about, and two persons of dissimilar character and unfriendly to one another might not arrive at the same conclusion and combine.

F

And that being so, I say you have not the materials of party, and unless you have the materials, if you attempt to construct a Parliamentary party, you simply succeed in creating a faction—a faction which has no motive except its own interest to pursue, or its own animosities to gratify. Now I was desirous to say so much on this general topic, because I wished to show what my conduct as a member of Parliament would be in this respect, if you do me the honour to elect me your representative. I will not join in any organised opposition to any government in which Parliament may have confidence, or the existence of which Parliament may be disposed to tolerate. If any individual member of a government acts in such a manner as to deserve and call for the censure of Parliament, I should endeavour to direct the censure so deserved against the offending individual member of the government, and wherever possible not to vote a sweeping censure, such as is now usually practised, on the whole government, most of the members of which may be wholly undeserving of it. It seems almost intolerable, because one member of a government may have acted in a way to call for the censure of Parliament, that, therefore, the country should be thrown into confusion for six weeks or two months, and that anarchy should exist in the legislature and the government. Why should we not maintain the government as a consistent and continuous body, altering its structure from time to time as occasion may require; turning out, as occasion may require, those members calling for censure, or who may prove themselves unfit for office? I do not deem it necessary, on every occasion when a cause of complaint arises, to pass a sweeping vote of censure upon the whole of the members of a government; and, therefore, whenever I can possibly avoid joining in it, I shall certainly refrain from doing so. I shall endeavour to direct censure to that particular quarter where censure is called for; and I believe if that course were adopted by members of Parliament, more would be done than can be done by other means to effect the desire we all have at heart—the establishment of a really strong government—strong in the support of Parliament, and at the same time closely watched, and carefully, though liberally and fairly, criticised by the representatives of the people.

Mr. Higinbotham's views on immediate questions of the day may be briefly stated. He was in favour of assisted immigration on two conditions—the first, that the immigrants assisted should be those able to support themselves on arrival in independence, and by preference those whose relatives in the colony send for them; the second, that no money should be spent to benefit one or more classes, and at the same time produce a directly and largely injurious influence upon any other class, for instance, lowering the wages of the labouring class. The assistance of the unemployed by the government except in case of absolute necessity was a very serious blow inflicted upon the cause of government. Then followed a long passage on the land question, and the claims of the squatters. The speaker was anxious that these claims should be publicly made and settled.

If the squatters have rights, and if the State has broken its engagements, let the squatters go into a court of law and prove their rights, and let them be paid the legal damage which they can prove they have sustained by a breach of the contract. . . . Waste lands of the Crown ought to be held as property by individuals and not in commonage. . . . There ought to be security of tenure. . . . The runs ought to be let by tender.

Next came the subject of education. Mr. Higinbotham drew a distinction between education and instruction.

Education, both in its grammatical meaning and ordinary acceptation, means something more than mere instruction in the rudiments of knowledge. It means the development of all the faculties of the child —the spiritual and moral, as well as the intellectual faculties : and when we have arrived at the conclusion that it is the interest and duty of the State to educate the children of the country, we necessarily conclude that that duty is very imperfectly fulfilled if we only succeed in teaching the child to read and write. I think that, in all cases, the duties of a state are limited by the powers of the State ; and I think it requires very little reflection to show us that in a community like this, where differences of opinion of the highest nature, both in religion and morals, all stand on an equal footing in the eye of the State, it is wholly beyond the power of the State to educate the children in the proper sense of the word " education." I believe the most the State can do—and, therefore, all that the State ought to attempt to do—is to instruct the children.

From the subject of education to that of religion is an easy step. Mr. Higinbotham was in favour of the continuance of the grant in aid of religion, though entirely opposed to the union of Church and State.

There is no conclusion which I have drawn from the study of history more confidently, or which has stood the test of experience and observation more permanently, than this—that nothing has been so injurious, either to the State or the Church, as the union between the Church and the State. In all European countries, for instance, except in the earliest times, when the Church was able certainly to render valuable assistance to literature and liberty by means of its connection with the State, the union of the Church and State has tended to make the State despotic and the Church tyrannical. Now, if the grant of £50,000 in aid of the different denominations recognized in any way the union between Church and State, if it were even a relic of that union, I should unhesitatingly oppose it.   But I do not think it does. I do not think the State acquires the slightest possible power from any religious denomination by means of this State grant, nor do I think that any religious denomination acquires any influence from the State by means of its acceptance of the grant.

In the course of his speech Mr. Higinbotham had made no allusion to two questions of the day, then only beginning to become burning questions, payment of members and protection. He was mildly "heckled" about them.   With respect to the former he thought there was something to be said in favour of recompensing those who had to leave the place where their business was carried on and remain a large portion of the year in Melbourne, but at the same time he saw overwhelming objections to the principle of payment of members by the public at large.   Some one called out, "Let those who send them pay them!" and Mr. Higinbotham added—"I was just going to make that suggestion."   He then stated his objection to payment of members by the public at large—

A perpetuation of the worst Parliamentary evils that exist at present.   Instead of having sittings for nine months in the year, you will have sittings all the year round ; and party warfare will be carried to a degree that it has never been carried before.

When an elector asked "Are you in favour of protection?" direct came the answer—

I am not.   I am a free trader.   At the same time I believe the question of protection has not deserved the contempt which has been thrown upon it in some quarters.   I believe it is an arguable question, and ought to be entertained and discussed.

On the nomination day, five days later, Mr. Higinbotham's proposer took the opportunity to advocate a protectionist policy, whereupon the candidate further expounded his views on free trade.

I certainly do not share the opinions he has expressed on the subject of protection, and if my friend will permit me to refer to one of the passages in the article in *Blackwood's Magazine*, from which he has quoted, I think I will be able, from a single word by Lord Overstone, to point out the fallacy of the doctrine of protection. This is the passage : Lord Overstone says—and the passage is quoted by

M‘Culloch—"It is important that a country should clearly understand the true meaning of free trade. It means trade freed, not from those necessary duties which are raised only for the purposes of revenue, but trade freed from all charges or duties that arise either from an ignorant jealousy of other countries, or from an equally foolish impression that it is our interest to foster unnatural productions in our own country rather than receive them from other countries." Now I think that clearly points out what free trade is, and for what purposes only duties ought to be levied. Where duties are for the purposes of revenue they may be imposed, and raised or lowered as necessity demands, but in no case should duties be imposed for the mere purpose of conferring a benefit on any particular interest as against every other interest in the community. I am a free trader, but I have not hastily or theoretically, or simply from the reading of books only, as my friend Captain Cole seems to think, formed my opinions on free trade. I have certainly given my attention to the writing of some eminent political writers on the subject of free trade ; but I have also sought to correct my views by the results of free trade as represented in the vast progress England has made from the time she unhesitatingly adopted the system. So I am strengthened in my views not only by the abstract opinions of eminent thinkers, but as far as the practical experience of our country is concerned it justifies me in holding that the principle of free trade is beneficial to the country at large.

There was no other candidate. On May 17th according to *Hansard*—

The new member for Brighton was introduced by Messrs. Mollison and Martley, and was duly sworn at the table. The honourable and learned member was warmly congratulated by the occupants of the Treasury benches, including the Chief Secretary, the Attorney-General, and Messrs. Grant and Brooke. He then took his seat below the gangway on the Opposition side of the House.

Mr. Richard Heales was Chief Secretary and Premier, and Mr. R. D. Ireland Attorney-General ; and their government was in office altogether a year. The middle of its somewhat troubled course had just been reached. On the whole it may be described as a Democratic cabinet with one or two members of a more Conservative tendency.

The Second Parliament of Victoria was drawing nigh unto its close. Parliament was prorogued on the 3rd and dissolved on the 11th of July. So that Mr. Higinbotham was not seven weeks in session, and not eight a member. In his first division he voted with the Government. It was proposed to increase the salary of a geodetic surveyor then in temporary charge of the observatory. The Government opposed the increase, and Mr. Higinbotham supported the ministers. His maiden speech was concerned with a similar question—an increase of salary. It occupies a column in *Hansard*. He showed the difficulty of dealing with such questions, and quoted the practice of the House of Commons, which refrains from interference. Feeling this difficulty, he should vote with the Government; at the same time he found fault with the Government because salaries had been reduced on no apparent principle, "except the unsound rule that the domestic circumstances of the officers should be considered." The House, being near the fag end of the session, was in a somewhat demoralised state. Personal recriminations were not uncommon, and there are also manifest signs of log-rolling. One page of *Hansard* is quite amusing, in which about fifteen members proposed, each in turn, an increase to the amount set down for the hospital or other charitable institution in his district, whilst the Government was powerless to prevent the increase.

The member for Brighton had not been a month in the House before he had an opportunity of showing that he was in earnest in the views as to party government which he had placed before his constituents. The bane of colonial parliaments is the frequent motion of want of confidence. On June 13th such a motion was proposed, and a debate ensued which lasted nearly twenty-one hours. The Government would not consent to an adjournment, and a great deal of time through the night was wasted in the struggle, motions to adjourn the debate and the House being moved alternately. Mr. Higinbotham had spoken rather early in the debate and had set forth such a view as might be expected after his Brighton speech. Stability of government being precious in his eyes, he was against motions of want of confidence and against frequent changes of ministry. The following sentences concluded the speech :—

We repeatedly hear that it is thought that these changes exhibit a vacillation and a want of political ability in our statesmen. That is bad. It should not be forgotten that it is still a disputed question whether Parliamentary government be good for a people or not. It is a question not forgotten in England, and much debated in other countries, and so far as our example is concerned, it will lend an argument either for or against Parliamentary government. So long as I have a seat in this House, so long will I oppose changes of government unless for more urgent and stronger reasons than those now alleged.

Those near whom the speaker sat on opposition benches did not like that doctrine, for they wanted his vote. His later conduct, during the debate, they were unable to make out. On the first two motions for adjournment he voted against the Government, for he thought that the debate should be concluded, as such debates were a hindrance to the business of the colony. On the next two motions he voted with the Government, as he thought it was not receiving fair play. Then having, as he always had, a strong feeling that all speaking against time and similar devices were an insult to the House, he paired and went home to bed. He was not in the chamber when, at a quarter past one on Saturday afternoon, the division was taken, and the Government was defeated by a majority of eighteen (thirty-seven to nineteen). The Governor, Sir Henry Barkly, granted the ministry a dissolution.

At this General Election Mr. Higinbotham was defeated for Brighton. He was too reasonable. True to his view that ejecting a ministry unless upon good cause shown was factious and wrong, he refused to pledge himself to vote against the Government; nor, on the other hand, would he promise to vote for it. His answer was that he had not made up his mind, but would decide on the point when he had heard the charges brought against the Government, and knew who were to be the successors. Neither side was pleased with this independence, and each brought out a party candidate, so that there was a triangular contest. Mr. J. G. Burtt was the Government candidate, and Mr. W. A. Brodribb, who had been a squatter for a quarter of a century, was put forward by the Opposition. The nominations were made on July 29th, and the poll took place on August 2nd. The result was :—

Brodribb 292
Higinbotham . . 227
Burtt 191

Strangely enough, Mr. Brodribb stood second on the poll in each division of the electorate, but at the head when the votes were added together.

Mr. Higinbotham's banishment from politics was not however for long. In the following March Mr. Brodribb resigned his seat in order that he might go for a trip to England, and

Mr. Higinbotham was again elected member for Brighton—not however without a contest. His opponent was Mr. W. J. Clarke, later created a baronet. In the meantime a new ministry had succeeded to power, which, with Mr. O'Shanassy as Chief Secretary and Premier and Mr. Haines as Treasurer, may be described as a coalition ministry. Mr. Clarke was a supporter of the ministry. Mr. Higinbotham again declared his independence, and so vigorously, that at a meeting of electors called to hear him speak a vote adverse to his candidature was carried. The election took place on April 8th, 1862, with the following result:—

$$
\begin{aligned}
&\text{Higinbotham} \quad . \quad . \quad . \quad 394 \\
&\text{Clarke} \quad . \quad . \quad . \quad . \quad 296 \\
&\overline{} \\
&\text{Majority} \quad . \quad . \quad . \quad 98
\end{aligned}
$$

That evening, introduced by Messrs. Service and Howard, he took the oaths. His seat was on the ministerial side below the gangway, and that very evening he made a short speech in committee on the Crown Land Sales Bill, usually called the Duffy Land Act. It was intended to encourage small holdings, but can hardly be regarded as having effected its object. The motion for the third reading came on almost immediately afterwards, and Mr. Higinbotham voted with the Government, which carried its bill by twenty-two votes (forty-five to twenty-three). As governments were not to be ejected, but improved by support, he gave the Government an independent support for the next fifteen months. He spoke occasionally, not very frequently. Education led to several speeches on different occasions, as the question came up. On Dill's case, a case of breach of privilege in which the printer of the *Argus* was brought before the Assembly for speaking evil of a member, Mr. Higinbotham was entirely opposed to the privilege of the House, and thought it should be abrogated. This, it is needless to add, was remembered on a similar later occasion when Hugh George was brought before the House. At the end of May he brought in a little bill to amend the law relating to conveyancers. In the next session this private member carried against the ministry this measure, which was to admit to the status of attorneys and solicitors nine conveyancers—who because of the new Real Property Act were, like Othello, with occupation gone. The Upper House threw out the bill without a division.

A speech towards the end of the first session is a case of coming events casting shadows.

In June [1] Mr. Verdon proposed and carried a resolution, "That in the opinion of this House it is expedient to consolidate and codify the statute law of this colony." On this motion the future consolidator of the Victorian Statutes spoke :—

He should be glad to see a sum placed on the estimates, under the control of the law officers of the Crown, for the purpose of effecting this work. The law officers could not, of course, be expected to do the work themselves, but they might superintend its performance by others. He could not conceive any work which would be more honourable to the law officers or more useful to the public than this. As to the usefulness of consolidation there could really be but one opinion. He agreed that the work of codification was much more difficult, or, rather, that the prospects of success attending it were not so great. He believed that even codification might ultimately be carried out.

The following strongly-worded extract from a private letter written from Victoria in the middle of 1862 was handed by the recipient to a member of the family :—

The position of Mr. Higinbotham and his brother, in the present state of affairs in the colony, is very high ; the engineer being one of two or three heads of departments at most, who to a high character in their profession join a repute of integrity of purpose. The brother who is a member of the Lower House has I may say the eyes of every well-wisher hopefully turned towards him. His high character and talent are a phenomenon in the House ; he holds the ministry in awe. I do not think they like him, but they fear him—which is better ; and the Opposition respect him, which they do not any other member of the governing party. A friend of mine, who watches the machinations here pretty closely, says he has but one failing, and that is that he is too scrupulous for the country !

At the opening of the second session in November, Mr. Higinbotham being opposed to the administration of the Land Act, spoke against the Government in the debate on the address, and ten days later voted against them. They however held their ground by forty votes to thirty.

[1] June 13th, 1862.

In a debate on a Partnership Bill he said:—"They should keep their legislation on the same footing, and as far as possible adopt the same acts as those put in force in England." Several times he spoke in committee on a long Local Government Bill. During the first half of the year 1863 he was prominent in the House. Having brought forward a grievance he accepted the Minister's explanation with the utmost frankness. He spoke against public nominations on the hustings, and in favour of an educational test for voters. He carried a motion about mail subsidies in favour of the Cape route, the journey not to exceed forty-five days. He opposed an Immigration Bill which seemed to favour employers of labour. One of those strange but not uncommon contests breaking out, in which a minority uses the forms of the House to delay a measure—a process known in later times as "stonewalling"—Mr. Higinbotham

agreed with the objections taken to the clause by the members on the Opposition side, but he deprecated the manner in which those hon. gentlemen were endeavouring to attain their end. Speaking against time and threatening to protract the debate until ten o'clock in the morning were unseemly proceedings. . . . It was evident discussion was at an end, and it appeared to him that the influence and character of the House were not raised by a contest as to which side possessed the greater power of physical endurance.

That sitting of the House terminated at 4.20 a.m.

In June of that year, 1863, the O'Shanassy *cum* Haines administration was defeated. The previous year it carried its Land Act by a majority of twenty-two; in November it carried its Address by ten. But the feeling against the administration of the Act, if not against the Act itself, was increasing, and in June, 1863, the ministry was defeated on a motion in connection with that subject.

The Governor sent for Mr. McCulloch, who forming a new ministry offered the post of Attorney-General to Mr. George Higinbotham.

CHAPTER IX

ATTORNEY-GENERAL

Mr. Rusden's Comments criticised—Colleagues in the new Cabinet—
Ministry of All the Talents—Mr. McCulloch, Mr. Verdon, Mr.
Francis—The Cement of the Ministry— Legal opinions— Consoli-
dation— Queen's Counsel—Letter to Mr. Ireland.

THE most important *History of Australia* hitherto published
is that written by Mr. George W. Rusden, who was for a
long time Clerk of the Parliaments in Victoria. His work
is the history composed on the largest scale and with most
literary pretensions. Probably the author would not claim
to be an impartial historian. He claims to tell the truth,
and always takes a side vigorously, after the pattern of
Macaulay rather than after that of Hallam. Even he must
be aware of the bitterness of tone that he has infused into
many parts of his book. The particular portion of his *History
of Australia* which deals with the tariff, the tack, and the
Darling grant in Victoria is especially full and violent,
opening almost with the following account of Mr. Higinbotham :—

A theoretical enthusiast, steeped in a mixture of the ideas of John
Stuart Mill and the French iconoclasts of 1789. His personal character
was so much respected that the Cascas of Victoria sheltered themselves
under his name, knowing that what would appear offence in them, "his
countenance, like richest alchemy, would change to virtue and to
worthiness."

The imputation against friends and supporters robs the
personal eulogy of its honey, but the details of the blame
should be examined. During the eighteenth century and the

first half of this the word "enthusiast" was used in a disparaging sense, from which some writers have tried to rescue it. No bad force is attached to "the enthusiasm of humanity." Mr. Higinbotham, whilst a member of the ministry, developed a remarkable power of influencing others by the persuasiveness of his speech and the fire of his oratory: but, unless all inspiring orators are to be condemned as enthusiasts, it is an open question whether he was an enthusiast at all. He had a legal mind, and loved precedent. It is true that he had an enthusiast's objection to any form of compromise, and when certain he was right, nothing could make him give way. Is it wise to oppose theory and practice? They must go hand in hand. An opponent is usually called theoretical, if he has thought out the reasons of his opinions. Practice unless based on reason is empiricism. Unless theory will bear to be carried into act, it is mere foolishness and idle dreaming. The word theoretical is used in the sense of unpractical. The volumes of statute law twice consolidated, five years of excellent administration of office, twelve and a half years of judicial life prove that it would be ridiculous to call Mr. Higinbotham unpractical.

Nor is Mr. Rusden more happy in tracing the source of Mr. Higinbotham's political ideas. Most thinking men in the middle of the century were more or less influenced by the writings of John Stuart Mill. Probably Mr. Rusden's reference is not so much to the *Elements of Logic* as to Free Trade views in the *Political Economy*, or perhaps to the work on *Representative Government* and *On Liberty*. When England adopted Free Trade, Mill's treatise became the text-book of Political Economy, superseding Adam Smith and Ricardo; and now, as is natural, a later generation turns to newer books. Mr. Higinbotham certainly began political life as a free-trader, but he was hardly a disciple of Mill, and later he drew away from Mill's individualism, as indeed the world seems to have drawn. The other fountain of influence is not very judiciously selected. It may be doubted whether there were French iconoclasts in 1789. Writers on the French Revolution distinguish the ideas of 1789 from the ideas of 1792.

> "Bliss was it in that dawn to be alive,
> But to be young was very heaven,"

was Wordsworth's description of the feelings of the earlier period. "Liberty, fraternity, equality" were the ideas of the time,—the abolition of serfdom, a new social spirit, and equality before the law. At first there was very little of hostility to existing institutions, and the new importance attached to the States-General was brought forward as a revival rather than as a novelty. No doubt iconoclasm was not unnaturally developed out of these ideas, and went to fearful lengths, but Mr. Higinbotham was never an iconoclast. Did the French Revolution influence him greatly? Unless all democracy be due to the French Revolution,—a proposition that can hardly be maintained,—there are but slight traces of such influence in his speeches or writings. It is far more true to say that his mind was saturated with the teaching of the great opponent of the French Revolution, Edmund Burke. The British Constitution, precedents drawn from English politics and from the practice of the House of Commons, not abstract principles, were always on his lips. If any French writer has had a special influence on him, it is M. de Tocqueville, whose great analytical work on *Democracy in America* was much read and carefully studied for at least a quarter of a century after its appearance in 1834. It is our misfortune that the book is not studied still. M. de Tocqueville was assuredly not an iconoclast.

Mr. Rusden is as hostile to Mr. Higinbotham's colleagues; indeed he is more offensive in describing them, but his remarks may now be put on one side. This ministry has been called a "ministry of all the talents," and it certainly comprised many able men. The Premier was Mr. James McCulloch, who took the office of Chief Secretary. He was of Glasgow birth,—a Melbourne merchant, shrewd, hard-headed. Twice over—in two previous ministries—he had had a year's experience of office; once as Commissioner of Trade and Customs, the second time as Treasurer. Few politicians in Victoria had enjoyed a longer experience, for it must be remembered that responsible government was still young, being not yet eight years old. Mr. George Verdon, the Treasurer, was the son of an English clergyman, educated at Rossall under Dr. Woolley, afterwards the first Professor of Classics in the University of Sydney. Mr. Verdon came out to the colony in 1851, and engaged in commerce. In November, 1857, the following eulogy of him appeared in the *Argus*, perhaps from the pen of his new colleague :—" Mr. Verdon deserves some expression of approbation as presenting a spectacle too rare in these colonies, that of an energetic, young and educated gentleman, who has steadily devoted himself to public affairs, without suddenly pushing himself into undue prominence, but with the apparent determination of winning his way step by step to an honourable position." Such a position certainly came to him early. Having graduated in the Municipal Council of Williamstown, in 1860, being not twenty-seven years of age, he became Treasurer of the Colony. He was now a second time at the Treasury. Mr. Verdon was the diplomatist of the new Cabinet.

Mr. Richard Heales, the Premier under whom Mr. Verdon had been Treasurer, was now one of his colleagues, having accepted office as President of the Board of Land and Works. The versatile and witty Mr. Michie was Minister of Justice. One of the most remarkable men in the Cabinet was Mr. James Goodall Francis, Commissioner of Trade and Customs. Like Mr. McCulloch he was a successful Melbourne merchant. He had been four years in the House and once before in office. An extraordinary speaker, he would invent words on the spur of the moment, would blunder in his grammar, would begin a sentence and, weaving in clause after clause and parenthesis upon parenthesis, would never complete the unfortunate sentence. The reporters were however very kind to him, and dressed his grammar, for his meaning was never far to seek. From his first entrance into politics he had convinced himself that some measure of protection to native industry was advisable.

When the present author was new to the colony, he ventured with all the rashness of a " new chum " on a correspondence with Mr. Francis on fiscal matters ; and he can remember the following passage from Mr. Francis' reply : " I am neither a Protectionist, nor a Free-trader, but a citizen of a young country." The reply seems at first sight ridiculous, but its meaning is quite clear. It is eminently the voice of the practical man. "As an abstract doctrine, I support neither Protection nor Free Trade, but I am prepared to accept a certain measure of protection for a time, to establish industries whilst they are young—such protection at a later period to be withdrawn."

One of the ablest of the ministers soon left the ministry. Mr. Thomas Howard Fellows was afterwards so vigorous an opponent of the McCulloch ministry that it is often forgotten that for the first five months of its existence he was Post-master-General.

The question naturally arises, what was the connecting bond of this Cabinet? In England, where there are generally two well-defined parties facing each other, homogeneous cabinets are the rule. In the colonies, parties are not so well defined; and, as Mr. Higinbotham said over and over again, there is hardly the material for party government. For this reason, in every ministry men of widely different views are included. The McCulloch ministry was no exception. There were in it both Protectionists and Free-traders, Liberals and Conservatives. If parties had been sufficiently definite, the Cabinet might have been called a coalition. It was formed to create a strong government, ability and fitness for office being more considered than similarity of views.

In spite of all differences this ministry held together. Previous to the formation of this Cabinet, there had been seven ministries in less than eight years—an average life of a year and a month. This ministry remained in power for nearly five years. Never in the history of the colony since has a ministry been so long in office. There must have been some strong cement to keep together men who differed so widely; and it is probably no exaggeration to say that a powerful element in that cement was the admiration felt for the character of George Higinbotham.

Sir George Verdon thus speaks of him as a colleague :—

For those who knew Mr. Higinbotham by his speeches in Parliament or from public platforms, it would be difficult to realise the kindness, gentleness, and forbearance which marked his conduct towards all those with whom he had to do in close personal association.

These qualities were specially shown in Cabinet and in his depart-ment. His colleagues regarded him not only with the deep respect which his great capacity, acquirements, and integrity of purpose com-manded, but with a personal affection seldom bestowed upon any man by his associates. He made allowances for others which he never would make in his own case, and his unselfishness, devotion to duty, and kindness, gained for him the love of his colleagues and the devotion of all who served under him.

During the early part of the life of the ministry, the Attorney-General does not seem to have taken an especially prominent part in the Government, though he worked very hard in his own office. Many points of practice were unsettled, and the Attorney-General was often called upon for his legal opinion. A record of these opinions is preserved at the Crown Law Offices in Melbourne; and it is quite evident that Higinbotham had harder work to do than his successors. Very soon also, he began the heavy work of consolidation of the statutes, which occupied a great deal of time.

> " What are ye fear'd on, fools? 'od rot 'em—
> Were the first words of Higinbotham "-

was the friendly comment of the Melbourne *Punch*, afterwards bitterly hostile. The lines are set beneath a picture of the Attorney-General as a cobbler at work on the statutes. In peaceful, though arduous, tasks of administration the first eighteen months of office were spent, giving no promise of the coming storm.

The Cabinet, it seems, generally met in the chambers of the Attorney-General. No notes or minutes are kept of Cabinet meetings, so that it is often impossible in the aftertime to bring evidence that any one idea was due to a particular man. The historian would be glad of some record of Pitt's cabinets to know who suggested the idea of colonising Australia. Was it Pitt himself, or that subordinate minister, the Secretary of State, who gave his pleasant-sounding title as the name of the mother-city of Australia, Thomas Townshend, Earl of Sydney?

Perhaps the view must be accepted with limitations, but the popular belief was that after a short period of its history when its fighting began, George Higinbotham became the central figure of the McCulloch ministry. A member of the Legislature at the time thus describes him at a little later date :—

> He was the brains, the heart, and the right hand of the Ministry. He was the Wellington of the small army. And he was *such* a man that to say this rather conveys honour than reflects discredit on his colleagues.

One of the earliest of Mr. Higinbotham's acts in his office as Attorney-General was the appointment of two Queen's Counsel,—his colleague, Mr. Michie, on his acceptance of the office of Minister of Justice ; and his predecessor, Mr. Ireland, on his retirement from the office of Attorney-General. Such appointments had evidently been contemplated at an earlier date, for five and a half years earlier, when Mr. Fellows was Solicitor-General, he had prepared regulations for the appointment, which are here given :—

Regulations to be observed on the appointment of Queen's Counsel :

(1) Except in the case of barristers who shall have held the office of Attorney—or Solicitor-General, no barrister shall be appointed Her Majesty's Counsel except on the recommendation of the Chief Justice to the Governor in Council.

(2) On every such appointment the usual fee of five guineas shall be paid for the patent at the office of the Chief Secretary.

(3) For every license to appear against the Crown in cases in which the services of any of Her Majesty's Counsel may be dispensed with, a fee of one guinea shall be paid at the same office.

(4) That a copy of these regulations be forwarded by the Attorney-General to His Honour the Chief Justice.

These regulations were submitted for the approval of His Excellency the Governor in Council, by Thomas Howard Fellows, on December 5th, and approved by the same on December 7th, 1857. No appointments had however been made, until the date of Mr. Higinbotham's letter to Mr. Ireland, which, as entering more into detail than the letter to Mr. Michie, is here appended :—

Crown Law Offices,
July 18th, 1863.

My dear Sir,

Will you do me the favour to inform me whether you would be disposed to accept the office of Queen's Counsel in the event of the Governor in Council being advised to confer the distinction on you upon your retirement from the office of Attorney-General ?

No Queen's Counsel have hitherto been nominated in this colony. I believe that such appointments would be acceptable to the profession, and would prove beneficial to the Bar by bringing it into closer correspondence with the state in which the profession exists at home. But if Queen's Counsel are to be introduced here, I think that care must be taken that the office shall exist in reality as well as in name ; and that the conditions which are understood to be attached to the office, and which may in some cases be felt to be onerous, shall be accepted together with the title of distinction.   A silk gown is, I believe, always given at home on the understanding that it is to be retained for life, or given up only under special and unforeseen circumstances.   A Queen's Counsel, moreover, is forbidden by professional usage to practise in inferior courts, to draw pleadings, and generally to undertake business which commonly falls to the share of the junior members of the profession.   I am aware that their Honours, the Judges of the Supreme Court, concur in the opinion that these and all other obligations attached to the office of Queen's Counsel in England and Ireland, ought to be observed and enforced in Victoria.

Considering the extensive jurisdiction at present possessed by the Courts of Mines, and the great importance of many of the suits brought in them, I think that these courts should, so long as they continue to be constituted as they now are, be an exception to the general rule, which forbids a Queen's Counsel to practise in an inferior court.

If you should be willing to accept an appointment upon the terms I have mentioned, and subject to the Regulations made on the 7th of December, 1857, I shall have pleasure in recommending your name to the Governor in Council.

I am, my dear Sir.
Yours faithfully,
GEO. HIGINBOTHAM.

The Honorable Richard D. Ireland.

The two barristers accepted the offer, and the appointments were made by the Governor in Council on the 10th of August, 1863.

CHAPTER X

The American Civil War—Confederates recognised as a Belligerent
Power—The Rules of Neutrality--The *Shenandoah*, Confederate
steamer, arrives in Hobson's Bay, January 25th, 1865 ; departs
February 18th—Hospitality shown--Protest of American Consul,
who wants the *Shenandoah* seized as a Pirate--The Vessel's History
—Enlistment of British Subjects—Mischief done by the *Shenandoah*
even after close of War—The Ship surrendered at Liverpool—Mr.
Cardwell approves action of Victorian Government—The *Times*
also—Protest of United States Government—Treaty of Washington—Geneva Arbitration--The Decision by three to two against
England.

BETWEEN the Governor's speech, which heralded the revision
of the tariff, and the contest, to which the tariff led, inter-
vened the incident of the *Shenandoah*. On the 25th of
January, 1865, the war-steamer *Shenandoah* arrived in
Hobson's Bay, destined to give trouble not only to the
Governor of Victoria and his advisers, especially the Law
Officers of the Crown, but to the British Empire. The
incident terminated nearly eight years later with the
payment of the indemnity awarded by the International
Conference at Geneva.

It was the last year of the American Civil War between
the Federals and Confederates—North and South. Not quite
four years had elapsed since the seizure of Fort Sumter,
which may be regarded as the opening scene of the war, but
the Confederate cause was already languishing. The great
Battle of Five Forks was yet in the future, so that the brave
Lee was still in arms ; but it was clear by this time to all

who had eyes to see that, however brave the final resistance
might be, the Confederacy was doomed, and that the end was
nigh.   During the war, the sympathy of the English world
had been much divided.   The working classes, in spite of
the Lancashire cotton famine, were true to the North, but
society, the clergy, and gentry, guided by the *Times*, had
taken the side of the South.   As, however, the conflict proceeded, the issues became clearer, and the falsity of the
English statesman's epigram, "The North are fighting for
empire, the South for freedom," was more and more recognised.   Many English thinkers and leaders of public opinion
were convinced that the cause of the Union was the cause of
humanity, and that whatever may have been the original
intentions of the Northern States, their victory in the
struggle meant the extinction of slavery.

When the war broke out, Great Britain and France recognised the Southern States as a belligerent power, but
decided to observe the duties of neutrality between the
hostile parties.   A proclamation signed by Earl Russell,
Minister for Foreign Affairs, was sent round to the Governors
of all colonies, setting forth the rules of neutrality, which
may be reduced to the three following :—

(*a*) No ship of war, privateer, or other armed vessel belonging to
either of the belligerents which shall anchor in any British port shall
be allowed to quit her anchorage within twenty-four hours after any
vessel belonging to the adverse belligerent, whether armed or unarmed,
shall have left the same port.

(*b*) In any other case every ship of war or privateer shall be required
to depart and to put to sea within twenty-four hours after entrance into
any British port, roadstead or waters, except in case of stress of weather,
or of her requiring provisions or things necessary for the subsistence of
her crew, or repairs, in which case she must depart as soon as possible
afterwards.

(*c*) Such ship may take in no supplies, except provisions and such
other things as may be requisite for the subsistence of her crew, and
so much coal only as may be sufficient to carry such vessel to the
nearest port of her own country, or to some nearer destination.

The commander of the *Shenandoah* said he had come
to have some machinery repaired, and to procure coals and
provisions.   This was what he wrote to the Governor of
Victoria :—

C. S. Steamer of War, *Shenandoah*,

PORT PHILLIP, *25th January*, 1865.

SIR,

I have the honour to announce to your Excellency the arrival of the Confederate States steamer *Shenandoah*, under my command, in Port Phillip, this afternoon, and also to communicate that the steamer's machinery requires repairs, and that I am in want of coals.

I desire your Excellency to grant permission that I may make the necessary repairs and supply of coals, to enable me to get to sea as quickly as possible.

I desire also your Excellency's permission to land my prisoners. I shall observe the neutrality.

I have the honour to be, very respectfully,

Your obedient servant,

JAS. J. WADDELL,

Lieutenant-Commanding.

The Governor of Victoria and his advisers did their utmost to observe the rules laid down for the observance of a strict neutrality. A board was appointed to inspect the ship and see what repairs were necessary. These repairs were permitted, and effected. The Governor pressed the captain to name a day for his departure. The *Shenandoah* took on board the necessary supplies of provisions, coals, etc., but no munitions of war; and she thereupon left the port of Melbourne, and passed through Port Phillip Heads on the 18th of February, 1865.

Whilst the Governor and his ministers observed strict neutrality, many of the citizens of Melbourne, especially those belonging to "good society," were anxious to show their sympathies with the Confederates. They left cards on the captain and officers; they entertained them. At the Melbourne Club a dinner was given to the officers of the ship; the Mayor of Melbourne paid them some attention. But, of course, a dinner at the Melbourne Club is a private, not an official entertainment, and the Mayor is a municipal officer altogether independent of the Government.

The day after the arrival of the *Shenandoah*, the Consul of the United States forwarded a protest to the Governor. It ended thus :—

I avail myself of this opportunity to call upon your Excellency to cause the said *Shenandoah*, alias *Sea King*, to be seized for piratical acts, she not coming within Her Majesty's neutrality proclamation, never having entered a port of the so-styled Confederate States of America for the purpose of neutralization, and consequently not entitled to belligerent rights.

Table service, plate, etc., on board said vessel bear the mark *Sea King*, and the captain should bring evidence to entitle him to belligerent rights.

I therefore protest against any aid or comfort being extended to said piratical vessel in any of the ports of this colony.

The Consul followed this letter up with other and more detailed letters to the same effect, and with affidavits from prisoners who had escaped from the *Shenandoah*. All the letters were referred to the Crown Law Officers, Mr. Higinbotham and Mr. Michie, who advised that there was no evidence of any act of piracy committed by any person on board the *Shenandoah*, that this vessel purported to be, and they thought she should be treated as, a ship of war belonging to a belligerent power.

The history of the ship as detailed by the American Consul was as follows, and the facts are undisputed :—

In October last, the *Sea King* cleared from England, ostensibly for Bombay, loaded with coals, and further equipped with guns, sails, stores, etc., for a long voyage ; crew ample, and besides the regular officers of such a vessel, a lieutenant in the so-called Confederate service.

Proceeding upon her cruise, she, after a few days, by a preconcerted arrangement, falls in with the *Laurel*, also from England, and receives from her upon the high seas a further armament, munitions, etc., and the remainder of her officers. This being done, the *Sea King* hauls down the British flag, and hoists that of the so-called Confederacy, assumes a new name, and commences more active hostilities upon the commerce of the United States.

Continuing her cruise, after the destruction of several vessels [1] she enters this port, the first one since clearing from England, and drops anchor in Hobson's Bay, flying the so-called Confederate flag, and styling herself the *Shenandoah*, a Confederate vessel of war.

The Government of Victoria was called upon to seize the *Shenandoah* as a pirate, and was told that if it failed in this duty the consequences, that is to say, all later depredations caused by the ship, would be visited on the British Government. The Government of Victoria, acting chiefly upon

[1] Nine, seven of which were destroyed and the others ransomed. Century Company's *War Book*, vol. iv., p. 599,

the advice of Mr. Higinbotham, declined. Another matter complicated the case.

It is contrary to the law of England that any of her subjects should enlist under an alien flag, the particular statute that forbids this being called the Foreign Enlistment Act, dating, like the poet Burns, from "the hindmost year but ane" in good King George's reign; but this George is George the Third, whereas Burns spoke of the Second. The Act is "59 George III., cap. 69." The *Shenandoah* wanted men, and there were plenty of adventurous men in Melbourne only too anxious, if the pay or chances of prize-money were good enough, to enlist under the Confederate flag. It was the duty of the Government and the police acting under its orders to prevent any enlistment of British subjects. Information having been laid before a magistrate that a British subject had enlisted, a warrant for his arrest was issued. Captain Waddell refused to allow the police officers to search for him. He said, "I pledge you my word of honour as an officer and a gentleman that I have not any one on board, nor have I engaged any one, nor will I while I am here." Further pressed, he said he would "fight his ship rather than allow it." This was on the 14th of February; and in consequence of Captain Waddell's action, permission to repair and take supplies was cancelled. In reply, he asserted the inviolability of the deck of a man-of-war, and positively denied that any one had been enlisted since his arrival in the port. The night of the day on which he wrote, four men were seen stealthily leaving the ship, were followed, and arrested by the water police. One declared he was an American subject; another was a young lad about fifteen; but the two others were tried for a breach of the law, and sentenced to a short imprisonment. Waddell's friends maintained these were "stowaways" who had been discovered.

There were many rumours of enlistment, but though the police authorities were vigilant, no other breaches of the law were discovered. The Government claimed to have exercised watchfulness to the fullest extent in its power. After the departure of the *Shenandoah* the Government received information confirming in a manner the truth of the rumours. There is very good reason to believe that as many as forty-two recruits went in another vessel, and joined the

Shenandoah outside the Heads. This would seem to have been Captain Waddell's intention, for he wrote a brief letter to the Attorney-General :—

> Be pleased to inform me if the Crown claims the sea to be British waters three miles from the Port Philip (*sic*) Head lights, or from a straight line drawn from Port (*sic*)[1] Lonsdale and Cape Schank ?

At the last moment the American Consul tried to stop some of these men by laying an information and obtaining warrants against them. Unfortunately, instead of going before a magistrate, he went to the Crown Law Offices; but the Attorney-General was not there, and the Consul meeting the Crown Solicitor was told—apparently abruptly—to go to a magistrate. When the Consul did go to a magistrate he found difficulties still. Complaint was made that the Crown Solicitor had insulted the Consul. This is the answer of the former: "I positively assert that neither in language or (*sic*) manner did I insult him. I was in a hurry to catch the train, and may perhaps have left more suddenly than I otherwise should have done." An American gentleman, who accompanied the Consul, described his manner as sneering and insulting, his words being, " I don't care : I want my dinner." It has been remarked that the Crown Solicitor's dinner cost his nation dear, for the *Shenandoah*, when she passed through Port Phillip Heads, by no means passed out of history, Victorian or British, with the same rapidity with which the Crown Solicitor hurried away to his dinner.

Before the 2nd of August this Confederate privateer captured and destroyed many Federal vessels, especially whalers, near Behring Straits. The number of ships is estimated at thirty, and the most were captured after the close of the war. Lee surrendered on the 9th of April, and the last Confederate general on the 26th of May. On that date the war ended ; but it was not until the 6th of November that Captain Waddell brought his ship into Liverpool, where he surrendered her to the British Government, and stated that he had not heard of the close of the war until August 2nd, and had then

---

[1] The letter is copied from the American Blue Book : " Papers relating to Foreign Affairs accompanying the Annual Message of the President." Washington, 1866, p. 504. Philip should be Phillip, and Port, Point Lonsdale.

hastened to Liverpool. The vessel was then handed over to the Consul of the United States.

The most striking evidence that the Governor and his advisers, in their efforts to observe neutrality, were moving in a diagonal between two extreme views was the fact that neither party was pleased. On the one side the American Consul was frequent and loud in protest. Meanwhile the more fiery spirits among the Americans in Melbourne were plotting to scuttle the ship whilst in Hobson's Bay, or to blow her up whilst she was still upon the slip. According to one story a contrivance with this design was actually fastened to the ship; a train was to be fired by a pistol, but the pistol missed fire. On the other side Captain Waddell considered the tone of one letter "remarkably disrespectful and insulting to the Government I have the honour to represent, and I shall take an early opportunity of forwarding it to the Richmond Government." Three months later that Government ceased to exist. Meetings of sympathisers with the Confederates were held in Melbourne, and some strangely ignorant speeches made. With one marked exception [1] the members of both Houses of Parliament were strongly with the Confederates.

The Secretary for the Colonies was satisfied:

DOWNING STREET,
26th April, 1865.

SIR,

I have to acknowledge the receipt of your despatches of the numbers and dates noted in the margin, with their several enclosures, relative to the visit at the Port of Melbourne of the Confederate States Steamer, *Shenandoah*, and the alleged enlistment of British subjects to serve on board that vessel.

These papers have received the fullest consideration of Her Majesty's Government and the Law Officers of the Crown; and I have much pleasure in informing you, that Her Majesty's Government are of opinion, that under the circumstances stated, you acted with propriety and discretion, and that there does not appear at present to be a necessity for any action on their part.

With regard to your request, that you may receive instructions as to the propriety of executing any warrant under the Foreign Enlistment Act on board a Confederate (public) Ship of War, Her Majesty's Government are of opinion, that in a case of strong suspicion you

---

[1] Mr. (now Sir) Graham Berry.

ought to request the permission of the commander of the ship to execute the warrant, and that if this request be refused you ought not to attempt to enforce the execution; but that in this case the commander should be desired to leave the port as speedily as possible, and should be informed that he would not be re-admitted into it. Of course in any such case you will take the earliest opportunity of reporting the circumstances to me.

I have, &c.,
(Signed)   E. CARDWELL.

Governor Sir C. H. Darling, K.C.B.,
&c., &c.

And the *Times* at a later date approves—

It was not Captain Waddell's respect for English hospitality, but the vigilance of the Colonial Government, that alone prevented a gross breach of our laws when the *Shenandoah* lay in Australian waters.— The *Times*, September 11, 1865.

But the Government of the United States was not so well satisfied, and when the war was at an end, summed up its frequent protests to the British Government " against armed vessels being permitted to issue from British ports to cruise against the commerce of the United States." Feeling in the United States ran very high against England. Mr. James Russell Lowell, in his well-known essay "On a Certain Condescension in Foreigners," written in the full tide of this irritated feeling, which he himself afterwards did so much to soften, has the remark, " I never blamed her [England] for not wishing well to democracy—how should she?—but *Alabamas* are not wishes."

The mischief done by the *Shenandoah* was decidedly smaller than that done by the *Alabama*, which ship was built in Birkenhead and sailed from the Mersey under a false name in July, 1862. She was sunk by a Federal iron-clad, the *Kearsarge*, off Cherbourg in June, 1864. Three officers in the *Alabama* on that occasion were in Melbourne with the *Shenandoah*. For two years the *Alabama* had preyed on American commerce, destroying nearly a hundred ships, and almost sweeping it from the sea. The American Government contended that the English Government was criminally negligent in allowing the *Alabama* to sail. Indeed, the Government meant to interfere, but postponed interference until it was too late. Under pretence of a trial trip the ship escaped. In the case of both ships, as well as of others of less importance, the English Government claimed to have done all that was incumbent upon it, but in this view the Government of the United States refused to concur. Over and over again representations were made: much diplomatic correspondence was interchanged. At length in 1871, the Treaty of Washington was signed, by which the matter was referred to arbitration. Lord Canterbury, the Governor of Victoria, was then requested to have a statement of the facts with respect to the *Shenandoah* transmitted to England. A paper was drawn up, chiefly by Mr. Higinbotham, with all the correspondence appended, and printed. From this paper, which curiously enough bears no imprint, the above narrative has been mainly compiled, its very language being employed without quotation marks. In 1871 Mr. Higinbotham was working at the Bar, no longer even in the Assembly; but he positively refused to accept any fee for his work, although payment was pressed upon him by Lord Canterbury. The completed statement was signed by James McCulloch, J. G. Francis, Archibald Michie, and George Higinbotham.

By the Treaty of Washington (8th May, 1871), it was agreed that the Tribunal of Arbitrators should consist of five, nominated—one by Her Britannic Majesty, one by the President of the United States, one by the King of Italy, one by the President of the Swiss Confederation, and one by the Emperor of Brazil. Sir Alexander Cockburn, Lord Chief Justice of England, was arbitrator for Great Britain. Mr. Charles Francis Adams, who had been ambassador for the United States in England through the whole time of trouble and knew every turn of the negotiations, represented his country. The King of Italy nominated Count Sclopis: the President of Switzerland, M. Jacques Staempfli; and the Emperor of Brazil, Viscount d'Itajuba. Count Sclopis was elected President of the Tribunal. The Conference, which met on the 15th of December, 1871, at Geneva, sat on thirty-two days, and the last day was the 14th September, 1872. The "decision and award" is published in the Supplement to the *London Gazette* of Friday, the 20th of September. It occupied five pages, and is signed by four of the arbitrators. Sir Alexander Cockburn stated at great length his reasons for dissenting from the award. These reasons occupy 254 pages. Mr. Adams' statement occupies forty pages, and a similar space is covered by the statements in French of the other three arbitrators. This is not the place for setting forth the whole of the interesting history of the Geneva Conference, and the cases, counter-cases, documents, and evidence brought forward. The general decision was in favour of the United States, and the award was 15,500,000 dollars in gold. The decision in the *Alabama* case and in several others was by a majority of four voices to one. But in the *Shenandoah* case the ultimate decision was by three to two. One of the two was Sir Alexander Cockburn,[1] who can find nothing in all that took place in Melbourne to justify the charge against the colonial authorities of negligence. Two passages from his statement may be quoted. It closes as follows :—

I cannot agree that where the government of a colony is honestly desirous of doing its duty and maintaining neutrality, the fact that men anxious to ship on board a belligerent vessel elude the vigilance of the police in the night time, is to make the parent state liable for all the damage such vessel may afterwards do. And I protest, respectfully but emphatically, against a decision based on grounds to my mind so wholly untenable.[2]

The other quotation is :—

The honour of the commander of the ship having been pledged, ought the search of the ship to have been further insisted on? By the comity of nations the word of a commissioned officer is held to be sufficient guarantee for the truth of anything to which it is officially pledged. The rule is a sound one.[3]

The violation of his word by Captain Waddell strikes all the judges ; and to excuse him the doctrine that " all is fair in war " must be widely stretched so as to include false swearing to a neutral.

The second dissentient was Viscount d'Itajuba, and these are his words :—

Considérant, Que, si d'un côté, de tous les faits relatifs au séjour du *Shenandoah* dans le port de Melbourne, il ressort qu'il y a eu quelques

---

[1] It is a little distressing to find the Lord Chief Justice of England speaking of " the Governor of Melbourne."

[2] P. 4334.   [3] P. 4327.

irrégularités commises, telles surtout que l'augmentation de l'équipage—d'un autre côté, il n'est pas prouvé que ces irrégularités puissent être mises à la charge du Gouvernement de Sa Majesté Britannique et imputées à la négligence des autorités anglaises, mais qu'elles ont été la conséquence de la violation de la parole d'honneur donnée par le Commandant Waddell, et des difficultés exceptionelles de surveillance que présentait la conformation du port ; Considérant en outre, Que le Gouverneur de la Colonie, ayant appris après le départ du *Shenandoah* la violation de neutralité dont ce navire s'était rendu coupable, décida de refuser dorénavant l'hospitalité au Lieutenant Waddell et aux autres officiers du *Shenandoah*, et écrivit dans ce sens aux autorités navales et civiles de l'Australie en les priant d'agir de même, ce qui contribue à dégager la responsabilité du Gouvernement de Sa Majesté Britannique, est d'avis, Que la Grande Bretagne n'a pas manqué aux devoirs prescrits dans les régles établies pas l'Article vi. du Traité de Washington, et que par conséquent elle n'est pas responsable des faits imputés au croiseur Confédéré le *Shenandoah*.[1]

Not only was the *Shenandoah* case decided by a bare majority of one, but from the statement of Count Sclopis, it is very clear that he was long in doubt and very near voting on the other side. He stated his difficulty to his fellow-arbitrators, heard what they had to say, took a day to think it over, and then voted against the British view.

Mon opinion, chancelante avant-hier, arrêtée aujourd'hui par suite de la discussion que j'ai soulevée et que vous avez su rendre féconde et décisive par vos lumières.[2]

It is advisable to remember these facts in considering the question whether the advice of the Attorney-General to Sir Charles Darling was blameworthy because of its consequences.

[1] P. 4411.   [2] P. 4439.

CHAPTER XI

TARIFF AND TACK

The Governor's Speech—The Budget, January 19th, 1865—
Higinbotham's Speech in the Debate—Is this Protection?—The
Legislative Council—The Tack—Was it Premature? Was it a
true Tack?—The Bill is "laid aside"—Bitter Contest—Conference
on Water Works Bill—Resolutions of Assembly—Collection of
Customs on Resolution of Assembly declared illegal—Agreement
with London Chartered Bank—Mr. Cardwell censures the
Governor—The Tack is removed, and Legislative Council rejects
the Tariff.

A NEW parliament, the fourth in the history of Victoria,
met at the end of November, 1864. In the ministerial
programme, as declared in the Governor's speech, was
included "a measure having for its purpose the readjustment
of the tariff." The next paragraphs in the speech explained
as follows :—

It is proposed by my advisers that the revenue to be collected
through the medium of the Custom House shall be levied partly by
reduced duties upon objects already chargeable, and partly by duties,
moderate in amount, on various commodities which as yet have been
altogether exempt from taxation.

The effect, it is conceived, of this proposed measure will be to
decrease the burden of taxation hitherto borne by the mining and other
industrious classes, and to distribute it more equitably among all classes
of society.

This was generally interpreted as foreshadowing a measure
of Protection. Many advocates of Protection had been
returned at the General Election, and there were some in
the Cabinet. On the tariff question the members of the
Cabinet had met with open minds. Some were Free-traders

and some Protectionists, though the latter were hardly to be counted extreme, and mostly under the influence of Mr. Mill's exceptional case, viz., granting protection in a new country to rising industries for a limited time.

The Budget was submitted on the 19th of January, and contained proposals that the duty on tea, sugar, and opium, as well as the export duty on gold, should be reduced, and that a duty small in amount should be imposed on a great many articles hitherto duty-free. The Treasurer, Mr. Verdon, avowed that, revenue being needed, the Ministry had "selected those articles which compete with our own articles rather than those which do not." The debate on the Budget lasted a dozen nights, all of which fell (January 24th—February 15th) during the time that the *Shenandoah* was in port. In committee of the whole, members can speak more than once; and Mr. Higinbotham spoke several times in the course of the long debates, but his views are most fully expressed in the speech of January 31st. . . . He spoke of "the intellectual puzzle "—

Was the tariff a Free-trade or a Protectionist one? One member for Ballarat, speaking as a Free-trader, objected to the tariff as Protectionist, while his colleague, a Protectionist, objected to it as a Free-trade tariff. Again, the member for Kilmore told the Protectionists that the tariff would not carry out their views. They found the member for Collingwood also speaking of the tariff as a Free-trade one, and yet declaring that although a Protectionist he would support it. He confessed that he was lost amidst these conflicting views, but he felt bound not to maintain a disingenuous silence. . . . Unless members were prepared for direct taxation, they had no right to complain of the present as a Protectionist tariff. . . . An hon. member had given a definition of Protection he could readily accept—a system of Customs duties not necessary for the purposes of revenue, and deliberately imposed for the purpose of excluding or of discouraging the introduction of foreign commodities in cases where the same commodities could be introduced at home. Well, if that were a true description of Protection, could the tariff on any ground whatever be called a Protective one? He maintained that it could not come within that classification. For what purpose then was the change made? . . . He believed that although the tariff would not meet the views of those who desired to foster native industry, it would help to cast the burden of taxation upon classes who had not hitherto borne their fair share of it.

The conclusion of the speech was a defence of Protection from the intellectual scorn of its opponents, coupled with a repudiation of the policy as mischievous and only leading to disappointment and disaster.

In the *Punch* of the day the "intellectual puzzle" is put in a different way: the Treasurer is represented as shifting the pea from thimble to thimble, and the three thimbles are labelled Protection, Free Trade, and Revenue. It was certainly a Revenue tariff, but there was also a small measure of Protection, which was regarded by the mercantile community with the utmost disfavour. "Thin end of the wedge"; "it is the nature of the beast to grow," were the familiar answers given to those who urged that the Protection was very small.

The stronghold of the Free-traders and of the mercantile class was the Upper House, the Legislative Council. At that time the members of the Council were elected on a strictly limited franchise, and it was pre-eminently the house of the wealthy. When the Tariff passed the Assembly, its enemies, about a third of that house, were thanking God that there was an Upper House, which would know how to do its duty. By the Constitution Act the Upper House is assigned the privileges of the House of Lords, the Lower House those of the Commons. It is a commonplace of English politics that the power of the purse rests with the latter, who would never dream of allowing the House of Lords to throw out a Tariff Bill. In England these are matters of unwritten law. Unfortunately in the Victorian Constitution Act it was put down in black and white that the Upper House might reject though not amend a Money Bill.

Mr. Higinbotham admitted that they had the right to reject it— so had the Queen or His Excellency; but the legal right and the constitutional exercise of that right were different questions. It was admitted over and over again that the Lords had the legal right to reject the Paper Duty Bill, but yet the Commons continuously denied their right to do so.—Hansard, *March 9th*, 1865.

The Legislative Assembly was determined that the Council should not exercise this legal but unconstitutional right, and tacked the Tariff to the Appropriation Act. In the first place it is doubtful whether this action was not premature— jumping before coming to the leap. The Council had not thrown out a Money Bill. Perhaps it would have been wiser not to have listened to the vapouring talk of the lobby, the library, and the refreshment-room, for in the colonies the two Houses have these conveniences in common—wiser to have waited until the Tariff was thrown out. On the other hand it is a question whether the tack was a real tack at all. A tack is where two distinct matters are united in one bill. A popular illustration used to be given, when the last clause of a Turnpike Bill in England ran—" And that the Warden of Wadham College, Oxford, be permitted to marry." The Appropriation Act deals with money just as a Tariff Act does, and it might fairly be contended that the two subjects were at least germane.

The talk that the Tariff Bill would be thrown out by the Council was met by the threat of the tack. Before the tacked bill, if it was a tacked bill, reached the Council, that body had appointed a committee, and, as a result of its report, had determined on resisting any encroachment on its rights.

The Appropriation-*cum*-Tariff Bill was sent to the Council, and by it on the 25th of July—after a single night's debate—" laid aside."

Sir Charles Darling, when reporting the matter to the Secretary of State for the Colonies, wrote :—

The difficulty has been brought about by an overstrained exercise of their powers on the part of both the deliberative chambers, which appears to me to be at variance with the true spirit of a constitution, based and modelled in its main features upon that of the mother country ; concession on either side adopted in that spirit will immediately remove the difficulty and remove the course of legislature to its accustomed channel.

But there is a homely proverb which says that if two men ride on one horse, one must ride in front. If two houses have powers in all respects equal, sooner or later a deadlock must ensue. The House of Lords alters and rejects many of the less important measures that have passed the Commons. It can delay a measure of chief importance ; but if the nation is resolved on any measure, it is well known that the Lords will and must yield. It is specially true that the Commons will not brook the least interference with money matters. Could the Legislative Council of Victoria, because elected on a narrow franchise, expect to be stronger than its prototype, the House of Lords ?

When constitutions were given to the colonies, it was thought good to model them on the British pattern. The House of Commons it was easy to imitate, but the Upper House was a difficulty. It was generally agreed to be absurd to introduce hereditary legislators, and the choice lay between nominated life peers and some form of representation. The nomination system was adopted in several colonies; election on a limited franchise, in Victoria. But it was always contended by those opposed to the claims of the Upper House that election was merely a method of appointment. The number of those represented by the Council was less than 10,000, out of a population of 600,000; so that a contest between the two Houses, if the Assembly was supported by the constituencies, meant a conflict between the will of the people and the will of the moneyed class.

The contest that began with the laying aside of the bill in July was a very bitter contest. It and its direct effects lasted for three years. The first part of it lasted nine months, and was simply an obstinate struggle between the Houses. If two obstinate men have a difficulty, each maintains that the other is obstinate and he himself firm. The firmness is not blamed for unpleasant consequences, the obstinacy is.

Both Council and Assembly were so desperately in earnest that it was not proposed that an attempt should be made to remove the difficulties by the obvious expedient of a conference. But, curiously enough, there was an analogous question at issue between the Houses at the very time, called the Water Works Bill, as to which a conference was held. The report, being a summary, though hardly a short summary, of the views on each side, is very instructive reading; for it is quite evident that although the conference seemed to be concerned with the power of the Legislative Council to make amendments in a bill that imposed a rate, the graver question of the deadlock was really in the minds of the six members of each House who met on six days in August in the Parliament library. Without mentioning the Appropriation-*cum*-Tariff Bill the whole matter as to the privilege of the Assembly was both ably and amicably discussed. Mr. Higinbotham was one of the six champions of the Assembly, but Mr. Michie, the Minister of Justice, seems to have been the Protagonist. A short extract from Mr. Higinbotham's first speech may be quoted :—

The second principle in England is that the House of Commons is the author of all taxation and the grantor of all supplies to the Crown. It has always claimed the right—the sole right—to impose taxation upon the people. That power too appears to be, to some extent at all events, intended to be conferred by these sections of the Constitution Act upon the Legislative Assembly. That right of the House of Commons is a limitation of the power of the House of Lords, which has, in practice, been always submitted to by that body, that it shall not alter or reject either bills, the main purpose of which is to impose taxation, or bills in which taxation is proposed as an incidental part.

That is to say, the House of Lords would not reject either the Tariff or the Water Works Bill. One cannot but wonder whether a conference on the former might not have opened out some way by which the coming troubles might have been avoided. In the case of the Water Works Bill the Council practically gave way; and a little later it, or rather a modified edition of it, became law.

When the news that the more important bill had been laid aside reached the Lower House, the Prime Minister, Mr. McCulloch, moved four resolutions,—drafted, it was generally thought, by the Attorney-General—and they were adopted without a division.

1. That the right of granting aids and supplies to the Crown is in the Legislative Assembly alone.

2. That the power conferred by the *Constitution Act* on the Legislative Council to reject bills for appropriating the revenue and bills for improving any duty, rate, tax, rent, return or impost, is justly regarded by this House with peculiar jealousy, as affecting the right of the Legislative Assembly to grant and appropriate supplies and to provide the ways and means for the service of the year.

The third and fourth resolutions were of similar purport, closing with the

determination not to entertain any further or other bill for the appropriation of supplies for the service of the year 1865 until the rightful control of this House over taxation and supply shall have been acknowledged by the adoption by the Legislative Council of the Tariff approved of by this House.

So now the two Houses stood "like cliffs that had been rent asunder." The Treasury had money, which could not legally be paid for services that had been rendered to the State. There were certain special appropriations under other acts which do not require the passing of the Appropriation Act—the salaries of the Governor, the Judges of the Supreme Court, the Ministers, and certain high officials, as well as sundry purposes, including the interest on the loan, and amounting in all to £1,133,502. But the civil servants could not be paid; contractors could not be paid. The head of the Executive was "without funds," he said himself, "to keep up the gaol and police establishments, to pay the pledged allowances to the Queen's troops." The cruelty of the situation lay in the fact that innocent people were suffering whilst the Houses fought. Those who read the story will differ, as those who then lived in the colony differed warmly, on the question who was to blame for this dangerous state of things. The Upper House had no constitutional right to reject the Tariff. The Lower House was coercing the Council by the tack, and it is natural that coercion should be resisted. Honourable citizens might fairly side with either party.

The problem that arose for the consideration of Ministers was to find some means of carrying ont he Queen's Government. Revenue was raised on the resolution of the Assembly. To explain this, an English precedent should be adduced.

The moment that the Chancellor of the Exchequer has finished his Budget speech, and told the world what are to be the changes in the duties, the House of Commons passes resolutions to protect the revenue, and at all the ports the increased duties are collected from the next morning. The propriety of this course is self-evident. If any delay were permitted, merchants could import large stocks at the lower duties, and gain from the public some at least of the profit of the higher rate, whilst the revenue would lose. A similar practice has prevailed in the colonies. On January 19th, 1865, on the occasion of the Treasurer's Budget speech introducing the Tariff which caused all the trouble, Mr. Francis, the Commissioner of Customs, said :—

At that moment an officer of the Customs was in attendance at the House, ready to send off by telegram to the outports any alteration made in the Tariff; and the Customs Department was ready to make the necessary arrangements for Melbourne in the morning. The Customs Department, on the one hand would at once proceed to the collection of the new duties; and on the other, reduced duties would be received on a bond being given that the money would be refunded in the event of the Tariff not being granted by Parliament.

Mr. Francis was not a clear speaker, but his final clause probably means that in the case of reduced duties, the smaller amount would be collected on a bond that the balance would be paid by the importer, if Parliament retained the higher rate.

On January 19th it was not possible for Ministers to foresee what would be the fate of the Tariff. The new duties were collected and brought in revenue, described by the Governor in one despatch as "overflowing." No one protested. It is difficult to say exactly at what point the collection of these revenues became illegal. They were all collected subject to a pledge that they would be returned if the law were not passed.

The term used by the Legislative Council had been that the bill should be "laid aside." It was not finally rejected. Much later it was explained that laying aside was equivalent to rejection. The collection continued for nearly six months. Petitions were filed by merchants in the Supreme Court, where the judges decided that "the demanding of duties under the mere resolutions of the Legislative Assembly was illegal." And yet similar demanding is continued in the colony, as it is in Great Britain, to this day.

Another device for raising money is thus described in one of the Governor's despatches :—

One of the six banks in Melbourne, with which the public revenue is by law deposited, had agreed to make advances equal to the amount at the credit of the colony, upon no other security than the pledge of the Government that the amount advanced would be repaid under the Governor's authority whenever the existing dispute between the Council and Assembly should be arranged.

The bank was the London Chartered Bank of Australia (reconstructed in 1893 as the London Bank of Australia, Limited), and its only resident director was Mr. McCulloch, the Prime Minister.

Any man to whom the Government owes money can, in the Law Courts, sue the Government for payment as he can any other debtor. If the Court decides that the money is due, it must be paid independently of any Appropriation Act, for the Law Courts must be obeyed. The London Chartered Bank brought its action for the money due to it; the Attorney-General confessed judgment, so that the case never came before the Court at all, but the effect was just the same, and the money was paid. Thus for the remainder of the year 1865 all claims upon the Crown were met, and salaries paid. His Excellency the Governor sent despatches to Downing Street detailing these steps. In reply, he was told by the Secretary of State for the Colonies that he had been conniving at breaches of the law.

The despatch is dated Downing Street, 27th November, 1865. A paragraph near the end may be said to sum up Mr. Cardwell's view :—

I am of opinion that in these three respects—in collecting duties without sanction of law, in contracting a loan without sanction of law, and in paying salaries without sanction of law—you have departed from the principle of conduct announced by yourself and approved by me, the principle of rigid adherence to the law. I deeply regret this. The Queen's Representative is justified in deferring very largely to his Constitutional Advisers in matters of policy, and even of equity. But he is imperatively bound to withhold the Queen's authority from all or any of those manifestly unlawful proceedings by which one political party, or one member of the body politic, is occasionally tempted to endeavour to establish its preponderance over another. I am quite sure that all honest and intelligent colonists will concur with me in thinking that the power of the Crown ought never to be used to authorise or facilitate any act which is required for an immediate political purpose, but is forbidden by law.

The comment on this that naturally rises is that it was very easy for Mr. Cardwell in the safe distance of Downing Street to criticise the means adopted to carry on the Queen's Government. He condemns what Sir Charles Darling did; he does not show how else the desired end could have been attained—how the Queen's Government could have been carried on.

During the contest it was often said that the whole trouble was due to the obstinacy of the Ministry and its supporters in the Lower House, who persisted in the tack, thereby coercing the Council. Some of those who held this view acknowledged that, according to constitutional precedent, the financial policy of the Colony should be regulated by the Lower House, and by it alone. In the month of November the Ministry decided to retrace its steps as far as the tack was concerned, and to try now what should have been tried earlier. On November 7th, a Tariff Bill was introduced into the Assembly and read a first time. On the next day the second reading was carried by thirty-nine to fourteen (without pairs), and the measure was passed through its remaining stages. Eight days later the Upper House rejected it by a majority of fourteen, only five being reckoned as "Contents." The Upper House uses the phraseology of the Lords.

It was now quite clear that it was not the tack which was standing in the way; and in order to make it equally clear that the colony was behind them, Ministers advised the Governor to grant a dissolution. In the Governor's speech at the prorogation (28th November), there came the clause—it is easy to imagine from whose pen—

The vital principle of representative institutions is the enlightened will of the community.

As the Speaker, on return from the Council, read the speech at the table, this clause was received with cheers and counter-cheers. And thus they made them ready for battle.

CHAPTER XII

ELECTION OF 1866 AND END OF DEADLOCK

Excitement over General Election—Election at Brighton—Opponent, Mr. J. Wilberforce Stephen—Mr. Higinbotham's address—Extract from Mr. McCulloch's—Charge of inconsistency—Legislative Council again rejects Tariff Bill—Case of Mr. Hugh George—A new session of Parliament—Conference and settlement of contest—The trouble begins anew.

OVER the General Election held early in 1866 the excitement was tremendous. For months the colony—it has been said, like one large debating society—had been discussing the crisis, which had been acute as well as prolonged. Everywhere men took sides with the Council or with the Assembly. Hardly any one was neutral or prepared to allow that truth could lie between the extremes. Now an opportunity was given at the polling-booth and the ballot-box to make opinions felt. Hardly a constituency was without a contest. But the interest culminated in the places where the Ministers were contending, especially in Mornington, Richmond, St. Kilda, and Brighton. The Chief Secretary, Mr. McCulloch, was opposed at Mornington, but had not much difficulty in securing his seat. Mr. Francis, the Commissioner of Customs and reputed author of the Protectionist element in the Tariff, had still less trouble at Richmond, for many of his constituents were, as he himself was, Protectionist. Their desire was not so much for the thin end of the wedge, as that the wedge should be driven further in. Mr. Michie, the Minister of Justice, suffered defeat at St. Kilda, for the residents in villas were, as usually, Conservative. It is perhaps no exaggeration to say that eyes were more closely fixed on the Brighton election than on any other.

Mr. Higinbotham was personally very popular, and in accounts of the elections in many constituencies it is recorded that the proceedings were interrupted, when his name was mentioned, by the proposal to give "three cheers for the Attorney-General." The candidate selected to oppose him at Brighton was a foeman worthy of his steel. Mr. James Wilberforce Stephen, barrister-at-law, was a member of the well-known family of Stephen that has for several generations given distinguished lawyers and judges, not to mention men of letters, to various parts of the Empire. Conspicuous ability, legal and literary, has been combined in them with a sturdy independence of character. Mr. Wilberforce Stephen was a son of Sir George Stephen,[1] knighted in 1837, the year of the Queen's accession, after taking a prominent part in the suppression of slavery throughout the British Dominions. At this Brighton election Mr. Stephen came forward as a strong supporter of the Legislative Council, but he made much of the Protectionist element in the Tariff, whilst his opponent would only argue the constitutional question.

Hence the simplicity of the following :—

To THE ELECTORS OF THE DISTRICT OF BRIGHTON.

GENTLEMEN,—

In compliance with a requisition, numerously signed, of electors of Brighton, I have the honour to offer myself again as a candidate for the representation of your district in the Legislative Assembly.

I thank you for the approval of my past conduct conveyed by this requisition. In the event of your again electing me, I will give my support to all measures which the Legislative Assembly or the Government may find it necessary to adopt for the purpose of maintaining and securing for the Assembly the exclusive control of the public finances and taxation, which I believe it to have been the intention and the effect of the Constitution to confer upon that body. The first of these measures will be the Tariff, in the same form in which it has been already adopted by the Assembly, and unconstitutionally rejected by the Council.

After the rights of the Assembly shall have been vindicated by the enactment of the Tariff, and conditionally upon that event, a proposal for the reform of the Legislative Council will receive my support.

---

[1] Sir George Stephen was a brother of Sir James Stephen, long Under-Secretary for the Colonies, Professor of History at Cambridge, father of Sir James FitzJames and Mr. Leslie Stephen.

I am unwilling to divert your attention from these questions of paramount importance by alluding to other topics. I desire that my success or failure at this election should turn upon your approval or disapproval, as well of my past acts as of my views and intentions with respect to the question of the constitutional rights of the Legislative Assembly. It is my earnest wish, in the event of my being again returned to Parliament as the member for Brighton, to be assured that I shall have the approval and support of your Conservative district in reference to a question which, in my opinion, vitally concerns public rights and public liberties.

I have the honour to be, Gentlemen,
Your obedient servant,
GEO. HIGINBOTHAM.

Brighton, 14*th December*, 1865.

Side by side with this it may be as well to quote the opening paragraphs of the Chief Secretary's address, which clearly states the issue before the Colony :—

TO THE ELECTORS OF THE COUNTY OF MORNINGTON.

GENTLEMEN,—

The rejection by the Legislative Council of the financial measures of the year submitted by the Government and passed by large majorities in the Assembly, has raised the question as to whether the right of taxation is to be in the Legislative Assembly, by whom the people is represented, or whether it is to be handed over to the Legislative Council, which represents only a small section of the community.

Had it been a matter of general legislation which was thus rejected, I should have deemed it to be the duty of the Government to yield, and to reintroduce the measure in another session ; but believing as I do, that to have taken any other course than that which has been taken, would have been virtually surrendering the rights of the House of Legislature which represents all classes of the community, the Government was bound to resist to the utmost the claim made by the Council to control the finances.

The Legislative Assembly having done all that it could in the maintenance of the rights entrusted to it, two courses were open to the Government resignation, or an appeal to the country. The adoption of the former would have been to acknowledge that the Council has the power of making and unmaking administrations—an acknowledgment which could not have been made without giving up one of the most important rights of the popular branch of the Legislature. The Government, therefore, resolved that the rights of the Assembly should not be sacrificed in their hands, and determined on submitting to the country the issues that have been raised between the two Houses.

The constituencies are now asked to decide whether the right of taxation is vested solely in that branch of the Legislature which represents all classes of the community, including the constituents of the Council ; whether taxation and representation are to go together ; whether the people, through their representatives, are to tax themselves, or are to submit to the dictation of the other branch of the Legislature, in whose election they have no voice, and over whose actions they have no control.   If there is to be taxation either without representation, or with a nominal representation without real responsibility, it is for the people at the ensuing election to say so.

At this election the grave charge of inconsistency was brought against Mr. Higinbotham, that he had changed his mind on certain questions during the four years in which he had been actively engaged in politics.   Early in 1894, the most respected of Victorian statesmen, who admired Mr. Higinbotham—then a year in his grave—but had opposed him steadily through his political career, was asked the question, " Did you think Mr. Higinbotham inconsistent ? "   His answer came : " Of all the adjectives in the English language that is the last of which I should have thought in connection with his name."

Opponents at Brighton reprinted Mr. Higinbotham's card of 1861, placing side by side with it two of his votes.   To show how little there is in this charge of inconsistency this card is here copied :—

<table>
<tr><td>

1861.

MR. HIGINBOTHAM'S
ELECTION CARD OF JULY, 1861.

—◆—

BRIGHTON ELECTION.

MR.
George Higinbotham
IS IN FAVOR OF

Free Trade.
Revision of the Road Tolls.
Torrens' Act, and Simplification of Transfer of Real Property.
Endowments to Municipalities.
Retention of the Gold Duty.
Extension of the Present Plan of Assisted Immigration.
A National System of Education.
The Civil Service being Regulated in Conformity with the Report of the Commissioners.

AND IS OPPOSED TO

Payment of Members.
Protection.
Conferring upon the Governor the power of Dissolving the Upper House.

</td><td>

1865.

MR. HIGINBOTHAM'S
Votes in Parliament.

— —

PAYMENT OF MEMBERS.

7th April, 1865, Mr. Higinbotham voted at the rate of £300 for each Member.

GOLD EXPORT DUTY.

Feb. 2, 1865, Mr. Higinbotham voted for the Abolition of the Duty.

—◆—

Mr. McCULLOCH, the Chief Secretary, in his Address to the Electors of Mornington, says :—

" The Government is prepared to give the Governor power to dissolve the Council."

—◆—

ELECTORS OF BRIGHTON.

Reflect before you promise your Votes.

</td></tr>
</table>

Free Trade.—As much has been made of this difference, it is worth while to examine it more closely. Mr. Higinbotham was a general believer in Free Trade, and did not regard the Tariff as Protectionist.

Gold Export Duty.—This was not a matter of great importance.

Payment of Members.—On this he had an open mind. He at first disliked the general principle, but saw that it might admit of modifications. This was just the kind of question on which experience of actual politics would modify views.

Dissolution of Upper House.—This was suggested as a safety-valve. In 1861 no one dreamt that the Upper House would claim powers greater than the House of Lords. In England the power to create peers is the safety-valve. Were the Upper House in the colony nominated, without the number of members being fixed, a similar safety-valve would be possible. But in 1861, as later—as always—Mr. Higinbotham held that the popular will should prevail.

Before abandoning this question of consistency it may be as well to remark that the charge and its repetition hardly come well from a supporter of Mr. Stephen. On the main point at issue no one could think Mr. Higinbotham inconsistent. From first to last he presented an unchanged front to the claims of the Legislative Council. Mr. Stephen, in January, 1866, was a strong supporter of those claims. In 1873 he was Attorney-General, when a bill of the Ministry to which he belonged was "laid aside" by the Upper House. Did he support the claims of the Council then?[1]

The polling at Brighton took place on January 29th, 1866, and Mr. Higinbotham defeated his opponent by 46.

Higinbotham	396
Stephen . .	350

The first session of the Fifth Parliament was short. It began on February 12th and ended on April 5th. The followers of the Ministry numbered fifty-eight out of a House of seventy-eight members ; that is to say, the majority was about half the House. In the House of Commons it would be a majority

---

[1] See Rusden's *History of Australia*, vol iii., pp. 385, 386.

of 330 members.   An English Premier would be in rapture at such a majority.   A Ministry with that force behind it could carry any reform that it desired.   The position taken by the Victorian Upper House may be seen from the address in reply to the Governor's speech.

It was thus briefly put by the leader of the Opposition (the Hon. T. H. Fellows) :—

We are ready to concur in a Protective tariff, even if it includes a duty on wheat ; . . . we disclaim any undue interference with the fiscal system, but shall insist on adherence to Parliamentary usage in regard to bills, and will not consider any bill of supply which deals with land revenue.

It would thus seem that what was left of the great dispute was matters of form.   The Legislative Council contended that it was justified in rejecting the Tariff Bill, even untacked, towards the close of 1865 ; not on the ground that it did not like Protection, but because the constituencies had not been definitely consulted.   There was no longer this excuse.   Yet on the 13th March the Upper House again, on the motion of Mr. Fellows, threw out the Tariff, avowedly on the points of form.   Hereupon the Ministry resigned, forwarding to the Governor a long minute setting out the reasons for such action.   Sir Charles Darling sent a short note to Mr. Fellows requesting " to be informed whether Mr. Fellows is prepared to undertake the duty of forming a new administration."

Complaint has been made that his Excellency did not *send for* Mr. Fellows.   The reason why he did not will soon appear. When Mr. Fellows was unsuccessful in forming an administration, the Governor asked Mr. McCulloch and his colleagues to remain in office.   The situation was again becoming strained, and the Upper House showed symptoms of a willingness to enter into conference ; but the bill had been rejected, and could not be brought in again in the same session of Parliament.   It was therefore decided to prorogue Parliament, and to summon it again for a new session on the following day, April 11th.

The conclusion of the short session that ended on 10th April was marked by an incident, which, on account of its personal character, attracted more attention than questions far more important often do. The *Argus*, having declared that the statement of the Chief Secretary "bristled with falsehoods," the indignant majority in the Assembly ordered that the printer of the *Argus*, Mr. Hugh George, should be summoned before it, and later should be committed to the custody of the Sergeant-at-Arms. It was on the motion of the Attorney-General that Mr. George was committed, and when the imprisonment became a farce, "a means of personal recreation and enjoyment," the Attorney-General called for stricter discipline. A piquancy was given to these facts by the knowledge that Mr. Higinbotham and Mr. George were personal friends. The dissolution of Parliament gave Mr. George his release. On an earlier occasion, the case of Mr. Dill, also printer of the *Argus*, Mr. Higinbotham had warned the Assembly not to exercise its privileges against perfect freedom of the Press. No doubt the latter case was worse, both in the strength of the language employed and in the fact that the head of the Government was assailed. But in contests between Parliament and the Press, which are perhaps inevitable, it is more dignified for the former not to assert privileges unshared by citizens at large. There are law courts where every citizen has his remedy.

In the new session a conference was held between the two Houses. Amongst the seven members representing the Assembly, Mr. Higinbotham was not included, evidently for the reason that he was not prepared to make concession. The seven consisted of two members of the Government, the Premier and the Treasurer, three gentlemen who joined the Government a few months later, one who succeeded Mr. Higinbotham as Attorney-General in the next McCulloch Ministry, and another.

After some debate concessions were made on both sides ; both sides claimed a victory, and taunted their opponents with defeat. In matters of form it may be said the Upper House won, in substance the Lower. How far in such cases form can be separated from substance is another question.

To help to decide the question with which side the honours of victory lay, the report of the Conference as laid before the Legislative Assembly is here given :—

Your Committee have conferred with the Committee of the Legislative Council on the subject of the said differences, which your Committee ascertained from the Committee of the Legislative Council were comprised under three heads, viz:

1. The form of the Preamble.

2. The inclusion of the repeal of the Duty on the Export of Gold in a Bill imposing Duties of Customs.

3. The limited duration of the measure.

And your Committee have now the honour to make the following recommendations to your Honourable House :—

1. That the Preamble be as follows :

MOST GRACIOUS SOVEREIGN,—
    WHEREAS we Your Majesty's most dutiful and loyal subjects, the Legislative Assembly of Victoria in Parliament assembled, did on the eleventh day of April in the year of our Lord one thousand eight hundred and sixty-six freely and voluntarily vote that a Supply be granted to Your Majesty and whereas towards raising such Supply we did on the said eleventh day of April vote that the several duties hereinafter mentioned be charged. We do therefore most humbly beseech Your Majesty that it may be enacted and be it enacted, &c.

2. That so much of the last clause of the Bill as limits the duration of the Bill be omitted.

After much deliberation upon the subject, the Committee of the Legislative Council stated that they would " no longer insist upon their objections to the inclusion of the repeal of the Gold Export Duty in the Bill of Supply, upon the assurance of your Committee that it was inserted in the Bill as a tax, and not as territorial revenue, and upon your Committee disclaiming any intention on the part of your Honourable House of tacking it, with the view of coercing the Council to pass it" ; to this proposal of the Committee of the Legislative Council, your Committee acceded.

In accordance with this report matters were settled. On 17th April, 1866, a new bill with the preamble agreed upon was introduced, and although the debate did not lack taunts and acrimony, a Supply Bill and an Appropriation Bill at length passed both Houses.

It seemed as if the strife in the colony were at an end, and the healing process might begin ; but on that very day, 17th April, the Premier announced in the House that a despatch had been received from Mr. Cardwell, recalling Sir Charles Darling. That recall led to a renewal of the strife, and to the second deadlock.

CHAPTER XIII

JUDGES' RIGHTS

THE affair with the Judges is frequently mentioned in connection with Mr. Higinbotham's Attorney-Generalship, chiefly because of one expression often quoted, and also because he was afterwards a Judge himself. It is of importance chiefly as indicating his strong and clear views on Responsible Government. The controversy began with a brief note from Sir Redmond Barry to the Governor :— "January 4th, 1864. I do myself the honour to inform your Excellency that I leave Melbourne this day for Sydney and Brisbane, to enjoy a short holiday trip." The Governor referred the letter to the Attorney-General : "I presume the Judges have a legal right to take the step adopted by Sir R. Barry. C. H. D." The Attorney-General gave his opinion that they had not a right to take leave, nor to report it to the Governor direct. More letters ensued. Sir Redmond Barry asserted his right, and refused "to acquiesce in submission to the authority of the Executive Council." Then (April 16th, 1864) came a minute from the Attorney-General, in which occurs the famous expression about the "officer in his Department." This paragraph of the minute is quoted unabridged :—

The Attorney-General begs leave to inform His Excellency that it has been the practice since the coming into force of the *Constitution Act* for all judicial and other officers in the public service of Victoria to communicate upon all questions affecting their official rights or responsibilities with the Minister of the Crown who is charged with the duty of advising the Governor in each particular case. Neither the principles on which the independence of the Judges is secured by law, nor (so far as the Attorney-General can learn after careful enquiry) the usage which has hitherto prevailed, authorise a departure from this practice in the case of the Judges of the Supreme Court. The Attorney-General is not aware that the Judges of England enjoy the right, beyond the other subjects of Her Majesty, of submitting their claims to the cognizance and decision of the Queen in person. The Judges of the Supreme Court do not possess higher rights in this respect than the Judges of England, and the Attorney-General cannot permit any officer in his Department—no matter how eminent the position of the officer may be, or however independent the law may have made him in the exercise of his official functions—to place himself outside the limits of the system of responsible government, and communicate with the Attorney-General on an official subject by means of letters addressed to the Governor in person. The Attorney-General does not know whether Sir Redmond Barry intends to assert a right of this nature as belonging to himself and the other Judges of the Supreme Court, but the Attorney-General feels that he should give a tacit assent to an unconstitutional and an inconvenient practice if he were to submit an opinion to His Excellency founded on His Honour's letters in reference to the important subject which has been brought under Sir Charles Darling's attention by Sir Redmond Barry. He has felt bound, therefore, to regard His Honour's communications as private and unofficial, and in the absence of a command from His Excellency he has no observation to offer on the subject of the right of the Governor and the Executive Council to suspend a Judge of the Supreme Court.

More letters followed, Sir Redmond Barry continuing to claim the right for Judges to communicate direct with the Governor, and not through a Minister. At length on August 22nd, another minute from the Attorney-General was forwarded to the Governor setting out the views of the Members of the Cabinet. This minute was accompanied by a joint opinion of the Attorney-General and the Minister of Justice; and as a result of the minute the Executive Council made an order, which was formally communicated to each of the Judges of the Supreme Court :—

That the Governor and Executive Council direct that all official communications by their Honours the Judges of the Supreme Court, respecting the rights, privileges, or duties of their offices, and intended to be brought under the consideration of the representative of

I

the Crown, or the Government, or Executive Council, shall in future
be addressed to the Attorney-General, as the Responsible Minister
at the head of the Department to which the Supreme Court is
attached.

J. H. KAY,

5th September, 1864.   Clerk of the Council.

Sir Redmond Barry, on behalf of his brother judges and
himself, then once more wrote direct to the Governor asking
that the question might be submitted to the Secretary of
State for the Colonies, and the law point referred to
the Judicial Committee of the Privy Council. He was
informed that any documents would be forwarded if submitted in accordance with the order of the Executive.

That ended the first act. The second is more painful.
One of the Judges was petitioner in a divorce suit, and public
feeling was strong as to the retention of his office of judge in
such cases. Expecting that questions would be asked, or a
motion made in Parliament, the Attorney-General wrote to
him to suggest that the Divorce and Matrimonial causes
jurisdiction should be administered by a brother judge. The
answer that came was twofold,—a denial of any right to
interfere, and a statement that the judge had already done
what was suggested.

The third act is connected with a Consolidation Bill.
In an Act, 15 Victoria, No. 10, section 5, there was a clause
giving the Executive power to suspend judges. The Judges
of the Supreme Court maintained that this clause was not in
force. The law advisers were of opinion that it was. When
the consolidation came on, the Attorney-General included the
clause in his "Supreme Court Statute"; but the Chief Justice
on behalf of the judges claimed that he ought not so to do.
That was a very pretty controversy. An able communication
from the Chief Justice (Sir William Stawell) closes the
correspondence for the year 1864.

The bill came before Parliament, and the Judges of the
Supreme Court petitioned both Houses. The Legislative
Assembly, as was not unnatural, took the view of the
Attorney-General, and passed the clause: the Legislative
Council took the view of the judges, and amended the measure
in accordance therewith. The Assembly refused to accept
the amendments, and when the bill returned to the Council

it was thrown out. In one of the debates in the Assembly the Attorney-General commented on the much-quoted phrase in a manner which, whilst the phrase has clung to memory, has been completely forgotten :—

He would say that an expression used by him in the correspondence before the House was one the use of which he regretted. He meant the expression in which the judges were designated "officers in the department of the Attorney-General." He regretted it, not because he did not believe it to be a strictly accurate expression, and one easily to be defended as appropriate, but because he believed the use of it had tended to strengthen the impression or prejudice that there was some covert design on the part of the Executive, either in this bill or in the proceedings on which the correspondence had arisen, to interfere with the independence of the judges. A more unfounded impression never existed, and he believed that it was one which had been sedulously cultivated in order to disguise and conceal the true relations of this question. He wished to express a desire in which all united, that the judges should be, in the exercise of their judicial functions, independent.[1]

The final act of this little drama was a petition signed by the four Judges of the Supreme Court to the Queen's Most Excellent Majesty, asking that the point at issue should be referred to the Judicial Committee of the Privy Council. This petition was forwarded to England with many documents at the end of September, 1865, and the reply was received in the following March. The Judicial Committee is a law court, and English courts will not pronounce an opinion on abstract questions of law : to which effect wrote Mr. Henry Reeve, " Reg. P.C."[2] to Sir F. Rogers of the Colonial Office : " The question raised by the judges is as yet entirely of an abstract and theoretical character." The Secretary for the Colonies obtained an opinion from the Law Officers of the Crown in England (Sir Roundell Palmer and Sir R. P. Collier), and this opinion coincided with that of the Law Officers in Victoria, and was not in accordance with the claim put forward by the judges. Abbreviated it runs :—

1. The Governor and Council can still "amove" Judges under the Imperial Statute, 22 George III., cap. 75.

---

[1] *Victorian Hansard*, vol. xi., p. 779. (May 18th, 1865.)
[2] Registrar of the Privy Council.

2. We also think it is the better opinion that they can still suspend Judges under the Local Act, 15 Vic., No. 10, section 5, the power of suspension for the causes therein mentioned being not inconsistent with the tenure of the office during good behaviour.

The question was now practically set at rest. Since that time the Judges of the Supreme Court have without demur corresponded with the Attorney-General's department, and not with the Governor. But there is a characteristic conclusion to the controversy, a memorandum by the Attorney-General, dated April 25th, 1866, objecting to the interference of the Imperial Law Officers:—

Neither the Judges of the Supreme Court nor the Government of Victoria expressed a desire to submit the legal points at issue to the determination of the Law Officers of England. The opinion which has been given, while it is unfavourable to the claim of the Judges, is in no way binding upon their Honours. If on the other hand the opinion had been favourable to the claims advanced by the Judges, the Law Officers of the Crown in Victoria could not have permitted it to influence their advice on the conduct of the Government towards the Judges, unless the reasons by which it was supported were sufficient to convince the judgment of His Excellency's legal advisers.

This is dated one week after the recall of Sir Charles Darling was known.

CHAPTER XIV

Despatches—Mr. Cardwell on Free Trade in the Colony—Position of
Governor under Responsible Government—How far is it compatible
with Instructions—Sir Charles Darling's despatches—The petition
of twenty-two Executive Councillors, and his comments on it—
Unwise Clause 74—His consequent recall—Address of Legislative
Assembly—Proposed grant to Lady Darling.

IT has always been and still is the custom for the governor
of a colony to send numerous despatches to the Colonial
Office, in which he narrates the history of the colony. The
Secretary of State for the Colonies comments on these despatches, approves or censures the conduct of the governor, and
frequently expresses an unfavourable comment on the conduct
of the Legislature or of the constituencies. In the year 1865
Mr. Cardwell was Secretary of State for the Colonies. At
the end of November, 1864, Sir Charles Darling wrote a
despatch reporting the General Election, in which he said he
thought Protection to native industry was in favour with the
constituencies. At the end of February, Mr. Cardwell says
in reply :—

It will be a subject of sincere regret to Her Majesty's Government if
the result of the new elections shall lead, as you appear to anticipate,
to any desire, on the part of your prosperous and intelligent community, to depart from those principles of commercial freedom which
have been so universally adopted and so successfully applied in this
country. I trust that the Legislature of Victoria will see that nothing
would be so much calculated to obstruct the progress of the colony
as the enactment of laws having it for their object to induce the
colonists to desert more profitable for less profitable branches of
industry.

Nothing could be more true nor more calmly expressed, and yet it was a perfectly gratuitous, and in the strict sense of the word, impertinent, remark.

When the English Parliament established Responsible Government in the colonies, it abandoned all right to interfere in the domestic affairs of the colony. When Mr. Cardwell penned his dignified sentences, he must have known that they could have no weight beyond the weight that would attach to them, if uttered by any prominent public man, member of Parliament, or journalist. His office gave him no right to intrude advice.

It may be that the English Parliament did not see the full effect of its grant of Responsible Government, for if that means anything, it means that, as far as internal affairs are concerned, the governor of the colony is in the position of a Constitutional Monarch. The wholesome doctrine that "the king can do no wrong," and that if he does anything which in another would be wrong, his ministers are to be held responsible and not himself, is accepted in England as the basis of the monarchy, under which, according to the Frenchman's epigram, "the king reigns, but does not govern." It ought to have followed as a corollary of Responsible Government, that the Colonial Office should have changed its instructions. The logical instruction would have been, "Your capacity is twofold. In certain matters you are an agent of the Imperial Government; in these matters you will receive instructions, more or less minute, and on these you will correspond with us; but in other matters you are a constitutional sovereign—accept the advice of your ministers, or change them. If the colony is behind the Ministry, follow their advice. If you have reason to doubt, dissolve Parliament and let the country speak."

It has been said on the highest authority that "no man can serve two masters": but a colonial governor is constantly trying the experiment. From Downing Street he receives instructions, advice, reprimand. This advice may not consort with the advice of the Ministers through whom he is supposed to govern. The wonder is that this dual control has not led to greater troubles. It certainly produced the second deadlock in Victoria.

Mr. Cardwell, as an English Liberal, and one of the most

accomplished of the followers of Sir Robert Peel, naturally held the doctrines of Free Trade. He was shocked at the smallest fragment of Protection, and so, early in the battle, his sympathies were ranged with the opponents of the Ministry. He tries, honestly tries, to be impartial; but it never occurs to him that he has nothing to do with the battle, that he may look on from the shore, but that he has no business even to express his sympathy. This unfortunate system of despatches gives the Secretary for the Colonies or his subordinates, the permanent officials, frequent opportunity to express views. They have to write and must say something. In the last chapter but one it is recorded how the Colonial Office and Mr. Cardwell expressed a condemnation of Sir Charles Darling. Had the Governor been wise, he would have said very little, but he wrote long exculpatory minutes. It was hinted that Mr. Higinbotham helped him in the composition of many of these, in which the arguments for his actions are expressed with great ability. Later in life it is certain Mr. Higinbotham would not have consented to enter into argument with the Colonial Office; but his regard for the Governor was great, and it is possible that in this as in other matters he tried to help him. Sir Charles Darling held firmly that it was the duty of a governor to govern according to the advice of his ministers. As long as he held to that doctrine he was safe. Unfortunately, instead of standing by that simple axiom he defended his conduct as Governor, that is, the advice of his Ministers, in detail. Defence in detail is entering into a fight; and in a fight, defence soon becomes attack.

In December, 1865, Sir Charles received a petition to the Queen signed by twenty-two Executive Councillors.

It may be as well to explain that the Executive Council in Victoria consists of all who have been Cabinet ministers, unless they have resigned their seats on the Executive. Ex-ministers are generally members of the Opposition. If the list of twenty-two be scanned, it will be found to contain the names of many eminent and able Victorian politicians, either active and sitting on Opposition benches, or retired from politics and holding the views of the Opposition. The petition contained very strong charges against the Ministry and against the Governor for acting in accordance with the advice of his

Ministers. It is evident that the Governor was very angry. According to his instructions he sent the petition home, but with it he sent a long report, controverting the statements of the petition. Had it been briefer, he would have been wise; had he simply made it clear, "this emanates from the Opposition; the facts are such and such, and I am bound to act in accordance with the advice of my Ministers or to dismiss them," he would have been safe. But in his wrath he stepped out of his defence, and hit out. Here are some of the most pugnacious and unguarded clauses of his long despatch:—

56. But I must now reverse the position in which the gentlemen who have signed the Address, and I, as Her Majesty's Representative, have stood in relationship to each other in this matter.

57. I accuse these gentlemen, one and all, of conduct highly discreditable to them as members of the Executive Council of this Colony; and I respectfully submit my opinion that they have proved themselves to be unfit to hold Her Majesty's commission in that capacity, and to enjoy the precedence and distinction which attach to it.

58. I might rest this opinion solely upon the fact that the course which they have pursued amounts to a treacherous conspiracy against the Governor.

66. I charge the members of the Executive Council who have addressed Her Majesty in this instance, with having suppressed—and wilfully suppressed—every material fact and circumstance upon which it is well known that my justification of the proceedings they impugn is based.

74. Whatever course in the exercise of your judgment you may see fit to advise Her Majesty to adopt, it is impossible that the relations between the petitioners and myself can, in the face of this conspiracy, be such as ought to subsist between the Governor and gentlemen holding the commission of an Executive Councillor, whether occupying or not occupying responsible office; and it is at least to be hoped, that the future course of political events may never designate any of them for the position of a confidential adviser of the Crown, since *it is impossible their advice could be received with any other feelings than those of doubt and distrust.*

This despatch (dated December 23rd, 1865) was certainly unwise in many of its parts, most unwise in the words now printed in italic, with which the last quoted clause concludes.

A constitutional sovereign has to act now with one party, and now with another. It was therefore remarkable unwisdom, accounted for, though not excused, by a strong feeling of resentment, that made Sir Charles Darling say that if the Opposition came into power he could not work with them.

He had thus identified himself with a party. One member of the Cabinet saw the despatch after it was sent, and when it was too late to modify it, and he at once prophesied to his colleagues that it would lead to the Governor's recall.

For Clause 74, Sir Charles Darling was recalled.

Pope says that "blindness to the future" is "kindly given." But it may well be doubted, whether, if Mr. Cardwell could have foreseen the trouble which the recall would cause, he would not have adopted a different course, such as in such a case a modern Secretary for the Colonies would probably now pursue. He would have written to Sir Charles, and pointed out the error of his ways, and would have suggested that as Clause 74 had been evidently penned under feelings of exasperation, it would be better to withdraw it. He would then, when all was over, have contributed a long State paper, reviewing the situation, distributing praise and blame with an even hand, and rejoicing that the wise moderation of both parties had stayed the strife. Unfortunately, Mr. Cardwell's line of action prolonged the strife in a new form for two years and a quarter.

Sir Charles Darling was recalled nominally for one unwise remark. The punishment was so disproportionate to the offence that it was generally believed that he was being punished for following the advice of his Ministers. Now the Ministers had the support of the country. Therefore Sir Charles Darling became more than ever endeared to the people of the colony.

A Select Committee was appointed by the Legislative Assembly to prepare an Address to His Excellency, and to consider and report on the steps the House should take with reference to his being relieved from his position as officer administering Her Majesty's Government in this colony.

It prepared an Address which was adopted, and is here given :—

To His Excellency Sir Charles Henry Darling, *Knight Commander of the Most Honourable Order of the Bath, Governor and Commander-in-Chief of the Colony of Victoria, &c., &c., &c.*

May it please Your Excellency—
We, the Members of the Legislative Assembly of Victoria in Parliament assembled, have learned with extreme regret that Her

Majesty has been advised to recall you from the Government of Victoria.

2. We cannot be unmindful of the great and unprecedented difficulties with which Your Excellency has been beset, nor of the fact that had Your Excellency adopted any other course of administration, the unhappy differences between the Houses of Legislature would not have been satisfactorily adjusted.

3. We are greatly beholden to Your Excellency for your steadfast adherence to the principles of Constitutional Government, and recognize in Your Excellency's conduct a determination to rule by the advice of your responsible Ministers. We do not hesitate to express our conviction that if Your Excellency had adopted the opposite course—if you had attempted to give effect to the opinions of the minority—the political contest, now happily at an end, would still be raging to the great injury of the country.

4. We therefore thank Your Excellency for having saved the colony from anarchy, and for having effected a settlement of the serious political differences from which we have just emerged. Especially we thank Your Excellency for not having interposed to influence the operation of Responsible Government, to the possession of which, as British subjects, we have never ceased to be entitled.

5. We beg, at the termination of Your Excellency's official connexion with this colony, to express the deep and sincere interest we feel in Your Excellency's future welfare and in that of your family, and we desire also to express our belief that the widespread regret publicly manifested at Your Excellency's recall from the Government, will afford to Your Excellency the best assurance that you leave these shores possessed of the general respect and sympathy of the people of this colony.

In consideration of the services which His Excellency Sir Charles Darling has rendered in the administration of the Government of Victoria, from which he has been recalled for political reasons only, and seeing that his removal will entail upon his family very heavy pecuniary loss, the Committee recommended further, that a grant of twenty thousand pounds be made to Lady Darling for her separate use.

CHAPTER XV

SPEECH ON DARLING'S TREATMENT

THE following speech was delivered by Mr. Higinbotham on
the second night of the debate upon the Governor's recall
(2nd May, 1866). It is reprinted from the *Victorian
Hansard* :—

We are invited by this motion to join in voting an address to the
Governor of this colony when leaving our shores under circumstances
not only unusual, but unprecedented, for I believe I am correct in
saying, that this is the first occasion on which a Governor holding
Her Majesty's commission in a colony possessing Responsible Government has been recalled from office during his period of service.
It is not my intention to offer any reply to the remarks of the honourable members who have preceded me, upon the conduct and acts of
the Government during the last fifteen months, either with regard to
the verbal criticism of the honourable member who has resumed his
seat, or the more elaborate comments of the honourable member for
East Melbourne. I do not complain of those remarks. They are
naturally awakened by the consideration of the despatches before us.
I am sensibly reminded, that the acts of the Government and the advice
of legal advisers, are subjects intimately connected with the question
at present under the consideration of the House, and I do not complain of honourable members departing from the strict terms of the resolution, to indulge in oft-repeated criticisms on the conduct of the
Government. On the contrary, I was glad to hear some honourable
members, and especially the honourable and learned member who
immediately preceded me, address themselves to the conduct of the
Government, for I felt that if by diverting those comments from the
Governor to the Government, I could induce the honourable and learned
member to abstain from addressing a wounded and ruined man in terms
of coarse jest, of cruel insult, and malignant triumph, I would gladly
bear in silence any commentary, however adverse. Let honourable
members address themselves to the Government.

In nos convertite tela.

For this night, but this night only, we will not reply. On no other occasion have we refrained from meeting you in fair debate, on no other occasion have we shrunk from encountering your attacks. For the last fifteen months we have engaged in a conflict, opposed by men whose every other blow has been a foul one. We have never flinched from that contest, and I feel that at present we may cheerfully bear in silence any remarks the honourable and learned member has it in his power to make, provided that by drawing them on ourselves, we can shield if possible the character and name of the Governor, who is leaving this colony. I confess that there is another reason which leads me to abstain from entering into a defence of the conduct of the Government. I am bound to say that I decline to enter into a justification of any of my acts, or of any advice I have tendered His Excellency the Governor, in consequence of any criticism which the Secretary of State may have been pleased to make. I am not responsible to the Secretary of State. It is in that gentleman's power to recall the Governor; it is not in his power to censure the Government. I deny his authority to criticise my acts. I assert that, as a person holding a high but still a lay office, he is not a competent authority to question my law. I say it with all deference for the Secretary of State, and with the more confidence because I do not shrink from admitting my liability to competent critics in this colony. I say to them, "You are our natural and legitimate critics; we have never shrunk from meeting you." We have eminent barristers in the colony; I never denied their right to criticise, and I never was afraid to meet their criticism; but I totally deny the right of the Secretary of State to pronounce, in terms of authority, by virtue of his office, on the legality or illegality of the advice which the advisers of a Responsible Government tender to the Governor. So much for the comments of honourable members on the acts of the Government.

I now desire to address myself, shortly, to the real question before us—the duty of this House on the occasion of Sir Charles Darling leaving the shores of Victoria. I have listened for any possible reason for withholding from Sir Charles Darling the usual testimony, the usual mark of courtesy which colonial Legislatures pay to retiring governors. I have not heard any reasons. I have heard many comments on these despatches, and I must say that, after making every allowance for the excited party feelings of gentlemen who have been in opposition to the Governor and to this Government, I am unable to understand how even they can say that Sir Charles Darling does not leave this colony a deeply injured man. There is no person with either a generous heart or a mind acquainted with the first principles of constitutional government, who will say that Sir Charles Darling is not now being punished, his prospects ruined, his character—his long-sustained character—damaged, and, it may be, his fortunes destroyed for the acts of others. I challenge honourable members to meet that view of the question. It has not yet been touched upon. For the purpose of this part of my argument, I will admit that all the acts of the Government, all the advice we have tendered to him, have been illegal and unconstitutional. Charge us, if you please, not only with faults, but crimes. Why should he be the sufferer?   What has he done to deserve at your hands, and at your instigation, the treatment he is now receiving.   On what principle, I will not say of constitutional government, but of common equity, can you seek to make a man, who yourselves declare fills the post of a responsible Governor, responsible for the acts of his advisers? How can you seek to punish him for the acts and the advice of others? Can that question be answered?   I have listened with attention to hear whether honourable members would even approach this side of the subject.   They themselves admit that a governor, in a colony like this, holds a similar position to that occupied by the Queen in England —that the Governor, like the Queen, cannot be visited with personal consequences. (" No.")   Well, sir, I thought honourable members entertained that belief.   Certainly I have heard honourable members on the other side (including the honourable and learned member who last addressed the House) advance views on this particular subject very far in advance of those I have been able to assent to.   The honourable and learned member for Kilmore spoke on a former occasion in reference to the position and liability of the Governor of this colony, and he made partial quotations from *Merivale* and other English authorities with the view of showing that a Governor of a colony like this occupied no other than a merely irresponsible position—that his dual character of agent of the Imperial Government and responsible Governor was a character that could not be recognised by the Parliament of this country.   I have heard that argument advanced not only by the honourable and learned member, but also by the head of the Government with which he was connected.   But this was at a time when circumstances were different to what they are at present.   At that time those honourable gentlemen were Ministers of the Crown, and in hostility to the Governor ; and part of their policy was to endeavour to show that the Governor was absolutely subject, in all things to be bound by the advice of his responsible Ministers for the time being.   I have never been able to accept that doctrine.   I have always recognised the double position of Governor in this colony.   I have recognised his opinion as subject to be bound at once by the written instructions he receives from the Secretary of State in connection with imperial interests, and at the same time by his duty to the Parliament and people of this country as a responsible Governor.   I have always believed the Governor of this colony to be under an obligation to obey first of all his written instructions, provided—and this is matter for the consideration of Parliament and the people of this country—that those written instructions do not interfere with the public liberties of the people ; and in the absence of written instructions he is bound, only in reference to internal affairs, by the advice he receives from his Ministers. Now, it is not pretended that the written instructions Sir Charles Darling received were departed from.   The acts complained of by the Secretary of State are acts not covered by his instructions.

The substantial ground of complaint against Sir Charles Darling is, not that he knowingly violated the law, but that he did not anticipate the views of the Secretary of State in reference to the law.   (" No, no.")   I am aware that the Secretary of State has founded Sir Charles

Darling's recall on a sentence—it may be an impolitic sentence—in one of the despatches relative to the petition of the Executive Councillors. I think I am not expressing an unfair view when I say that that sentence has been made the occasion, and that it was not the cause, of Sir Charles Darling's recall. I recollect that, before the sentences reached the eyes of Mr. Cardwell, it was publicly stated in this colony that reliable information had been received that Sir Charles Darling's recall had then been determined upon. I heard the honourable and gallant member for West Melbourne declare last night, by way of exculpating a subordinate member of the Government to which Mr. Cardwell belongs, that the gentleman, although supposed to be one who influenced Sir Charles Darling's recall, had not, in fact, exercised any influence in that direction; but the honourable and gallant member did not go on to say, as I expected he would, that that gentleman, who enjoys a pension from this colony, had not been the channel of information respecting the intentions of Mr. Cardwell, in reference to Sir Charles Darling's recall. Now, if I am not misinformed, the statement publicly made in this city of the intention to recall Sir Charles Darling, was made on the authority of that gentleman; and I say, if there be any foundation in the report, published in a journal which claims credence for not publishing statements without foundation, it is not the fact that Sir Charles Darling has been recalled in consequence of a sentence which, at the time the report was published, had not reached the eyes of Mr. Cardwell. I am bound, therefore, to assume the real cause of Sir Charles Darling's recall is to be found in the series of acts which are made the subject of complaint in Mr. Cardwell's despatches—that Sir Charles Darling is recalled really because he assented to acts of his Ministers which Mr. Cardwell declares to be illegal. Well, Sir, I accept that view, and I again ask upon what principle of justice can honourable members defend the treatment which Sir Charles Darling has received, inasmuch as those acts, which are made the ground of his recall, are acts for which he is no more responsible than the honourable and gallant member for West Melbourne himself. Nay, more, they are acts which, according to the usage and practice of government in this colony, there was no necessity for Sir Charles Darling to be made acquainted with before they were done; with many of which he was, in fact, not made acquainted, and for none of which, except one, I believe, was his authority, consent, or permission asked. If that be so, what is the position of those persons in this country who have devoted their energies to effect the recall of Sir Charles Darling?

The honourable and gallant member for West Melbourne endeavoured last night, I thought, to excuse the memorial of the Executive Councillors, to which he had been a party. He said that the avowed object of that memorial was not to effect Sir Charles Darling's recall. I was glad to observe that the honourable and gallant member seemed to feel a touch of shame for the act to which he had been a party; but I failed to find in the remarks of the honourable and gallant member any explanation of the fact that the memorial had been sent home at all. With what purpose was it sent, except to procure the recall of Sir Charles Darling? What other object had it? What other object could it have?

(A MEMBER.—To have the law maintained.)

But the law, according to the honourable member's view of law, can only be maintained in this case by the recall of the Governor; and the only way to effect that object was to petition for the recall of Sir Charles Darling. The honourable member appears to differ from the honourable and gallant member for West Melbourne, and though no party to the memorial, appears to assent to the proposition that the necessary effect, if not the object of that memorial, was to procure the recall of Sir Charles Darling. But is my recollection deceived when I say that, in another place, when a similar memorial was under consideration, the object—to effect the recall of Sir Charles Darling—was openly avowed? Well, Sir, the object has been successful. Sir Charles Darling is recalled. Mr. Cardwell has made himself a party to the designs of those persons in this country who wished his recall; and now we are asked to express an opinion upon the subject. I think we are entitled to express an opinion. I think whatever may be the dependence of a colonial governor upon the Colonial Office in England, those over whom he presides have at least a right to be permitted to express their opinion of his conduct. In some respects a governor is intimately connected with the people of the colony over which he presides. They are charged with the expense of providing the governor's salary. They are deeply interested in the character of the governor—more deeply, I am inclined to think, than is commonly known, for upon the personal character of the governor, particularly in a colony like this, the public interests vitally depend. We are called upon, I say, to express an opinion. It was suggested by the honourable and gallant member for West Melbourne that this motion of the honourable member for East Bourke had a further object, which does not appear on the face of it—that not merely would it be proposed to this House, to pass a vote of confidence and of thanks to Sir Charles Darling, but that probably the House would also be invited, by the report of the committee, to compensate Sir Charles Darling for the heavy pecuniary loss which, in addition to his injured reputation, he will have to endure in consequence of his recall. I hope, Sir, that the suggestion of the honourable and gallant member is well founded. I hope the honourable member for East Bourke is prepared to assume the responsibility of suggesting to the committee, and that the committee will not shrink from recommending to this House, the adoption of that course. I believe, Sir, it will be a course that will speak in significant tones, not only to the people of this country, but also to those persons at home who take an interest in our affairs. I think we have a right, and that it is our interest, to place side by side with the unjust condemnation of Mr. Cardwell, the expressed opinion of the people—an opinion which once expressed by us, I take leave to say, may, if anybody has the power to represent the voice of the people of this country, be taken to express the views of this community—and, in addition to that, I think we should do ourselves honour, and we should only be doing justice to Sir Charles

Darling, we should only be giving a proof to the whole world that we were determined to be not merely generous, but just, if we say, " Sir Charles Darling shall not leave these shores ruined in fortune or in reputation, so far as it is in the power of the people of this colony to prevent it."

I am sorry at this late hour to occupy the attention of honourable members, but I must be permitted to ask the indulgence of the House for a few minutes longer. There is one aspect of the case which I cannot overlook, which I confess preoccupies my mind, even to a greater extent than the personal aspect of the case. I feel deeply the injury done to Sir Charles Darling : I should be sorry to be behind any honourable members in expressing, as distinctly as I can, my personal sympathy with that gentleman in his present position ; but I believe that the question disclosed by these despatches has an interest more permanent and deep than even the personal question connected with Sir Charles Darling. I think, Sir, and I would say it in a word—I think these despatches threaten danger to the public liberties of this people. (Dissent from the Opposition.) Will honourable members allow me to ask them whether they are prepared to accept the doctrine that, on all questions relating to the internal affairs of this colony, the Secretary of State is to be permitted to pass an opinion upon the legality or illegality of the acts of the Colonial Government ?

(SEVERAL HON. MEMBERS.—Certainly.)

I asked the question from some curiosity, and I am glad to have the answer of honourable members. I think the views of honourable members opposite, as expressed by that answer, differ altogether from the views which most persons in this colony entertain of their position as a people living under a system of responsible government. I find that Mr. Cardwell instructs the Governor of this colony as to the illegality of acts of the Government—acts relating purely to domestic and internal affairs, not in any way involving imperial policy, not in any way connected with English interests. On affairs purely domestic and internal, Mr. Cardwell instructs the Governor—that is the expression—that the acts of the Government are illegal ; he begs the Governor not to permit a continuance of those acts ; and he states what a future Governor should do if an occasion arose in which it would be " clear to his judgment "—I ask honourable members opposite to mark the words—" clear to his judgment," apart from all advice, free from all control, responsible to no authority, " that the advice of his Ministers for the time being would involve a violation of the law." Do I rightly interpret the views of honourable members on the other side if I suppose that, in their opinion, it is the duty of the Governor, in all cases, to form a personal opinion of the legality of the advice presented to him ? The previous answer implies that it is the opinion of honourable members. But that is not my opinion. I do not believe that it is consistent with the bare existence of responsible government; and I confess I look, under present circumstances, with very serious alarm upon the expression of the opinion of the Secretary of State in this direction.

We were told last night by the honourable and gallant member for

West Melbourne, who furnishes us with information, not derived from any public sources— for I believe the information has not been communicated to the public journals—that the Imperial Parliament is about to undertake an investigation of our affairs, and to inquire into the condition of responsible government in this colony. When, Sir, we are informed of this, upon the private authority of the honourable and gallant member, who receives his communications on this subject, I have no doubt, from reliable sources at home ; and when we take this information in connexion with the opinions of the Secretary of State, as expressed in these despatches, I say it is time for the people of this colony to consider under what form of government they are living. I should not fear either a parliamentary inquiry or the hostile views of a Secretary of State, if we were a united people among ourselves. I should view with utter unconcern the illiberal or harsh views of a Secretary of State, provided that we ourselves fully understood and duly valued the principles of responsible government. If we were a united people, bound to the soil and to the constitution of this country, by a lengthened enjoyment of both, I should not care what opinion the Secretary of State held. But, unfortunately, that is not the case. Unfortunately we are a divided people, with hostile interests against one another. There is in this country a large class—large, not, indeed, in the numbers of those who belong to it, but large in varied influence and in great power—which, I believe, is now hostile to the continuance of responsible government in this colony. The general mass of the people—the mass that never take a prominent part in politics, that are not heard of in public life, that cannot easily be designated by any special name, except it be one of those opprobrious terms which vile persons sometimes attach to them—terms which only recoil in shame and dishonour upon those who use them—this general body of the people are, I believe, perfectly satisfied with the system of government under which we live. I believe more. I believe—and I say it without flattery—that there is not a community on the face of the globe that may be more safely entrusted with constitutional liberties than this community; not one that will more wisely use, or is less likely to abuse, that gift of perfectly equal political as well as civil rights which it was the intention and design, although it has not yet been the effect, of our constitutional system to confer upon every member of the community. But, Sir, we have amongst us discontented classes, we have thwarted interests, we have disappointed politicians, and we have dissatisfied officials ; and the discontent and dissatisfaction of all these classes and individuals has recently taken the form of disloyalty and disaffection to our form of government—disloyalty, not, indeed, to the throne or to the Queen—there is plenty of lip loyalty to the throne—but disloyalty to that of which the throne and Her Majesty are symbols and signs—disloyalty to the authority of fundamental law and to the principles of our free constitution. Do honourable members opposite question that statement? Am I wrong ?

(Yes.)

If I am wrong I shall be very glad to be corrected. I certainly do not desire to utter a slander on any class of my countrymen.

K

(A MEMBER.—We say you are violating that constitution.)

I contend that the honourable member and those who entertain the same opinion have adopted a course which shows they are not only indifferent but hostile to the continuance of our free government. If my opinion be well founded, the honourable member is bound to give me an explanation of the fact that for the last twelve months no party has been satisfied to fight out its battle on our own soil—that every discontented class has resorted to an appeal to England, and has endeavoured to secure, by English interference, the object which might be legitimately sought for by colonial action. I ask honourable members to explain on what grounds, and for what reason, the traders of this city got up a petition to Her Majesty against the Governor and his Government? How are we to explain the fact that a legislative body has followed the same course?—that twenty-two gentlemen occupying the highest position in this country, and likely at any time to be called upon to take part in the affairs of government, can be found so far forgetful of their duties to responsible government here as to seek to create an appellate jurisdiction in the mother country? If honourable members will explain these facts to me, I shall be prepared to reconsider my opinion.

And (addressing the Opposition) how can you explain this additional fact, that for many months past the press of this country—the press which exercises a great influence over human intelligence, and a far greater, and even an awful influence over the larger mass of human ignorance—has teemed with articles and letters which, under the guise of political speculation, have been nothing else but sedition and disaffection? I observe that every writer who has just sufficient capacity to misunderstand De Tocqueville, and to misquote Mill or Hare, pours forth speculations, in newspaper articles and letters, which I cannot distinguish from rank sedition; which manifest a persistent hatred of free government, and an anxious desire to establish an inequality of political rights. If this be so, I say it is a subject for grave reflection to find a Secretary of State willing to lend himself to aid and to abet this class of opinion in the country. It is a subject not merely of regret but alarm, because, I frankly admit, the party in whose interests this is done is a most powerful party—a party which has all the power that wealth can confer. I am speaking of the party which consists of every discontented class, interest and official. I am speaking of the class which includes the Melbourne merchants. I believe at this moment—and I hope I do them no injustice—that the Melbourne merchants would gladly purchase a continuance of their importing monopoly by the surrender of our civil government. I believe the pastoral class would gladly, on the same terms, effect the defeat of the agricultural interest. I believe there is not a discontented official, from the judge on the bench of the Supreme Court—("Oh, oh" and "Shame" from the Opposition). I will justify the observation. One of the most significant circumstances, though not one of the most prominent, which has occurred within the last twelve months, is the fact—a fact, important from the quarter whence it came, and from the bad example which it set—that these officials, of whom I speak, actually presumed to disobey the Government of this country, and to appeal to the Home Government upon a question of mere official routine. And I say that, as with the merchants and squatters, so with the officials. There is not in this country at the present minute a dissatisfied official who would not procure the redress of his grievances, whether real or imaginary, by the sacrifice of all public rights, and by the destruction, personal and political, of every public reputation.

(A MEMBER.—That is a libel.)

It may be a libel. The honourable member for the Wimmera says so; but if so I regret that close observation of public affairs has led me to a state in which libel and my mind are identical. I cannot think, except I think a libel. Your party (addressing the Opposition) is a powerful one; you have all the power that money can give you; you have all the power that the persistent influence of continuing interest can give you; you have all the power that the English Government can give you: and, if you have not been completely successful in your designs upon the public liberties, the reason is to be found in the fact, not that we are strong, not that you are weak, but that you have not yet evinced the capacity to use your superior power in such a way as to lead to success.

On this occasion, as I understand it, we are asked to express personal sympathy with an injured man. We are also asked to put on the records of this House an expression of opinion which will indicate the views of this House, speaking in the name of the people, on the subject of our public rights under responsible government. I believe that this is a most important occasion, and that an opportunity rarely offered, and certainly not to be lightly used or thrown away, is now presented to us. We have now the opportunity, and I hope we shall use it, of setting right those who have suffered wrong through you. I refer not merely to the Governor, but to his family, and all who are dependent on him. We have the power, at all events, to declare our opinion on this matter—to declare that, whatever the opinion of Mr. Cardwell may be, Sir Charles Darling will be held in grateful memory by the people of this country; and further, we have it in our power—a power that cannot be interfered with—mark that—of doing what an honourable and learned member has said we had formerly disavowed—namely, of making a grant of public money to Sir Charles Darling. We also have it in our power to place upon record not in violent or menacing language, but by a significant act, our firm determination to maintain in their integrity the self-governing rights of independence in this country. I trust, Sir, that this Assembly will know the value of the opportunity which it now possesses, and will use it to the uttermost.

In the debate that followed, one member spoke of "the highly treasonable and traitorous speech made by the Attorney-General. (A laugh.) Honourable members may smile, but I think that he ought to be denounced as a traitor. I denounce him as such." There is absolutely nothing treasonable in the speech. Nonsense about separation was talked in connection

with it.   There is nothing about separation from the Empire
in the speech.   If a minister interfered with another minister's
department in England there would be nothing treasonable in
the latter crying " Hands off."   The view here adopted is that,
Responsible Government once unequivocally established, the
Secretary of State for the Colonies has nothing to do with the
internal affairs of the colony.   That is logical or illogical ; but
talk of treason does not touch it.

CHAPTER XVI

THE DARLING GRANT

Sir C. Darling's departure—Petition to the Queen—Lord Carnarvon's
despatch—The new Governor, Sir J. H. T. Manners Sutton—Sir
C. Darling quits the Queen's service—The Legislative Assembly
passes and tacks the Darling Grant—The Council rejects the Appropriation Act—A second session—Council rejects it again—
Short Duke of Edinburgh session—Alcock *v.* Fergie—Dissolution
—Brighton Election—A " disloyal man "—The Duke of Buckingham and his two despatches—Governor acting on instructions,
Ministers resign—Parliament meets, but no speech is ready—Attack on Duke of Edinburgh—Sir Charles Sladen's ministry—The
grant about to pass, untacked—Sir C. Darling re-enters—The
great strain and the relief—Nineteen months later death of Sir C.
Darling—Letter from Mr. Higinbotham.

On the 5th of May, 1866, Sir Charles Darling left the colony
amidst many expressions of regret. His departure was made
the occasion of a demonstration on the part of his personal
and political admirers. It was more like a triumphal procession than the retirement of a governor in disgrace.
Crowds attended to the wharf, cheering. A very general
feeling was entertained throughout the colony that Sir
Charles was an ill-used man ; but in all the crowds and
throughout the colony no one held that view so strongly as
the Attorney-General, late his chief legal adviser.

Sir Charles Darling went first to Sydney, whence he
addressed a letter to the Secretary of State, enclosing a
petition to the Queen, in which he asked that a tribunal
might be appointed to inquire into the whole of his conduct
as Governor of Victoria. On his return to England he
found that a new Secretary for the Colonies, Lord Carnarvon,

had succeeded to Mr. Cardwell. But the new Secretary of State felt as his predecessor, and neither would grant an inquiry. It seems that Sir Charles did not proceed to petition Parliament. Papers were presented to Parliament, but no action was taken upon them. What did either Lords or Commons care? To us, who look back upon the events, the request of the recalled Governor does not seem unreasonable, nor would compliance with it have been unwise.

Before leaving the colony Sir Charles sent a message to the Legislative Assembly to the effect that he

desired to express his deep and grateful appreciation of the generous consideration for his family evinced by the recommendation of the Committee ; but that he felt it to be his duty, while yet administering the Government, to intimate that his family would not feel at liberty to accept the bounty of the Parliament and people of Victoria, until he should know the Queen's commands, and have submitted his petition for " the most rigid inquiry and investigation."

After receipt of this message the Assembly petitioned the Queen to permit Lady Darling to accept the grant. This petition was duly fowarded by General Carey, the Acting Governor. The answer came to the new Governor, and was laid before the Assembly on February 19th, 1867. Here is its important part :—

I request that you will inform the Speaker of the Assembly that the Address has been laid before the Queen, who was pleased to receive it very graciously, but that I am unable to advise Her Majesty to accede to the request which it conveys.

The rule that a governor should not receive pecuniary or valuable presents from the inhabitants of the colony over which he presides, either during the continuance of his office or on leaving it, is expressly laid down in the Colonial Regulations, and, for obvious reasons, it has always been rigidly enforced. It is plain that such a rule would be merely nugatory if it were held that what the Governor was precluded from receiving might properly be given to his wife.

It is, under these circumstances, impossible that Her Majesty should be advised to sanction the literal, or substantial violation of this rule by any of her servants, or, on the other hand, that the acceptance of the proposed gift should be regarded otherwise than as a final relinquishment by Sir Charles Darling of that service, and of all the emoluments or expectations attaching to it.

I have, &c.,
(Signed)   CARNARVON.

The new Governor was Sir John Henry Thomas Manners Sutton, afterwards, through the death of his brother, Lord Canterbury ; and it may here be added that seldom did any man accept a position of greater difficulty and delicacy, or fulfil his duty with a more determined desire to do what seemed to him right.   A scrap from a letter written to the *Times*, in 1888, by Sir Charles Gavan Duffy, gives a clue to the reason of his selection :—

I was in England when Darling's successor was about to be selected, and I called on Mr. Disraeli at Downing Street to urge that it was a fatal mistake to entrust the control of a Parliamentary system to a man who had never seen a Parliament. " Well," he replied, smiling, " next time you will not have that complaint to make, as we are sending out the son of a Speaker who was bred up in Palace Yard."

There is no doubt the new Governor needed all his Parliamentary knowledge. The only complaint ever made against him was that, as a constitutional ruler, he hardly attached enough importance to his own House of Commons.

A reply was made by Lord Carnarvon to Sir Charles Darling to the same effect as that to the Legislative Assembly. He took the latter part of it as a suggestion. Reduced to something bordering on poverty, he relinquished in April his position in the service of the Queen. Whereupon the Victorian Ministry, considering that the regulations of the service no longer touched the case, renewed the question of the grant. In order to make a money-grant, a message from the Governor is necessary ; and on July 23rd, 1867, the Governor sent a formal message to the Legislative Assembly. His conduct in so doing was afterwards violently attacked, and some ten months later Sir Roundell Palmer tabled a motion that the House of Commons should condemn his conduct. The Governor's explanation, as contained in despatches, was that he regarded the message as formal, and he had made it clear that it was "not to be regarded as implying any personal opinion with respect to the policy of the proposal." In other words, it was one of those matters in which a governor accepts the advice of his ministers.

On receipt of the message the Assembly included the grant in the Appropriation Bill, and sent it to the Council, whereupon, on August 20th, by twenty-three votes to six, that body rejected the Appropriation Bill. Thus on that date began the second and severer deadlock, which lasted 322 days, or nearly a year.

The conduct of the Legislative Council was not unnatural. It had no reason to be fond of Sir Charles Darling, but the whole question was now revived. Had the Assembly, like the Commons of England, the sole power of the purse? If so, had the Council any right to reject the grant because of its own likes or dislikes? To include a money-grant in the Appropriation Bill, could that be regarded as a tack and an unfair means of coercing the Upper House? All the trouble that had distressed the colony during the former deadlock was brought back again through the rejection of the bill in the Upper House. The civil servants and the creditors of the State were left unpaid.

The first proposal of Ministers was that Parliament should be at once prorogued, and then called together for a new session, when the same bill would be introduced again. The Governor refused to accept this advice. Then the Ministers resigned, whereupon the Governor did his best to find others to take their places. His efforts having proved unsuccessful, he then accepted the advice of the former Ministers, prorogued Parliament on September 10th, and called it together again on September 18th.

In the new session the Appropriation Bill, including the grant, was passed by the Assembly, and again it was rejected by the Council. This time the Ministers advised a dissolution; and the Governor, seeing no other course open, accepted the advice. The House was prorogued on November 5th, and dissolved on December 30th, the General Election following in February.

In the earlier interval fell a curious little session that lasted less than an hour. The visit of Prince Alfred to the colony made it advisable that the Houses should meet in order that each should adopt an address to his Royal Highness. The Houses met at 10 a.m. on November 25th. A Governor's speech was delivered, an address in reply adopted, an address to the Prince was carried, and a little other business accomplished, and each House had adjourned before the clock struck eleven. Had it not been for the Prince's visit, the General Election would have come sooner. Meanwhile much of the necessary business of government was carried on in the way indicated during the former deadlock by the system of "confessing judgment" for salaries, and paying without further authority. But in December that plan was upset by the decision of the Supréme Court, in the case of Alcock *v*. Fergie. When judgments were confessed, the cases did not appear before the Court; but the barristers, who wished to embarrass the Government, arranged that a case should be brought into court which indirectly involved the question of the legality of these judgments. The decision of the Court in this important case was that the recovery of a judgment against the Crown did not authorise the payment of the amount of such a judgment unless Parliament had previously voted the amount.

The year 1868 opened with the fierce excitement of a General Election. The only result was that the Ministerial majority in the Lower House was made a little larger. Before the election, Ministers commanded fifty-eight votes, and after it sixty. An incidental result of the election was that the opposition in the Assembly was strengthened by one strong champion. Mr. Fellows resigned his seat in the Council and was elected to the Assembly.

So decidedly was Mr. Higinbotham looked upon as indispensable to the party, that a proposal was made to him to stand for Collingwood, a sure seat, as well as for Brighton. Standing for two places, in order to secure a leader's return, is not uncommon in England, as Mr. Gladstone's parliamentary history shows; but after consultation with friends Mr. Higinbotham declined the offer from Collingwood. The selected opponent at Brighton was Mr. K. E. Brodribb, younger brother of the Mr. Brodribb who defeated Mr. Higinbotham at the second election in 1861. On 14th February, 1868, at a meeting of the electors in his constituency, Mr. Higinbotham made a speech which occupies six columns of the papers. An elector moved that Mr. Higinbotham had forfeited the confidence of the electors, whereat the latter's supporters were so angry that, in spite of his own urgent appeals to hear the speaker, the meeting howled him down. After this it is recorded that the Brighton election passed off quietly on the 20th. The confidence of the electors was thus shown :—

Higinbotham	. 468
Brodribb . . .	. 378
	90

A characteristic utterance at the declaration of the poll has been preserved : " I have been told, gentlemen, that I am a disloyal man. Well, gentlemen, I congratulate the electors of Brighton on being also disloyal men." It would seem well-nigh impossible that this remark could be misunderstood, but it has been by one of the Brighton opponents. Having often denied the disloyalty the speaker means, " You know that the accusation of disloyalty is so ridiculously unjust that you are willing to share it with me."

Meanwhile the master of the Colonies, the man whose province it was to instruct governors and tell them how to rule, had been changed. His Grace the Duke of Buckingham and Chandos had succeeded to Lord Carnarvon. The difficulty of attempting to govern a colony by despatches that took about two months to come, and started at intervals of a month, written by some one at a distance from the scene of action, who could hardly be fully informed, could not be better illustrated than in the two despatches, penned, or, it would be more correct to say, signed, by his Grace on the 1st of January, and on the 1st of February 1868. The former said :—

You ought not again to recommend the vote to the acceptance of the Legislature . . . except on a clear understanding that it will be brought before the Legislative Council in a manner which will enable them to exercise their discretion respecting it without the necessity of throwing the colony into confusion. If I refrain from giving you a positive instruction to this effect, it is only because I am unwilling to bind you irrevocably to a specific course of conduct under circumstances which may have materially changed before this despatch reaches you.

The latter said :—

The proposed grant, whatever opinion may be formed of its policy or propriety, is not so clear and unmistakable a violation of the existing rule as to call for the extreme measure of forbidding the Governor to be party, under the advice of his responsible Ministers, to those formal acts which are necessary to bring the grant under the consideration of the local Parliament.

The second despatch went on to suggest that the Legislative Council should no longer continue to oppose itself to the ascertained wishes of the community. His Grace had no right to advise the Council.

Had the despatches changed places—and there seems little reason why they should not—the Darling Grant would probably have passed as the Ministers wished. The first of these was handed to Ministers shortly after the General Election; and as it told the Governor that "he ought not again to recommend the vote to the acceptance of the Legislature," Ministers resigned. The Governor again did his best to fill their places. When the time came for meeting Parliament arrangements were not completed, and seldom did any Parliament meet under stranger circumstances. Mr. McCulloch, the Premier who had just resigned, was ill, and Mr. Higinbotham acted as leader of the House. The Speaker was elected, but no Governor's speech announcing a policy was ready. How could Ministers, only holding office until their successors were appointed, prepare a speech? It reads like a parody of popular government that a Ministry commanding sixty votes should yet be powerless.

The evening before the meeting of Parliament news had arrived that Prince Alfred had been shot by a Fenian at Clontarf, on the Sydney harbour; and Mr. Higinbotham, after congratulating the Speaker on his re-election, proposed that, as the House could not constitutionally do business, a meeting of members should be held to adopt an address expressing horror at the outrage. The "disloyal" member for Brighton spoke of "the outrage—the cruel outrage—inflicted upon his Royal Highness the Duke of Edinburgh by the hand of an assassin. I believe, Sir, that that event will have excited in the mind of every man in all these colonies one universal thrill of horror and indignation."

For two months, whenever the Houses met, there was merely a motion for adjournment. In the Lower House it was moved regularly by Mr. Higinbotham. Many of the members were recalcitrant against the delay, and tried to oppose the adjournment or to shorten the period over which it was asked. It is a rule of Parliament that no business can be proceeded with until there is a speech from the Throne, or in the colonies from the Governor. Such speech is impossible unless there is a ministry to be responsible for it. Meanwhile the Governor was doing his utmost to obtain ministers. At length on May 6th a ministry was formed, under the Hon. Mr. Sladen, afterwards Sir Charles Sladen. And let it be said here that there never lived a more loyal, honest, upright gentleman. All shadow of self-seeking was far from him. He was only anxious that the Queen's government should be carried on, and for that reason alone he accepted the uncomfortable task of trying to govern supported only by a minority in the Assembly, so small in numbers that the Government and all its supporters actually could not form a quorum of the House. On May 6th the Sladen Ministry accepted office ; but its members had to go before their constituents for re-election, when two, including one of the ablest, that is two out of seven, were defeated. The Governor's speech on the opening of Parliament was read on the 29th of May. During June Mr. Fellows, Minister of Justice, the leader of the Ministry in the Assembly, for Mr. Sladen sat in the Council, offered to introduce the Darling Grant in a separate bill ; and it had been ascertained that, if it were presented in that shape, a majority of the members of the Upper House were prepared to accept it. It is probable that this solution of the difficulty might have been accepted, when news arrived from England which caused the swords to drop, the fight to cease. Sir Charles Darling had re-entered the service.

His Excellency the Governor had striven in every way to be impartial ; but he was becoming very anxious. The great majority of the inhabitants of the colony desired to make the grant, and the question was how long the Council and Downing Street would be permitted to stop it. The strain was very severe. Ten years later in a similar crisis some confidential despatches from the Governor were published. A summary of them is given in Todd's *Parliamentary Government in the Colonies :* [1]—

The Governor could not but confess that, without undervaluin the status of the Legislative Council, they were, in their persistent

[1] Edition of 1880, p. 121.

opposition to this grant, asserting a claim which the House of Lords, under similar circumstances, would not have preferred. The legitimate exercise of the legal rights of a Legislative Council should be defined by the practice, rather than by the abstract claims or undefined powers, of the House of Lords.

It might almost be imagined that this last sentence was written by Mr. Higinbotham rather than by Governor Manners Sutton.

The severity of the strain was duly represented to the Colonial Office, with the prayer that some way should be found out of the trouble.

Sir Roundell Palmer has in the colony the credit of finding the way out. When in the House of Commons he tabled his motion, Sir Charles Darling entered into correspondence with him. Then Darling forwarded a copy of the same to the Secretary of the Colonies, with a letter in which he said that the suggestion he should leave the Government service had been made by the Colonial Office.

To this an answer came amounting to this—"Was it all a misapprehension? Will you re-enter the service unconditionally?"

Sir Charles Darling wrote: "I learn I have been under a misapprehension as to the views entertained by Her Majesty's Government. Under that misapprehension I was led to relinquish the Colonial Service, and I have now to ask the permission of Her Majesty's Government to withdraw my relinquishment upon the ground that it was made under the misapprehension referred to."

This was sent off by the mail; a final declaration by Sir Charles Darling of his inability to accept the proposed grant to Lady Darling being telegraphed to the Consul at Alexandria, and forwarded by the mail.

Sir Charles Darling, upon his return to the fold, received certain lapsed emoluments from the Victorian Government, and a pension of £1,000 a year from the Colonial Office, dated back from October 24th, 1866. In January, 1870, he died at Cheltenham. It is creditable to the good feeling of the former opponents of the grant that, immediately on the news of the late Governor's death being received, a bill was passed through both Houses, conferring a pension of £1,000 a year on Lady Darling, together with a sum of £5,000 for the education of her children.

A copy of the following letter has been kindly sent by Lady Darling :--

MELBOURNE, VICTORIA,
April 22nd, 1870.

MY DEAR LADY DARLING,—

I have had the honour to receive your note of February 16th. The intelligence of the death of Sir Charles Darling was received in Victoria with feelings of general regret for the loss of a brave, noble-hearted man (who had suffered much only because he was true to his Sovereign and also to the people committed to his charge), and of very deep and sincere sympathy with you. You will have learned ere now the form in which this feeling of sympathy has been expressed by the Legislative Assembly. It will be gratifying to you to know that the wishes and intentions of Sir Charles Darling's former ministers were anticipated by one who had been a political opponent, and that the prompt and generous action of Mr. Fellows was the means of averting all difficulty and delay in the passing of the bill.

Permit me to assure your ladyship that the memory of Sir Charles Darling will be cherished in the hearts of many persons in this country —certainly in mine, and, I hope, in those of my children, with honour and affection.

Believe me to remain,
My dear Lady Darling,
Your faithful servant,
GEO. HIGINBOTHAM.

It is extraordinary in how. many accounts of the contest, professing to be historical, it is stated that the contest was closed by the death of Sir Charles Darling. As a matter of fact he lived for nineteen months after its conclusion. Though when he died he was nearly sixty-one, there can be little doubt that his death was hastened by the worry of the long-continued crisis.

When the deadlock was brought to an end there was naturally a general feeling of relief in the colony, but in this feeling Mr. Higinbotham did not share. A characteristic story, told in a footnote to Mr. Rusden's *History of Australia*, evidently applies to him.

Amongst these a recent colleague of McCulloch (too amiable to desire to injure any one unless to serve a political purpose) must be included. The equally amiable Mr. T. T. à Beckett hastened to congratulate him on the happy termination of the crisis. They were in public view on a railway platform. " Are you not delighted ? " said the Councillor, who had so vainly striven to form a conciliatory ministry. He shrank back from the countenance by which he was confronted. In deep emotion, the adviser of Sir C. Darling ejaculated, " Mr. à Beckett, I can't speak to you," and moodily turned away. " Can you understand that ? " said Mr. à Beckett to a friend. " Quite," replied he ; " and also that you do not understand it."

George Higinbotham was a man who, when principle was involved, was never willing to admit of compromise. The matter in dispute was not settled, it was only avoided ; and that to his logical mind was eminently unsatisfactory. If this be a blemish, let it be openly stated. George Higinbotham of all men would prefer to be painted with his warts.

CHAPTER XVII

THE EDUCATION COMMISSION

Royal Commission appointed September 4th, 1866—Mr. Higinbotham, chairman The members Celerity Statistics of meetings—Testimony to the work of the Chairman—A Draft Bill—Framework of Report— Recommendations— Compared with present law—Rejection of Bill through influence of denominations—Higinbotham's support of *national* system of education—His attack on the sects. (By Mr. David Blair) Herculean The Roman Catholics stand aloof—The Five Years' Truce—Bishop Perry - Chairman strongly in favour of religious education—Report written by Chairman—" Of whom the world was not worthy."

In the interval between the two deadlocks—that which led to the recall of Sir Charles Darling and that which was caused by the recall—the Attorney-General was busily engaged upon the question of Public Education. He had always taken an interest in the subject, and in his first speech to the electors at Brighton had dwelt upon its importance. On September 4th, 1866, a Royal Commission was appointed " to inquire into and report upon the operation of the system of Public Education " in the colony of Victoria. Of this Commission Mr. Higinbotham was appointed chairman. It consisted of eleven members, of whom three, including the Chairman, were members of the Legislative Assembly, whilst a fourth was elected during the sitting of the Commission, and another had formerly been a member of that body and was still an Executive Councillor, two were members of the Legislative Council, one was a County Court judge, and three had practical knowledge of education, being the headmasters of the Church of England Grammar School, of the Scotch College, and of the Wesley College.

The terms of the Commission commanded the Commissioners to report "with as little delay as possible." These words were taken very literally. The celerity with which the work was begun and carried through offers a great contrast to the proceedings of sundry other Royal Commissions. From the date of the Commission to the day when the Report was submitted "under hands and seals" (January 29th, 1867) is a period of less than one hundred and fifty days. Within this time the Commission held fifty-two meetings, and examined thirty-seven witnesses, questions being put only by or through the Chairman. The examination of witnesses occupied exactly half the number of meetings, and in several cases the meetings were held on two successive days. The Chairman never missed a meeting, and was well supported, as there was an average attendance of eight members of the Commission. After the Chairman, the schoolmasters attended best. The five months of the time occupied may be thus divided : three weeks, preparing questions for circulation amongst teachers and others ; two months, taking evidence, and, after three weeks interval, three more days of evidence ; the last six weeks, preparing and considering Report. The Report is signed by all eleven Commissioners without a single dissent as to even a single clause. One of them told me that he thought most of the members entered upon the work with a prejudice against the Chairman. His courteous charm of manner and his earnestness were such that they all ended with enthusiastic admiration.

The President of the Legislative Council, Sir J. F. Palmer, who, it is easy to believe, could not have loved the chief opponent of certain claims of the Council, spoke publicly about a year later of

the remarkable unanimity of the eleven commissioners, and the confidence with which they recommended fundamental changes. . . . I should not do justice to those gentlemen who composed it, nor to my own strong convictions, if I did not bear testimony to the assiduity and indefatigable zeal which they displayed, and especially to the conspicuous talents of the gentleman on whom, as chairman of the Commission, the labour of the inquiry principally devolved.

Some comments on the work of the Commission have been kindly supplied by Mr. David Blair, who was Secretary to the Commission, and are printed as an appendix to this chapter. The report was drafted by the Chairman, and its main features must be stated here. Annexed to the report is a Draft Bill, ready to be presented to Parliament. This is an example which may well be followed as a part of common practice. Every Royal Commission of inquiry should be allowed the services of a draftsman, nor should its work be regarded as complete until a Draft Bill embodying the recommendations forms a part of the Report. This is much more important than the printing of all the evidence. Independently of the Bill and the Evidence, the Report itself occupied some forty-five folio pages, ten of which are occupied with the question of religious instruction. The following is the framework of the Report :—

I. Present Extent :—

    (1) Number of children under instruction.
    (2) Education in Town and in Rural Districts.
    (3) Compulsory Education.
    (4) Aborigines and Chinese.

II. Nature and Quality :—

    (1) Religious and Secular Instruction.
    (2) Mixed Schools, and Amalgamation of Schools.
    (3) Examination under Standards and Payment by Results.
    (4) Higher Class Instruction in Public Schools.
    (5) Physical Training.

III. Machinery :—

    (1) Governing Body and Officers.
    (2) Local Committees.
    (3) Teachers, Assistants, and Pupil Teachers.
    (4) Training School.
    (5) School Lands and Buildings.
    (6) Cost and Revenues of Public Instruction.

The following is a brief statement of the Recommendations:—

    (1) Enactment of a law making instruction of children compulsory upon parents.
    (2) Appointment of a Minister of Public Instruction.
    (3) Establishment of Public Schools from which sectarian teaching shall be excluded by express legislative enactment, and in which religious teaching shall be in like manner sanctioned and encouraged.

(4) Local committees to be partly nominated by ratepayers and parents.

(5) Teachers to be under local committees, subject to authority of Minister.

(6) Payment by results to be retained, but modified.

(7) Establishment of a training school for teachers.

(8) Annual exhibitions at grammar schools to be given to pupils of public schools.

(9) For five years capitation grant to be continued.

(10) Encouragement to be given to denominations to surrender their schools.

(11) Separate grant for aiding instruction in rural districts, to aborigines and Chinese, and for ragged schools.

(12) Levying a rate in aid of public instruction upon land.

The Commission was unanimous that education should not be gratuitous.

Five of these recommendations (the 1st, 2nd, 6th, 7th, and 8th) are now part of the national system of education, though owing to retrenchment training at the Training College has been, to the great danger of future education, for a while suspended. Three (9, 10, and 11) are temporary.

The 4th and 5th form an attempt to preserve local control, but have not been carried out, for the so-called Boards of Advice are practically powerless. The colony has a highly centralised system of education, and many would gladly see a reversion to some larger degree of local control. In the last recommendation a wrong word has been employed, as it is usual to keep the word "rate" for local as opposed to general taxation. The Commission recommended a land tax, and cannot be quoted in favour of the proposal to follow England in throwing part of the burden of the schools on the rates.

When the Draft Bill, which had received the unanimous support of the eleven commissioners, was brought into Parliament by the Chairman, in spite of admirable argument and oratory, it was decisively rejected. The reason is to be sought in the third recommendation. The Report received the approval of all who cared more for education than for the success of the denominations. But the more influential religious bodies would have none of it. They practically said in defiance of the experience of teachers that it was impossible to have religious teaching which was not sectarian, and that the Christianity which is common to all the sects cannot be taught.

The churches were successful in throwing out the measure ; but with what result, and with what cost ? Half a dozen years later an Act was passed making education in Victoria compulsory, gratuitous, and secular. The Commission would have given Victoria religious instruction such as that imparted in the schools under the Irish National Board, or in those under the London School Board. Dr. Perry, the Anglican Bishop of Melbourne, opposed the Commission's Bill. His successor, Dr. Moorhouse, was ready to purchase just such religious teaching as it offered by consenting to a separate grant to the Roman Catholics. This however was what the colony would not accept. Remembering the past, it will not permit a return to denominational education in any form or shape. That in the language of the Report is "anti-social." The affection for the present system, in spite of its expense, is based on the fact that it is national and not sectarian. Strongly preferring religious to secular education, Mr. Higinbotham felt so keenly against any return to the broken-up, divided, and imperfect education given by the churches and sects, that a near prospect of the repeal of the present Education Act, or its modification in the denominational direction, would have caused him to resign his seat on the Supreme Court Bench and return to the political arena. He said this definitely to two of his former colleagues in the Cabinet.

Even after the unanimity of the Commission Mr. Higinbotham could hardly have expected that the country would accept his measure. Too well he knew the power of the denominations, and spoke strongly about it in his opening speech :—

I believe that the denominations really deal with the matter of education as a simple question of property. They have received certain lands ; they have been assisted, partly by private contributions and partly by State aid, to build schools upon these lands ; they desire to keep these schools chiefly as nurseries of their sects, and as proofs and marks of their prosperity ; they attach the highest possible value to the material property which they collect, and they are animated by such intense rivalry and bitterness that they cannot bear their property to be reduced, unless the property of other sects be reduced in the same proportion. Each sect clings closely to its property, and, at the same time, desires the assistance of the State in order to maintain that property. Each sect desires to retain its school buildings in its own hands, and also desires to extract assistance from the State in order to keep its schools in operation. This conclusion will not be found to be very distinctly and expressly avowed by the clergymen of different denominations in their evidence. I confess that the reserve with which the different clergymen spoke on the subject appeared to me even more eloquent than their words ; but while they showed a natural reluctance to trace the evil to its true source, they were induced, in some instances, to refer to the true cause of the defects in our system of education. In one case in particular, a clergyman—a gentleman of very large experience and very enlightened views—put the matter shortly, and, as it seemed to me, most pithily and truly. He said—"The truth is, we don't like—the denominations don't like—to give up our little bit of land." That seems to me to contain in itself the real explanation of this difficulty. These religious sects desire to keep their lands. And it is not merely in the matter of education, but in other respects, that we see the mischievous effects of this deadly rivalry that exists among religious sects in this country. I own that I do not think a more melancholy spectacle can be presented than that which is presented by these religious bodies, when viewed merely as competing companies or corporations. Whether you look to the spirit in which they work, or the objects which they desire to attain, their existence appears to me to be one of the darkest blots on our civilization. These sects are animated, I am compelled to say, by a spirit of intense bitterness and hostility to one another—a bitterness and hostility which is usually in inverse proportion to the extent of the differences by which they are separated. And when you look to the objects which they seek to accomplish, the spectacle is equally melancholy. They seem to me to be desirous merely of collecting real and personal property ; and they seem to measure their prosperity by the amount which they can show on their annual balance-sheets as compared with rival sects. They call themselves churches, and, no doubt, they believe that the pestilent energy which they display in collecting property is a proof of vitality. They do not know, and they will not learn, that they have not, and that they cannot have, as sects—for sects they are—anything of the organic life of the Christian community, of which they are the self-dismembered fragments. Their proceedings are not only injurious to the cause of education, but a disgrace to our social and political system ; and the matter of education, which does concern the State, these sects must not be permitted to regard as their exclusive property. This is the problem we have to consider : how we may get rid of the sects in dealing with education. The State in this country has dismissed from its service the sect which, in the mother country, still is willing to occupy that humble position. It has admitted all sects in this country to a position of perfect equality. It has admitted them to its table, if I may so say, and distributed in equal amounts, and with a most liberal hand, the bounty of the State. And the real problem which the State now, after ten or twelve years, has to address itself to is— how to get rid of these turbulent intruders upon the peace and welfare of the State household ? This conclusion was arrived at by the Commissioners of Education. It was a conclusion arrived at not merely by laymen, but also by gentlemen who occupy the position of clergymen in some of

the largest sects in this country. The Commission were unanimously
of opinion that, until the connection which now exists between the religious sects in this country and the State is absolutely, finally, and for
ever put an end to, you cannot establish in this country a sound or successful system of public education. This, Sir, is the primary principle
of the report of the Commissioners, and of the Bill which I have to ask
leave to introduce.

The Sects however are very powerful, and much of the
bitterness with which Mr. Higinbotham's name has been in
certain quarters regarded was due to his denunciation not of
religion but of the denominations. So strong was the opposition to the measure, shown in the debate on the Second
Reading, especially by the Roman Catholics and the Church
of England, that the Attorney-General with the consent of
his colleagues withdrew the bill.

(By Mr. David Blair.)

A personal association with the late Chief Justice Higinbotham, extending over the whole period of his political
career, was made still more intimate by my appointment as
Secretary to the Royal Commission on Education in 1867.
He was then Attorney-General, and the time had come, by
universal admission, for the institution of a uniform system
of primary instruction. Of that Commission Mr. Higinbotham was the originator, as he was subsequently its very
life and soul during its existence. He had evidently bent
all his intellectual and moral energies—it may even with
propriety be added, all his physical energies as well—to the
accomplishment of what may fairly be termed a Herculean
task of statesmanship. My own appointment, I may be
allowed to explain, was due to no impulse of political favour-
itism, but came to me as the natural sequel to many years of
public advocacy in the press, in the Assembly, and on the open
platform, of a general system of free education for the
children of the State. Such a system is one of the indispensable requirements of a free democratic constitution like our
own. The *personnel* of the Commission was selected with
the greatest carefulness. It included every one of the
leading practical authorities upon Education, as well as lay

representatives of the various religious denominations, with the exception of the Roman Catholics. This marked omission, as I learned, was owing to the point-blank refusal of the head of the Roman Catholic denomination to name a representative from the laymen of the body to sit on the Commission. As soon as I entered upon my duties as Secretary, I found that Archbishop Goold maintained to the last the same attitude of disdainful rejection of all overtures from the Government to enter into friendly and wholly impartial deliberation on the subject. My letters as Secretary were either left unanswered, or were replied to by the Archbishop's Secretary with sarcastic, even contemptuous brevity. The Archbishop, it was intimated, disowned the authority both of the Commission and the Government in relation to the instruction of the children of the religious communion of which he was head. He was sole guardian of faith and morals for the Roman Catholic Church in Victoria, and the action of the Government in this matter, in so far as it included the children of that Church, was simply an insolent and unwarrantable intrusion upon his exclusive domain of power.

The work of the Commission proceeded, therefore, without reference to the Roman Catholic denomination. The Chairman, I observed, was in no manner or degree influenced by the Archbishop's refusal. But, in spite of it, when the general heads of the Report came to be considered, he proposed a clause embodying what was termed around the table "the Five Years' Truce." This was a proposal that the Roman Catholic body should be allowed to maintain their own schools separately for that period after the passing of the new Act, and should receive a capitation grant for each pupil passing the Government Inspector's examination, equal to the sum paid for each scholar in the State schools, *minus* 20 per cent. This offer was duly embodied in the Report, and was rejected with silent contempt by the Archbishop. When, a couple of years afterwards, I went up to stand for re-election in my old constituency at Stawell, I found the Roman Catholic electors in furious hostility. I had been guilty of the unpardonable sin of conspiring with the Attorney-General and others in the design to throw their Church overboard in the matter of State-supported education, to deny them their fair share of the public endowment, and to subject them to the glaring injustice of taxing them for the education of Protestant children! They had never learned, I found, of the proposed Five Years' Truce, never seen a page of the Commissioners' Report, and were as ignorant of the real facts of the case as if they were still in Munster or Connaught. Of course I lost my election, but that was a very small matter, since the long-standing conflict for the principle of free State education had been at length practically ended. To the close of his life Archbishop Goold repeated, with monotonous persistency, in his periodical pastoral letters, the version of the story held by the Roman Catholic electors of Stawell. And the Attorney-General was held up to public reprobation as the instigator of a measure of flagrant injustice-to the Roman Catholic body—a measure which, whether it deserved to be so characterised or not, he was the first to provide against, and which he would have been just as incapable of framing, or supporting, as he would have been of proposing the exclusion of Roman Catholics from all the rights of free citizenship on the ground of religious disqualification. If the heads of that body still hold the opinion that their Church is suffering from a grievance inflicted on it by the passing of the present Education Act, they may at least console themselves with the reflection that the evil arose solely and exclusively from the rejection by Archbishop Goold of the (then) Attorney-General's friendly and generous overture of the Five Years' Truce.

A second incident in the history of that memorable Commission must, in the interests of justice, be recorded. When the question came on whether any elements of specially religious instruction should form part of the daily teaching in the new schools, it was unanimously resolved in the affirmative. The decision that the religious teaching should be distinctively Christian was similarly given, but with the reservation of a conscience clause, to save the rights of parents objecting to Christian teaching for their children. It was at first assumed as certain that none of the religious denominations, not excepting even the Roman Catholics, would raise objection to the adoption of lesson books similar to those used in the Irish National schools when the Protestant Archbishop Whately and the Roman Catholic Archbishop Murray were colleagues, in complete official accord, on the governing Board. But the appeal to the denominations on this point proved that this supposition was quite unwarranted. A conversation held by the Secretary with the Rev. Dr. Bleasdale, the Archbishop's Secretary, on the matter simply ended in nothing. The head of the Roman Catholic Church would listen to no proposals or overtures from the Commission, repudiated its authority, and denied its right to concern itself with the education of the children of his communion in any way whatsoever. At the same time he firmly maintained the right of that body to its full proportion (in respect of population) of the State subsidy in aid of elementary education, but without Government inspection or control of any kind. The heads of the Protestant denominations were, with one marked exception, unanimously and earnestly in favour of a common system of simplified religious instruction drawn from the Bible. That exception was the Protestant Bishop Perry, who pointedly declared his inability, as head of the Church of England in the colony, to join with any religious bodies outside his own communion in this important matter. Without going so far as Archbishop Goold in the assertion of his episcopal claims and responsibilities, Bishop Perry was equally firm in his refusal to meet on grounds even of common citizenship, in respect of this all-important question, the members of religious denominations not connected with his own Church. I well remember the shock of painful surprise that the Bishop's statement of his final and unalterable decision on this point gave to the members of the Commission, especially those of them who were adherents of the Church of England, including the Chairman himself, the late Rev. Dr. Bromby, and the late Judge Pohlman. And I also well recollect the grave solemnity of tone—the passionate earnestness of pleading—which the Chairman evinced, while, with his exquisite gentleness of manner, he questioned the Bishop closely, evidently with the hope of winning his assent to some form of honourable compromise. The effort was vain, and the Commissioners were therefore reduced to the last resource of allowing the clause embodying the Five Years' Truce to remain in the Report, and framing a clause providing that all reasonable permission should be given to ministers of religion to visit the schools at certain hours daily for the purpose of giving religious instruction to the children of their several communions.

As a matter of course, I had many private conversations with the Chairman on this subject, and I can bear testimony to the intense earnestness of his convictions upon the question of the supreme importance of education for all the children of the State in a free democracy like our own, and upon the paramount necessity of giving to that education a distinctively religious and Christian stamp. No man who ever called himself a Victorian colonist worked longer or more strenuously to gain those inestimable ends. He failed, as to the second of them, despite his quite heroic labours to accomplish it. The fact may appear incredible, but it is true all the same, that the Attorney-General was declared to be mainly responsible for the exclusion of the specific religious element from the State system of education ; and his accusers were the very men through whose resolute impracticability that omission (not exclusion) became imperative ! I suppose the case is rare in history that a particular class in the State will put forth all their energies to prevent the accomplishment of a certain high State object, and then, when their opposition has proved effective for its purpose, turn round on the party they have successfully opposed, and charge *them* with the serious political crime of deliberately plotting and working to bring about the result which their own opposition has produced ! Yet this is exactly what has taken place in relation to the secularisation (as it is termed) of the State school system in Victoria. The name of George Higinbotham is still linked with an accusation which has precisely the same foundation in truth as would have the charge against Mr. Gladstone, if brought by the Peers themselves, that to *him* was owing the rejection of the Irish Home Rule Bill by the House of Lords.

These two incidents in the history of the Commission on Education are deserving of permanent record, because it is within my personal knowledge that they both deeply and permanently affected the Chairman's views and convictions upon certain questions of the first importance. And I may add, for myself, that his conclusions were well sustained by evidence. Amongst these questions the following may be mentioned : (1) The difference between the two leading religious denominations is final, precluding the possibility of their ever combining for any common purpose of moral or spiritual advancement. (2) The clergy of all denominations are, as a class, passively indifferent to the obligation of providing education for children outside their own communion. (3) Even within those limits their exertions for the promotion of education are, as a rule, reluctantly given. (4) To share liberally in the State endowments for educational objects is, with them, a far more powerful motive than the promotion of education itself. (5) In the case of the clergy of some denominations the spread of general education is rather dreaded as an evil than regarded as a benefit and blessing. In support of these conclusions, it may be mentioned that the evidence before the Commission abundantly established these two facts : first, that under the old denominational system there were maintained by the various denominations, in small country townships, from two to half a dozen small and inefficient sectarian schools, all kept rigorously apart, where one good school would have sufficed for all the local requirements ; but each set stood stoutly upon its claim to a share in the State subsidy, and its right to a separate grant of land ; and, secondly, that religious instruction in the schools under their own control, and situated close by their own dwellings, was seldom or never given by the clergy. These facts, which had become grave public abuses, made the public demand for the abolition of the denominational system imperative and irresistible. After an existence of more than twenty years, the State system of education is still roundly denounced by the clergy as a fruitful cause of pagan ignorance, godlessness, and immorality, amongst the juvenile population ; but in no instance have these denunciations been accompanied with even the most remote acknowledgment that the effort to remedy those evils rests, at least in some degree, with the churches and the clergy themselves.

The Commission sat for five months, and in that time held fifty-two meetings, some of them from six to eight hours of unbroken length. This was an amount of work two or three times greater, within the time, than is usually performed by Royal Commissions. The unremitting zeal of their Chairman acted like a charm on the Commissioners. Not so short an interval as five minutes was lost through want of a quorum, delay, or confusion, during the whole period. The Chairman was at that time fulfilling punctually the duties of his high office from day to day, and in addition was bearing almost the whole burden of directing the government of the country. Yet he never was absent from his post for a moment; and when the business of the Commission had advanced so far as the preparation of the draft Report, he sat up night after night at the task until it was completed. Usually, as Secretary to several Royal Commissions, the task of preparing and completing the Report has fallen to me; but in this single instance the Chairman himself undertook that duty. The Report—which has always seemed to me an admirable model of what a great State document ought to be—was exclusively the composition of the Chairman. My duty was limited to putting it through the press. But in order to keep pace with the unwearying energy of the Chairman I was obliged to work eight hours a day at least, and on the days when the Commission sat I was at the desk ten or twelve hours. Never did the slightest "hitch" in the proceedings occur—a circumstance which gave the Chairman much satisfaction. When the work was finished, I remarked to him: "Now are you satisfied?" With a pleasant smile he replied: "I must say that the whole thing has gone on like clockwork." Let it be added that the cost of the Commission to the country (apart from the printing of the Report) was limited almost entirely to the half-year's salary of the Secretary at a very moderate rate of remuneration. There was no bill for "extras" in the line of travelling expenses, luncheons, &c. When their sittings lasted for six or eight hours the Commissioners usually adjourned to some near hotel for half an hour to take some slight refreshment, and each of them punctually paid his own scot.

The newspapers, on receiving their several copies of the Report, fell as is usual with them to criticism. A single small blot was hit by one of them in respect of its literary quality. The name of Sir John Pakington, occurring in a footnote, was misprinted "Packington." Upon reading this criticism, the Chairman looked at the Secretary very gravely, as if some serious *lapsus* had been detected. Thereupon the Secretary wrote out a memorandum and despatched it to

the Government printer by a messenger. He returned in a
few minutes with the "final revise" proof of that part of
the Report, which, unrolling, the Secretary handed to the
Chairman, showing him the intrusive "e" struck out for
correction in the Secretary's handwriting. This minute
incident also gave him visible pleasure, as showing patient
and careful attention to the smallest details. With the
exception of that superfluous letter, the Report is as faultless
as regards the typography as it is perfect in respect of its
statesmanlike style and quality.

I may be allowed to supplement these slight recollections
with a brief statement of the personal estimate I formed of
the late Chief Justice, from a prolonged acquaintance with his
career as a public man of the foremost rank amongst us. He
was, in my opinion, a man endowed with all the qualities of
a true statesman, both intellectually and morally. In this
respect he stands first, without an equal, amongst Victorian
politicians. His habit of mind and cast of thought were
essentially those of a man fitted to guide the councils of a
nation. Had his career been fixed in the old country, there
can be little doubt that he would, in due course, have risen
to the very highest position. As a parliamentary speaker,
when at his best, he would certainly have taken rank amongst
the leading debaters in the House of Commons. He was
one of those very rare men in whom their fellow-citizens
instinctively recognise their natural leaders. In respect of
his moral qualities, he was simply above criticism. No man
ever surpassed him in self-sustaining loftiness of character, in
the resolute determination to attain, and maintain, the moral
ideal. To me he seemed, indeed, a faultless character. And
I say this all the more unaffectedly, because I never was on
terms of private companionship with him, and never either
asked or received from him a personal favour. Of the very few
men with whom I have been well acquainted, and in whom I
discerned, or thought I discerned, elements of *greatness* of
character, he stands foremost. Naturally, he was never
appreciated at his true value by the world around him.
George Higinbotham was, emphatically, one of that exalted
class of men "of whom the world was not worthy."

CHAPTER XVIII

THE RESOLUTIONS

Defeat of Sladen Ministry—Mr. Higinbotham takes a subordinate place
in Second McCulloch Ministry ; after seven months retires—Has
no love of office—Retires from Executive Council—Not " Honourable "—Unofficial invitation to a conference—Proposes five resolutions, which are carried—His speech on the subject.

THE day after the reception of the news that Sir Charles
Darling had re-entered the service, a vote of want of confidence in the Sladen Ministry was carried. Mr. McCulloch
returned to power, but with different colleagues. His former
Attorney-General refused to return to his former post. Rather
than appear to desert his old colleague he accepted a nominal
place in the Ministry. He became Vice-President of the
Board of Land and Works without salary but with a seat
in the Cabinet. But his connection with the Ministry was
very slight. He hardly ever attended meetings of the
Cabinet, and about seven months later he retired from even
this nominal connection with the Ministry.

There is no doubt that he was thoroughly tired of the
whole contest, and sore that his principles had not really tri-
umphed. It was in his mind to retire from politics altogether,
but from this step he was dissuaded by his friends, especially by
Mr. Francis. But he never desired to return to office. " At
last there's a jubilee for the slaves," he had said on his release
in May. " They talk of the sweets of office ; I don't know
in what they consist," he said to a friend. John Bright, in
the House of Commons, once parodied the well-known lines in
Gray's *Elegy* :—

> For who, to dumb forgetfulness a prey,
>   This pleasing, anxious office e'er resigned,
> Left the warm precincts of the Treasury,
>   Nor cast one longing, lingering look behind ?

There have been some who cast back no longing looks on the ministerial benches. John Bright himself was one, George Higinbotham another.

After leaving office Higinbotham was yet some years in the House as a private member—about two years as member for Brighton, and then, after an interval, rather more than two and a half years representing the East Bourke Boroughs. During this time he was most assiduous in his attendance watching the course of legislation, especially taking the utmost interest in education. But his thoughts were chiefly concerned with the later developments of the two great earlier contests. He was determined to permit no encroachment on the part of the Upper House, and equally resolute against the interference of Downing Street. The two questions were closely connected and interwoven. The fact that his thoughts were concerned with these matters, whilst other members were thinking of the topics of the day, gave him a certain aloofness from his neighbours. He had always held strongly that mere fights for office were unworthy of politicians. Most of his neighbours were defending their own rights to the Treasury Benches, or attacking opponents already seated there, whilst he was thinking of the rights and privileges of the Assembly, or of the logical consequences of Responsible Government.

On the 1st of February, 1869, George Higinbotham ceased to be connected with Mr. McCulloch's Ministry. During that month he also resigned his seat on the Executive Council. Most retired ministers continue to be members of this and to be called "Honourable," although never summoned to meetings, just as in England ex-Cabinet ministers remain members of the Privy Council. But the reason that drove Mr. Higinbotham out of the Cabinet made him also resign his seat on the Executive—viz. the interference of Downing Street in local affairs. The letter from the Governor, informing him of the removal of his name from the roll of Executive Councillors, in accordance with his own wish, was dated 1st March, 1869. After this date he disliked any one to address letters to him as " Honourable," or to use the title of him in any way, as it was something to which he had no claim. Ten years later the notice of a prospective marriage was sent to England for insertion in the *Times*, to be inserted on receipt of a single word by telegraph. At Mr. Higinbotham's request the word was not sent after the marriage had taken place, because this title had through inadvertence been employed.

Towards the close of the year 1869 a very important full-dress debate took place in the Legislative Assembly on certain resolutions proposed by Mr. Higinbotham. A letter from London led up to the debate, asking that representatives of the colony should be sent to a conference on colonial affairs summoned, not by the Government of the day, but by certain unofficial persons. As any one can summon spirits from the vasty deep, so, apparently, any one who likes can call a conference; and as a matter of fact this particular meeting led to the establishment of the Royal Colonial Institute, excited interest in the colonies and in colonial questions, and has helped forward the desire for the cohesion of the Empire. But it was hardly to be expected that the colonial governments would consent to be represented at a gathering not summoned by responsible authorities. Mr. Higinbotham's resolutions were debated on five nights[1] in the House, during the month of November, and were then discussed again in committee on December 22nd. No fewer than seventeen speeches were made in the formal debate, and the record of what was said would fill a good-sized octavo volume. Here are the resolutions :—

(1) That the care of the political rights and interests of a free people can be safely entrusted only to a body appointed by and responsible to that people ; and that the Legislative Assembly declines to sanction or to recognise the proceedings (as far as the same may relate to Victoria) of the conference proposed to be held in London, at the instance of a self-constituted and irresponsible body of absentee colonists.

(2) That the people of Victoria, possessing by law the right of self-government, desire that this colony should remain an integral portion of the British Empire, and this House acknowledges, on behalf of its constituents, the obligation to provide for the defence of the shores of Victoria against foreign invasion, by means furnished at the sole cost, and retained within the exclusive control, of the people of Victoria.

(3) That this House protests against any interference, by legislation

[1] 2nd, 3rd, 10th, 16th, and 24th.

of the Imperial Parliament, with the internal affairs of Victoria, except at the instance or with the express consent of the people of the colony.

(4) That the official communication of advice, suggestions, or instructions, by the Secretary of State for the Colonies to Her Majesty's representative in Victoria, on any subject whatsoever connected with the local government, except the giving or withholding of the Royal assent to or the reservation of Bills passed by the two Houses of the Victorian Parliament, is a practice not sanctioned by law, derogatory to the independence of the Queen's representative, and a violation both of the principles of the system of responsible government' and of the constitutional rights of the people of this colony.

(5) That the Legislative Assembly will support Her Majesty's ministers for Victoria in any measures that may be necessary for the purposes of securing the recognition of the exclusive right of Her Majesty and of the Legislative Council and Legislative Assembly "to make laws in and for Victoria in all cases whatsoever," and putting an early and final stop to the unlawful interference of the Imperial Government in the domestic affairs of this colony.

The history of these resolutions in committee is worth following. The Chief Secretary, Mr. Macpherson, proposed an amendment to the first making its terms milder. He was beaten by forty-five to fifteen. He proposed an amendment to the second, to insert the words "in concert with the Imperial authorities." He was defeated by forty to twenty-one. The third was passed without comment. The fourth was opposed by the Government, but was carried by forty to eighteen, or, if we change a mistaken vote, thirty-nine to nineteen. The proposer offered to withdraw the fifth, if any one desired it to be withdrawn. It was then carried without comment.

These five resolutions thus adopted by the Legislative Assembly of Victoria sum up Mr. Higinbotham's views on Downing Street interference. In the face of the second it is ridiculous to call him a separatist, or to say that he favoured the disruption of the Empire. The best hope for the continuance of the Empire is that each part should mind its own business, and the special business of the Colonial Office is not to touch the internal concerns of the different colonies, but to reserve its strength for the great questions that affect the Empire as a whole.

Mr. Higinbotham's speech is long, but it is full and very explicit. To omit parts of it would have the effect of mutilation.

It was my intention to bring the question referred to in these resolutions under the attention of the House at the commencement of the present session. But a consideration of the state of public affairs induced me to refrain from doing so at that time, and the same consideration would now have induced me again to delay asking the House to deal with this subject, had it not been for the despatches from the Agent-General and the Secretary of State for the Colonies, which have been laid upon the table, and the invitation contained in the letter of certain colonists resident in London addressed to the Chief Secretary. Sir, that invitation compels the House, or at least compels the Government—who will, I apprehend, be glad to be assisted with the opinion and advice of the House upon this most important question— to return a distinct answer, and also to express an opinion upon the subject referred to in that invitation. The letter of the Agent-General, which I may say, in passing, evinces a very commendable discretion on the part of that gentleman, calls attention not merely to the invitation, but also to the difficulties that may arise in the colony on the subject of that invitation. I believe there are very few members of this House, if there be any, who entertain any doubt as to the answer which should be given to that invitation. I think there are hardly any members of this House who are of opinion that we should accept an invitation, which is virtually a request to transfer the seat of government from this country to England. Melbourne is the seat of government of this country, and of the legislation of this country—not London ; and Her Majesty's Ministers for Victoria and the legislative bodies elected for Victoria are the only powers known to me who have legal authority to deliberate, to consult, and to decide as to what shall be the political position which this country shall hold, either in relation to the mother country, or in regard to its own domestic and internal relations. I apprehend there will be no difference of opinion that the answer to be returned to this invitation is an answer in the negative.

I confess it appears to me that this invitation is one that indicates, on the part of those who have made it, either very lamentable ignorance, or something which I cannot help designating as very gross presumption—lamentable ignorance of their own position, and of the estimation in which they are held in this colony and in the neighbouring colonies, or gross presumption, if knowing their position, and knowing the rights of this country, and the estimate in which they themselves are held by this country, they presume to ask the Government and the Legislature of Victoria to send a delegate to London, invested with plenipotentiary powers, to alter or arrange, in his discretion, and in concert with the Colonial Office, the basis of government in this colony. Sir, I am glad the names of the persons who have made this invitation are not appended to it—it might then be an invidious task to criticise the terms in which the letter is framed—but, although we do not know the names of those persons, we know, at all events, the class to which they belong. We know who they are. Sir, the gentlemen who send this invitation are persons who have made all the fortune they possess—and in many instances it is a large fortune—

in these colonies.   They are men who have abandoned their duties to
the country to which they owe their prosperity.   And it appears to
me to be a surprising and marvellous thing that persons should take up
a permanent residence in a foreign country, and then venture to ask
the people of the country from which they come, and which they have
deserted, to surrender into their hands the government and legislation
on fundamental matters which belong to that people.   I do not envy
those persons who have deserted the sphere of their natural duties, in
order that they may have an opportunity of hunting tufts in the
neighbourhood of the Palace Hotel, at Westminster, or who conceive
that they achieve the proudest moment of their lives when they are
permitted to sit down to a subscription dinner at the London Tavern
in company with half-a-dozen English noblemen ; and yet I cannot help
fearing that the persons who have sent this invitation are persons, many
of whom, at least, can be actuated by no other motives and no other
ambition in life.   The answer to their invitation is prompt and easy.
It is not necessary to discuss that at length ; but I must say that the
honourable gentleman to whom this invitation is addressed will, I think,
lose an opportunity which does not often fall to the lot of the Chief
Secretary of a colony if he fail, in his reply, to point out to these
persons what is their true position, and what are their real duties.

Sir, the Chief Secretary has now a legitimate occasion presented to him
of telling persons who are constantly in our thoughts—of whom we are
perpetually thinking, with the view, if we can, of, if not recalling them,
at least retaining in these countries a part of the property which they
improperly withdraw from it—what are their duties to these
countries, and what these countries expect of them.   In reply to
this invitation, the honourable gentleman may tell these absentee
colonists that he invites them to return to their colonial homes, and
there discharge their colonial duties.   He may tell them also that, if
they return, they will enjoy, in common with all their fellow colonists,
the legitimate, natural, and individual share of political power which
belongs to all persons who have property in, or who belong to these
countries ; and he may hold out to them the hope that they may yet
have the opportunity of atoning in some degree, during the rest of
their careers, for the misspent time, the ill-used wealth, the low and
vulgar tastes, and the vagabond habits of their past lives.   These
persons have, however, raised a question which we cannot refuse to consider, nor, I think, to express an opinion upon.   It is proposed to hold
a conference in London, in the beginning of next year, on the subject
of the relations between these Australian colonies and the British
Empire.   The House will remember the occasion and the circumstances
which have given rise to this proposition.   A neighbouring colony has
been recently exposed to great danger, from which it is not yet
relieved.   I do not propose to discuss the causes of the unhappy
circumstances in which our countrymen in New Zealand now find themselves, further than to say that I believe in the opinion that our
countrymen themselves may at a future time be constrained to admit
that the contentions which now expose them and their families and
their fortunes to great and imminent risk are not entirely free from

connexion with their own defaults. I believe that the rising of the
noblest race of uncivilized men known in the world against our New
Zealand fellow countrymen has been, at least in part, occasioned by the
crimes of English civilization. But this it is unnecessary to consider.
Perhaps it would be improper and presumptuous to press the consideration of this part of the question. It is sufficient to say that at this
time, under existing circumstances, our countrymen in a neighbouring
colony are exposed to great and imminent risk from the insurrection of
the numerous and powerful uncivilized inhabitants of that island. Now
how have the complaints of our fellow colonists been received? Sir, the
colonists of New Zealand asked, in the first instance, that the English
troops might be retained in that colony. It is reported that the
Commander-in-Chief, who temporarily granted that application, and
delayed the removal of the troops, has been censured by the Home
Government for that concession. They also applied to the English
Government for the aid of English troops, and for the guarantee of a
loan to enable them to defend themselves. Both of these applications
have been refused, and upon what ground? It was stated, in the
House of Commons by Mr. Adderley and Mr. Monsell, and in the
House of Lords by Earl Granville and Lord Carnarvon, that the
application of the New Zealand colonists could not be granted, for this
reason—that they, as well as all other Australian colonists, possess in
full measure the privilege of self-government, and that, having self-
government, it was a duty of which they could not clear themselves,
that they should be able to defend their own country against aggression, whether it came from hostile native tribes or from a foreign source.
That is the distinct plain principle on which this most ungracious
refusal has been founded. Ungracious, I say, for I venture to believe
if a similar application had been made by a weak independent
state to a neighbouring powerful country, that, under ordinary
circumstances, the application would not have been refused. I am
prepared to show and I will show before I sit down, that the
reason given, both in the House of Commons and in the House of
Lords, is, in the mouths of those who utter it, an untruthful reason.
And therefore I say that if this principle, propounded by the English
Government under circumstances so ungracious, and even so offensive,
can commend itself to our judgment as a true principle which we
ought to accept, which we cannot dispute, it must be a principle of such
high and commanding truth as, if we adopted it, shall serve as a basis
for our political action in this colony for all future time. Sir, the
question thus raised is this—Shall these Australian colonies continue
their connexion with the mother country or not: and, if they do, upon
what conditions?

Now there are other outlying questions, indirectly connected with
this question, which I have designedly omitted from these resolutions. There is the question of the union of these colonies with one
another. That is a question which, I think, these colonies must
settle for themselves and by themselves, before it can be permitted
to be entertained or discussed either by the English Parliament or by
the English Government. We are not now in a position to settle that.

For myself, I believe it is a question which we should give the greatest and most patient consideration to before we rashly enter into any combination among these colonies. However, it is sufficient for the present to say that it is a question which has not yet been settled by ourselves, and which, therefore, cannot now be discussed either by this conference or by the English Government or by the English Parliament. There is also the question which has been raised, and which, I know, has presented itself with great force to the minds of some honourable members - namely, whether we should not claim on behalf of these colonies exemption from hostile attack upon the part of powers with which Great Britain may be at war. That, too, is a question which we cannot now discuss. I believe it to be a question involved in the greatest difficulties. I think that at the present time, in the present relations of the nations of the world towards one another, it can hardly be expected that foreign countries will readily or willingly accept a principle which would deprive them of much of their power in time of war against the country with which they were at war. We have lately seen that a proposition to exempt private property from the usual terms and conditions of warfare has been rejected by the most civilized countries in the world ; and we can hardly expect that foreign countries will consent to exempt English colonies from the natural consequences and conditions of warfare simply because it is the desire of English colonies that they should be so exempt. However, it is a question which may fairly form a subject for discussion ; but it can be discussed only between the English Government and the English colonies on the one hand, and the governments of all civilized countries of the world on the other hand. It is a question that cannot be discussed now. It can be discussed only at a sort of congress of the nations.

The question raised at home, which we have to consider here, is simply and solely the question of the relations which should be permitted to exist between Great Britain herself and these colonies, which enjoy, under English laws, the right of self-government under a responsible form of government. Sir, I should be extremely reluctant to place in the resolutions an expression of my own individual feelings and opinions upon this great subject. My own opinions and feelings are very strong ; but I do not think that a member of the Legislature who asks the Legislative Assembly to assent to a proposition of this kind, would be justified in placing in a resolution his own individual opinions or convictions. However, I am encouraged to propose the second resolution by the fact that I really believe it is the honest and ardent desire of ninety-nine men and women out of every hundred in this colony, that the connexion which now exists the formal connexion, and still more the real and substantial connexion between Great Britain and her colonies, should continue for an indefinite length of time to come. It is little more than a year since members of this House who claimed for this colony the right of self-government were taunted with a desire for separation from the mother country. Sir, that time has passed ; and it is now easy, and unattended by any embarrassment, for any member or any individual in the community to express, if he please, his desire that Victoria may be separated from the British Empire. There is nothing to prevent it. In the House of Lords, in the House of Commons, and in the English press, the question of casting off the colonies is freely discussed; and I cannot see why a question so freely considered in England should not be as freely considered in this country. Therefore, any member of this House, or of this community, who believes that it will be better for us that we should be separated from Great Britain may now freely and fearlessly express that opinion. I fearlessly express the opinion and ardent desire that we should not be separated from Great Britain, provided that the conditions which render real connexion and sympathetic and lasting union possible be conceded freely on both sides; for, although I desire that the connexion between this country and Great Britain should continue, I freely admit that I believe it is not desirable for either country that England and the Australian colonies should continue to be united by a formal bond of union, unless those conditions exist and are recognised in both countries which will make that union not merely formal but real.

Now, the English Government has stated a condition which, on the part of the English people, it claims as a condition of union. It has stated on behalf of the English taxpayers and our own countrymen at home, whom we are bound to consider, and whose interests it is our duty not to forget, that colonies which possess the absolute and entire privilege of self-government under a responsible system, shall defend themselves from foreign aggression. I do not know whether there is any one who can dispute the abstract justice of that proposition, although I admit there are very few who will feel the extremely unfavourable circumstances under which that proposition is now expressed. The condition seems to me to be absolutely true—to be entirely undeniable and indisputable. I do not know how a country which lacks the power or the will to defend itself can rightfully claim independence. If a country wants the power to defend itself I don't know that, in the existing state of the world, it has any right to be independent. At present, the affairs of the world are governed by force. Aggressive and unjust war is still the law which governs the world. We cannot dispute it. During the more than eighteen hundred years that Christianity has existed in the world, it has indeed done something to mitigate the horrors of war, but it has done hardly anything to prevent the recurrence and occasions of war. International law has done equally little. A system of private international law has been created and administered by the courts of different countries. But public international law does not exist in the world. More than a hundred years ago, Montesquieu observed that the principles of international law had been all corrupted by the passions of princes, the patience of peoples, and the servility of writers; and, since then, I don't know that public international law has made a single step in advance, or done a single thing to prevent the recurrence and continuance of wars in a world that calls itself civilized. Therefore, in the present state of the world, we must accept the conditions of the world, and those conditions, I think, require that a people that would be independent must be able to defend themselves. If they cannot defend themselves, they must attach themselves to

some superior state, and, by attaching themselves to a superior
state, they must accept the obligation of submitting their interests and
the control of their policy to the interests and the policy of the state
on which they are dependent. If a nation wants the will to defend
itself, of course it is a proper subject for subjection. A nation
or community which has the power to defend itself, and not the will,
has no right to be independent at all—it is born to slavery. Therefore,
I accept this condition proposed by the English Government without
any reserve whatever : and I ask the House to express its assent to the
proposition in terms, because this country has, for some years past,
accepted the proposition in fact.

I observe that the English colonists say that the proposition made by
the English Government is a disclosure of a policy which will open "a
new view of the relations of the mother country" towards the colonies.
Sir, this is not the fact. We have been acquainted for years with this
demand made by the English Government, and, from the time it was
first made, we frankly and freely accepted it. In the year 1863, the
Duke of Newcastle, for the first time I believe proposed, in a limited
form, this same government to these Australian colonies, and we
at once accepted it. Sir, it would be fortunate, not only for these
colonies, but for England, I believe, if other Secretaries of State
were men of the same rank and class of character as the nobleman
whose name I have mentioned. The distinguishing characteristic
of the despatches of that nobleman is their perfect straightforwardness,
simplicity, and sincerity. He was always able to speak his mind
without reserve, and at the same time, so far as I know without giving
offence on a single occasion. He spoke explicitly, but with such real
and hearty good-will, as to disarm even the strongest expressions of
any offensive or disagreeable effect. The Duke of Newcastle, writing
in 1863, said :—

"In the colonies of New South Wales, Victoria, South Australia,
and Queensland, there are no exceptional circumstances to prevent the
free application on the part of the Home Government of those principles
which arise from, or are correlative to, the grant of responsible
government. That form of government being unequivocally established,
it is, I imagine, admitted on all hands that the Imperial Government
has no further responsibility for maintaining the internal tranquillity of
the country. The obligation, therefore, to contribute towards the
defence of colonies in full possession of internal self-government, and
unaffected by any exceptional circumstances of situation or population,
is limited to the contingency of war and danger of war. . . .
Those obligations will always be in the main sufficiently discharged by
Her Majesty's navy, which must form, both in peace and war, the true
Imperial contribution to the security and protection of Australia."

The House will observe that the claim of the English Government at
that time was limited to the defence of these colonies against aggression by land. The principle in its more general form was stated by the
head of the present English Government, in the evidence given by him

before a committee of the House of Commons some years ago. Mr. Gladstone then used these words :

"No community which is not primarily charged with the ordinary business of its own defence is really, or can be in the full sense of the word, a free community. The privileges of freedom and the burthens of freedom are absolutely associated together. To bear the burden is as necessary as to enjoy the privilege, in order to form that character which is the great ornament of all freedom itself."

And he added this remarkable expression :—

"I should like to see the state of feeling restored to the colonies which induced the first American colonists, when they revolted, to make it one of their grievances that British troops were kept in their borders without their consent."

When this proposal was made by the Duke of Newcastle, in a practical and limited form, in 1863, we at once accepted it ; and from that time to the present we have freely paid the amount demanded by the English Government for the presence in this colony of English troops. We have latterly, I think, extended our views ; and I believe we are now prepared, not merely to accept the obligation to defend ourselves from aggression by land, but I think we have also shown by our recent acts that we are prepared to accept, in its fullest sense, the obligation to defend ourselves against all external aggression, whether by sea or land.

Let it not be said that when, a few years ago, the Houses of the Victorian Parliament presented a petition to the English Government for aid in the naval defence of this country, we at all abandoned or violated that principle. It must be remembered that both Houses of Parliament based their application for aid to the English Government expressly upon the fact that, while we were willing to defend our own shores from aggression, we thought the English Government were bound to make a contribution to the defence of English commerce in our waters which might be affected in the case of war. Sir, any danger to this colony, in time of war, will result from our connexion with England. If English merchants send English ships to this colony, and if this colony, in consequence of its connexion with the mother country, be involved in war with any foreign country, it is surely not unreasonable to ask that England should defend from foreign aggression not Victoria, but her own ships, while they are in our waters ; and any concession made by the English Government in this direction is not a concession in violation of the principle now advanced by the English government, and which we have expressly and impliedly admitted to be true, but it is an admission of the obligation of the empire to defend the interests of British commerce, so far as those interests may be affected by their position in our waters in a time of war with foreign countries. Now if this principle be accepted, there is only one condition by which it should be limited ; and that is that either the land force or the naval force which is created and called into existence by our own means, and maintained at our own cost, should be kept under our own control. I do not think there is any one who can raise a rational objection to that limitation. It is a limitation prescribed by prudence. It is prescribed also, I think, by self-respect. Certainly it is prescribed by prudence, for I do not know what advantage this or any of the neighbouring colonies can gain by paying in time of peace for either a military or naval force which may be withdrawn in time of war. If a regiment or a ship of war kept here in time of peace be withdrawn in time of war, of what earthly use is it to us? And, if it is outside our own control, it may be withdrawn, and probably will be withdrawn.

In time of peace, so far as I have been able to observe, the presence of English troops here has not been of the advantage which the presence of troops in any of the older countries of the world confers upon the people. Soldiers in time of war are a defence; and, in time of peace, it is supposed they are an ornament. But I must say that the soldiers which the British Government have sent us have not served the purposes of ornament. The regiments sent to this country in later years have been amongst the most undisciplined and ill-conducted regiments in Her Majesty's service. In another respect we have just reason to take offence at the management of the military force in these colonies. In all the old countries of the world, including England, the soldiers who are an ornament in time of peace are so applied that they may appear to be an ornament, not merely to the head of the executive government, but also to all the highest offices of the public service. The gates of Her Majesty's palaces are guarded by soldiers, and so are the high offices of Her Majesty's Government. In this country I have observed, and I have not been able to guess at an explanation of the fact, that while the house of the representative of the Colonial Office is guarded and ornamented by the presence of Her Majesty's troops, that ornament has always been withheld from the chief offices of Her Majesty's Government.

Now I think it will be an advantage to us to alter the system, so far as that either the military or the naval defences which may be necessary for the protection of this country shall be wholly under the control of Her Majesty's Government for Victoria. I believe that the defences which we can create and maintain ourselves will be abundantly sufficient for the purpose. We are situated at a remot corner of the world, and certainly no land force which could attack this country could attack it in such power as to be able to resist the weakest of our colonial defences upon land. I believe that our police force would be able to annihilate any land force that might land and attempt to take possession of this country. But, if our land forces are not sufficient, we should increase them, but increase them upon this condition, and for this express purpose—that they be kept under our own control, as they are paid for by our own money. This question is one which I hope will not escape the vigilant attention of the Chief Secretary at the present time. I fear that a great mistake was made when the *Nelson* ship was accepted upon the terms that she should be commanded by English officers. I mention the matter now for the purpose of asking the Chief Secretary to take care that we do not commit that mistake a second time in the case of the *Cerberus*. It is said that the Admiralty are exceedingly desirous to appoint their own officers to the command of that vessel. I hope the Chief Secretary will not accept that condition—that, rather than accept it, he will be prepared either to leave the *Cerberus* in the hands of the English Government, and ask them to take it over into their own possession and apply it to their own uses, or to pay to the English Government the amount contributed by them to the building of the vessel, so as to obtain her and place her entirely under our own control, and leave no trace of foreign dominion in the matter of our naval defences. Now, sir, it appears to me that this frank and full acceptance of the duty of self-defence is one that our fellow countrymen at home may reasonably expect from us. On the other hand, we have a right to demand from our fellow countrymen at home another condition—the condition on which the English Government has based this demand that the colonies shall protect themselves—namely, that we shall possess the absolute and entire right of self-government. Sir, I am prepared to show by facts, which I believe no one will be able to dispute, that while we possess by law, in this country, almost absolute and entire powers of self-government, we do not possess, and never have possessed, self-government in fact.

What is the constitution of this country? I suppose it might be most shortly and fitly described by saying that we possess, by our constitution and by law, almost all of what are known as the absolute rights of independent states, subject to certain qualifications ; and that we possess none at all of what are known as the relative rights of independent states. We possess virtually, according to law —though not in fact—independence. We possess also the right of legislation, subject to a very anomalous condition, not accepted by ourselves, but imposed upon us by the English Government and the English Parliament, which enables an English minister—a foreign minister, I will say for this purpose—to advise the Crown either to accept or to reject any of our legislative measures. That, no doubt, is an anomaly—it is an anomaly which exists in law, and can be corrected only by the joint action of the governments and legislatures of these colonies. Again, we possess the right of property, which is also one of the rights ordinarily conceded to be the rights of independent government. We have power to dispose of our own lands, of our own mines, and, in fact, of all the abundant property with which Providence has blessed this country. This we possess in absolute measure. On the other hand, we don't possess what are known as the relative rights of nations. We cannot send an embassy that will claim official recognition, even to a neighbouring colony. We cannot make a peace or proclaim a war. These are relative rights outside ourselves, and we have no power to exercise them. Sir, it seems to me that this distinction between absolute and relative rights forms the clearest and most distinct description of the rights of self-government which this and the neighbouring colonies enjoy under their Constitution Acts ; and the form of this government, according to law, the House is of course acquainted with. It is the form known as the form of responsible government. Under this form there is a head of the executive government, who is absolutely independent of all foreign and external control, except in the particular case in which power is reserved by our Constitution Act to a minister to instruct the governor in respect to the reservation of bills. With that single exception, I venture to assert—and I challenge contradiction from any person acquainted with constitutional law, or who is prepared to argue points of constitutional law—that, in all the internal affairs of Victoria, the head of the Executive enjoys the same freedom and independence with regard to Victoria that Her Majesty does in Great Britain. Sir, this is the very keystone of the system of self-government under our system. If you take that away you destroy the whole edifice. If you make the governor dependent upon any one except his responsible advisers for advice, what becomes of the power of self-government of the people ? The responsible advisers are responsible to whom ? To the representatives of the people. The head of the executive, according to the principles of this system of government, is bound to listen to no suggestions, much less instructions, and still less censure, from any one else except his advisers : and if you place the head of the executive in such a position that he is constrained to listen to advice, or suggestion, or instruction or censure, from any external authority, you so far supersede the advice of his responsible advisers, and just in the same proportion, strike at the very root of self-government in this country.

There has been a despatch quoted, once at least, I think, in this House, which, with the permission of the House, I should like to quote again. It is a despatch very remarkable not only from the high authority from which it proceeded, but from the remarkable circumstances under which it was written, and the still more remarkable subsequent acts of the person by whom it was written. I refer to the despatch of Lord John Russell addressed to Mr. Poulett Thompson, in the year 1839, on this very question of the nature of responsible government. At that time Canada asked for a system of responsible government. The House of Commons expressed an opinion that it should not be granted. The English Government, through Lord John Russell, wrote to its representative in Canada, telling him that it should not be granted, that it could not be granted, and forbidding him even to entertain any application that it might be granted. And he wrote in these words :—

" The Constitution of England, after long struggles and alternate successes, has settled into a form of government in which the prerogative of the Crown is undisputed, but is never exercised without advice. Hence the exercise only is questioned, and however the use of the authority may be condemned, the authority itself remains untouched. This is the practical solution of a great problem, which, from 1640 to 1690, shook the monarchy and disturbed the peace of the country.

"But if we seek to apply such a principle to the colonies, we shall at once find ourselves at fault. The power for which a minister is responsible in England is not his own power, but the power of the Crown, of which he is for the time the organ. It is obvious that the executive councillor of a colony is in a situation totally different. The governor under whom he serves receives his orders from the Crown of England ; but can the colonial council be the advisers of the Crown of England ? Evidently not, for the Crown has other advisers for the same functions, and with superior authority.

"It may happen, therefore, that the governor receives at one and the same time instructions from the Queen, and advice from his executive council, totally at variance with each other."

Sir, we have had a very remarkable illustration of that fact. We now know what it means—to what results it may lead. Lord John Russell proceeded to say——

"If he is to obey his instructions from England, the parallel of constitutional responsibility entirely fails."

No doubt it does. The writer added—

"If, on the other hand, he is to follow the advice of his council, he is no longer a subordinate officer, but an independent sovereign."

Well, Sir, the Governor of Victoria, in 1855, became, upon the recommendation of Lord John Russell, addressed to the English Parliament, an independent sovereign in and for Victoria, subject to the condition which I have mentioned. Lord John Russell, who, in 1839, refused to any colony the gift of responsible government—who maintained that it could not be granted—granted it, in the year 1846, to the very colony whose governor he instructed not to entertain an application that it might be granted ; and in 1854 he received, accepted, and proposed to the English Parliament the constitutions forwarded from these various colonies by which the governors of these colonies were established in a position which he describes as one which a governor could not occupy, namely, the head of an executive government under a system of responsible government. I think that is a very remarkable expression of opinion, considering the quarter from which it came and the circumstances under which it was uttered.

And now, Sir, I will venture to assert that although this principle of the existence of responsible government has been admitted by the English Parliament in our various Constitution Acts, and has been admitted by various leading English statesmen, yet, from time to time, from that time to the present, that principle has been denied, as a principle, by the Colonial Office, and the application of the principle has been in practice, persistently, steadfastly, and assiduously disregarded. Sir, I assert that the principle of the existence of responsible government, although it is now convenient to state that principle and to enforce it against our unhappy fellow-colonists in New Zealand, has been denied in terms by those who represent the policy of the Colonial Office in England. And, in proof of this, I will invite the attention of the House to a debate in the House of Lords which took place so recently as the 8th of May, 1868. It was a debate upon a question which I can assure honourable members it is not my wish to revive the remembrance of in this Assembly at the present time. I only refer to the debate in the House of Lords for the purpose of showing what the principles avowed by the Colonial Office in reference to the rights of colonists in these colonies were, and not for the purpose of reviving any old animosities. It was a debate upon the question of the grant to Sir Charles Darling. Seven members took part in that debate. Six of them—six members of the House of Lords —denied the existence of responsible government in this colony, and four out of the six have been either Secretaries of State for the Colonies or Under-Secretaries. The seventh—the only member of the House of Lords who asserted on behalf of these colonies the right of self-government, and traced to its full and legitimate conclusions the effect of those rights—was the Lord High Chancellor of England, a man who is not only the head of the law, and a most able and distinguished lawyer, but who has also been a very eminent politician. I refer to Sir Hugh Cairns. The debate was opened by Lord Lyveden. Lord Lyveden is a new nobleman. He formerly, under the name of Mr. Vernon Smith—which, it is believed, he very painfully endured—was Under-Secretary of State for the Colonies. I remember it was said to be the ambition of Mr. Vernon Smith to change his patronymic. I believe that any person who has either seen or heard Mr. Vernon Smith will not be curious to learn what may be the opinion of Lord Lyveden on any subject of human interest; but, at the same time, as Mr. Vernon Smith was Under-Secretary of State for the Colonies, his opinion upon a topic of this nature, inspired as it must be by Colonial Office feeling and opinion, is not destitute of interest. Lord Lyveden gave an opinion upon the meaning and effect of the 57th section of our Constitution Act, a section, as honourable members will recollect, which directs that no grant of money can be made by the Legislative Assembly unless it is recommended by message from the governor. It is almost a copy of a standing order of the House of Commons, and is known, I believe, to nearly every schoolboy. Now this was the opinion of Lord Lyveden as to the meaning and intention of that section of our Constitution Act :—

" The object of the 57th clause of the Constitution Act was to prevent the governor—whoever he might be—doing exactly what Sir Henry Sutton had done, proposing any vote of money against the opinion of the Legislative Council and the Secretary of State."

Sir, I commend this opinion to the wondering attention of those grave and reverend gentlemen who framed our constitution, and especially would I commend it to the attention of the learned Chief Justice of this colony. The next time that learned functionary is called upon to give a judicial decision of the meaning and intention of the framers and

draftsmen of our Constitution Act, I venture to think that he will find
in Lord Lyveden's opinion a source of the most new and wonderful
views of our constitution. But Lord Lyveden was not alone in his
opinion ; Lord Lyveden had been, in the time of his manhood, little
more than a political fribble, but he did not stand alone in the opinion
he expressed about this clause of our Constitution Act. The then
Secretary of State for the Colonies (the Duke of Buckingham) was unwilling, in deference to the views of his office, to abandon any
advantage that might be gained from that opinion. The Duke of
Buckingham said

"Now it may be said that, under the operation of that clause, the
governor could have withheld his assent altogether from the vote
recommended by his responsible advisers, and he was not prepared to
contend that such a power might not exist. It was not, however, a
power which had been used in the way in which it had been suggested
it might have been used in the present instance."

That is the opinion of one Secretary of State for the Colonies as to our
constitution—that this clause of our Constitution Act was inserted for
the express purpose of enabling the Colonial Office, as well as the
Legislative Council, to prescribe what grants of money shall be made
by the people of Victoria for the public service. The Duke of Argyle,
another ex-Secretary of State, was the next speaker. The Duke of
Argyle is a nobleman of very great and cultivated intelligence, and,
considering that he is a Scotchman, his cultivation has considerable
breadth. Now hear what this most intelligent and highly-cultivated
nobleman—the author of the *Reign of Law*—thinks and knows of
the law that reigns in Victoria : --

"The statement of the noble duke had narrowed the ground of
difference to a point of the highest importance as regarded the administration of the Crown over colonies enjoying constitutional government.
The position of the noble duke was that, in dealing with a colony possessing a full constitutional system, it was impossible for the Crown to
resist the colony if such a vote were proposed to a governor acting in
accordance with the wishes of the Assembly. That was a very dangerous principle to lay down . . . If the noble duke felt so
strongly the unconstitutional form of attack, why had he not advised
the governor to insist, in the event of the vote being introduced, on its
being proposed in the form of a Bill, so as to place no unconstitutional
duress on the Legislative Council ? These were matters entirely under
the control of the Colonial Office."

This was a very frank avowal. He was followed by a nobleman who
had very recently filled the position of Secretary of State for the
Colonies—Lord Carnarvon—a nobleman who twenty years ago enjoyed,
I remember, the very doubtful reputation of carrying a very old head
on very young shoulders, and who, as is not uncommon in such cases,

now that his shoulders are no longer very young, carries on them a head not much wiser than when he was a boy. Lord Carnarvon said—

"When a superior officer informed his subordinate that he could not take a certain course without certain effects resulting, it could not be said that he thereby gave him an option as to which course he could pursue. He agreed with the noble duke that, at so great a distance as we are from Australia, it was impossible for the Colonial Office to regulate every minute detail in the conduct of the Governor of the colony ; but, at the same time, they should give him such general directions as would serve to guide him in the course he should pursue."

Sir, those who are advocating increased facilities for communication with England should, I think, reflect upon this. Possibly, in addition to a bi-monthly mail, we may have the inestimable advantage of having the conduct of the Governor of this colony regulated " in every minute detail " by the Colonial Office. That is the advantage which Lord Carnarvon holds out to us from increased facilities of communication. His lordship proceeded to remark :—

"The noble duke said that, whatever theoretical right the Colonial Office might have to interpose in such a case, such a right had practically ceased to exist. He begged to express his entire dissent from that view. The right of the Crown to interfere in such a case not only existed in theory but in practice ; and, if the advisers of the Crown were assured that any constitutional principle were being violated, it would be their duty to interpose the veto of the Crown."

Nothing can be more distinct than that. He went on to say—

" In view of all this correspondence, he must bear witness to the extremely difficult position in which colonial governors often found themselves. Questions must from time to time arise which required not merely general knowledge of constitutional law, but of technical and professional details, which few could command. Their advisers were taken out of their own governments, and pledged to one political party in the colony. It was his fixed determination, had he remained in office, to strive as earnestly as possible for the appointment of some one permanent and impartial legal adviser, who might be in a position to advise a colonial governor as emergencies arose."

Sir, I am not quoting I would remind the House, from the speech of some schoolboy, upon a public speech day, but I am quoting the words of a nobleman who had recently been the Secretary of State for the Colonies, and who was expressing opinions professedly deliberate, in the highest and noblest assembly in the world. I suppose that if the Chief Secretary of this colony were to get up in his place and say that, in view of the very difficult circumstances in which Her Majesty was placed, he must testify to the necessity that existed for some further advice and assistance beyond that offered by Her Majesty's Ministers ;

that unfortunately Her Majesty's Ministers in England were selected out of the British Empire ; that they were taken from one political party in the British Empire, and that it was his (the Chief Secretary's) fixed determination if he remained in office, to request the Agent-General of Victoria to act as a permanent adviser of Her Majesty in all matters relating to the colony as emergencies might arise—I suppose, Sir, if that declaration were made by the Chief Secretary in this House to-night, it would be received with a peal of laughter ; and yet I venture to assert that it would not be a more preposterous, nor a more illegal or absurd doctrine than that which Lord Carnarvon laid down in this speech.

The Lord Chancellor [1] followed in the debate ; and he shortly enlightened the ignorance of the learned lords who preceded him as to the meaning of the 57th section of our Constitution Act.   He showed them that it was merely a transcript of a standing order of the House of Commons, devised for entirely different purposes than they imagined. He pointed out that, if these colonies had in reality and in law the right of constitutional government, the Colonial Office had no power to interfere with them, except so far as that constitutional law permitted ; and he added these remarkable words :—

" If it was to be laid down, as a rule, that the Secretary of State at home was to hold in leading-strings the Ministry of the colony, then the pretence of free colonial institutions was simply a delusion and a mockery."

The Lord Chancellor was followed by Lord Salisbury, an exceedingly able man, and who was exceedingly wroth with the Lord Chancellor for rebuking his own colleague, the Secretary of State for the Colonies, and for informing the Lords of the true nature of responsible government in these colonies.   Lord Salisbury said :—

" I, for one, cannot concur in the estimate of a colonial governor's position which my noble and learned friend appears to have formed. He seems to regard a governor of a colony as a mere mute person—as a gentleman who is to have no will of his own, and who is to do, with a certain amount of obsequiousness and servility, whatever the Ministers who happen to be seated in his council chamber may bid him."

Sir, the Lord Chancellor might have replied to Lord Salisbury that he had advanced nothing in behalf of the independence of a colonial governor beyond that which might be advanced, and would be advanced, by Ministers of the Crown in England on behalf of the Sovereign. The representative of the Sovereign in a colony of this kind is not a more mute person, is not a more subservient person, than the Queen of England within the Empire of England.   Certainly, Lord Salisbury had not had, at the time he spoke, a long opportunity of acquainting himself with the real position of the Sovereign of his own country.   That noble lord had for thirteen

---

[1] Lord Cairns.

years been undergoing, with his party, an education at the hands of a political leader whose true character he had himself only recently discovered, and during that period of thirteen years, while he had unconsciously been receiving an education, he and his party had few opportunities of learning what the position of a Sovereign of England was. But, Sir, with further experience no doubt Lord Salisbury will learn the fact that, while neither the Sovereign nor the representative of the Sovereign in a constitutionally governed country has any power to wag the little finger officially, except by advice, both Sovereign and representative have very large powers, not merely social but political, in the administration of the affairs of a country—large powers, which are co-extensive with the capacity of the Sovereign and the representative, and with his or her ability to use them as a means of most legitimate influence. Lord Salisbury added that :—

"There is a large class of cases with regard to which it might be the distinct duty of a governor to impose a veto on the proposals of his constitutional advisers, and the duty of the Secretary of State to enforce the adoption of that course."

The last speaker in the debate was Earl Grey, who of course maintained the position of the Colonial Office in support of the views of other speakers. However, I must do Earl Grey the justice to observe that he at all events has been sincere and out-spoken in his views upon colonial government. From the very first he dissented from the notion of responsible government in the colonies. He always admitted that parliamentary government might be granted ; and by parliamentary government Earl Grey intended that a Parliament or an assemblage of political factions might be established in these colonies, who should exhaust their time and energies in fighting over the spoils and plunders of office. That was his idea of parliamentary government ; but, at the same time, he desired and counselled that the real power should be retained in Downing Street. Therefore, although he was one of the speakers in this debate, it is only due to that noble, aged, and able man to say that he only expressed opinions which he had always consistently avowed.

Well, now, I think that these declarations by secretaries and under-secretaries of state clearly show that the Colonial Office, from whom all of them derive their inspiration, deny to us absolutely the existence, in principle, of responsible government in this country. I cannot myself conceive how responsible government, in an Englishman's sense of the word—responsible government in which the head of the Executive shall be independent of all influences, except the advice of his advisers, who shall be responsible to Parliament - is to exist, or how it can be maintained at all, if it be asserted that a foreign and irresponsible person is to have the power of control over the acts of the representative of the Crown. While this principle has been disavowed by the Colonial Office, when occasions required, and also asserted by the Colonial Office, as we have seen within the last few months, when occasion served, the Colonial Office has always in practice, steadily, persistently, and designedly disregarded the existence of responsible government. It does so in various ways. It does so first in legislation, relating to the colonies, by the Imperial Parliament. The legislation in reference to the colonies is entirely prepared and passed by the influence of the Colonial Office. The single statement in the declaration of the views of the colonists which seems to accord with the facts is a statement not relating to the colonies but to England, with which these colonists are better acquainted than they are with their own country. They say :—

" The constitution of the Colonial Office is ill adapted for carrying on friendly intercourse with colonial governments or representing their wants and wishes, whilst the attention of the British Parliament is absorbed in affairs of immediate concern to the mother country."

It is perfectly true. The Colonial Office prepares all measures passed by the English Parliament, relating to the colonies, and, by an ingenious device, they confound and mix together not only those colonies which are under the control of the Colonial Office, but colonies which enjoy the right of self-government under a responsible system. There is usually, I observe, in all these colonial measures a clause defining what a colony or a colonial possession should be, and having lumped the forty-three colonies or colonial possessions of the British Empire under one distinctive title, they pass one sweeping clause which shall be applicable to them all.

There is a little colonial dependency of England called Heligoland, inhabited principally by Germans, who visit it from the mainland for the double purpose of gambling and bathing. That colony is governed by a governor who is, happily, perhaps, for himself, free from the encumbrance of a Parliament, and who receives his instructions (which he is to carry out with authority) directly and expressly from the Colonial Office. The position in which such a governor as that is placed is one free from all difficulty. He knows the purpose for which he is sent, he knows the authority which created him, he knows that it is his sole duty to obey that authority ; and the distinguished Crimean officer who is now the the Governor of that colony can never, I am sure, feel any sense of degradation and disgrace in obeying heartily and loyally the instructions he receives from the Colonial Office. I think, however, that the case must be very different indeed with gentlemen who have the ill fortune to preside over colonies possessing responsible government. But the effect of measures applicable to all colonies without distinction is that the English Parliament, at the instance of the Colonial Office, and in its disregard and inattention to colonial affairs, passes measures which really it has no constitutional right to pass at all. These colonies have been given the power to make laws " in cases whatsoever " in and for the colonies. Now what does that mean ? I do not dispute the mere power of the British Parliament to pass any law it pleases. It may pass a law making us all helots if it pleases. It has the power to do it. It may pass a law abrogating our constitution—it has the power ; but I deny its right to pass any law affecting the internal affairs of these colonies without the consent of the colonies themselves, simply because the English Parliament has already surrendered that power to the representatives of the people in these colonies. I do not believe that the English Parliament has any design or intention of interfering with our rights, but simply in its indifference, in its absorption in imperial affairs, it does not pay attention to these colonial bills. The result is that the Colonial Office may propose any bill it pleases in relation to colonial affairs, and it is passed. I verily believe that if it were to prepare a bill abrogating the constitution of all these colonies, that bill would have a very good chance of passing through both Houses of Parliament without a question being asked. But that is certainly something of which we have a right to complain. If we look back to the legislation of several recent years, we shall find abundant instances of this unconstitutional interference by legislation with our affairs. Why last year there was a bill passed by both Houses of the Imperial Parliament enabling the Governor, individually, with the consent of one of Her Majesty's Secretaries of State, to register any ships in any of these colonies, and to appoint inspectors of those ships. Where is our right of legislation in that? No doubt English legislation is entitled to provide for British ships ; but are we to have no power over colonial ships? Here is an express power given to the Governor individually to do an act which he has no power by law in this colony to do individually, namely, to register ships himself, appoint inspectors of those ships, and, I presume, to pay them by fees. I venture to say that this interference, directed by the Colonial Office, although it may be within the power of the Imperial Parliament—it is said there is nothing beyond the power of the Imperial Parliament—is certainly beyond the constitutional rights which they have conferred upon this colony, and outside the limits of their own constitutional rights.

But it is not by legislation, wholly or chiefly, that the Colonial Office denies, in practice, the right of self-government in these colonies. Its chief interference—the interference which we have most to complain of, and which I think we ought at once endeavour to put an end to—is the interference by instructions addressed to the Governor. If the proposition I have submitted to the House be well-founded in constitutional law, these instructions, except so far as they are authorized by terms of express legislation, are beyond the power of the Secretary of State to give. He has no right to give them. They are exercised in two ways. The Governor brings out with him to this colony a code of instructions under Her Majesty's sign-manual. These are to serve for his directions during the entire period of his government. I had some time since prepared a paper showing the different changes that have been made from time to time in these permanent instructions given to the Governor, and if time permitted I think I could amuse the House by reading some of the alterations which have been made in the Governor's instructions. They are really some of them difficult to understand. Some of them are absolutely trivial and literal. In some places words are introduced, in subsequent instructions the words are omitted, and afterwards re-introduced. They are very numerous, and they seem almost to be the

result of a sort of education for the boys of the Colonial Office by which
lads may be said to learn English composition by practising upon the
corpus vile of Her Majesty's subjects.   Now these instructions retain at
the present day some of the most offensive and unconstitutional
directions which are contained in the instructions given to the
Governor at the time this colony was a portion of New South Wales,
and both formed a portion of a convict colony.   Some of the instructions given to Sir Charles Fitzroy are repeated in the instructions given
to Sir Henry Manners Sutton.   Sir, it will hardly be believed, in the
face of our Constitution Act, that the Queen of England can be advised,
by her advisers at home, to insert in her instructions to the Governor
a direction to take care that all bills passed by Parliament shall be
prepared in a certain way, regardless of the advice of the executive
council, or that it shall be in the power of the Governor, on all matters
touching life or death, to act upon his individual opinion, without
regard to the opinions of his responsible advisers.   Are these instructions consistent with self-government ?   I really do not like to press
upon the House views which may appear abstract, but which I confess
seem to me to be connected intimately with the practical interests of
our daily lives.   Are these instructions consistent with the view which
any honourable member of this House entertains of what is known as
the system of responsible government ?   I do not believe they are.

But in addition to these instructions, given to each governor during
the term of his governorship, he receives, from month to month,
monthly instructions.   Every month the Governor of this colony has
to send home something like a diary of his daily political life.   He
has to send home to his master an account of the most minute acts that
he does in connexion with the political affairs of this country, and he
receives monthly a series of instructions and advices, admonitions and
warnings, and approvals or disapprovals.   I can easily conceive that a
system of that kind is very effective, though I cannot see how it is
consistent in any way with the independence of the Queen's representative, or with the existence of a system of responsible government in
this country.   It appears to me that interference of that kind, except
so far as it is authorized by law, and it is only authorized by law in
the particular matter of the reservation of bills for Her Majesty's
assent, is a system which necessarily degrades the representative of the
Crown, and that that degradation extends to his advisers and the
whole people of the country whose affairs he administers.   Indeed, Sir,
for my own part I do not shrink from saying that I do not know a
position which is more inconsistent with the delicate feelings of an
honourable and self-respecting man than that of a Governor of any of
these Australian colonies at the present time.   For what is his
position ?   He is not allowed to come here and tell the colonists that
he is sent here by men who claim the right of interference with his
acts, and who assert that it is their duty to interpose the authority of
the Crown if they believe the advice tendered to him is erroneous.
He does not come out here to tell the colonists that.   He dare not.
He is made to feel that he is the servant of the Secretary of State ;
but he must not tell that.   He would defeat the purpose for which he

is sent, if he were to tell it. He is made to feel, month by month, that he wears the livery of the Colonial Office ; but he must not show it. He must wear plain clothes ; he must walk about and endeavour to appear that he is a gentleman living on his means. He dare not show that he is what he really is—what he knows he is, and what he has no power to resist—the servant of the Secretary of State for the Colonies for the time being. It is part of his functions, and one of the most important of his functions, that he should appear to be the representative of the Crown : that he should talk to his Ministers ; that he should address the Houses of Parliament, just as though he were an independent sovereign in regard to Victoria, as he is by law ; but then he must not show that he is. I think we all felt last year a very sincere sympathy for the Governor of this colony when the inconsistent and contradictory character of his different functions were forced upon the public attention. The Governor received, last year, a despatch giving him a conditional instruction which was clearly at variance with our law. I did not hear in this House, during the whole of that time, an honourable member on one side of the House or the other stand up and assert that that despatch was other than unconstitutional and illegal. But the despatch was received, and had to be obeyed ; and I think we all felt a real sympathy with the gentleman who was compelled by stress of circumstances to obey a despatch which he knew, and his advisers admitted to be illegal. But he had to obey it. He could not resist it. So those advisers came down to this House, and what was their argument ? It was not an argument ; it was rather a wail of grief and shame on behalf of the gentleman they represented that he was compelled to forget his duty to his Sovereign, and the people over whom he was placed as the representative of the Sovereign, and was forced by stress of circumstances to obey an order admitted to be illegal. Sir, the governor of one of these colonies is wholly helpless to defend himself against this unlawful interference ; and it appears to me that, just in proportion as the governor is helpless, so it becomes a more imperative duty upon the governor's advisers to protect him from that illegal interference ; for certainly, while the governor's advisers have their duty to the representative of the Sovereign to consider, they have also their own self-respect to consider. If their position is affected by this illegal interference, if they are really not the responsible advisers of the representative of the Crown, but if they are the Ministers of a gentleman who is himself the agent of the Secretary of State for the Colonies, I believe that they would not venture to think of themselves with the same self-respect which they would naturally desire to entertain after they have reached the high position which they now occupy. And the same sense of general degradation, and imposture, and sham extends not only to the Ministers of the Crown—it extends to the entire people ; for when this system exists, I do not think that the people subject to it can really respect the Government they suspect to be a sham, and yet are forced to profess to be a reality. We all know, though we don't like to say it, that responsible government does not exist. We don't govern ourselves, and we know it. We are all ashamed of it, though we don't care to say it. The same sense of a want of respect extends from us to our constituents, and I believe that in time it will tend to degrade the national character, by extending this sense of shame and want of respect for our constitution. An eminent authority (Sir Robert Peel) once said :—

"The semblance of independence without the reality can only be an evil and a curse, cheating with vain mockery the people upon whom it is inflicted, and bringing into general disrepute and shame the character of representative institutions."

There is a description of Victorian institutions at this day. And it seems to me that this sense of failure, of which we are all conscious, and want of respect for the institutions which we all profess to respect, are very greatly increased when we remember that it is not even a Minister of the Crown in England who controls these colonies. I believe that the Secretary of State for the Colonies has little or nothing to do with the government of the colonies. There is not a department of the English Government which is controlled with less knowledge than the department of the Colonial Office ; and for a very simple reason. In other departments the Ministers derive, from their residence in England, from their acquaintance with English public life and institutions, more or less knowledge of the various departments of the Government ; but an English Colonial Secretary knows little about these colonies. I believe that, ever since the time of Lord Stanley, ten years ago, there has not been a Secretary of State for the Colonies who has visited, in the course of his life-time, half a dozen English colonies. What does the Secretary of State know about the colonies ? Nothing whatever. And if a Secretary of State enters the Colonial Office unacquainted with the wants, interests, institutions, and feelings of the forty-three colonies over which he is said to preside, what is the effect ? An ignorant Minister, and a transient Minister, quickly supplanted by the changes in party politics, certainly point to one conclusion, and that is that the permanent officers of the department are the real governors. I believe, myself, that it is not the Secretary of State for the Colonies, who appends his name to the despatches, who is the real author of them, but his clerks. I had several indications, while I was in office, of the control exercised by clerks of the Colonial Office over one who was nominally at their head. I have seen a bill objected to by the chief clerk in the Colonial Office, and the objection overruled by his Ministerial head, and the same objection repeated to a bill of the same character, a few years afterwards, under a new Colonial Minister, and the Royal assent refused to that bill on the suggestion of the same officer. It was said of the Athenian Republic, in its best days, that it was governed by the poodle dog of a courtesan ; and the *bon mot* was made out with great ingenuity. It was said that the poodle dog engrossed the attentions of its mistress ; the mistress of course engrossed her lover ; and the lover ruled the fierce democracy— controlled its policy. I believe that a similar remark—for history often repeats itself—might be applied with far more truth to the present relations between the Colonial Office and these countries. I believe it might be said with perfect truth that the million and a half of Englishmen who inhabit these colonies, and who during the last fifteen years have believed they possessed self-government, have been really governed during the whole of that time by a person named Rogers. He is the chief clerk in the Colonial Office. Of course he inspires every Minister who enters the department, year after year, with Colonial Office traditions, Colonial Office policy, Colonial Office ideas. His views form the law for his chief, while the chief writes in imperious, and almost imperial style to the representative of the Crown in these colonies, and the representative of the Crown—the agent of the Colonial Office—rules over this very patient people. Is this not a simple description of the actual fact? And if this be the state of things, are we to allow it to continue? How long are we to submit to this? If it be the law, let us yield to it, and let us cast upon England not merely the general obligation of defending ourselves from foreign aggression, but the responsibility of wisely ruling these colonies. Let us not accept the responsibility of defending ourselves and of governing ourselves, while at the same time we are deprived of the power of governing ourselves. Let us be placed in the one position or the other. Let us be either dependent or free. If we are free, let us have the rights of freedom under the form of government which exists by law. If we are not free, then I say the sooner we cast off the obligations of an apparent freedom, and cast upon England the general obligation to govern us and to defend us, the better for us all.

Sir, I have to apologize to the House for detaining it so long. There is just one subject more to which I wish to call attention. In the last resolution of which I have given notice, and which, I believe, is not approved of by some honourable members, I have endeavoured to submit to the Government, without embarrassing the Government, the views which I hope the House will entertain upon this subject. I might have put this resolution in a form which would be construed by the Government as an intimation of the wish and desire of the House, and which might therefore, in some sense, be considered as either binding upon or embarrassing the Government in its freedom of action. I will tell the honourable and learned member (the Chief Secretary), with perfect sincerity, that my sole object in drawing this clause in its present undecided form has been to avoid even the appearance of embarrassing the Government in a matter in which, I believe, it would be not merely impolitic, but wrong of me to do so. If I were to express distinctly the practical course which I wish the Government would take, and which I earnestly hope the Government will take—if I were to put this in practical form—I could well believe that the honourable member might with some though by no means complete justice answer me in this wise. He might, I think, say—" You ask us as a government to take a particular course; why did you not take it yourselves? You were five years in office; you professed to have strong opinions on this subject; why did you not take the course which you ask us to take?" The honourable and learned member might with some justice make that observation, and, if he were to do it, I would tell him, in reply, that, until the debate in the House of Lords, from which I have read extracts, was published in this country, I really was not aware of the extent of the pretensions of the English Colonial Office, and that it was not for some time afterwards, and until I found that I should not be enabled to take the course which I desired to take, namely, to submit the matter to the consideration of the House at the commencement of the session, that I took the only other course which from a sense of self-respect I felt bound to do. Sir, as soon as I formed the opinion that I now entertain, I felt that I could not, consistently with self-respect, continue to hold the office of an executive councillor in this country, and I resigned. I will tell the honourable gentlemen, further, that I shall never again occupy that office until either I, or some more capable person than myself, take that course which I venture to press most earnestly upon his attention, or until I can again accept office in company with colleagues, who, with the full approval of the House, will take office for the sole or principal purpose of carrying out those views.

But, although I believe that this would be, to some extent, a partial answer to any observation the honourable member might address to me, I wish so far to yield to the justice of this anticipated objection that I have desired, in this resolution, to avoid even the appearance of attempting to coerce or embarrass the Government. I desire to persuade them. I hope earnestly that they will not oppose the resolutions, and that they will feel themselves in a position to be able to act upon them. But still the form of the resolutions, especially of the last, is such that they really may accept the principles contained in the resolutions without acting upon the last. However, I am perfectly prepared to state to the House the course which I believe ought to be taken by a government at this time, and in face of the questions which are now raised. Sir, I believe that this whole system of illegal interference could be very quickly and simply put a stop to. Not by consent of the Colonial Office. I am sure that the Colonial Office will never give its consent. Rather than give its consent, I think you would find that the Colonial Office would advocate a separation of the colonies from England; but I believe that Her Majesty's Government for Victoria may carry the principle of these resolutions into effect without asking the consent of the Colonial Office on the subject. Sir, why should not the Government of this country— Her Majesty's Ministers for this country—place themselves in direct and immediate communication with Her Majesty's advisers of the British Empire on the subject of colonial policy? What is to prevent them? I dare say the Colonial Office would consider it a slight and an indignity to be called upon to communicate directly with their brother Ministers of the Crown in this colony; but the Government of this colony would not entertain that feeling. What is to prevent that course being adopted? And, if there be nothing to prevent it, would not its adoption cure all the evils of which we have now to complain? I suppose that if Her Majesty's Ministers for Victoria were in direct and immediate communication, on equal terms, with the Ministers of the Crown in England, on matters of colonial interest, it would be impossible for

there to be any interference with the independence of the representative
of the Crown by the English Government.   And if there could be no
interference upon ordinary occasions, still less could there be any upon
extraordinary occasions ; still less, I apprehend, could a crime like that
which was perpetrated two years ago, when an honourable gentleman
who desired to do his duty to his Sovereign, and who, unfortunately,
in the endeavour to do it, incurred the vindictive displeasure of a
Secretary of State—it would be impossible, I say, that a crime of
that kind, yet unavenged, could ever be repeated. 'Sir, the Chief
Secretary can do this if he please, once he obtains the assent of this
House.

Without the assent of the Legislative Assembly, of course nothing can
be done in the matter, and nothing ought to be done ; but I venture to
assert that if the Legislative Assembly, this evening, passes these
resolutions, the Chief Secretary can at once, at the cost only of a delay
of three months and of a sheet of foolscap paper, effect this object.
What is to prevent him sitting down to-morrow morning and writing
directly to Earl Granville, communicating to him the resolutions of this
House, and informing him that Her Majesty's Ministers for Victoria
intend to give effect to them, and offering to enter into a correspondence
directly with any member of the English Government on subjects
affecting Victorian interests or affairs, and also telling him that, after a
day to be named, no official communication addressed to Her Majesty's
representative on any subjects relating to Victorian affairs, except the
reference of bills home, would be entertained by Her Majesty's advisers,
would be received by them, would be permitted to have official publication in this country, or would be laid on the table of either House of
Parliament ?   If that were done, I think it would settle the question.
I have thought over the matter for some time, and the longer
I think the more it appears to me that it is easier to do
this thing than to say it should be done.   What conceivable
difficulty is there in the way of doing it ? Perhaps it may be
said that the Colonial Office would not consent to this correspondence.
I have not the least doubt that the Colonial Office would strongly
object to it.   I am sure the clerks of the Colonial Office would be dismayed at the idea of their chief corresponding on equal terms with Her
Majesty's Ministers for Victoria.   I have heard it said that the Christian humility of an English bishop cannot resist the temptation of
snubbing a colonial bishop, if he meet him before a club window in
Pall Mall ; and I have not the least doubt that the Colonial Office
clerks would be dismayed at the idea of the Colonial Minister in
England corresponding on terms of perfect equality with Ministers
of the Crown in Victoria, and that they would resist it as far as
possible.

Now I should like to know if there would be any practical difficulty
or objection to the suspension of diplomatic relations between these
countries for one, two, or five years ? I venture to assert that this
country would suffer absolutely nothing from such a suspension. I remember only three occasions during the period I held office on which this
country desired, in view of Victorian interests, to communicate with

the English Government. One was the occasion on which the Chief Secretary desired to inform Mr. Cardwell that, if the promise given by the English Government to stop transportation to the Australian colonies were not fulfilled, the grant for the mail service would be withdrawn. That was stated to be a threat—and a threat it was; and I will add that a threat is the only language that an Englishman, in his coarser nature, can understand. Well, Sir, that communication was instantly attended to. The promise, given in 1851 I think, was renewed immediately, and it has since been, I believe, faithfully kept. The other two occasions were occasions on which conferences of members of the various Australian colonies, assembled in Melbourne, desired that the Colonial Office would introduce into the English Parliament a bill extending the powers of extradition of criminals between these colonies—a measure which we could not pass ourselves. That suggestion was not, of course, accompanied by any threat ; and on both occasions when that suggestion was made, to the best of my memory, no acknowledgment of the suggestion was sent. And yet we were able to survive the want of it. Now I think that shows that, so far as we are concerned, we have no immediate or urgent interest in carrying on communication with the Government of England. But it is very different with the English Government. The interests of English commerce necessitate—as the Chief Secretary already knows, from his short experience of office—frequent communication with the Government of this country. The Board of Trade, the Customs, and various other departments of the English Government, make suggestions to the Colonial Office, which require to be conveyed to the Government of this country, and to be acted upon and published. Now if diplomatic relations be suspended, I think it is the English Government that will first feel the inconvenience of it. I think that if a similar despatch to that sent out at the end of last year, in which the Customs department in England, recommended the Colonial Secretary to instruct the Governor to instruct his customs officers to inspect the cargoes of ships for particular purposes of interest to the commercial community in England, were not given effect to in this colony, we should probably find a question asked in the House of Commons, of the Under Secretary of State, as to why the suggestion had not been carried out ; and the only answer that could be given would be that Her Majesty's Ministers for Victoria could only correspond with Her Majesty's Ministers for the Empire, and that the latter Ministers really could not find it in their hearts to condescend to communicate with their brother Ministers in the colonies. I should like the British Ministry brought to the pass of giving an answer of that kind to a question. An answer of that kind would not be given without the immediate renewal of diplomatic relations. Perhaps, also, it may be said that the English Government would go further. Perhaps they might send out instructions to their servant to dismiss his advisers. I wonder whether they would go as far as that. That is about the furthest point to which they could go.

I think, if they did that, the result would be rather gratifying—gratifying, I mean, to the honourable gentleman who now holds the position of Chief Secretary, as well as the general body of his countrymen, for I venture to tell him that, if that were done, he would be permanent Minister for an indefinite time afterwards. The representative of the Crown would not be able to find seven other gentlemen than those now occupying the Treasury bench, who would be endured in office. Let him dismiss you—[addressing Ministers]—and you are there for a permanence. These are the only practical inconveniences that we need anticipate, and neither appears to me to have any weight or force. I am sure, after the best consideration I have given to the subject, that this scheme is absolutely without flaw, provided the House authorize it, and provided that Her Majesty's Ministers can be induced so far to assert their own position, so far to feel an interest in the protection of the representative of the Crown, and so far to desire to vindicate the rights of the people of this country that they will not shrink from attempting it. At the same time I abstain from seeking to enforce it upon them. I only desire to convince them that by no other means could they so effectually secure for themselves the respect and gratitude of the whole people of this country—and not merely of this country, for if this colony take the lead in this matter we set an example to all the neighbouring colonies, and they will be sure to follow. Not merely will that be done, but I believe, by removing this real grievance which is now communicating a large and growing discontent to thinking men in this country, they will be securing the gratitude of the people ; and, above all, will be establishing, on a basis of firm and lasting friendly union, the relations between this colony and the mother country. Indeed this whole subject presents itself to my mind not so much in view of present events and circumstances, nor I hope—though no doubt they are not altogether absent—in view of past feelings or susceptibilities. I look at this subject in reference chiefly to the future relations of this country with the mother country, and it is from a desire to establish those relations on a permanent and lasting footing of friendly union that I desire that the Government of this country should assert its rights. There is one thing which I hope the Government will not do. I hope they will not argue or remonstrate. Let them do anything but that : let them postpone action—but don't let them reason. The present Ministers of the Crown are young and inexperienced in office, and perhaps they will let me tell them that, if they venture to argue or remonstrate with the Colonial Office, they will be thoroughly and most humiliatingly defeated. If—[addressing Ministers]—you merely send home a despatch presenting a statement of your grievances, and inviting the Colonial Office to consider them, the Colonial Office will consider them. The Colonial Office will consider them until you, and half-a-dozen sets of your successors, have gone "the way to dusty death," politically. There is nothing that the Colonial Office would so much desire—just as it would desire exceedingly that this self-constituted conference of delegates in London should enter upon the vast international question of the rights of colonies to be exempted from the natural consequences of war in case of war between England and other countries. But if you desire really to settle the question you will deal with it only as a matter which you have the right, by law, to deal with—that you will assert your own legal position, and that by your own unassisted acts. What is this Colonial Office system? It is a mere straw image of official intrigue, and unlawful arbitrary interference. If you reason with it, you degrade yourselves. If you go to it, and strike it in the face with the back of your gloved hand, you will see it tumble in a heap at your feet, and the morrow after you have done so you will be establishing in this country a government which has never yet existed.

I recently saw an extract from a book written by a very intelligent member of the House of Commons, describing the conclusions that he drew from a visit to all parts of the American Union, including some of the most distant of the western states; and he mentions a very remarkable fact. It is this—that the dislike and hatred of the British Empire and people, which he found everywhere, instead of diminishing with time, appeared, so far as he could judge, to grow with each successive generation of Irishmen, at all events, who inhabited that country. To me this is one of the most mournful and one of the most extraordinary statements that I have ever read. I could not have believed it unless I had seen it stated on the most respectable authority, that the remembrance of political grievances, and the memory of undeserved taunts, instead of wearing out by time, increased by time. He adds that he believes that, in the event of a war with England, hundreds of thousands of men would come thronging from the far western states of America to the shores of the Atlantic, animated by a desire to take an active personal part in a war with that hated country. Now I see, in this country, the elements of the very same results which exist in America. But not to be manifested in our day. We, the adults of this generation, have ourselves come from the mother country, and are still so closely allied to it by family and social and personal feelings and interests that nothing can shake our affection and respect for our countrymen and country. It matters little to us what the British press or a department of the British Government may do to insult our feelings, to injure our interests, or to encroach upon our rights; but that will not be so perhaps with the next generation. The next generation will not have a feeling of kindred for England such as we have; and perhaps, if this strange feature which has been remarked in American life by this author (Mr. Maguire) has operation here, we shall find, in one or two generations, that the Australians, who will then be counted not by hundreds of thousands but by millions, will be a power not merely estranged and alien from the mother country, but hostile and inimical. Surely it is our interest to prevent, if possible, this most unhappy consequence. Surely we should endeavour, if we can, so to adjust the rights of both countries, so to remove all cause of complaint on the part of our countrymen at home, and all cause of complaint that we have for ourselves, that in future the union of these colonies may be not only formal but real, and that in all time to come we may have not only a common language and a common history, but a common sense of nationality that will bind all English communities on the face of the earth in one common brotherhood. I believe that by these resolutions—if the House will adopt them, and if the Government can see their way to act upon them we shall be doing something more than merely establishing our own liberties and rights ; I believe we shall be establishing the rights and liberties of all these Australian colonies. I believe we shall be doing more than that. I believe we shall be tending to unite the feelings of all British communities on the face of the globe ; and in doing that, if we should do it, I believe we shall be doing something also in the distant future towards the advancement and well-being of mankind itself. Sir, I thank the House for the attention with which it has listened to me, and I beg to submit these resolutions to its consideration.

CHAPTER XIX

LATER POLITICS

Defeat at Brighton, March 17th, 1871—Election for East Bourke Boroughs, May, 1873—The Norwegian Scheme—Answer to an Address—Payment of members—History of events that led to withdrawal from politics—Last speeches in the House—Address to Electors.

At the General Election of 1871 Mr. Higinbotham received his release from the electors of Brighton in antique fashion by a slap in the face. The opponent chosen was Mr. Thomas Bent, who was well known in the constituency, for he had been rate-collector, and was a market-gardener. There can be no doubt that Mr. Higinbotham's supporters made the fatal mistake of undervaluing their foe. The Brighton electorate may be roughly divided into two parts—those who dwell in villas, and the market-gardeners. At previous elections the opponents of Mr. Higinbotham, Mr. W. A. Brodribb, Sir William Clarke, Mr. Wilberforce Stephen, Mr. K. E. Brodribb had been the chosen of the villas. In 1871 it seemed as if a great quiet reigned amongst the villa folk, for there was no very stirring question before the colony, and wherefore should they trouble? As a matter of fact this section had been diligently but quietly canvassed. Mr. Higinbotham's old opponents did not attend Mr. Bent's meetings, but none the less they were prepared to poll for him. Meanwhile in the more democratic portion of the constituency, Mr. Higinbotham's stronghold in the fighting days, a much more vigorous and open canvass was being carried on. The line taken was something like this: "We know that Mr. Higinbotham is a great gentleman, but you

know little of him, and he knows nothing of you. What
Brighton wants is not a great orator, but one who knows our
local needs. Market-gardeners should be represented by a
market-gardener, one of yourselves." Many of Mr. Higinbotham's supporters thought that he was quite certain of
victory until within a few days of the election. Waking up
they then found it was too late. A week before the poll Mr.
Higinbotham made a speech which was well received. It
was the speech of a statesman, thinking of principles and
looking far ahead. He revived the questions that arose out
of the Darling Grant, and asserted that the supremacy of the
Assembly as the people's House must be vindicated. He
stated plainly that he believed the views of the Protectionist
party to be wrong, but on that point he was prepared to give
way should that party be in the majority. When heckling
time came on, an elector asked the late member's view on
some small local question. Mr. Higinbotham did not understand him, and the matter had to be explained to him there
and then. The questioner was the other candidate's brother.
Careless contempt for their opponent on the part of supporters,
undisguised localism amongst some of the electors, and a
thirst for paying off old scores amongst others produced the
surprise of that General Election. Thus stood the poll :—

Bent 400
Higinbotham . . . 386

———

Majority . . . 14

" Well, how went the election ?" was the question asked at
home. " I am just fourteen votes on the wrong side of the
ledger," was the quiet reply. Freedom, even though somewhat roughly given, was yet not an unwelcome gift. Mr.
Higinbotham was not so well pleased with the turn that political
life was taking, as greatly to regret that for a while he should
be a spectator rather than a sharer in the fray. Since he
had ceased to be Attorney-General he had taken up his work
at the Bar. Even his political opponents allowed that he was
a good barrister, and for a little more than two years he was
only that and nothing more.

After this interval an opportunity was given to him to

enter the political field again. Since the General Election Lieut.-Colonel Champ had been member for the East Bourke Boroughs. It was his second experience of political life, for he had been the first Premier under Responsible Government in Tasmania, but he had abandoned that position in 1857; and coming over to Melbourne had succeeded Colonel Price after the latter's murder by convicts. For eleven years he had been Inspector-General of Penal Establishments in Victoria; then after his resignation, he was tempted in 1871 to make another incursion into politics, but the taste for it soon palled on him, and in May, 1873, he resigned.

Mr. Higinbotham was invited to stand for Colonel Champ's vacancy. After a little hesitation he consented, and addressed the electors on several occasions. At Alphington he strongly condemned assisted immigration, to which twelve years previously he had given a guarded support. The circumstances of the colony had changed. The population had so increased that now the assistance thus given by the State would tend to reduce the wages of the working classes. At Brunswick he strongly defended the doctrine that a member's first duty was to represent and attend to the requirements of the country generally, and only his secondary duty to attend to the needs of his constituency. At another meeting he expressed himself against any reduction of newspaper postage.

The polling took place on May 26th, with this result:—

Higinbotham   . . . 716
Allan Staley 478
                      ———
Majority   . . . 238

The principal measure before Parliament was Mr. Francis' proposal, known as "the Norwegian scheme," that if the Council rejected a measure twice passed by the Assembly, the two Houses should sit together and decide its fate. Mr. Higinbotham was not strongly enamoured of the proposal, but was prepared to support it as an experiment on the sole condition that all money bills should be exempted from its operation. His vote was thus given for the second reading of the measure; but the amendments that he desired not being made in committee, on the third reading he and six others over whom his influence was strong voted against the bill. This gave the Ministry only thirty-five votes against thirty-three for the third reading. According to the Constitution Act an absolute majority of the House was required for any measure effecting an alteration in the constitution of either Council or Assembly, wherefore the bill expired of insufficient support.

At the General Election in April, 1874, Mr. Higinbotham stood his last election, and secured his largest majority. The polling was on April 22nd :—

Higinbotham   . . . 757
Captain Dane   . . . 422
———
Majority   . . . 335

In July, 1875, an address was presented to Mr. Higinbotham thanking him for his statesmanlike conduct, and attacking the Legislative Council, and glancing at a certain weakness in the Assembly. The following was part of his reply :—

Your observations about the present attitude and condition of the Legislative Assembly claims a word in reply from one who is proud of the honour of being a member of that body. Permit me, then, to say to you, the Legislative Assembly has no faults and no shortcomings which are not also political faults and shortcomings of yourselves, and of all other adult men in this community. The Legislative Assembly is just what the people of Victoria have made it ; and although it may not be better, it is assuredly not worse than the source from which it has sprung. If the weakness and subserviency and demoralisation which you seem to think are observable in the Chamber which repre-sents the people should lead the general body of electors to reflect on the like defects in themselves, who are largely responsible as politicians for the consequences they notice and lament, your censure, though it be severe, and even harsh, may work good results ; while its more equal distribution will render it less unjust than, I venture to tell you, it nows appears to me to be in its application exclusively to the Legislative Assembly.

A question which frequently occupied the attention of Parliament and created discord between the Houses was the payment of members. The view of the Upper House and of Conservatives in the Lower was that members should serve from a sense of public duty as in England, and that paid members would be professional politicians. The view of the other side which prevailed in the Lower House was that there was not a sufficiently large leisure class in the colony to provide members as in England; that working men ought to be represented by men of their own class; and that payment of members would help the stability of government. If a government has the power of dissolution, members who care for their salary are reluctant to push it to use that power. The frequent proposal of a vote of want of confidence is the curse of colonial legislatures, and it must be allowed that in Victoria the remedy has been effective partly, but only in part. It is not necessary here to give the history of the struggle. Mr. Higinbotham did not like payment of members, but he voted for it on the grounds just stated, to strengthen the hands of Government, and to increase the power of the working men. Although he voted for the payment, he would never accept it. The money due to him accumulated in the Treasury in his name, until an act was passed sweeping it back into the common stock.

Early in 1876 Mr. Higinbotham withdrew from politics altogether. To understand his reason it is necessary to go back over the history of the preceding six months. Because of ill-health Mr. Francis had retired from the position of Premier, and had gone to England. He was succeeded by Mr. Kerferd, with Mr. James Service as Treasurer. Towards the end of July, 1875, this Ministry gained a victory which seemed no better than a defeat. In a division on an important item of the Budget the Government had a majority of one only in a very full House. Hereupon Mr. Kerferd asked the Acting-Governor, Sir William Stawell, for a dissolution; but he refused on the ground that the possibilities of the House had not been exhausted, for this was practically the same Ministry as that of Mr. Francis, which had been in power at the time of the General Election fifteen months earlier. On receiving this answer Ministers resigned, and His Excellency sent for Mr. Graham Berry. This Ministry remained in power less than eleven weeks, and left office very indignant with the Acting-Governor because to it also he had refused a dissolution, on the strange ground that it would be unfair to grant it after having declined to do so to the preceding Ministry, as there did not seem sufficient difference between them. Sir William Stawell must have afterwards regretted this decision, for the supporters of Mr. Berry began to show the difference that he had sought in vain. The new Premier was Sir James McCulloch, now Premier for the fourth time; but time had wrought a change, and Sir James was now the leader of the Conservative or Constitutional party. The country thought that Mr. Berry had been badly treated; and when the new Ministers sought re-election two of them were defeated by large majorities, in large and important constituencies, and the Premier himself had to fight for his seat. Moreover at the General Election in the following May Mr. Berry's supporters swept the constituencies, and he returned to power with an enormous majority. In the interval between October and March, as a protest against the action of the Acting-Governor, the "Stonewall" policy was invented and carried out. The Opposition determined not only that the Government should not carry its measures, but that no business should be done. The stonewall that they would erect was to strain with the forms of the House, and to talk against time. No true lover of Parliamentary institutions could see this unmoved; and Mr. Higinbotham, after ten weeks of it, resigned his seat, telling his constituents what he had done in a dignified letter.

The question may be asked why Mr. Higinbotham did not go with his former leader, Sir James McCulloch, and help to break down the stonewall. He had always avowed that his policy was to improve governments by support. Why did he not support and improve this? The answer is that there had been a breach between the two. When Sir James was about to form his Ministry after defeating Mr. Berry, Mr. Higinbotham spoke strongly on a constitutional question, finding fault with Sir James. Even his friends thought his remarks injudicious. Sir James was irritated, and in reply attacked his former colleague, accusing him of "placing sham motions on the notice paper to bring about an unsatisfactory state of matters with the Imperial Government." This reply sent Mr. Higinbotham into opposition to the new government, for it was not only unsatisfactory in substance, but offensive in manner. A member who was present says that the language as reported in the calm pages of *Hansard* conveys but little idea of what took place. The impression left on Mr. Higinbotham's mind was that the former leader had ceased to be true to the principles of his own side in the earlier contest.

On the last day (January 20th, 1876) on which Mr. Higinbotham spoke in the House, he spoke twice. He urged the Government to appoint a commission, or take some other means, to collect information which is obtainable in respect to school books, school furniture, and the training of teachers, for the purpose of applying that information for the benefit of the State schools of Victoria. Later he joined in the debate on the dissolution, speaking especially upon the conduct of the Attorney-General in taking office when his previous advice had not been accepted by the representative of the Crown. The concluding words have a pathos of their own, and a warning note that deserves attention :—

The fact is we have all been at it for the last twenty years. We have all been struggling for office—all of us—and in that struggle we have forgotten everything. We have forgotten our duty as legislators; we have forgotten our rights as a Legislative Assembly ; we have forgotten our duty to the representative of the Crown—to keep him and maintain him in the place where the law has put him ; and having forgotten all these things, why now we have nothing else to do, but to recriminate upon one another. (Hear, hear.) Oh yes, we are all guilty. We are all like common scolds in this House ; and I think the sooner we go back to our constituents and confess the grave offences that, individually and collectively, we have been guilty of, the better."

It takes away from the sting of a reproof if the speaker includes himself among those reproved. But in this case the orator did himself injustice. It is quite true that there had been, and there continued to be, much office-seeking and much contention for that end, but the bitterest opponent of Mr. Higinbotham, as a politician, could never say that he had fought to obtain office or struggled to retain it. He loathed such struggling, and never ceased to protest against it. When the House next met the Speaker announced that he had received the resignation of Mr. Higinbotham. Next morning the following letter was published :—

To the Electors of the District of East Bourke Boroughs.

Gentlemen,—

I beg respectfully to acquaint you that I have this day conveyed to the Speaker of the Legislative Assembly the resignation of my seat as the member for your district.

I have been constrained to take this course through the present state of affairs in Parliament and my own position as your member in relation to them.   A contest involving a single and now unalterable issue has been commenced between the Opposition in the Legislative Assembly and the Government, and the course of public business and the progress of legislation are in consequence suspended.   I concur with the Opposition in its desire that there should be an immediate dissolution of Parliament and an appeal to the people, but I am unable to approve the course which it intends to pursue for the purpose of attaining that object.   That a minority in a deliberative body should employ the forms which have been adopted to aid and guide its deliberations in such a manner as to defeat or coerce a hostile majority, appears to me to be a course inconsistent with the principles which lie at the foundation of all deliberative action and of political society itself, and to be one that may only be resorted to, if at all, for a limited time, and in very extraordinary circumstances, such as do not, in my opinion, exist at present.   I am therefore unable to co-operate with the Opposition. I have now as little difficulty in determining on the other hand that I ought not to join the side of the Government in this quarrel.   The explanations which the Administration at present in power has given, and the far more necessary explanations respecting its own origin, its party engagements, and its legislative policy, which it has persistently withheld from the public representatives, have convinced me that a Government so constituted and so supported is wholly undeserving of the confidence of Parliament.   My own feeling towards it is one of distrust so deep and confirmed that I cannot permit myself, as a representative, to follow its guidance for even the shortest time, or in order to effect the most legitimate purpose.

It is not permitted to a member of Parliament to be a mere onlooker in Parliamentary war.   It is his first duty to take his place and bear his part in the strife on the one side or the other, and the weight of this obligation increases in exact proportion to the importance of the issue.   I find that it is impossible for me, in the present emergency, to fulfil this duty by joining the ranks of either side, and I think that I should be doing a wrong to you if I continued at this time to hold the office, while I abstained from performing the duties of a representative. I have therefore resigned my seat.

Allow me to return you my sincere acknowledgments for the confidence you have reposed in me, and to express my grateful sense of the forbearing and generous consideration you have displayed towards me during the time I have had the honour to represent you in Parliament.

I remain, Gentlemen,
Your faithful servant,
GEO. HIGINBOTHAM.

Brighton, 24th January, 1876.

Within a week of his resignation, Mr. Higinbotham explained his conduct to his constituents at Brunswick in an interesting speech, which occupied six columns of next morning's papers. There is not room enough for it here, and the gist of it is contained in the above letter. One passage has been often quoted, but as it has been usual to stop the quotation too soon, the whole is given :—

Ever since I became a politician, if I disliked one thing more than another, was dissatisfied with one thing more than another in politics, it is what is called by the name of party government, which has assumed and has been assuming for years, the position of mere frantic struggles of conflicting factions. It matters little or nothing to the people of this country at this time, who is in the Government. I protest to you, gentlemen, that if you sent out the bellman into the streets, and let him select fifty men from whom to choose by ballot nine Ministers of the Crown, I believe that nine Ministers would be elected who would be quite as well deserving of the confidence of the people of this country as any of those Ministers who have been competing for power for years past. And I say that with no personal disrespect to those who have been competing for office, but for the purpose of expressing my conviction that official life does not demand the possession of those extraordinary qualities which are not to be found in the mass of our fellow-citizens.

Several later attempts were made to persuade him to come forward for different constituencies, but he declined all overtures. Even until in July, 1880, four and a half years later, he took his seat on the Bench, some of his admirers entertained a hope that he would come forward and lead a united Liberal party, but it was not so to be ; and the last day of January, 1876, witnessed his final retirement from the domain of practical politics.

CHAPTER XX

LATER DEVELOPMENT OF VIEW ABOUT THE COLONIAL OFFICE

The Morgan case—As to the Prerogative of Mercy—Three times put aside from acting as Governor—(1) Sir William Stawell appointed Lieutenant-Governor—Correspondence with Lord Knutsford—Is the first letter confidential?—Correspondence with Sir Henry Loch—(2) Sir William Robinson appointed—(3) Commission appointing Mr. Justice Williams—True Work of Colonial Office—Letter to Mr. Richardson—Letter to Lord Knutsford.

On leaving Parliament Mr. Higinbotham never would allow that he had ceased to be a practical politician. When he became a judge he still declared himself a politician first, not of course a party politician, but he claimed also and with justice, that he never had been that. The unlawful interference of the Colonial Office he resented from the Bench as from a seat in Parliament. When offered a judgeship he made it a condition with the Government that he was not to be called upon to obey instructions that seemed to him an illegal interference with responsible government.

The difficulty that he had anticipated occurred in the Morgan case. A man named Henry Morgan, who had committed a murder, was tried in May, 1884, at the Warrnambool Assizes before Mr. Justice Higinbotham, and received sentence of death. The instructions were very explicit as to the course a Governor was to pursue in the case of capital sentences. He was to require the judge "to make to him a written report of the case," and to cause the judge to be specially summoned to attend a meeting of the Executive Council, and to produce his notes. Finally, he was to decide either "to extend or to withhold a pardon or reprieve according to his own deliberate judgment." In other words he was not to play the part of a constitutional sovereign. Mr. Justice Higinbotham was perfectly willing to attend the Executive Council, to produce his notes, and to furnish a report, if he were required so to do by "lawful authority,"— that is, by Her Majesty's Ministers for Victoria. The correspondence between the judge and the Attorney-General was published. The judge's wish was respected, and no mention of the instructions given as the reason for his attendance; but the Attorney-General was thought to have "scored" in the following passage which seems a reminiscence of the famous "officer in my department":—

In my opinion it would be disastrous in the extreme if a government allowed any officer of the State, however highly placed, unasked, to indicate to the Government its duty, or to request an assurance that it had adopted a specific course. I respectfully but firmly submit that as a judge of the Supreme Court you are entitled to assume that Her Majesty's Government would make no improper request, and that the Attorney-General, in communicating with you officially, is doing so with a full knowledge of his constitutional responsibility.

On this point however the judge could easily allow the Attorney-General to score, for on the main point he had won. In no later summons to him were the instructions ever quoted. The offending instruction has since been cancelled, and the point for which Mr. Higinbotham contended, wholly ceded; but as late as September, 1885, in what is known as the Wantabadgery case, the Governor of the neighbouring colony of New South Wales, pardoned a criminal contrary to the advice of his Executive Council. Such an exercise of the Prerogative of Mercy would, in Victoria, have led to the resignation of Ministers.

In the middle of 1884 Sir Henry Loch arrived as Governor, and it is no breach of confidence to say that his manly, soldierly character soon attracted Mr. Higinbotham, whilst the undisputed charm of the latter's society gained the affectionate regard of Sir Henry Loch. A little after Sir Henry's arrival, Mr. Higinbotham became Chief Justice, but the late Chief Justice, Sir William Stawell, was appointed Lieutenant-Governor. At the time, it was made to appear that this was only a suitable compliment to pay to so old and trusted a public servant as Sir William Stawell, and the new

Chief Justice quite acquiesced in the appointment. In New South Wales a similar compliment had been paid to Sir Alfred Stephen.

It should be stated here that it is usual in the colonies for the name of the Chief Justice to stand in the Dormant Commission. In other words, if the Governor were suddenly to die, the Chief Justice would become Governor; and if the Governor goes out of the colony, unless for a very brief holiday, his place is taken by the Chief Justice. But this rule is by no means without exceptions, and then a Lieutenant-Governor is appointed.

After a while it became evident that Sir William Stawell's health would not allow him to hold the appointment and that if by any chance the governorship came to him, his medical attendants would have to recommend his immediate resignation. Sir Henry Loch, in the course of conversation with the Chief Justice, asked him if he would mind writing out for Sir Henry Holland, then Secretary of State for the Colonies, the grounds of his complaint against the Colonial Office. This Mr. Higinbotham consented to do, and he forwarded through the Governor a paper, which discusses the whole question with great fulness. After an interval of nearly two years it was published by the Chief Justice in the *Argus*, but no copy of the number of the newspaper in which it was printed can now be procured, and as the paper is of importance and has achieved results, it is given as an appendix to this chapter.

Nearly a year passed before any notice was taken of the letter, although in the interval an offer of knighthood was made to the Chief Justice, and courteously declined. When Lord Knutsford—under which title Sir Henry Holland had been raised to the peerage—did reply, he spoke of the letter as a "confidential report." Now this was the last thing in the world that the writer intended it to be. Correspondence then ensued, chiefly turning on the question whether the letter should be treated as confidential. The writer of a letter has the right to claim that it be confidential, but has the recipient? In a later letter by the Chief Justice occurs a passage in which his views about the Colonial Office are summed up in the words, "the sinister and clandestine policy which the office over which you preside has successfully pursued for the third part of a century." In the same letter he remarked, "no doubt you may probably consider the subject quite insignificant." Lord Knutsford replied :

> Where, or how, have I shown that I considered the subject "insignificant." ? So very much the reverse is the case that after consulting the law officers, I have redrafted "instructions," with a view of meeting many of the points which you brought under my notice, and of bringing them more into conformity with the existing state of things. I regret the use of such phrases as "clandestine" and "sinister" with respect to the policy of the Home Government.

It is only right to say that the phrases were applied not to the Government, strictly so called, but to the permanent officials of the Colonial Office.

Before this correspondence had closed, another connected with it was commenced by the Governor, Sir Henry Loch. He had tried to remove difficulties by asking the Chief Justice to express his views to the head of the Colonial Office. It was quite evident, however, this removal of difficulties was to be a matter of time, if it could be done at all. The Colonial Office does not move rapidly. In July, 1888, Lord Knutsford had redrafted instructions. He went out of office in 1892, and one of his last official acts was the issue of the new instructions. The new edition appeared in the *Melbourne Government Gazette* in September of that year. The improvement was enormous. For the first time Responsible Government is recognised. For the first time the Governor is instructed to accept the advice of his Ministers, whereas all earlier editions seem to imply that he is to be careful about accepting such advice and ready to oppose them.

The object of the new correspondence was chiefly to ask the Chief Justice whether, if he became Acting-Governor, he would be willing to communicate with the Colonial Office by despatches upon matters of domestic policy, as the English Law Officers maintained that such correspondence was not illegal. The Chief Justice said he would not correspond; and the Colonial Office decided that he was again to be superseded. Sir Henry Loch was anxious to visit England partly for a holiday, partly on public and private business. It should be added that the Colonial Office acted with delicacy in selecting an Acting-Governor from outside the colony. The term of office of Sir William Robinson as Governor of South Australia was drawing to a close. It was therefore decided that when Sir Henry Loch went, Sir William Robinson should take his place. When this decision was made known, the Chief Justice published the correspondence. He never for a moment disputed the right of the Colonial Office to appoint a Governor or an Acting-Governor, but he wished the public to know for what reasons his appointment was distasteful to the Colonial Office.

Towards the end of 1892 the case was repeated. Lord Hopetoun wished to go away for a holiday to visit New Zealand. His wish being made known to the Colonial Office, a commission appointing the Senior Puisne Judge, Mr. Justice (now Sir Hartley) Williams, to the position of Acting-Governor, was sent out. Lord Hopetoun's tour was to begin in January, 1893, and before that month opened the Chief Justice died, and his successor became Acting-Governor. Mr. Higinbotham had made arrangements to swear in Mr. Justice Williams, to whom, as to Lord Hopetoun, he explained that he entertained no personal feeling whatever about being superseded. George Higinbotham had not the smallest desire to be Governor of the Colony; but he resented the insult to his office of Chief Justice in being put aside, solely because he was resolute to uphold his view of the constitutional law. A remark to this effect was almost the last I ever heard from his lips.

It is sometimes said that Mr. Higinbotham wished to abolish the Colonial Office. Nothing would be further from the truth. He wished to confine it to its proper work, and believed, it is quite evident, that this proper work would be better done if it abstained from encroachments.

In November, 1888, the Government of Queensland protested against the appointment of Sir Henry Blake as Governor, and claimed that colonial ministries should be consulted before the appointment of a Governor. Colonial opinion varied on the subject; but Mr. Higinbotham, as well as all the Victorian statesmen, held that the Colonial Office was perfectly right in resisting this claim. The *Times* said: "If the right be once conceded to Colonial Ministers of laying objections to any appointment before the Secretary of State, it is almost inconceivable that a duty will not be inferred on the part of the Secretary of State to yield to those objections whether reasonable or unreasonable." Against this, Mr. Higinbotham wrote in the margin, " Right."

But on the Colonial Office's true position on this and similar questions, there is more definite evidence than a word scribbled on a chance-preserved fragment of newspaper. In 1885, when many in the colonies were eager and angry on the New Guinea question, how discriminatingly Mr. Higinbotham reviewed the position is seen in the following letter to a Victorian politician :—

Brighton, Melbourne,
April 6th, 1885.

My dear Mr. Richardson,—

I think it is probable that you have paid closer attention than I have done to the course of events connected with the subject on which you ask me for my opinion, and I fear therefore that I may not be able by communicating my views to aid you much in removing or lightening your difficulties. I am sensible that for more than a year past my sympathies have become more and more estranged from the claims and opinions which have been generally regarded as the prevailing claims and opinions of Australian politicians.

At the meeting in the Town Hall in July, 1883, to which you refer, two views were put forward by the speakers, and were cordially received and adopted by the meeting. One was a protest against the proposal of the French Government to send criminals in increased numbers to New Caledonia. With regard to that question I may say that I think that the Imperial Government, stimulated by the able and zealous Agents-General of the Australian Colonies, has done all that could fairly be expected of it. It remains for us, if the Récidiviste Bill should become law, to meet it by legislation of our own in the nature of quarantine legislation. We should be clearly within our rights in taking that course, and I hope that Victoria, if she should stand alone, will not shrink from taking it. The unauthorized annexation of New Guinea by the Queensland Government was also dealt with by the meeting. The speakers endeavoured to excuse that clearly illegal act, and to induce the Imperial Government to ratify it in view of the importance of establishing a more effectual control by England over the so-called labour traffic, and of preventing the slave traffic and slavery (we need not mince words) from becoming an Australian trade and gaining a footing on Australian soil. In view of these two objects, and these alone, the Town Hall meeting expressed its desire, which then and ever since has been the desire of all Victorians, that the Imperial Government should aid us in guarding against two great dangers, and that, if it should be found consistent with Imperial engagements and the maintenance of friendly relations with other European powers, it should annex or extend the protection of England to both New Guinea and the New Hebrides. The resolutions, subsequently passed at the Australian Convention held in Sydney in November and December, 1883, and afterwards approved of by the

Victorian Government, were passed upon the same lines, and while praying for annexation or the establishment of control for similar reasons, they expressly recognised and admitted the fact that the responsibility of extending the boundaries of the Empire belonged to the Imperial Government.

Up to this point no exception could be taken to our aims or to our expressed wishes. Subsequently a marked change took place. We have heard very little for a long time past of the measures to be taken to control the labour traffic. It even seems doubtful whether the colonies will faithfully carry out the limited promises of pecuniary contributions which were cautiously and somewhat grudgingly given to the Imperial Government. Writers in the public press after a time ceased to advocate merely, and began, frequently in intemperate language, to demand annexation. Claims have been repeatedly and publicly made in and on behalf of all the Australian Colonies of an alleged right in these colonies to insist upon Great Britain annexing New Guinea and all the islands of the Western Pacific, founded upon our prior possession of this Australian Continent. Not very long ago regret was expressed in the leading columns of the *Argus* that Queensland had not kept, by its own authority, possession of New Guinea, which it had taken in the name, but without the sanction, of Her Majesty. The New Zealand Government, you may remember, avowedly made preparations for annexing Samoa. Now these claims and acts are one and all of them open outrages upon the public law, international and municipal, which binds all these colonies. The seizure and occupation by a civilized nation of the territory of uncivilized men is a wrongful and a criminal act, certain to result in the debasement and ultimately in the extinction of the weaker people, and only to be excused by the very pressing needs of the occupying state. In this work of annexation all civilized nations alike are robbers ; but law holds its place even amongst robbers, and it is clear that according to this law no civilized people has a right to claim for itself without occupying a country unoccupied by civilized men to the exclusion of another civilized people who desire and intend to occupy that country. Priority of possession constitutes the sole title as between civilized nations. Yet this is the claim which we Australians in view of our own supposed future interests have presumed to put forward on behalf of England, and thanks to the imbecility of the Colonial Office we have been allowed to do so without a word of rebuke or disclaimer by the Imperial Government. Two courses were open to the Colonial Office ; one was to accede promptly to the wishes of Australia, and to annex or take under the protection of Great Britain the whole of the Eastern part of New Guinea. If that had been done Germany would have made no complaint because she had then advanced no claim. The other course was to tell us kindly but firmly and with all plainness that while our wishes should be considered favourably, they must be subordinated to the general policy and also to the existing special engagements of the Crown of England ; that we could not be permitted to advance claims and to commit unauthorised acts for which England might be held responsible by other

Powers, and that if we insisted upon acting independently in extra-territorial questions without the sanction of the Imperial Government, we must accept the responsibilities of complete independence and submit to be dis-annexed from the parent state. Frank language of this kind might have been addressed, I believe, without fear of ill consequences, to these communities. It would not have incensed the general body of the people in any of them. It would have opened the eyes of our politicians and awakened in them some sense of international responsibility and some recognition of the obligations of public law. Above all it would have anticipated and prevented the disaster which the arrogant words and acts of colonial politicians and public writers have brought about, namely, the just irritation and estrangement from England of that great kindred power whose cordial friendship and co-operation in every part of the world it should be England's constant policy to secure.

I think it is now demonstrated that our ill-advised and reckless acts and language, not corrected but tacitly encouraged by the vacillation and panic fears of the English Colonial and Foreign Offices, have contributed largely to producing in Germany a just sense of distrust of England. Happily they have not prevented Germany, whose good neighbourhood and friendship in this hemisphere we Australians should be first to welcome, from exercising her undoubted right of occupying that part of New Guinea which England had announced her intention not to occupy. As Englishmen we must all be humiliated to feel that in the diplomatic struggle that is just coming to an end those qualities which we should all like to claim for England and for English administration in the eyes of the world—justice, reasonableness, frankness, courage, vigilance, zeal, practical good sense—are all found upon the side of her successful and now contemptuous opponent. We Australians, who have been a principal effective cause of this national disgrace, have come off, in my opinion, far better than we deserve. Papua will not be a new hunting-ground for the slave traffickers. We shall have gained the best possible neighbours. That is the happy end of a piece in which Australia and England have each played a most sorry part.

The incidents of this New Guinea affair have a very important bearing, as it seems to me, on the subject of Federation, to which more immediately you call my attention. They present to my mind a powerful illustration of one aspect of a very remarkable fact which should not be lost sight of for an instant. When we are considering the various meanings of that ambiguous term "Federation," and the numerous and confusing forms in which the idea of Federation is brought before us, the fact is this: that in all these Australian colonies ever since they acquired responsible government (it was quite otherwise before that time) Australian politicians have been, as a rule, profoundly indifferent to the highest questions of public law; they have always been utterly careless about the intrigues that have been incessantly and most successfuly carried on by the officials of the Colonial Office against their legal rights of self-government in local affairs, while these recent events have shown that they can for an insufficient cause and on merely momentary impulse exhibit a reckless disregard of the obligations imposed upon them by that same public law, heedless indifference about our political rights, on which political progress and even material prosperity largely depend, light-hearted disregard of our political obligations, which may involve, according as they are observed or not observed, the union or the disruption of the Empire or the peace of the world. I would that we could efface from our minds as politicians these two most dangerous modes of thought or rather no-thought, and that we could substitute for them a jealous and ever watchful care of our rights of self-government against the slightest attempt at encroachment either by intrigue or open violence, and a loyal, cheerful and contented submission to those slight restrictions and practically unfelt limitations of equal rights which are necessarily attached to our position as members of communities, separated by space and by space only from our countrymen in the home household.

You are dissatisfied with the proposal for an Imperial federation. I fully concur with you, and I think there is ground for serious alarm as well as dissatisfaction in that proposal, but you desire, you say, a federation of the colonies, by means of which the colonies shall have a controlling voice—at all events a voting power --in all Imperial questions. We have not yet been told how this idea can be accomplished. The difficulties in the way appear to be inherent in the nature of the case and to be insuperable. I have yet to learn that any reason exists for attempting the task of accomplishing it. I venture to believe that the great bulk of the people in these colonial communities have no desire to be represented either in the British Parliament or in any Colonial Council on the subject of the campaign in the Soudan, or of the war with Russia, or even upon the question of German settlement in New Guinea. And why not? I suppose it is because we are content, with reference to all questions in which we have no separate or special interest, to leave the decision of them to the Central Government of the Imperial Parliament, while as regards matters on which we may have distinct interests or views we know that a representative could not by his single voice and vote—and ought not to be allowed to—do more than convey our wishes or views, and that we at present possess in our Agents-General and through the Press an equally effective and sufficient means of communication. As a colonist myself I do not feel, and until I received your letter I had not heard of any Victorian who did feel, the slightest desire to be represented in any colonial federative body created to deal with Imperial questions. It is a soothing and also a very sober-ing thought, that if any of these colonies at any time wishes to become independent and take a direct part in the affairs of nations and the world, it will certainly be allowed to assume independ-ence without any forcible opposition on the part of the mother country. The truth is that no sane politician who thought for a moment of the heavy burdens and the tremendous risk entailed by separation from Great Britain would dream of proposing it, even if he were not, as ninety-nine out of every hundred of us are, attached to and proud of the union that exists at present, and ready and desirous of putting up with a great deal for the sake of preserving it. War between Great

Britain and another great power, it is said, brings to us expenses and risks, and yet we have no voice in the determining whether there shall be peace or war. That is true, but it is also true that our country " seeks peace and ensues it " more than most of the countries of the world, and that during the lengthened period in recent times of England's peace as compared with the short period of her wars we enjoy supreme benefits from her protection. Deprived of the protection and alliance of England every community on this continent would be an almost helpless prey to any European power that might choose to pick a quarrel with it, and could, without impediment from England, transport an army to our shores. Apart from sentiment, we get from the old country many more benefits both in time of peace and of war than we give to her. It is our clear interest to cleave to her so long as she is willing to leave to us freedom ; and it is, in my opinion, quite an insignificant detraction from the advantages of union that the British Parliament, and not the Colonial Parliaments or Federal Assemblies, the head and not the extremities, must govern the movements of the colonial frame so long as it continues a living organism. You will see therefore that I cannot remove your difficulty upon this question of federation. I can only tell you that I am not myself sensible of it ; it is not a difficulty to me. You say that you are disappointed because you cannot act in the New Guinea affair. I can only reply that I have not the faintest desire to act in it, though I do wish, as an Englishman and a colonist, that some one else besides Lord Derby had had the conduct of it for the sake both of England and Australia.

I am very glad to learn that you distrust the Imperial Federation Scheme. You say that it appears to be popular. But for your statement I should not have thought that it had taken any hold on the public mind in Victoria. It seems to me to be a significant fact that this idea originated not in Australia but in London. Schemes professedly for the welfare of the colonies having this origin deserve to be regarded with deepest suspicion, even when they are supported, as this is, by men of indisputable integrity and good faith. Earl Grey's and Mr. Forster's proposals for a consultative council in London to confer with the Secretary of State with or without executive powers, carry their condemnation on the face of them ; the intention of their framers we are bound to believe is good, but the most certain effect of adopting them will be to transfer power from Melbourne and the capitals of the other colonies to London, and to hide a little longer by this new device the illegal assumption by the Secretary of State of a right of interference in our local affairs by the exercise of coercive authority over the Queen's Representative. Sitting at such a Council Board the Australian Agents-General would have really less influence than they have at present. They would in fact be subject in a greater or less degree, like the members of the India Board, to the control of the Secretary of State, and the Board, like our own Board of Land and Works, would serve the purpose of a screen, and shelter the Minister from responsibility and criticism. I earnestly trust that the members of our Legislative Assembly will jealously watch this movement, and that they will not tolerate the making of laws or regulations in England that will be used to undermine the foundations of our constitutional systems of government in Australia.

If I seem to have written to you as a politician with undue freedom about Australian politicians, I pray that you will pardon me. I claim the right of still calling myself a Victorian politician, though I have retired from active service, and you may regard what I have written quite as much in the light of confession as of criticism.

I should not have been able to trouble you with so long an answer to your interesting letter, if you had not addressed it to me immediately before the holidays.

Believe me, my dear Mr. Richardson,
Yours very truly,
(Signed)   GEORGE HIGINBOTHAM.

APPENDIX.

Letter to the Right Honourable SIR HENRY T. HOLLAND, BART., G.C.M.G.

MELBOURNE, VICTORIA.
February 28th, 1887.

SIR,—His Excellency Sir Henry B. Loch recently communicated to me your request that I would state confidentially for your information my opinion upon the subject of the instructions which are from time to time given to the Governors of Victoria and the other Australian colonies. I very willingly comply with your request, although I could have wished that the condition of personal confidence had not been attached to it by you, and notwithstanding the fear I entertain that such condition, if you think proper to adhere to it, may deprive my communication of some of the advantage which might be expected to be derived if public attention should be called through it to the subject to which it refers.

(1) Before proceeding to speak of the Governor's instructions it is due both to you and to myself that I should indicate the position I propose to take in endeavouring to comply with your request; and first, I desire that you will observe that I address you in your private capacity as an English politician interested in colonial affairs, and not in your character of Her Majesty's Secretary of State for the Colonies. I cannot allow you to suppose that I think I have any ground for addressing you in your official character, or that I have any intention of seeking or appearing to seek any explanation or redress of grievances (real or supposed) from the Ministerial head of the Colonial Office. Her Majesty's Ministers for Victoria possess the power, and on them alone devolves the supreme and the hitherto neglected duty of vindicating public law in this colony, and of protecting the exalted office of the

P

Queen's representative from the indignity of illegal invasion. I do not propose to present to you any claim or complaint from which it could be inferred that I attempted either to usurp their function or to anticipate their action, or that I am willing to assume any—the very smallest— share of the responsibility which in this matter rests upon them. I merely give you information which I happen to possess, and which I have learned that it is your wish to obtain. Secondly, it is right that you should know that the views which I in my private capacity offer for your information are the views of an individual member only of this community, and that they are not at present generally accepted by, or even known to, any considerable section or class of the population. My attention was first called to this question more than twenty years ago. During the period of five years when I had the honour of holding office as a Minister of the Crown in Victoria I had special and very un- common opportunities of becoming acquainted with the instructions transmitted to the representative of the Crown in this colony, and with the nature and objects of the Colonial Office policy which those instructions seemed to be intended to promote. Ever since that time I have been an attentive observer of their operation and influence. A strong interest was felt by the public in this and cognate subjects at the same comparatively early period. The reso- lution,[1] a copy of which I subjoin, which contains an accurate state- ment of this portion of the public law of Victoria, was submitted with others by me to the Legislative Assembly in the year 1869, and, after a lengthened and animated discussion, in which every prominent politician who was a member of that House of Parliament took part, was passed by a majority of more than two votes to one. But this debate took place after public opinion, clearly expressed at repeated general elections, had sustained a decisive defeat through the action of the Colonial Office. The resolution of the Legislative Assembly was disregarded, and the community, then disheartened, quickly became, and has ever since continued, profoundly indifferent. At the present time no intelligent opinion of any kind whatever exists upon this subject in any section or class of the community. I should mislead you if I allowed you to believe that my individual opinions possess any claim whatever upon your attention founded on their present popularity. I could not affirm that they are at this moment either intelligently approved or intelligently dissented from by a dozen persons out of the whole population of Victoria. Thirdly, any statement of my views on the subject you have indicated must necessarily imply, if it should not plainly express, my condemnation, unqualified and severe, of the con- duct of the Colonial Office, and of the policy which has dictated that conduct towards Victoria and all the other self-governing colonies of Australia during the last thirty years. I request that you will believe that my censure is directed against that policy and conduct, and that it is not intended by me to apply to or include Ministers of the Crown who have presided over that office, excepting those Ministers who, on certain occasions, have come forward, and have openly sanctioned and

---

[1] See p. 161 chapter xviii. Resolution No. 4.

defended the illegal action of their department. The Colonial Office i one of the least known to the public of all the departments of the British Government. Except upon isolated questions connected with, and springing from time to time out of, current events in the history of particular colonies, the action of the Colonial Office is free from public criticism. Its general rules of official conduct and policy are not thought of or inquired into outside the department itself. It is probably true that, owing to this and other causes, a Minister of the Crown is more dependent in this than in any other department upon the assistance and guidance of the permanent heads of his office. It would be unjust to hold such a Minister personally responsible for the effects of a policy of the nature and even of the existence of which he may not be aware. It would probably be no disparagement to even a capable ministerial administrator to suppose that he may be ignorant during his whole term of office of the policy which dictates many of the despatches that are addressed in his name to Australian Governors, or of the precise provisions, the true construction, and the proper application of that public colonial law which those despatches may be intended to overrule or subvert.

2. There are two classes of instructions to Governors of the Australian Colonies— namely, public instructions and private instructions. About the latter nothing is known to the colonial community except what may be inferred from the publication, formerly frequent, of particular despatches by the permission of the Secretary of State for the Colonies. It has been generally believed—and I have little doubt that the belief is well founded—that Governors are required by their private unpublished instructions to report periodically, minutely, and confidentially to the Secretary of State upon all subjects connected with the interests of the colony over which they preside, including all political events, and the acts and characters of persons coming within the sphere of the system of Responsible Government. In addition to these private instructions given from time to time to a Governor, there are general instructions which every Governor brings with him from England to the seat of his Government. It has been the practice in Victoria for more than twenty years, sanctioned, of course, by Her Majesty's Ministers for Victoria, that these instructions, together with the letters patent constituting and appointing the Governor the commander-in-chief —or, since the year 1879, permanently constituting the office of Governor and commander-in-chief —and claiming to confer, define, and prescribe the powers, authorities, and duty of the Governor, should be published in the *Government Gazette*. These general permanent instructions have undergone no substantial or real change for at least thirty-six years. Verbal alterations, numerous and frequent, indicating that constant and minute attention is paid in the Colonial Office to the form of the instructions, are to be found in them all. But a comparison of the letters patent, instructions, and commission issued to the last appointed Australian Governor, with the commission and instructions issued to Sir Charles A. Fitzroy as Governor-in-Chief of New South Wales in the year 1850, will show that no substantial alteration has been made since that year. I have not seen a copy of

an Australian Governor's commission and instructions of an earlier date than 1850. No legislative change necessitating a material alteration of those instructions occurred from the year 1829, when the first Constitution Act, 9 Geo. IV. c. 83, came into operation, down to the year 1850. It is probable, therefore, that the orders given to the officer of the Imperial Government at the time New South Wales ceased to be a mere military settlement, and acquired for the first time the most rudimentary form of civil government, were in substance the same as those which are now issued from the Colonial Office to Her Majesty's representatives in all Australian colonies as lawful, proper, and sufficient guides of their conduct. An English Minister (Lord John Russell), who introduced and carried through the British Parliament the Constitution Statute of Victoria—18 and 19 Vict. c. 55—recognised the fact that the fundamental change which was then made in the public law of this colony imperatively required a corresponding change in the Governor's instructions ; and he promised that the change should be made. The Colonial Office seems to have determined that the change should not be made. It altered the recitals and phraseology in part, but left the instructions unaltered in substance from that time until now.

3. Vast though gradual changes have taken place in the constitutional law of the Australian colonies since the year 1829. By various acts of the Imperial Parliament the self-governing powers of these communities have been from time to time extended, and representative government has been fully established. The last and by far the greatest change was made in Victoria in 1855, and about the same time in the other leading colonies of Australia, by the introduction of responsibility to Parliament of Ministers of the Crown, in addition to Representative Government, which all the colonies had previously possessed. By the terms of the Victorian Constitution Act power is given to the Crown, the Legislative Council, and the Legislative Assembly to make laws in and for Victoria in all cases whatsoever. Ministers chosen by the representative of the Crown advise him in all things relating to the conduct of the ordinary domestic affairs of State and the executive administration of existing laws, with the single exception created by statute law of the giving or withholding of the Royal assent to, or the reservation of, bills. Questions involving Imperial interests, including the control of Her Majesty's military and naval forces, and questions affecting relations with foreign states, do not come within the purview of the Constitution Statute. As regards all such questions, the Governor is still an officer of the Imperial Government, and is bound to obey the instructions given to him either directly from the Crown or through the Secretary of State. With respect to the same questions and interests, Her Majesty's Ministers for Victoria cannot tender responsible advice. They may, if they think fit—they will, so long as rational and friendly relations exist between the two Governments—assist the Imperial officer by all means in their power to perform his duties to the Imperial Government. But with respect to local affairs, subject to the single exception above mentioned, the case is wholly different. The statute does not by express grant convey any powers or

prerogatives to the Governor. But the creation by statute of the system of Responsible Government necessarily involves the vesting in the representative of the Crown, upon his appointment and by virtue of the statute, of all powers and prerogatives of the Crown necessary in the conduct of local affairs and the administration of law. Allow me to request your special attention to this point, that it is by virtue of the Constitution Acts themselves of the Australian colonies—assuming those acts to have created in each of the colonies the system of Responsible Government—that the prerogatives and powers which are necessary for carrying that system into effect and operation are transferred from the Sovereign, and are vested in the representative of the Sovereign. I am aware that it has been urged by those who have desired to uphold the Government by the Colonial Office of these colonies, and who have therefore supported the Governor's instructions in their present form, that, although Responsible Government has been created in the Australian colonies by the Imperial statutes, prerogatives and powers are from time to time conferred on the Governor by the Crown, according to its pleasures by a separate instrument, and not by force of the Act of Parliament. If the policy which the Colonial Office has steadily pursued for the last thirty years has sprung from a real but mistaken belief in this doctrine, and not, as has been more probably conjectured, from the natural but very censurable desire of irresponsible subordinate officers to retain for their department by stratagem a power which they know has been taken away from it by law, it is to be deeply deplored that the Colonial Office has not during that long period sought competent legal advice upon a subject which concerns so nearly its own duties as well as the highest rights and interests of these Australian communities. As a legal proposition, I venture to affirm that the doctrine is wholly untenable and false. If it were true, all the colonial Constitution Statutes would be a dead letter, and all public rights of these communities would depend not upon the grant of Parliament, but upon the will or caprice, exerted from day to day, of the Imperial Minister. Responsible Government cannot exist unless some powers and prerogatives are vested in the representative of the Crown, for the exercise of which Ministers of the Crown, appointed by the Crown, are responsible to Parliament. Hence it follows that the law which creates this system of government itself also conveys such powers and prerogatives as are necessary for carrying into effect the objects for which the system has been created. *Quando lex aliquid concedit, concedere videtur et illud sine quo res ipsa esse non potest.* This is a legal maxim founded on necessity, which, with slight variations of form, is of almost universal application in the construction of grants, of rights and powers, and of property. It applies to statutes as well as to deeds and other instruments. It applies not only to the subject, but also to the Crown, in all cases of statutes passed for the public good, or in which the prerogative is included by necessary implication. And the necessity which compels the application of this rule also supplies the limitation of the rule. The representative of the Crown has vested in him, by force of the Constitution Statute, and by virtue of his appointment as Governor, such powers and prerogatives of the Crown, and only such, as are necessary in the conduct of the ordinary duties and functions of government and the administration of existing laws within the colony. The Governor, in this character of the Queen's representative, and exercising the powers and prerogatives of the Crown vested in him by statute, is legally independent of all external influence and authority, and can be lawfully guided only by the advice of his responsible ministers. The Crown cannot resume to itself, or to its Imperial advisers, any powers which have been withdrawn from it or from them by a statute to which the Crown has been a party. Neither can the Crown or the Secretary of State lawfully impose any restriction upon the exercise of the Governor's inherent powers. Government by means of advisers responsible to Parliament exists in England by common law. In the Australian colonies that same system of government has been created by statute. There is a difference of historical origin, but with this exception, and the limitation to local affairs, and the exception of the reservation of bills passed by the Australian Parliaments, the analogy between the British and the colonial systems of government, and between the Sovereign in England and the representative of the Sovereign in England, is, I believe, complete.

4. The radical vice of the Governor's letters patent, commission, and instructions, both public and private, appears to me to be this—that they studiously and persistently refuse to take note of the fundamental change made in the public laws of the Australian colonies by the Constitution Acts of 1854-5. In particular, they pretend to confer powers and authorities which have been already conferred with others by the Constitution Statutes; they decline to recognise the dual character of the Governor, and, applying a misleading title to the advisers of the Governor in one of his two characters, they affect to ignore altogether the existence of Responsible Government. I will refer to particular clauses which present the most striking illustrations of a violation in these respects of constitutional law.

Clause II. of the letters patent —

" We do hereby authorise, empower, and command our said Governor and Commander-in-Chief (hereinafter called the Governor) to do and execute all things that belong to his said office, according to the tenor of these our letters patent, and of such commission as may be issued to him under our sign manual and signet, and according to such instructions as may from time to time be given to him under our sign manual and signet, or by our order in our Privy Council, or by us through one of our principal Secretaries of State, and to such laws as are now or shall hereafter be in force in the colony."

This purports to grant, subject to limitations, certain authorities and powers already vested in the Governor by the Constitution Statute. The grant is, in my opinion, void, and the limitations and the commands founded thereon are also void and illegal.

Clause VI. of instructions—

" In the exercise of the powers and authorities granted to the Governor by our said letters patent, he shall in all cases consult with the Executive Council, excepting only in cases which are of such a nature that, in his judgment, our service would sustain material prejudice by consulting the said council thereupon, or when the matters to be decided are too unimportant to require their advice, or too urgent to admit of their advice being given by the time within which it may be necessary for him to act in respect to any such matters—in all such urgent cases, he shall, at the earliest practical period, communicate to the said Council the measures which he may so have adopted, with the reasons thereof."

This is an instruction which a Governor does not, and cannot, obey. The Executive Council, in the proper sense of this expression, has never been convened in Victoria. Like the Privy Council, it could not be convened except by the direction of the Victorian Premier. If by the words " Executive Council " the " Cabinet " is intended to be referred to, this instruction is unmeaning and void. It is, doubtless, the duty of the representative of the Sovereign to consult his advisers, and it is their duty to advise him in all matters connected with local affairs, but the duty in neither case springs from this Royal instruction. If it be intended to direct the Governor to consult his advisers in matters connected with his duty as an officer of the Imperial Government, this is an indirect instruction, offensive in form and without either legal authority or means of enforcement to Her Majesty's Ministers to do something which they are not required by their duty as Ministers of the Crown to do.

Clause VII. of instructions—

" A Governor may act in the exercise of the powers and authorities granted to him by our said letters patent in opposition to the advice given to him by the members of the Executive Council, if he shall in any case deem it right to do so, but in any such case he shall fully report the matter to us by the first convenient opportunity, with the grounds and reasons of his action."

I think that this instruction can only be characterised as a distinct denial of the fundamental principle of the existing public law of Victoria. As a direct instigation to Her Majesty's representative to violate that law it offers a grave indignity and conveys an unmistakable menace to him and to his advisers, who are here and elsewhere misnamed the Executive Council.

Clause XI of instructions—

" Whenever any offender shall have been condemned to suffer death by the sentence of any court, the Governor shall call upon the judge who presided at the trial to make to him a written report of the case of such offender, and shall cause such report to be taken into consideration at the first meeting thereafter which may be conveniently held of the Executive Council, and he may cause the said judge to be specially summoned to attend at such meeting and to produce his notes thereat. The Governor shall not pardon or reprieve any such offender unless it shall appear to him expedient so to do upon receiving the advice of the said Executive Council thereon; but in all such cases he is to decide either to extend or to withhold a pardon or a reprieve according to his own deliberate judgment, whether the members of the Executive Council concur therein or otherwise; entering nevertheless on the minutes of the said Executive Council a minute of his reasons at length, in case he should decide such action in opposition to the judgment of the majority of members thereof."

This instruction presents a glaring instance of not less flagrant illegality. The prerogative of mercy is a prerogative essentially necessary to the administration of criminal law. The exercise of it in Victoria is therefore a matter in which the representative of the Crown can and ought to act solely upon the advice of his responsible advisers, and neither the Crown nor the Crown's Imperial advisers are legally competent to dictate or advise upon his action. By this instruction the Governor is personally ordered to call upon the judge to make to him a written report—an order which, if it were conveyed otherwise than through and by the advice of the Minister, it would be, I conceive, the duty of the judge to refuse to comply with. The Governor is further required to decide "either to extend or to withhold a pardon or reprieve, according to his own deliberate judgment, whether the members of the Executive Council concur therein or otherwise." This unjust and cruel as well as illegal order is not obeyed, and could not be obeyed, by any Governor in the only cases to which it could apply. It has been attempted to excuse this instruction on the ground that it is virtually obsolete, yet on two separate occasions long subsequent to the passing of the Australian Constitution Acts, the Colonial Office has expressed its approval of this instruction, and has repeated the injunction to the Governor to obey it.

Clauses VIII. and X. of instructions—

"VIII. In the execution of such powers as are vested in the Governor by law for assenting to or dissenting from or of reserving for the signification of our pleasure, bills which have been passed by the Legislature of the colony, he shall take care as far as may be practicable that in the passing of all laws each different matter be provided for by a different law without intermixing in one and the same law such things as have no proper relation to each other; and that no clause be inserted in or annexed to any law which shall be foreign to what the title of such law imports, and that no perpetual clause be part of any temporary law." "X. The Governor is to take care that all laws assented to in our name, or reserved for the signification of our pleasure thereon, shall, when transmitted by him, be fairly abstracted in the margins, and be accompanied, in such cases as may seem to him necessary, with such explanatory observations as may be required to exhibit the reasons and occasions for proposing such laws; and shall also transmit fair copies of the journals and minutes of the proceedings of the legislative bodies of the colony, which he is to require from the clerks or other proper officers in that behalf of the said legislative bodies."

These clauses are not illegal because they relate to the reservation of bills for the signification of Her Majesty's pleasure. I refer to them only as showing the almost contemptuous disrespect and want of consideration displayed by the Colonial Office towards Australian Parliaments and Imperial officers in Australia. To order a governor to take care that in the passing of all laws each different matter shall be provided for by a different law may at one time have been proper and not unnecessary. Addressed, as the order indirectly is, to Legislatures consisting of two Houses of Parliament like the Legislative Council and the Legislative Assembly of the various Australian colonies, it is an insult to all of those bodies. And it has proved on one occasion, at least, a cause of actual embarrassment to Her Majesty's Government in Victoria. When the Governor is ordered to require from the clerks in Parliament fair copies of the journals and minutes of the proceedings of the Legislative bodies, he is humiliated by being needlessly instructed to make a requirement which, if disputed, he could not enforce, and for the fulfilment of which he is in any and in every case indebted to the aid (which is, of course, never withheld) of a Minister of the Crown.

5. I cannot allow you, Sir, to suppose that I waste time and attention upon the obscure phraseology of documents which do not in fact possess most real influence, and have not been and are not attended with important practical consequences. It has been alleged by way of excuse for the culpable inattention of all Australian Governments to this question that the instructions to a governor are, as a whole, obsolete, and that they are not intended by the Colonial Office, which continues to issue them, to have effect, or to exercise controlling influence on the action of the representative of the Crown. If such be the views of the Colonial Office, infinite relief would be afforded by an official and public intimation of them. I have a confident assurance that the Colonial Office entertains no such views, and that it will not, unless it is compelled, give such an intimation. I entertain no doubt whatever that the published instructions have been maintained by the Colonial Office in their present form for the last thirty years solely for the purpose of asserting, and with the intention of enforcing whenever it is deemed possible and prudent to do so, the claim of this department of the Imperial Government to control the representative of the Crown in the exercise of all his functions and authorities alike, and that it is the wish and intention of the Colonial Office that the Governor shall always and in everything fulfil the oath which he has taken to obey his instructions, whether they be legal or illegal, up to the point, but no further, at which compliance with his instructions and disobedience to the law of the land consequent thereon might involve the risk of comment, followed by exposure and rejection of the illegal claim of the Colonial Office. But whatever may be the views or intentions of the irresponsible officers who from time to time, as permanent heads, administer the policy of the Colonial Office, there is no doubt that that policy has

had, and still has, a vast, though at present silent, influence upon the national life of this and all the other Australian communities, and that that influence has been, and is, exercised chiefly by the instructions, public and private, which have been issued to governors from the Colonial Office. It is a fact within my personal knowledge that Colonial Office influence was strenuously exerted in this manner in Victoria from about the year 1864 to the year 1868. At that time the Colonial Office first endeavoured by means of instructions to the Governor to check and prevent legislation on the subject of the tariff. When that question led to a contest between the two Houses of the Victorian Legislature the Colonial Office influence was exerted in favour of one House as against the other House, and against the will of the great majority of the people repeatedly expressed at several general elections. It was owing solely to the influence of the Colonial Office that the claims of the Legislative Assembly to the exclusive control of the public finances received at that time a decisive check, from which they have never since recovered, and that the current of national political thought was then turned into new channels, in which it still runs. During the same period the Colonial Office effected the recall and ruin of the representative of the Crown in Victoria, than whom Her Majesty never had a more faithful and loyal servant, nominally upon a pretext known to both the contending political parties to be fictitious, and really because that Governor performed his plain duty by retaining and acting on the advice of Ministers of the Crown in whom alone at that time the representative House of Legislature had confidence. There was, and there still may be, a difference of opinion as to the character of all these acts and events. To some persons all or some of them have been matter of congratulation. In other persons they produced at the same time very deep regret and displeasure. But all would agree that they were acts and events of great moment and of enduring influence upon the national life of this community. No one who is acquainted with the history of the time can doubt that they all sprang from, and were mainly determined by, the interference of the Colonial Office, exercised by and through instructions to the Governor of Victoria.

6. The same influence, founded on the same policy, and exerted by the same means, still exists, though in times of political quietude it is silent, and it is not apparent to superficial observers. It is a fact well known to those who are acquainted with the inner life of Australian Governments that every Governor arrives in these colonies imbued with erroneous impressions of his legal and constitutional rights and duties. It cannot be known whether he derives these impressions solely from his written instructions, or partly from misleading oral instructions. There is consequently always more or less friction between a representative of the Crown and his advisers, until the former has learned that there is a public law in partial force in the colonies, superior to, and sometimes directly at variance with, the instructions of the Colonial Office. He has contracted a solemn obligation to obey them both, and he is then compelled to find out for himself the limits and the sphere of each. His responsible advisers cannot, or, I should rather say, will not help him. Resembling, in

this respect, their brother Ministers of the Crown in England, they are chiefly desirous of avoiding questions of which politicians, warned by past experience, are afraid, and to which the general body of the people are for the time indifferent. Ministers of the Crown will acquaint the Governor with the law only just so far as they are themselves compelled by the necessities of their position as administrators of the law to constrain him to sanction the observance of it by them. In the meantime the public mind is either completely ignorant and indifferent, or it labours under partial but grave misapprehension. For example, many educated persons at this moment have the impression that they are entitled to communicate directly with the representative of the Crown upon matters of public business without the intervention of the Governor's responsible advisers. A still larger number of persons believe, in accordance with the doctrine of the eleventh clause of the instructions, that the Governor, without or in opposition to the advice of his Ministers, can exercise the Royal prerogative of mercy. Hence it has followed that the representative of the Crown is sometimes exposed to the gross indignity and the very painful embarrassment of being compelled on the eve of the execution of a criminal to apologise—at one time to a crowd collected from the street, at another time to an equally ignorant crowd of clergymen and laymen - for his Ministers in allowing the law to take its course, and refusing to transfer to incompetent and irresponsible persons the most delicate and responsible duty connected with the exercise of this prerogative. Illustrations of the continuing influence of the policy underlying the instructions to Governors might be multiplied indefinitely.

7. The systematic violation of the public law by the Colonial Office has recently led to more extended consequences, and is likely to involve new dangers. These Australian communities have external as well as internal interests of the highest importance. They all are interested in banishing from the Southern Hemisphere the injurious system of transportation of criminals from other parts of the world. It is the opinion of many persons— in which I do not myself concur—that these Australian colonies have a species of right to exclude other civilised nations from the islands remaining unoccupied in this part of the Pacific Ocean, and that they are entitled to demand Imperial aid in asserting that right. Upon both questions these colonies are undoubtedly justified in claiming to be heard by the Imperial Government. Their views and arguments should receive patient, earnest, and sympathetic consideration, and, if Imperial interests concur and the rights of other nations permit, the wishes of these colonies should be carried into effect by the prompt, open, and fearless action of the British Government. To more than this the Australian colonies are not and cannot be entitled so long as they remain parts of the British Empire, and are unable or unwilling to assume to themselves the burdens and the responsibilities of national independence. But Australian communities are at present almost totally ignorant of the existence of any legal or constitutional limit to their freedom of speech and action. The line at which the self-governing

powers of a colony end and its duties and obligations as a component part of the empire begin, if not quite unseen is now wholly disregarded. Language is not unfrequently used by public writers and by politicians which is not only calculated to disturb the susceptibilities of foreign nations, and thus to increase the difficulties of dealing with international questions, but which also involves a denial of the exclusive necessary right of the central Imperial Government to determine for itself, and in view of the interests of the whole empire, all questions arising between it and the governments of other independent countries. I conceive it to be an object of the very highest importance that this ignorance should be dispelled, and that Her Majesty's Imperial Government, while giving its earnest attention to the wishes and views of the Australian colonies, should convey to them in unmistakable terms its determination to perform its own duty to the empire by refusing to recognise or permit any direct interference with international questions by the Government or the people of any part or parts of the empire. I believe that a candid and bold policy of this kind might be adopted towards the Australian colonies with perfect safety, and that, so far from alienating or irritating them, it would tend to conciliate and permanently settle public opinion and sentiment by engaging the attention and satisfying the reason of communities which are, as a whole, keen-witted and sensible. It is quite manifest that the Colonial Office is at present unequal to the discharge of this or of any other great duty. Its sole apparent purpose in the past has been to covertly advance its unlawful claim of right to interfere in the domestic affairs of these colonies, and to conceal from the colonies the fact as well as the extent and the grounds of its claim. The Colonial Office knows that discovery of its designs against the intra-colonial rights of these communities would probably quickly follow any attempt it might make to fulfil its own duties and to assert its own constitutional right with regard to extra-colonial and Imperial interests. To this as the probable cause, I suppose, may be traced the recent vacillating and imbecile conduct of the Colonial Office with regard to New Guinea, resulting in disappointment of the wishes and hopes of these colonies, and in a display, deeply painful to all Englishmen everywhere, of angry contempt in foreign countries directed against British institutions, and the feeble and timid modes of action of a British department of state.

8. In view of past consequences, of present embarrassment, uncertainty, and public ignorance caused by the instructions to Governors and the policy they have been maintained to promote, and of future dangers to the empire as well as to these colonies from the same source, I am of opinion that a partial alteration of the public instructions will be of little value. Her Majesty's Colonial Ministers in the Australian colonies ought, I presume to think, to insist upon a new and very clear delimitation of relations with the Imperial Government. The claim of the Colonial Office to interfere in local affairs by indirect coercion or control of the representative of the Crown in the exercise of his powers in that character must be once for all officially and openly withdrawn. All existing public and private instructions to the Governor should be recalled, and instruc-

tions addressed to him solely in his character as an officer of the
Imperial Government should be substituted. Such an authoritative
acknowledgment of the true legal relations between the Governor and
Colonial Ministers of the Crown on the one hand, and Imperial Ministers of the Crown on the other hand, would, in addition to other great
and lasting benefits, contribute materially to facilitate the carrying
out of the arrangements which henceforth must be made and maintained by direct mutual agreement between the Imperial and the
Colonial Governments for the purpose of joint action in all matters of
common interest.

9. Before I conclude this letter I shall be glad if I can gain your brief
attention to a subject not entirely unconnected with that to which
you have invited mine. I mean the bestowal by the Crown of titles
of honour upon Australian citizens. The existing practice in this
matter by which the Imperial Government advises the Crown is not
open to objection on legal or constitutional grounds. The exercise of
this prerogative is not absolutely necessary in the conduct of local
affairs, and consequently the prerogative is not vested in the representative of the Crown by force of the Australian Constitution Acts. But
the present mode of exercising this prerogative is regarded in Australia
with only cold indulgence. It does not and cannot in any case express
spontaneous national sentiment. It may sometimes, through mistaken
representations conveyed to the Imperial Minister, have resulted in
giving offence to the public judgment. I do not think that it has
hitherto had the effect of increasing the just influence of those Australian politicians who have been objects of the Royal favour in this
respect with the communities to which their services have been
rendered. It is not quite certain, perhaps, that public opinion, if it
could be ascertained, would favour the continuance in any form of the
system by which titles of honour are conferred upon Australian citizens.
But, assuming that the existing practice ought in some form to be maintained, it might probably be asserted with confidence that the great
preponderance of opinion in Victoria would be decidedly adverse to the
grant of any hereditary titles of honour whatever, as being opposed to the
spirit of our laws and to the principle of equality which is the foundation of the theory of our political system. Life titles of honour, on
the other hand, are not open in an equal degree to this objection.
And if life titles of the highest rank could be awarded by the Crown in
such a way as to express the public sense of honour for meritorious
public services, while at the same time they should be effectually
guarded against becoming the prize of personal or party intrigue, it is
probable, I think, that they would be regarded in Australian communities with cordial welcome instead of with coldness, and that they might
become important and most valuable factors in the formation of national
character, while they would also be an object of the most legitimate
individual ambition. It appears to me to be a suggestion that deserves
the attention both of English and colonial politicians, that it would be
greatly for the advantage of these colonies if Her Majesty should be
advised to vest this prerogative in the representative of the Crown in
each Australian colony, to be exercised upon the advice of colonial

advisers of the Crown, and upon the recommendation of both Houses of the Colonial Parliament.

10. I have marked this letter "confidential," in accordance with what I have understood to be your wish.   It would be more agreeable to my own inclination if no such restriction were imposed on either of us, and you have my permission to make any use you may think proper of this letter.   If you should determine not to regard it as strictly confidential, I shall, of course, claim a like discretion.   I shall be glad to learn and willing to comply conditionally with your decision upon this point, and for the present I will observe a strict confidence.

I have the honour to be, Sir,
Your faithful servant,
(Signed)   GEORGE HIGINBOTHAM.

CHAPTER XXI

POLITICIAN

THE training of a lawyer certainly gives a bias towards Conservatism. An English lawyer, at any rate, is taught not to settle questions upon a general principle, but to seek for precedent. The result is that comparatively few lawyers have been really Radical in politics. Fortunately English precedents make for freedom, and therefore many and distinguished English lawyers have been on freedom's side in the political strife. To those who have merely a superficial acquaintance with Mr. Higinbotham's character and career, the remark that his mind was essentially Conservative may seem paradoxical ; but it is true. History— the history of political struggle—was the great armoury whence he took his weapons. The influence of general principles was also strong upon him, as it must be upon all reasoning men. Precedents may usually be quoted on both sides, and in his precedents Mr. Higinbotham sought for those that were guided and decided by the general principle. More than most men, he possessed the faculty to discern " the law within the law."

In politics his instincts were opposed to the arts of the demagogue. He hated humbug, shams, and charlatanism as strongly as Carlyle, but, believing more strongly in the human race,[1] he was not so ready to discover them. He certainly held a strong belief in man as man, stripped of all trappings, class distinctions, and artificial differences, what Carlyle calls "clothes." These, with Carlyle, he despised. George Higinbotham measured others by himself, and this made him a democrat.

Chaucer speaks of those "who demen gladly to the badder ende"; that is to say, always look on the worst side of their neighbours. Higinbotham was rather accused of an incurable optimism : he always looked on their best side.

Of this an amusing illustration may be quoted.

One day at his table an officer of a ship was describing how, when the ship came into port, there were so many rats on board that rat-catchers were sent for to clear it. "But it is my belief," he added, "that they leave a few rats on board so that there may be work for them at the end of the next voyage also." "Oh ! do not say that," said Higinbotham, in a pained tone. "He means," was the comment of one at table who knew him well, "that he would not do it if he were a rat-catcher ! "

Higinbotham certainly should be written "as one who loved his fellow-men."

One reward of this belief in and love for his fellow-man was that he possessed the gift of gauging popular feeling in a degree which did not come to many who prided themselves on knowing the world far better than he did.

Higinbotham would have been as willing as Carlyle to have the world governed by its best, but his experience of public life, especially in a colony, convinced him that there was no short and easy road of discovering who were the best. The fascination of politics was not so great that he would not willingly have buried the whole of it, if with perfect certainty some system of government could have been evolved without it that could not fail to be just. Oftentimes Higinbotham lamented the decline of authority throughout the world ; he valued authority so highly that he would gladly have made sacrifices to retain it, or to induce it to return to earth. The fact that everything has gone into the melting cauldron—

---

[1] He could never have chuckled over Friedrich's *Diese verdammte Race*, as Carlyle did.

theology, philosophy, science, art, even grammar—distressed
him.   But in a young colony no reasonable method of
government, except democracy, seemed possible, unless it were
to assign political power to money ; and from that he shrank
with unmixed loathing.   In a new colony birth has no power ;
education, unless it will take trouble to persuade, very
little.   Money soon lifts up its head, soon asserts itself, and
claims a right to govern.   All the teachers of religion and
philosophy tell men to despise money.   George Higinbotham
carried out their precepts.

Of all the phrases that he coined none had more point and
sting, none has had more life, than the phrase the " wealthy
lower orders." [1]   It is a phrase worth thinking about.   Poli
tical opponents acknowledged its power ; though only by
misunderstanding can they say that it was " somewhat ludi-
crously applied to the professional and educated classes who
were his opponents." [2]   Granted that the professional classes
in Victoria, as elsewhere, were Conservative, the phrase was
never intended to apply to all the opponents, but to some.   Its
truth was the very reason of the epigram's sting.   Those
who had made money in Victoria were not as a rule educated, and the stronghold of the Council lay in the moneyed
men who had risen.   The airs of the local aristocracy in
the early days—not best ($\ddot{a}\rho\iota\sigma\tau o\iota$) at all, but solely wealthiest
—excited Mr. Higinbotham's contempt ; their claim to control
and rule the colony, his indignation.   These feelings gave
quite a marked bias to his political thought ; and the phrase
about the " wealthy lower orders " is a key to it.

How high Higinbotham's standard of political purity was
may be seen from the following extract.   There was a railway
for which his constituents were anxious, and they wanted to
know why their member had not supported it.   He said :—

I now wish to tell you the motives of my silence, in order that
you, having heard them, may judge whether you approve or not of
my conduct.   That route was first suggested to the Government by
an officer in the railway department who is a relative of mine, and
who is something more than a relative— who, and I say this in order

---

[1] Speech at Brighton, October 22nd, 1864.   No notice was taken of
the phrase at the time.   It has stuck like a bur.
[2] Timotheus, in *Argus*, January 7th, 1893.

that you may fully understand my motives, who is a very dear and lifelong, intimate friend of mine, a man of whose judgment upon questions of this nature, and upon not a few other subjects of a like kind, my own judgment would be greatly influenced, if not, indeed, controlled. I have always known or believed it to be a rule of parliamentary prudence and propriety, that a member should not be forward to speak or vote upon subjects or questions on which he may be, or may reasonably be supposed to be, subject to private influences. or controlled by personal feelings or interests. And if he do so, gentlemen, he will soon find that when he speaks his voice lacks the influence that every man who speaks in public should seek to have, and that every man who represents others should insist upon maintaining. In accordance with that rule- an unwritten rule, I admit I have from the time I first entered Parliament down to the present time. both as a private member and as a Minister of the Crown when I was one, abstained altogether from interference, direct or indirect, in any matter or question connected with the railway department of the Government. There was also another feeling in my mind. I was jealous of the honour of one whose good name is quite as dear to me as my own, and no man in this community can say, no man shall ever with just cause be able to say, that the professional opinion or official interest of the Engineer-in-Chief of Railways has received political support or aid from his relative who happens to have the honour of a seat in Parliament. It was under the influence of these feelings that I deliberately abstained from speaking or voting as your member.

The fights in which Mr. Higinbotham was engaged were the most bitter party fights in the history of the Colony of Victoria. Strange irony of fate that the leader in these party fights was one who deprecated party altogether; who on entering politics declared that Victoria had not the material for party government; who always would have worked for its annihilation. He simply loathed the constant struggle for office. In a speech on the Education question (May 30th, 1867) he spoke of

the accepted system of government by party or faction, as I prefer to call it. . . . There has always been in the country, and in a less offensive form in the mother country, a political party who are endeavouring at all hazards to eject a government, in fact to " upset the coach," to " stab the man at the wheel, and throw his body overboard." . . . The British public generally view political struggles in the same way that they view prize-fights ; they look upon them either with feelings of stolid apathy, or with a sense of brutal enjoyment.

On November 30th, 1875, speaking on a very different subject, he spoke of the accursed system under which the party on this side of the House are always striving to murder the reputation of the party on the other side, in order to leap over the dead bodies of those reputations into the seats on the Treasury Bench.

These are two strong instances; there are many more. His ideal for the State was that with certain limitations every man and every woman should have an equal vote, the whole colony be one constituency, and that the Executive should be selected quite without reference to party, or faction, as with truth he used to call it. Of this ideal Mr. Higinbotham never lost sight, but the desire to take sides, and the clinging together of allies in one combat, when they came to another and different fight, proved too strong for it and him. Protesting against party he entered politics; and protesting against party he quitted the political arena. Strongly convinced as he was that the intrusion of party lowered politics, he never accepted the excuse that it was the fault of the politicians. The House is what the electors make it, and the electors cannot screen themselves behind unworthy representatives. If these prove unworthy, it is the duty of the electors to find worthier.

For a while at least he was a party leader. As to his merits in that capacity this distinction must be drawn. To excite enthusiasm on his own side it may be doubted whether any one was ever his superior. In a battle, or in a campaign, he was like a dashing leader of cavalry, and none hesitated to follow where he led the way. For several years after he had left office many hoped that he would organize and lead the Liberal party, not for one political object but for many-headed reform. These have since regarded him as a "lost leader"; but it may well be doubted whether he was adapted for such a position, where the need is not so much for a grasp of principle and vigorous support of it as for the political tact which makes concessions in one place, whilst it is firm in another. In politics you must be politic. There are those who say that compromise is the very essence of political life. Now Higinbotham abhorred compromise as a thing in itself evil. Like one who was in many respects his master in politics, he was

Too fond of the right to pursue the expedient.

With all his greatness, Edmund Burke could not have led a party for a continuance. One cannot but think the same about George Higinbotham.

As a member of Parliament he was impelled by a strong sense of duty to constant and regular attendance. When Attorney-General he was regularly on the Ministerial bench, ready to answer questions and to take his part in all the work of the House. As a private member he was equally regular in his attendance, though much of that attendance must have been irksome to him. It is contrary to the strict rule of the House to read a book, but the rule was seldom enforced, and Mr. Higinbotham when a private member read frequently. When attention was needed, the book was quickly laid aside. No work was too much for him. The phrase, " There were giants in the land," springs to the mind confronted with the work he eagerly undertook.

It has sometimes been said that Mr. Higinbotham's political career was a failure, by which is meant, not that his political influence in raising the tone of public life was unavailing, but rather that the causes for which he cared were not gained. His influence is written on every page of the Victorian statute book ; even independently of his work in consolidation, there is no legislator who has done so much for legislation. But if attention be confined to the two main political questions for which he cared, opposition to the interference of the Upper House in financial matters, and opposition to the interference of Downing Street in colonial affairs, and if thus only the main position be considered, has his influence been for nought? A career is not a failure because the extremest victory has not yet been won. In 1893 the Government prepared a small measure to enable the Trustees of the Melbourne Public Library to fine for default in returning books on loan. As the Legislative Council had not much to do in the early part of the session, the measure was introduced in the Council. On its reaching the Assembly, the Speaker proclaimed that it was an infringement on the rights of the Assembly, and the bill was at once thrown out. The Speaker, it may be mentioned, was Mr. Thomas Bent, member for Brighton since 1871. The Lower House is as jealous of its financial rights and of the power of the purse as ever.

The measure of the victory with respect to Downing Street is to be found in the altered instructions. The Home Law Officers told Lord Knutsford that it was not illegal for Governors to correspond with the Colonial Office; but the tone of that Office is not now the tone of Mr. Cardwell, nor of the Duke of Buckingham, but rather this "involves no question calling for the intervention of the Imperial Government; it is not one on which it seems to me incumbent to express an opinion." Contrast the Instructions to Sir Charles Darling, signed "V. Rg.," of June 23rd, 1863, with those published in the *Victoria Government Gazette* of September 2nd, 1892, signed, July 9th of that year, "V. R. I." The difference is enormous. The Victorian newspapers of that September commented on the change, and praised the wisdom of the Colonial Office in making it; but no one remembered the Victorian politician whose persistent efforts were at last successful. That number of the *Gazette* was published only four months before his death.

But even if it had to be granted that on his two main contentions the people's champion was defeated, there remains his influence. "I was almost always opposed to him," said a high authority, whose Parliamentary experience was of the highest; "but from the day he left the House it began to descend."

The following is an analysis of Mr. Higinbotham's influence in Parliament, written by a leading member of the Victorian Legislative Assembly:—

The peculiar influence which George Higinbotham exercised upon our politics was connected with the two questions of resisting the interference of Downing Street and the encroachments by the Legislative Council, but it had a wider scope, and impressed those who were opposed to him in these points. This influence is hard to define, because it was composed of several elements. There was, first, the lawyer's respect for the law, the habit of mind which turns at once to the text, and seeks to construe all rights from the terms in which they have been embodied. This textual loyalty is always repugnant to the lay mind, and particularly to the impatient politician, who seeks the shortest cuts that will meet his immediate needs without regard to the consistency of the means he employs with the charter from which he professes to draw them. Of the legal aspect there will always be exponents, but they are generally mistrusted by their associates because supposed to be wholly governed by mere technicalities of phrase and desirous of splitting straws with or without justification.

Higinbotham by the sheer weight of personal character rose above this suspicion, and made strictly legal rendering less unpopular with us than it would otherwise have been.

The next element was also professional.

For interpretation it was necessary to lay down principles so that the readings of the Constitution Act might be coherent, and that any questionable occurrences might be tested not merely by reference to the letter of the Act, but by that letter read in the light of broad constitutional doctrine. His great knowledge of the principles of Constitutional Law awoke many echoes, some of which still remain. Again, those principles require for their application constant historical reference, and here too a tendency was imparted which left a distinct mark upon the Assembly, and forced even members of the Council to seek for precedents to justify their claims.

In one sense the smallest of the avenues in which his influence was exercised most discovered it. This was in knowledge of the forms of the House and pious adherence to them. Some of the checks upon individual license imposed by them are severe, and many of the provisions relate simply and solely to what might be termed the bare ceremonial of procedure. Nevertheless as laws of the House they were sacred to George Higinbotham, and through him a sense of their sanctity passed to those who surrounded him. In all these respects his was more or less a legal influence, but it was gained upon wholly extra-legal grounds. His popularity arose as a champion of the rights of the people and of their chamber, but this was built upon his character. It was his individuality which impressed all, —not only his brilliant oratorical powers, but the almost overwhelming weight and force, which were expressed in his eloquent words with perfectly natural but marvellously telling deliberation and precision. Even in his most fiery passages there was everywhere a judicial element, in the background perhaps for the moment, but presently reasserting itself, a thoughtfulness and thoroughness betokening the balance of opinions in a ripe judgment and the careful preliminary survey of a wide field and from a high standpoint of the whole situation of which he was dealing only with a passing phase. This intellectual rectitude and capacity, supported by the blameless political and private record (*sans peur et sans reproche*), made him by right of quality and strength the natural leader of his party and an irresistibly dominant personality. Hence he was imitated consciously or unconsciously by the most dissimilar men. What breathed through the whole and rendered it harmonious was the keen and abiding sense of the importance of the work of Parliament, the dignity of its practice, the magnitude of its opportunities, the loftiness of its authority. Fully imbued with the wisdom and supremacy of the Commons, the antiquity of its rights, and the majesty of its achievements, he contrived to pour into the shallowest and meanest minds some of the overflowing reverence and pride with which he regarded the People's House. This influence was moral rather than legal. It gave a gravity of tone to our debates which has been steadily lowered since his departure His contempt for mere wealth, disdain for class prejudices, and unconcealed dislike for the uncultivated *nouveaux riches*, were based on moral grounds also, adding the spice and barb of invective, which contrasted so forcibly with his expressions of almost religious awe for constitutional principles and popular rights. His loyalty to the throne and his feeling for Imperialism were but imperfectly understood in his political days, and were an occasion of astonishment to some who confused his resistance to the Colonial Office with resistance to the mother country, than which nothing was further from his feeling. It has to be remembered that a great struggle such as was waged here in the sixties always has an elevating effect in politics. It has also to be remembered that in New South Wales and other colonies the Upper Chamber is nominee. Only South Australia resembles Victoria in its Upper Chamber. But making all allowance for these facts, I believe that, during George Higinbotham's term of office, and indeed for some time afterwards, the Victorian Assembly was distinguished from its fellows by a higher standard of discussion, a better demeanour of members, a stricter sense of the value of the forms of the House, and a far superior grasp of all constitutional issues. Even in the Convention of 1891 it was noticeable that the relations of the two Houses were discussed coldly and on mere academic grounds by all the representatives of the other colonies, with perhaps two exceptions, while the Victorians one and all flung themselves into the discussion *con amore*, and with the readiness of men experienced in the question. This knowledge, especially essential in young Parliaments, and the higher class of debate and higher sense of responsibility in members and in Parliament, I attribute almost solely to the immense personal influence of George Higinbotham. I believe the able men of his time were abler than those who fill their places, and certainly more individual and more various ; but I know none of them to whom can be attributed the propagation of the ideal which Higinbotham held except himself. Some were brilliant soldiers of fortune, some had brisk, keen, and able intellects, some had a grip of principles, but none of them approached Higinbotham either in intellectual or moral stature, or in the training which made him *par excellence* the Parliamentarian, the representative of the representative principle, spirit, and method, who imparted to that period of our political history a certain greatness of style which has been sadly wanting since, and is conspicuously wanting now.

It may be added that Mr. Higinbotham's profound belief in the House of Commons was due to his study of history, but his knowledge of the very forms and life of that great assembly may rather be traced to his early experience as a reporter in the gallery.

It may naturally be asked what were Mr. Higinbotham's views on certain prominent questions of modern politics, that word being used in its widest sense. In English politics he was a Liberal Unionist, strongly opposed to granting Home Rule to Ireland. With respect to the connection between

England and the colonies, he was strongly averse to the idea of separation, but

prepared [1] to admit that if there was no very active feeling in favour of separation there was no very strong sentiment amongst the younger generation in favour of continuing the British connection. This he attributed to the ignorance of England amongst the young colonials, who, he thought, would look at matters differently if they could all have the advantage of a trip to the old country. Whilst deploring this ignorance, which he spoke of as the main cause of misapprehension between nations, he attributed it very much to the neglect and selfishness of the older generation of emigrants, who had devoted all their energies to money-making, and had taught their children neither loyalty to the old country nor an enlightened patriotism in regard to the new. . . . His idea was that the colonies should be told that they could " cut the painter " at any time they liked, with the certain result, as he contended, that they would pause long before terminating a connection involving so many practical advantages and so much valuable prestige.

To the idea of Imperial Federation he was also opposed, fancying that it would lead back to rule by Downing Street, and " government by despatches." He had fought too much and too bravely against this to see any advantage in schemes of closer connection. And yet every scheme of Imperial or Britannic Confederation implies complete self-government of each part as to its own affairs. " The future can take care of itself," was his answer, when pressed as to what would be the state of affairs when the colonies had a population equal or nearly equal to that of Great Britain. Australian Federation he supported, but not so warmly as many. He told the visitor who reports the above opinions on the English connection that he " saw no necessity for hurry in the matter of Federation, and would consent to any postponement rather than see Responsible Government in the British sense weakened in the least by its adoption. On this point I found him as Conservative as the most true-blue Constitutionalist could desire."

Lastly, his attitude toward socialism.

On this point a personal reminiscence may be permitted. A friend had once been talking to me, and had declared that in future the political world would not be divided between

[1] An interview described in the *British Australasian*, January 11th, 1893.

Liberals and Conservatives, but between Individualists and Collectivists. I said I could not make up my mind which side I should then take, and I carried my difficulties to Mr. Higinbotham. I pointed out how my early Liberalism had been fed upon Mill *On Liberty*, and on the book to which Mill owed so much, Humboldt *On the Sphere and Duties of Government*; that I still believed the individualist system would produce the finer type of man, the self-reliant; but that in many later matters I had seen the good effected by collective action, and wavered in my allegiance: even Mill allows that the State should undertake education, but that personally I should be sorry to limit the State's action where Mill did. Higinbotham said he thought we had all passed through the same struggle, that he had left the Individualist camp with regret, quite seeing its merits, but that now he hoped more for humanity from collective action.

A few more words may be quoted from the same conversation with his visitor from England :—

The greatest doubter about human perfectibility could not be faint-hearted as to the future of labour after he had been for a few minutes under the optimistic spell of the Victorian Chief Justice. He revelled in the fact of the growing solidarity of labour, which served to checkmate the grasping employer when he sought to call in the glutted wealth of one part of the world to aid him in crushing the rising tide of working-class emancipation at another.

APPENDIX.

A.

THE OLD INSTRUCTIONS.

I. [Very long and formal. Here omitted.] You shall then and there take the oath.

II. And We do authorize and require you from time to time, and at any time hereafter, by yourself or by any other person to be authorized by you in that behalf, to administer and give to all and every such person or persons as you shall think fit, who shall hold any office or place of trust or profit, or who shall at any time or times pass into Our said Colony, or be resident therein, the said oath of allegiance, save only in cases wherein any other oath or oaths is or are prescribed by the Statutes in that behalf made, or by any of them, in which case it is

Our pleasure, and We do hereby direct, that you do administer, or cause to be administered to such persons, such oath or oaths as aforesaid.

III. You are to communicate forthwith to Our said Executive Council for Our said Colony these Our instructions, and likewise all such others, from time to time, as you shall find convenient for Our service to be imparted to them.

IV. And We do hereby direct and enjoin that Our said Council shall not proceed to the despatch of business, unless duly summoned by your authority, and [1] unless two members at the least (exclusive of yourself or the member presiding) be present, and assisting throughout the whole of the meetings at which any such business shall be despatched.

V. And We do further direct and enjoin that you do attend and preside at the meetings of Our said Executive Council, unless when prevented by some necessary or reasonable cause, and that in your absence the senior member of the said Executive Council actually present shall preside at all such meetings, the seniority of the members of the Council being regulated according to the order of their appointments as members of Our said Council.

VI. And We do further direct and enjoin that a full and exact journal or minute be kept of all the deliberations, acts, proceedings, votes, and resolutions of Our said Council ; and that, at each meeting of the said Council, the minutes of the last meeting be read over, confirmed, or amended, as the case may require, before proceeding to the despatch of any other business.

VII. And We do hereby direct and enjoin that, in the execution of the powers and authorities committed to you by our said Commission, you do in all cases consult with our Executive Council, excepting only in cases which may be of such a nature that, in your judgment, Our Service would sustain material prejudice by consulting Our Council thereupon, or when the matters to be decided shall be too unimportant to require their advice, or too urgent to admit of their advice being given by the time within which it may be necessary for you to act in respect of any such matters :   Provided that in all such urgent cases you do subsequently, and at the earliest practicable period, communicate to the said Executive Council the measures which you may so have adopted with the reasons thereof.

VIII. And We do authorize you, in your discretion, and if it shall in any case appear right, to act in the exercise of the power committed to you by Our said Commission in opposition to the advice which may in any such case be given to you by the members of Our said Executive Council: Provided nevertheless, that in any such case you do fully report to Us, by the first convenient opportunity, any such proceeding, with the grounds and reasons thereof.   And We do further direct that twice in each year a full transcript of all the minutes of the said Council for the preceding half-year be transmitted to Us through one of Our Principal Secretaries of State.[2]

---

[1] In the instructions to Governor Manners Sutton " and " was altered to " nor."

[2] This sentence was omitted in the next instructions.

IX. And whereas it has been appointed by Parliament that such of the provisions of the Act of the fourteenth year of Our reign, chapter fifty-nine, and of the Act of the fifth and sixth years of Our reign, chapter seventy-six, which relate to the giving and withholding Our assent to Bills, the reservation of Bills for the signification of Our pleasure thereupon, and the instructions to be conveyed to Governors for their guidance in relation to the matters aforesaid, shall apply to and be in force in Our said Colony : We do, in the exercise of the powers in Us vested, by these Our instructions under Our Sign-Manual and Signet, declare Our pleasure to be, that until further orders shall be made by Us in that behalf, you do, in the exercise of the powers vested in you, of assenting to or dissenting from, or of reserving for the signification of Our pleasure such Bills as may be passed by the Legislative Council and House of Assembly of Our said Colony, guide yourself, as far as may be practicable, by the following rules, directions, and instructions (that is to say) :-

X. You are, as much as possible, to observe, in the passing of all laws, that each different matter be provided for by a different law, without intermixing in one and the same Act such things as have no proper relation to each other ; and you are more especially to take care that no clause or clauses be inserted in or annexed to any Act which shall be foreign to what the title of such Act imports, and that no perpetual clause be part of any temporary law.

XI. If any Bill of any one of the clauses hereinafter specified should be presented to you for Our assent, you are (unless you think proper to withhold Our assent from the same) to reserve the same for the signification of Our pleasure thereon : subject, nevertheless, to your discretion in case you should be of opinion that an urgent necessity exists requiring that such Bill be brought into immediate operation ; in which case you are authorised to assent to such Bill in Our name, transmitting to Us, by the earliest opportunity, the Bill so assented to, together with your reasons for assenting thereto (that is to say)-

[The reservations are practically the same as in the new instructions.]

XII. You shall take care that all laws assented to by you in Our name, or reserved for the signification of Our Royal pleasure thereon, shall, when transmitted by you, be fairly abstracted in the margins, and accompanied with explanatory observations upon each of them, exhibiting the reasons and occasion for proposing such laws ; and you shall also transmit fair copies of the Journals and Minutes of the Proceedings of the said Legislative Council and House of Assembly, which you are to require from the Clerks or other proper officers in that behalf of the said Legislative Council and House of Assembly.

XIII. And whereas We have, by Our said Commission, authorised and empowered you, as you shall see occasion in Our name and on Our behalf, to grant to any offender, convicted of any crime in any court, or before any judge, justice, or magistrate within Our said Colony, a pardon, either free, or subject to lawful conditions. Now, We do hereby direct and enjoin you to call upon the judge presiding at the trial of any offender who may from time to time be condemned to suffer death by the sentence of any court within Our said Colony, to make to you a written report of the case of such offender, and such report of the said judge shall by you be taken into consideration at the first meeting thereafter which may be conveniently held, of Our said Executive Council, where the said judge shall be specially summoned to attend, and you shall not pardon or reprieve any such offender as aforesaid unless it shall appear to you expedient so to do upon receiving the advice of our Executive Council therein, but in all such cases you are to decide either to extend or to withhold a pardon or reprieve, according to your own deliberate judgment, whether the Members of our said Executive Council concur therein or otherwise; entering nevertheless on the minutes of the said Council a minute of your reasons at length, in case you should decide any such question in opposition to the judgment of the majority of the members thereof.

XIV. And it is Our further will and pleasure that you do, to the utmost of your power, promote religion and education among the Native Inhabitants of Our said Colony or of the Lands and Islands thereto adjoining, and that you do especially take care to protect them in their persons, and in the free enjoyment of their possessions, and that you do by all lawful means prevent and restrain all violence and injustice which may in any manner be practised or attempted against them.

XV. And whereas great prejudice may happen to Our service and to the security of Our said Colony by the absence of the Governor, you shall not, upon any pretence whatever, quit Our said Colony without having first obtained Our leave for so doing under Our Sign Manual and Signet, or through one of Our Principal Secretaries of State.

(Signed) V. Rg.

B.

THE NEW INSTRUCTIONS.

I. In these Our Instructions, unless inconsistent with the context, the term " the Governor " shall include every person for the time being administering the Government of the Colony, and the term " the Executive Council " shall mean the members of Our Executive Council for the Colony who are for the time being the responsible advisers of the Governor.

II. The Governor may, whenever he thinks fit, require any person in the public service to take the Oath of Allegiance, together with such other Oath or Oaths as may from time to time be prescribed by any Law in force in the Colony. The Governor is to administer such Oaths or cause them to be administered by some Public Officer of the Colony.

III. The Governor shall forthwith communicate these Our Instructions to the Executive Council, and likewise all such others, from time to time, as he shall find convenient for Our Service to impart to them.

IV. The Governor shall attend and preside at the meetings of the

Executive Council, unless prevented by some necessary or reasonable cause, and in his absence such member as may be appointed by him in that behalf, or in the absence of such member the senior member of the Executive Council actually present shall preside; the seniority of the members of the said Council being regulated according to the order of their respective appointments as members thereof.

V. The Executive Council shall not proceed to the despatch of business unless duly summoned by authority of the Governor nor unless two members at the least (exclusive of the Governor or of the member presiding) be present and assisting throughout the whole of the meetings at which any such business shall be despatched.

VI. In the execution of the powers and authorities vested in him, the Governor shall be guided by the advice of the Executive Council, but if in any case he shall see sufficient cause to dissent from the opinion of the said Council he may act in the exercise of his said powers and authorities in opposition to the opinion of the Council, reporting the matter to Us without delay, with the reasons for his so acting.

In any such case it shall be competent to any member of the said Council to require that there be recorded upon the Minutes of the Council the grounds of any advice or opinion that he may give upon the question.

VII. The Governor shall not, except in the cases hereunder mentioned, assent in Our name to any Bill of any of the following classes :—

1. Any Bill for the divorce of persons joined together in holy matrimony.

2. Any Bill whereby any grant of land or money, or other donation or gratuity, may be made to himself.

3. Any Bill affecting the currency of the Colony.

4. Any Bill imposing differential duties (other than as allowed by the *Australian Colonies' Duties Act* 1873).

5. Any Bill the provisions of which shall appear inconsistent with obligations imposed upon Us by Treaty.

6. Any Bill interfering with the discipline or control of Our forces in the Colony by land or sea.

7. Any Bill of an extraordinary nature and importance, whereby Our prerogative or the rights and property of Our subjects not residing in the Colony, or the trade and shipping of the United Kingdom and its Dependencies, may be prejudiced.

8. Any Bill containing provisions to which Our assent has been once refused, or which has been disallowed by Us -

Unless he shall have previously obtained Our Instructions upon such Bill through one of Our Principal Secretaries of State, or unless such Bill shall contain a clause suspending the operation of such Bill until the signification in the Colony of Our pleasure thereupon, or unless the Governor shall have satisfied himself that an urgent necessity exists requiring that such Bill be brought into immediate operation, in which case he is authorized to assent in Our name to such Bill, unless the same shall be repugnant to the law of England, or inconsistent with any obligations imposed upon Us by Treaty. But he is to transmit to Us by the earliest opportunity the Bill so assented to, together with his reasons for assenting thereto.

VIII. The Governor shall not pardon or reprieve any offender without first receiving in capital cases the advice of the Executive Council, and in other cases the advice of one, at least, of his Ministers ; and in any case in which such pardon or reprieve might directly affect the interests of our Empire, or of any country or place beyond the jurisdiction of the Government of the Colony, the Governor shall, before deciding as to either pardon or reprieve, take those interests specially into his own personal consideration in conjunction with such advice as aforesaid.

IX. All commissions granted by the Governor to any persons to be Judges, Justices of the Peace, or other officers shall, unless otherwise provided by law, be granted during pleasure only.

X. The Governor shall not quit the Colony without having first obtained leave from us for so doing under Our Sign Manual and Signet, or through one of Our Principal Secretaries of State, except for the purpose of visiting the Governor of any neighbouring Colony for periods not exceeding one month at any one time, nor exceeding in the aggregate one month for every year's service in the Colony.

XI. The temporary absence of the Governor for any period not exceeding one month shall not, if he have previously informed the Executive Council, in writing, of his intended absence, and if he have duly appointed a Deputy in accordance with Our said Letters Patent, be deemed a departure from the Colony within the meaning of the said Letters Patent.

V. R I.

CHAPTER XXII

IT is difficult formally to express in words wherein consists the art of an orator; yet George Higinbotham's fame as an orator is such that some expression of it cannot be omitted. Friends may claim that in his oratory there was no art at all, that it was all nature, and that he was too sincere a man to employ art or, what the word art suggests, artifice. In that objection there is embodied a truth, and it is quite clear that the speeches are not cast in one mould, and that they are singularly free from the tricks of the trade. One characteristic is apparent, the absence of peroration. In no respect is the artful orator, the orator who is made not born, more manifest than in the peroration, carefully studied and ingeniously introduced. No doubt much depends on the ending of a speech, the words that linger in the ear, and perhaps Mr. Higinbotham's endings may be criticised as too careless of effect; but the elaborate peroration that savours of the lamp is a more offensive fault. For the great speeches there was careful preparation. He respected his audiences too highly to insult them by giving what had cost him nought, but the preparation was of the matter, the sequence of thought, the arguments, and not of the words. He was not, however, dependent on preparation, for his contemporaries allow that he was ready in debate. Some parliamentary speakers confine themselves to the formal debate, the debate of great speeches, when an allusion or two to former speakers may be woven almost as an ornament into a speech the main web of which is independently prepared. But the true power of the debater is seen in the skirmish rather than in the field-day, in the quick parry and thrust, for which no preparation is possible, and in this respect Higinbotham's fame is almost equal to that of his great orations.

It is natural there should be a difference between forensic and political oratory. Certainly there was in his case. At the bar he was persuasive and argumentative, as, of course, he frequently was in the Assembly also, but it was not persuasion nor argument that won him renown. "He always speaks best at a white heat," was often said of him, and once in my hearing his only rival in Melbourne oratory, Bishop Moorhouse, expressed surprise thereat. The reason lies in the sincerity of the man; he could not assume a passion if he did not feel it. Only therefore when he felt strongly could he put that fire into his speeches which seemed to carry all before it. It was his "terrible earnestness" that impressed his listeners. His persuasive speeches were meant to convince : the greatest speeches, to rally when there was no hope to win. On smaller matters, cases laid before a jury, proposals to modify legislation, a gentle voice might persuade. On the political questions, when the country was divided into two camps, the speeches were rather like a trumpet-blast, putting heart into the combatants on his own side, not conciliating nor converting, but dismaying his opponents. This marked difference in his styles of speaking made his oratory uneven.

The manner with which a speech began was always most gentle : the voice, low and hardly audible. This was partly due to nervousness, from which no experience, no practice, ever gave freedom. Mr. Higinbotham has confessed often to the desire felt just before beginning that the earth would open and swallow him ; but before two sentences were uttered this feeling wholly passed away. The gentle opening, however, was very telling : it produced the effect of a *crescendo* movement in music, the effect also of surprise. Soon the nervous, almost hesitating opening is forgotten ; ingenious argument, cutting sarcasm, appropriate literary illustration are being poured forth, and the audience grows warm with excitement. Yet the manner is still most deliberate. It is almost as if the words of Hamlet to the players were borne well in mind : "In the very torrent, tempest, and (as I may say) the whirlwind of passion, you must acquire and beget a temperance, that may give it smoothness." Mr. Higinbotham was never in a hurry, and never spoke fast. Excitement, which hastens most men, made him more deliberate and slow.

" He understood the value of the pause," is the comment of a friend, who went on to add : "I only heard him twice, in one important speech, and once he charged a jury on which I sat. Both times I noticed his masterly use of the pause. It was as if he would say, 'There, let that sink in.'" Some speakers pour forth their fiery sentences, one close upon the other without an interval, so that each seems to remove the effect of the other. No one had that impression with Higinbotham. It was rather as if each sentence pressed its predecessor home. Of a general comment like this, concerning manner rather than matter, it is not easy to adduce a satisfactory example. The following is from a speech on behalf of the Working Man's College.[1]

Frederick Denison Maurice came to the conclusion that the failure of the mechanics' institutes was "the result of the exclusion from their studies of both politics and theology. In the forefront of the curriculum of his college he put both politics and theology." (Cheers.) " Not party politics." (Renewed cheers.) " Not sectarian theology." (Renewed cheers.)

The applause of the audience marks the effectiveness of the pauses.

In the days of his prime a writer compared our Victorian orator to John Bright, whom he closely resembled in "many curious personal respects. His was the same flow of vigorous Saxon ; the same terrible sarcasm, the same precision of epithet, the same fondness for scriptural illustrations, and the same clear, clarion voice." There is something in the comparison, but like all comparisons it must not be pushed too far. Mr. Higinbotham's language is often as vigorous as Bright's, but it is not so largely drawn from the "early

[1] Melbourne Town Hall, June 26th, 1882.

English " element of our speech, nor is he so scriptural in his illustrations. In the build of his sentences, certainly in his writings and to some extent in his speeches, he might rather be compared to Mr. Gladstone.

Elsewhere [1] a speech is given in full upon the treatment of Sir Charles Darling. It was selected by a great admirer who had heard all the great speeches. This gentleman, then a member of the House, corrected and supplemented Hansard by describing the action of a part near the close, where the speaker said that the officials of Victoria cared so little for the principles of responsible government that in violation of them they would always like to appeal to Downing Street, and a member opposite interjected "It's a libel!" "A libel," repeated the orator in a silvery voice little more than a whisper, but a whisper that could be heard in every part of the chamber. Then he drew himself up until, short as he was, he seemed to tower over everybody, and stepping forward to the table flung forth both hands with a gesture of contempt. "I declare to God, I cannot think of them without thinking libel." At the close of the speech an astute opponent moved the adjournment of the debate upon the ground that the House was too excited to do business. "We are still under the wand of the enchanter," he might have quoted from the words that Pitt used after Sheridan's great speech in the House of Commons upon the Begums.[2]

There is no doubt that as a speaker Mr. Higinbotham owed much to the clearness and the musical tone of his voice. Yet "beautiful as was his oratory," said a strong admirer to me, "it was not the manner but the matter that made the speeches valuable. What he said was so sound and true, that I was often reminded of what the Yankee said of Daniel Webster: 'His words were so weighty. Each of them weighed a pa-ound.'"

One word more. The language that fell from Mr. Higinbotham's lips was couched in perfect grammar. He never "broke Priscian's head." Every sentence was completely formed. The reporters all testify that they had nothing to

---

[1] Chapter xv.
[2] Not to be confused with the later speech on the same topic in Westminster Hall.

do but to report. The kind offices that they perform for many another speaker were never needed.

Mr. W. V. Robinson, Clerk of the Legislative Assembly has kindly contributed the following :—

REMINISCENCES BY A REPORTER.

" As a reporter it was my good fortune to hear and record a large number of the speeches delivered by the late Chief Justice Higinbotham, both in Parliament and on the platform. I was not in 'the gallery' when he first became a member of the Legislative Assembly, but from the time of his second election, in the year 1862, until the close of his parliamentary career, in 1876, my duty called me there every night the Assembly sat, and therefore I very frequently heard him address the House during that period. I recollect no man whose oratorical powers I so greatly admired as I did those of George Higinbotham, though I have listened to addresses from many of the most eminent platform speakers of their day in England. In the deep earnestness of his manner, the powerful simplicity of his language, and the general arrangement of the matter of his speeches he was very like John Bright : while the vehement eloquence with which he denounced what he regarded as iniquitous reminded me of thrilling utterances I had heard years before from the lips of Samuel Wilberforce when Bishop of Oxford.

" From a professional point of view it was impossible for an efficient stenographer to have a more delightful speaker to follow than Mr. Higinbotham. He spoke so deliberately, and with such a clear, distinct voice, that it was a perfect pleasure to follow him : and his fervour seemed so to communicate itself to the reporter that even when in the very whirlwind of his passion it was comparatively easy to take down accurately every word he said.

" No doubt his most impassioned parliamentary oratory was displayed in connection with the various debates arising out of the rejection by the Legislative Council of the Appropriation-*cum*-Tariff Bill, the proposed grant of £20,000 to Lady Darling, and topics of a kindred character : but on all occasions he was a singularly able debater. Whenever it was his function to explain the provisions of a bill, or to take part in discussing any ordinary question, his remarks were a model of perspicuity and lucidity. His trained intellect and cultivated mind manifested themselves in every one of his deliverances deserving the title of a speech. Some of his parliamentary addresses—such, for instance, as his speech, in 1867, when introducing a bill to amend the law relating to public instruction, and again on the second reading of that measure—were most admirable treatises on the subjects with which they dealt.

"In this connexion it may not be inappropriate if I quote an extract from one of his speeches in 1867, to show the value he attached to religious education—a matter on which, I believe, a good deal of ignorance exists in some quarters.

"'I am here to avow,' he said 'the belief that religion, not merely as differing from, but as contrasted with, sectarianism and dogma, is an essential part of a sound education. (An Honourable Member: 'It will be difficult to define.') It may be difficult, sir, to define it, it may be impossible to define it. I grant that, perhaps, it is; but, Sir, the State is not called upon to define it by this bill. That is left by the bill to those who are most deeply interested in the giving of religious instruction—namely, the parents. And I freely admit that the religious instruction which will be sanctioned by those parents will depend, for its character and results and value, entirely upon the degree of religious cultivation amongst the parents who prescribe and authorize it for the schools. No one pretends, in the present day, to say that the State can or ought to attempt to construct a religious system of opinion or practice for the people of a community; but I have yet to learn that the people themselves, who profess to desire religion as a part of education, should be prohibited from making it part of education; or why, because the State has abandoned the patronage of any one of the sects, it should therefore be supposed to have renounced religion altogether, and be precluded from even allowing persons aided by the money of the State, to give their own children the religious education in which they themselves believe. Sir, those who advocate a purely secular system appear to me, if I may venture to say so, to separate from education that which cannot be separated from it. If I exclude from my mind the idea of dogma or sectarianism in connexion with religious teaching, I find that the remainder is necessarily connected with every act of life, and especially with the communication of instruction. I do not think, Sir, that you can communicate even secular knowledge without imparting to it either a religious or an irreligious tone. You must have the one or the other: I believe you must have either. If this be so, and if you attempt to separate two things which cannot be separated, and endeavour by absolute prohibition to exclude a religious tone from your secular instruction, I say you maim education of a portion of its chief value.'

"Some specimens of, perhaps, as splendid invective as was ever known in a British Parliament might be culled from Mr. Higinbotham's speeches in the Legislative Assembly of Victoria during the Darling grant controversy; but I will not unearth more than one or two, of which I have a vivid recollection. On the 1st of August, 1867, the Committee of Supply discussed a proposal to vote £20,000 to Lady Darling in accordance with the resolution of the Legislative Assembly, adopted on the 9th of May, 1866. In the course of his speech in support of the vote, Mr. Higinbotham said :—

"'What is this vote now? It is not merely a compensation to Sir Charles Darling. It is not merely a renewal of the expressed opinion of this House upon his merits, but when it is passed it will be a decisive condemnation of those who pursued Sir Charles Darling through his whole political career, and who now avow themselves his unrelenting enemies. This vote when passed will be something more than a vote of money to Sir Charles Darling: it will be the censure of the Legislative Assembly upon the constitutional faction of 1865. . . . I rejoice that this vote will brand the enemies of Sir Charles Darling who pursued him while here, and who do not desist from that pursuit now. I will tell those honourable members that I have always considered the faction to which they belong as the very vilest faction by which this country has been cursed.'

"And in another part of the same speech he thus further denounced the same 'faction.'

"'The constitutional party was the most pretentious party which ever existed in this country. It included, according to its own account, all the self-styled respectability, the wealth, and the intelligence of the country. Wealth it certainly had, and it grossly abused that wealth; respectability—why, its respectability was the mere unfounded insolent pretence of a class; intelligence—well, Sir, its intelligence, I suppose, is fitly represented by honourable members I see opposite. That party, Sir, it will not be denied even by its members themselves in their calmer moments, has been a party more basely subservient to external influences, more hypocritical in its professions, more unprincipled in its acts, more outrageous in its language, both printed and spoken, than any party by which this country has ever been cursed.'

"Mr. Higinbotham's defence of Sir Charles Darling, after the latter had been recalled from the Governorship of Victoria, was as eloquent a tribute to the good qualities of the unfortunate Governor as one man could possibly pay to the merits of another.'

"'I believe,' said Mr. Higinbotham, 'that the feeling of this country, now as then, is one of sincere respect and sympathy for Sir Charles Darling. In one respect, Sir, I believe the feeling has changed. I believe that a reflection on the undeserved misfortunes of that gentleman has altered the sentiments of many towards him, that it has made many, even of his enemies, to be at peace with him, and to be willing that this vote should be passed even though they were opposed to his policy. The opinions of his friends and admirers—and they, I believe, are nine-tenths of the people of this country—remain unchanged. . . . I assert that the despatches show demonstratively that Sir Charles Darling was removed from office on account of an expression which may have been incautious, but which was never charged with being illegal. . . . Sir, I do not believe that a want of caution—and that is the only offence which has ever been charged against Sir Charles Darling by his ill-informed critics in England—I do not believe that an incautious expression will outweigh the sense of other and greater merits. Caution and prudence in a person holding the high office which he filled are qualities of a high order, but they are not the highest qualities. They may not be incompatible with higher qualities, but they do not often—they certainly do not always—accompany them. Sir Charles Darling possessed qualities with which caution and prudence are not always associated, but which are far higher qualities. He possessed intense hatred of wrong; he possessed a profound contempt for the persons who conspired against the public law; and he possessed the greatest determination to resist their designs at all hazards and risks.'

"This last sentence very felicitously expresses some of the traits of the character of the late George Higinbotham, as well as of Sir Charles Darling.

"Some observations made on different occasions by Mr. Higinbotham about the press are noteworthy, especially as proceeding from one at one period of his career a distinguished journalist. Addressing the Legislative Assembly on a motion for committing to the custody of the Sergeant-at-Arms, Mr. Hugh George, for publishing an article which the House declared to be a scandalous breach of its privileges, Mr. Higinbotham remarked :—

"'A person who asserts, when endeavouring to explain such a statement as that a person's speech "bristles with falsehood," that he merely intended to state that the speech was "not consistent with truth," endeavours to avail himself, as it seems to me, of the next least offensive expression that he could possibly use; and in making use of that less offensive, but still highly offensive expression, I say he aggravates the original offence. It is also declared by Mr. George, "in vindication of the liberty which the press of right enjoys, that, as thus understood, the article referred to is no more than a fair criticism upon a statement made by a servant of the Crown in his public capacity, and in a public place." That is to say, that the press of right enjoys the liberty of asserting of a public man that his words uttered in a public place, and on a public question, "bristle with falsehood." If that be the liberty of the press, I say the liberty of the press must be suppressed.'

"While supporting the action which the House was resolved to take on that memorable occasion, Mr. Higinbotham clearly showed that personally he cared nothing for any calumnies which the press uttered against public men.

"'For my own part,' he said, 'I am quite habituated to the use of such terms as "chicanery," "lawlessness," "revolutionary," and so forth, whether applied to this Ministry or to any other; for it has become the habit of the degraded press which now exists in this colony—it is simply a form in which personal passion, unguided either by reason or conscience, gives vent to its own baseness. . . . I do not hesitate to say that if the language which has been complained of had been applied to me, instead of the Chief Secretary, I should not have dreamt for a moment of appealing to this House. . . . I believe there is no epithet of vilification in the whole gamut of calumny, from the top to the bottom, that I would not allow to be used with respect to myself, for the simple reason that I agree with the hon. member for the Ovens, that these things do no personal harm to any one.'

"On one occasion, speaking of the attitude of a section of the press towards Sir Charles Darling, Mr. Higinbotham evoked the humour of the House by saying that—

"'In another country a Government warns the press—once, twice, thrice; but here, Sir, the press warns the Governor, and only gives him the benefit of a single warning.'

"Many of the memorable utterances of Mr. Higinbotham, both in Parliament and on the platform, were very epigrammatic. His reference to a certain section of politicians as the 'wealthy lower orders' is still as familiar in the mouths of the people of Victoria as household words. On one occasion, seeing that members made words spoken at one time apply to different and unsuitable circumstances, he characterised *Hansard* (the authorised version of the Victorian Parliamentary Debates) as a 'barren and mischievous publication.'

"In 1867, during a debate on a motion by Mr. Macpherson, against a contemplated dissolution of the Legislative Assembly, Mr. Higinbotham referred to the English Constitution as 'a constitution which has been described as a democracy in disguise, and which seems at the present time in England very much disposed to strip off that disguise.'

"Some of Mr. Higinbotham's expressions have been misquoted so often, or quoted apart from their context, as to convey a very erroneous notion of the sentiments he really intended to convey by them. One conspicuous example is the well-known allusion to Sir Frederick Rogers, subsequently Lord Blachford. The quotation is almost invariably given as 'the man Rogers.'"

[The whole speech is given elsewhere,[1] and it will be seen that the exact words are "a person named Rogers.'

[1] Chap. xviii. p. 183.

People often say Mr. Higinbotham "used to speak" of him as the man Rogers. He only alluded to the gentleman on this one occasion.]

"A very simple remark made early in the first session of the Parliament elected after the McCulloch Government appealed to the country on the Appropriation-*cum*-Tariff Bill has been singularly perverted. A well-known writer has credited Mr. Higinbotham with declaring on one occasion that 'members were returned to vote, not to discuss,' and substantially the same thing has been asserted times out of number; but by quoting Mr. Higinbotham's own language it will be seen that his words have been greatly distorted. *Hansard* reports him thus:—

"'The Government, if he rightly understood the effect of the elections, came into Parliament not to discuss the tariff, but to pass it. . . . As soon as that House passed the tariff, and as soon as it was laid aside and afterwards rejected in another place, all the members of the Assembly, excepting a small minority, were agreed on this— whether the tariff was protective or free trade, whether it contained within it a vicious system of financial policy or a wise one, the interests and rights of that House were bound up in that Tariff, and that if an appeal were made to the country at all—if the members of the Assembly were put to the trouble and expense, and the indignity, under the circumstances, of having to go to the country, they would go for the purpose of carrying this tariff into law. They were now in the House for that purpose, and they were not there to discuss the character of the tariff.'

"As far back as April 1869, Mr. Higinbotham felt constrained to speak from his place in Parliament in these terms:—

"'It sometimes seems to me that political life is, I would almost say, a sort of pandemonium, in which a number of lost souls are endeavouring to increase one another's tortures.'

"It is not surprising, remembering the sensitive nature of the man, and how many things occurred between that time and 1876 to shatter his political hopes and aspirations, that in the latter year he resigned his seat in the Legislative Assembly and retired altogether from political life.

"I will close these reminiscences by mentioning an incident which caused some amusement at the time it occurred. Besides the blemishes on political life indicated in the quotation just given, the time of Parliament was frequently wasted in Mr. Higinbotham's day by futile discussions arising out of some misunderstanding between the two sides of the Assembly—a state of affairs not wholly unknown even now. A debate, already somewhat prolonged, would be adjourned to some future evening on the assurance given to the Government that it would be finished at an early hour on the night appointed for its resumption. Almost invariably, when that night arrived, a conflict of testimony ensued as to the precise nature of the agreement, the result being irritation and squabbling. With wisdom begotten of experience, Mr. Higinbotham on one occasion, in consenting to the adjournment of a debate, quietly remarked, more in sorrow than in anger, 'Let it be clearly understood that there is no understanding.'"

CHAPTER XXIII

BARRISTER

GEORGE HIGINBOTHAM was a practising barrister for nearly twenty years. From the date of his admission to the Victorian Bar to his acceptance of a seat on the Supreme Court Bench is more than twenty-six years, but from this number must be deducted part of the time when he was editor of the *Argus* and the time when he was Attorney-General. Of course as Attorney-General he was not absent from the Courts, but he would only appear in his official capacity. He regarded his salary as a retainer which entitled the Crown to the whole of his services. Before his time barristers in the position of Attorney-General took outside work as in England, but since his time the example which he set has been generally followed.

When a barrister commences work, he naturally is unable to choose the kind of practice that he would prefer. He takes the briefs that come to him, now in the County Court, now in Chambers, now in the Supreme Court, civil cases, criminal cases ; but soon, if he be even moderately successful, the work has a tendency to sort itself, and the kind that fell to Mr. Higinbotham in his earlier years was chiefly pleadings. One who was often his junior speaks of the result of this work shown in " his profound knowledge of pleading and of the law of evidence."

When Mr. Higinbotham emerged from office in May, 1868,

with a great reputation as an orator, the coast was clear for him. Many of the brilliant advocates and able lawyers were gone who made the fifteen years of the Victorian Bar following the discovery of gold famous in its forensic annals. Mr. Higinbotham at once stepped into large practice. His able political opponent, Mr. Fellows, was the recognised leader of the Bar; and when in 1872 Mr. Fellows accepted a judgeship Mr. Higinbotham certainly filled that position,[1] until on the death of Mr. Justice Fellows, though not immediately thereon, Mr. Higinbotham succeeded that distinguished judge upon the Bench.

A man naturally takes into his profession the characteristics that mark him as a man. The qualities that mark Mr. Higinbotham the barrister are conscientious thoroughness, a high sense of honour, love of justice, courtesy in word and deed. Nothing was more characteristic than the elaborate pains with which he studied every case, and this careful preparation guarded him against surprises in the court. One who was often his junior speaks of his

invariable and thorough study of both the facts and the law of the cases in which he was retained. His study was minute and accurate. On more than one occasion he has asked me to work out some point which might possibly arise at the trial, and more than once this working-up was fruitless, as the opponents did not take the point.

Another writer says, "he was certainly one of the most minute thinkers and workers that ever graced the Victorian Bar. To such an extreme was this carried that his briefs were invariably expanded and epitomised in the form of a genealogical tree, the arguments being committed with immense care to paper." The adverb "invariably" and the epithet "immense" push this statement to an extreme: docked of those two words, it is true. This carefulness was so natural to him that it may be said he was never in a hurry. The same former junior says that Higinbotham was frequently

afraid that evidence would be given too fast to allow of its being fully grasped not only by the jury but by the judge. Often and often,

---

[1] On December 12th, 1870, a general retainer was given to Mr Higinbotham as Standing Counsel for the Corporation of the City of Melbourne.

both in court and in private conversation, he would chide me for hurrying on the answers from a witness, and no doubt he was right.

Later comment will be made on the development of this feeling in his judicial work.

Mr. Higinbotham was slow in making up his mind on legal as on other questions, but when once he saw his way clear it was difficult, if not impossible, to shake him. When certain he was very certain. The following story is told by a political opponent,[1] and, as he acknowledges, is probably apocryphal. It is however eminently characteristic, and it may be added that the trait is exactly what we are called upon to admire in *Athanasius contra mundum*.

An insurance director in Parliament used to tell the story that a judge and jury decided against the company in an action in which Mr. Higinbotham had advised. "Well," said counsel, "the judge and jury are wrong." On this the company went to the Full Court, which was against them. "Well," said Mr. Higinbotham, "the Full Court is wrong." The company therefore went to the Privy Council, which was unanimously adverse. "Well," said Mr. Higinbotham, as his final word, "the Privy Council is wrong." Probably the tale is apocryphal, but it exemplifies the firmness and fervour of the hon. gentleman when he had made up his mind.

So high was Mr. Higinbotham's sense of honour that he would never take up a case unless he was satisfied that it was right. Attorneys in consequence naturally refrained from bringing him doubtful cases.

Instance after instance (writes the same political opponent) could be mentioned in which he refused briefs because he was by no means satisfied with the equities of the case. The professional man who abuses his client out of court, and his client's adversary in court, was not his type. On the contrary, a business interview, or a friendly chat about a case would reveal to the most obtuse the inherent probity and the essential delicacy of his character.

The doctrine that a barrister owes a double duty was held by him in contradistinction to Erskine's view that the advocate has a duty only to his client. Higinbotham held that a barrister was bound to believe his client until the evidence was too strong against him, but he also held that truth and

[1] "Timotheus" in the *Argus*, January 7th, 1893.

right should limit and guide his conduct. This latter view indeed he pushed, as some would think, almost to an extreme. A logical mind combined with courage leads to extreme views. Once when Higinbotham was defending a bank clerk, evidence of a convincing nature being given, he persuaded his client to withdraw his plea of "not guilty," and those who held the opposite view of an advocate's duty were shocked. Yet another case may be quoted. "An illustration of his lofty view of the responsibilities of an advocate was afforded during the progress of a case of great magnitude in which he was engaged. After the case had been on for some weeks Mr. Higinbotham suddenly discovered that certain steps had been taken on behalf of his clients of a more than doubtful nature. He at once demanded an explanation, and none satisfactory being offered he at once resigned his brief." The ethical tone of the Bar on such points is not very certain. Since Courvoisier's case most barristers repudiate the extreme doctrine of Erskine, but they certainly refrain from the opposite extreme.

George Higinbotham's inborn courtesy was as remarkable as his lofty sense of honour. His manner towards other counsel was most just and pleasing, gentleness with perfect firmness towards his opponents, and a delicate and kindly sympathy towards juniors. *O si sic omnes!*

A suggestion from a junior (writes the same friend already quoted) has often brought down on me a snub from my leader in court : but Mr. Higinbotham, on hearing the suggestion, would either adopt it, and in open court give me the praise for it, or would quietly lay his hand on my shoulder to imply that he understood, but did not agree with my idea.

Anything that approached discourtesy to women disgusted him. There was one case in which he was second counsel with a leader (since dead) and a junior. His client, the defendant, was being examined by the leader, and in his evidence used a vulgar expression of the plaintiff, a lady. Higinbotham made an exclamation of disgust, and said to the attorney opposite, "I really think that I had better return my brief." The attorney pacified him as well as he could till the client got out of the box and took a seat at the table. Higinbotham glared at him, and expressed his disgust at the use of such an expression of a woman. "Why, my goodness gracious," said he, " Mr. — —" (the leading counsel) " told me in consultation that that was the best expression possible to use."

The most formidable case that ever fell to his lot was Cornish and Bruce v. the Queen. The plaintiffs were railway contractors on a very large scale, and had retained all the leaders at the Bar. Mr. Higinbotham defended as Attorney-General, having, with one exception, only juniors to assist him. The case lasted two months, and was of an intricate nature. One of the juniors, Mr. (now Sir) Henry Wrixon, testifies to "the marked ability and astounding capacity for work which the Attorney-General displayed. He had all his heavy work as Attorney-General as well. We juniors felt done up by the case alone." Tradition in the family speaks of the great physical exhaustion of the Attorney-General, as well as of his brother, the Engineer-in-Chief, who was the most important witness for the Crown.

It fell to his lot as Attorney-General to prosecute a well-connected young fellow who went out bush-ranging, and whilst robbing a place shot in a scuffle one of the inmates of the house. It was not deliberate murder; but robbery under arms is, in Australia, a capital offence. Mr. Higinbotham put the case skilfully, but quite fairly. The jury convicted, and sentence of death was passed. A friend writes : "I was with the Attorney-General alone in the robing-room after we had left the court at about ten o'clock in the evening. He expressed deep pity for the young fellow in quite an involuntary manner. He had that knack of keeping his feelings distinct from his sense of duty. The youth was hanged, but at the Council the Attorney-General voted to spare his life."

With juries Mr. Higinbotham was very successful. His manner was so persuasive, earnest, and dignified. It is true that he did not put the same fire into forensic speeches as into his great political orations; nor was the court thronged with listeners as in the days when Dawson or Ireland were indulging in impassioned oratory. A gentle persuasiveness of manner, a "sweet reasonableness" of tone, are not attractive of crowds; but the jurors liked to hear him. They felt he helped them. Indeed a barrister once complained that it was not fair of juries to pay him such attention : Higinbotham was only an advocate, and they paid as much attention as if he were a judge.

The most famous speech that Mr. Higinbotham made at the Bar was the defence of Supple, a barrister and journalist, who shot at Mr. G. Paton Smith, a brother barrister, who had been Attorney-General, and killed Mr. J. S. Walshe, a publican. The *Argus*[1] described Mr. Higinbotham's speech as a splendid specimen of forensic eloquence. He spoke with extreme pathos, and at times was so much affected that his voice almost broke down. The line of defence was that Supple was not sane.

There was no sufficient motive for the crime. He was suffering from short-sightedness, which had been rapidly increasing until it had resulted in almost absolute blindness. A young man, dependent on his own exertions not merely for success but for existence, he found himself, after a long struggle with life, with prospects marred by that sad affliction. With such a future before him, it could not be wondered at that a sensitive, despondent man should altogether give way and lose his faculties. Various cases might be quoted that of Lord Ferrers, of Bellingham (in whose case subsequent reflection had shown that justice was too hasty, it was a legal murder), of McNaughton, who shot Mr. Drummond, the secretary for Sir Robert Peel, under the delusion that he was the victim of a widespread persecution and conspiracy. The jury had to consider what was the state of the prisoner Supple's mind. There was no doubt that there was a difference between legal and medical authority on the subject of insanity. By the law a man was supposed to be sane if he knew that the act he was about to commit was unlawful. Medical authorities declared with one voice that there was another kind of insanity where a man was dragged on by an irresistible impulse and overwhelming control to do wrong. Medical authorities, also, with one voice declared that such persons were not only capable of distinguishing right from wrong, but used the utmost cleverness and ingenuity in endeavouring to avoid the restraints which they know will follow their acts.

Such is a very brief outline of the arguments by which Mr. Higinbotham sought to prove Supple insane.

The profession of barrister was not by any means so lucrative to Mr. Higinbotham as to others in a leading position. It has often been said that he made a patriotic sacrifice in taking a judgeship. As a matter of fact it was no

[1] July 21st, 1870.

sacrifice at all. The salary of a Judge of the Supreme-Court is £3,000 a year : and only in one year had his practice at the Bar brought in as much. It is well known that many practising barristers in Victoria have earned much larger incomes, rising in a few cases even to three times the amount. There were two special reasons why Mr. Higinbotham's professional income was not so large as that of others, besides his attitude towards doubtful cases. He himself kept fees low. If a solicitor marked a brief at so many guineas and he thought the work was not worth the sum, he would scratch it out and write a smaller sum. Secondly, because of the relations between himself and some of the judges, he refused to take Chamber business, and, as lawyers can testify, that "leads to so much." It was not, however, the increased income nor its regularity that tempted him, to the surprise of the profession, to accept a seat upon the Bench, but rather the fact that he was growing tired of advocacy.

With a very keen feeling for the honour of his profession and a very high standard in its practice, he had not a real liking for the law, as generally followed. Sir Henry Wrixon says that once Mr. Higinbotham told him that he believed that in time the world would come to having a class of advocates paid like judges, by the State, and not by clients, and that to them causes would be assigned to conduct fairly. Then the truth and only the truth, not victory for a client would be sought. This seemed to him a much more satisfactory system.

CHAPTER XXIV

PUISNE JUDGE, AND THEN CHIEF JUSTICE

Appointed Puisne Judge by Service Ministry (1880)—The difficulties
Answer to letter of congratulation (1886)—Made Chief Justice
by Gillies-Deakin Coalition—Conscientious—Some said "too
slow"—Great worker—"What you believe to be right"—
Judicial dignity—No lounging nor flippancy—The oath—
Unsuitable garb—Prison dress—Manner towards counsel—
Women in court—Extra pay—The dinners—Case of Ah Toy.

In the year 1880, Mr. Service being Premier and the Marquis
of Normanby Governor of Victoria, George Higinbotham was
promoted to the "splendid obscurity" of the Supreme Court
Bench. The appointment was actually made when the short-
lived Service Ministry of that year was moribund, but the
retiring Premier was able to prove to the Governor that
negotiations had been going on with Mr. Higinbotham for
some time prior to the vote of want of confidence, and that
the appointment would be extremely popular with the people
of the colony of every shade of opinion. Mr. Higinbotham
had once previously been offered a judgeship, but the offer
had been made by a Premier who had grossly insulted his
brother, and on that account he had refused it. The negotiations with Mr. Service, in which his old friend Mr. Francis
had also taken part, entirely turned upon the Governor's
instructions, and Mr. Service had undertaken that if the
Executive had need of the Judge's presence he should be
summoned without any reference to the instructions. When
the news was announced that Mr. Higinbotham was to be the
new judge, the satisfaction felt throughout the colony was
both general and sincere.

Here is an answer to one of the many letters of congratulation received :—

BRIGHTON,
July 29th, 1880.

MY DEAR MR. RICHARDSON,

I thank you most sincerely for your very kind letter. Your approval of my acceptance of the office of Judge is peculiar gratifying to me. Recently I have often had an uneasy feeling that I was a skulker from duty as a politician when hard fighting was going on close at hand, and I have only reassured myself (not always quite to my own satisfaction) by the thought that I was not, and could not be, a faithful soldier on either side, and that I might fairly be shot down as a suspected interloper by the combatants on both sides. Your words fortify me in the belief that I have not erred in accepting work when it was offered to me in the narrower but yet honourable sphere of judicial duty.

But I shall never cease to be a politician, in the sense in which you and I have understood the term, to my life's end, and as a Victorian politician I shall continue to watch your course in Parliament with close attention and interest, and with the warm sympathy which springs from feelings nearly identical, I believe, in reference to matters of the highest concern.

Believe me,
Yours very faithfully,
(Signed)   GEORGE HIGINBOTHAM.

In September, 1886, Sir William Foster Stawell, who had been Chief Justice of Victoria since 1857, retired. Mr. Justice Higinbotham, although only six years on the Bench, was the Senior Puisne Judge. During the six years there had been many losses. In November, 1880, Sir Redmond Barry, after nearly twenty-nine years of judicial life, had died. In the following year fell the death of Mr. Justice Wilberforce Stephen, who was a judge for seven years only.

In 1886 two veterans retired in the persons of Sir William Stawell and Mr. Justice Molesworth. The latter had been thirty years a judge, and was close upon eighty years of age when he determined to spend the remainder of his days in well-earned rest. On his retirement (May 6th, 1886) he was knighted, and as Sir Robert Molesworth lived until October, 1890.

Thus Mr. Justice Higinbotham became the Senior Puisne Judge ; and the Ministry of the day, the Coalition under Messrs. Gillies and Deakin, hesitated not an instant to

s 2

appoint him Chief Justice. Once more public opinion and the goodwill of the profession ratified the appointment.

As a judge Mr. Higinbotham showed the same characteristics that he displayed as a barrister, the same qualities that he had as a man. He was conscientious, painstaking, and filled with a high sense of duty. A charge is often made that he had the defect of his quality. It was said that he took too great pains, that his elaborate note-taking, even though for criminal cases in shorthand, was the cause of delay, and that justice should not be delayed. In cases where other judges would say " Are the affidavits right ?" he would say " Read the affidavits." There is something in the charge, and certainly it is true that the slowness increased in the last year or two of the Judge's life. Not that there was any mental failing ; against this he was, and he charged his medical attendant to be, ever on the watch : but it is true that the deliberateness grew more deliberate and the slowness increased. His judgments were long, chiefly because he liked to set out all the facts of a case for the Reports.

There can be no doubt that he worked too hard. The work of the second consolidation by itself would have taxed the strength of a younger man. The Chief Justice added it to his judicial work, from which he was never absent. At a time when he needed more rest, he would work at reserved judgments late into the night. The custom of the Bar is that when at a consultation there is substantial agreement upon an opinion the junior counsel writes it out. *Juniores ad labores*,[1] is within limits a sound doctrine in life. Mr. Higinbotham never held it. When he was Chief Justice, if the judges agreed on an opinion, he would write it. His colleagues were most ready and willing to help him, but such was his appetite for work he preferred to do it himself. Once, about three months before the end, when a cold detained him a day from the courts, three of the Puisne Judges called in the after-

---

[1] When, twenty-five years ago, I was a master at Radley, I rode one morning to Cuddesdon to let the Bishop of Oxford know that the floods would not prevent his crossing the river at Sandford to a confirmation. The Bishop (Wilberforce) and his chaplain rode back with me. They talked high and not interesting theology. When I dismounted to open a gate, the Bishop called out, "Juniores ad labores." "Yes," said his companion, afterwards also a bishop ; " but the eldest pays the turnpike."

noon begging each for himself that he might be permitted to take an approaching circuit for the Chief, who, however, would not hear of it. Indeed it is not too much to say that he was beloved by his brother judges and by all who came into contact with him at the courts "on this side idolatry." No man could be more careful of the reputation of others, of county court judges and police magistrates, from whose decisions an appeal could come to him. If he thought a mistake had been made, it was in the gentlest terms rectified.

"How do you like the work?" he asked once of a judge who was new to the Bench. "I feel the responsibility," was the natural reply. "It is so hard to be sure that I am doing what is right." "You are not here to do what is right," was the seemingly strange answer; and to the look of astonishment the Chief continued, "You are here to do what you believe to be right." "Thank you; that is very helpful," said the younger judge.

Was Higinbotham a great lawyer? Where there is certainly a difference of opinion, it is difficult for a layman to decide. One who had the capacity and some opportunities for judging wrote :—

If I had ever been before Higinbotham as a litigant, I should probably have felt a doubt as to his law. I often did. I think he was too great a man to be a great technical lawyer. He could not lose sight of the object in the instrument. But I should have had no feeling of soreness. From——, (and here a name is given which must not be printed) a decision in my favour would be only one degree less unsatisfactory than a reverse, because I should suspect the process by which he arrived at it.

Upon the other hand a brother judge declares that Higinbotham's knowledge of the law, especially case-law, was profound, whilst few could doubt that the consolidator of the statutes knew the statutes, and that laws were familiar to the legislator who had borne his part in making many laws. It cannot be denied that as a general rule Higinbotham's decisions gave satisfaction to suitors, and it is not altogether easy to give satisfaction to suitors. His painstaking and manifest desire to decide aright impressed them.

The Chief Justice was a great believer in judicial dignity, insisting upon the etiquette of the courts and all due observance of external formalities. Surprise has not seldom been expressed that one who was acknowledged a true democrat should insist on such matters. Surely the surprise is shallow; but the feeling is so common that it needs an answer. Democracy does not mean anarchy; it literally means government by the people; that is, it finds the basis of government in the popular will, and it is little more than ridiculous to suppose that this means the abolition of form and ceremony. So far from meaning the removal of government the danger of democracy rather lies in the contrary direction, too much interference. The ideal of a true democrat is perfect simplicity in private life, a simplicity that is in strict accord with dignity, and in public life everything that wins respect for the power and authority that the people have given.

The Associates have told me that the Chief Justice was very particular that the oath should be administered carefully and solemnly to juries and to witnesses. There was to be no gabbling over so serious a business; but the juryman or witness was fully to understand its sacred import.

In his Court everything went smoothly, and there was an atmosphere of calm and dignity. Not only did the Chief shrink from slang, but he never used colloquial language in a judgment. When the Chief was summing up, the barristers would crowd into the court. He was always clear and lucid, and frequently eloquent.

Believing that respect is due to a court of law, the Chief Justice would never permit a witness to adopt a lounging attitude in the witness-box, and the more highly placed such a witness was, the more likely he was to be called sternly to attention. One story is told about a medical man, one of the leaders of his profession, being suddenly checked when the attitude he adopted was free and easy. "Take your hands out of your pockets, sir." There is another story about a less eminent doctor in an assize town, who ventured to be flippant in his answers. My informant was so seated in the Court that he could not see the Chief's face, but in the doctor's he saw a look of abject terror suddenly succeed the flippancy. No word had passed, but afterwards my friend heard the doctor explain how he had meant to brazen it out, when "suddenly a lightning flash darted from those clear blue eyes," and he was overpowered. In the Chief's presence ever "the flippant put himself to school." If in court he neglected so to do, he was quickly brought to his bearings.

As one method of maintaining the diginity of the Court, the Chief would rebuke witnesses who appeared before him in an unsuitable garb. In an assize town a carter about to give evidence entered the witness-box without a coat. He was sternly rebuked. "Are you aware, sir, that you have come before the highest tribunal in the land?" Perhaps a better instance is that of the policeman who appeared to give evidence in mufti, and being asked by the judge why he did not appear in uniform, replied that he only wore it on duty. He was promptly told that the duty on which he was then engaged, giving evidence so as to secure the ends of justice, was the highest duty that he could be called upon to perform. It was the Chief Justice who formulated the rule about prisoners wearing prison garb.

There is no objection from a judicial point of view to a prisoner who is undergoing sentence being brought up in the ordinary prison dress for the purpose of giving evidence. It is expedient and right in my opinion, that a prisoner should not be allowed to enter the witness box except in his prison dress. The fact that he is a convicted offender justly detracts from his credit as a witness, and that fact should not be concealed from the jury by permitting the prisoner to adopt a dress other than that usually worn by offenders undergoing sentence.

The case of a prisoner placed in the dock to take his trial on a second charge is wholly different. The judges do not approve and they probably would not permit an accused person to be placed at the disadvantage and exposed to the humiliation and prejudice of having to plead and defend himself while dressed in prison clothes. His previous conviction should not weigh with the jury in considering the new charge brought against him and they should not be constantly reminded by his attire of a fact prejudicial to him and irrelevant to the issue they have to try.

I think it is desirable that the practice should be settled. It is of the highest importance that the rule adopted should be observed with strict uniformity and that there should be no departure from it in the case of particular prisoners.

(Signed)   GEO. HIGINBOTHAM,
Chief Justice.

21st November, 1889.

With respect to the question of the demeanour of witnesses, the Chief Justice concurred with his predecessor in the view that witness-boxes should be so constructed that the legs of a witness should be visible. From demeanour it is often necessary to judge whether witnesses are speaking truth. The false witness fidgets, is uneasy, and shuffles his feet; therefore let legs be visible.

The manner of the Chief Justice towards counsel was ever a model. Studious politeness and unwavering courtesy marked it. It cannot by any means be said that he did not interrupt counsel during the course of an argument. He knew that sometimes an interruption by showing to the barrister the direction of a judge's thought may be of great assistance. On the other hand he recognised that the practice should be rigorously kept in check, as it is unfair to a counsel to take him off the main line of his argument on to a by-way, where perhaps there is no thoroughfare. All judges know this, but they are sometimes carried away, and the Chief Justice used to confess that he interrupted too much. Altercations with counsel Higinbotham would carefully avoid, though sometimes his patience was sorely tried, but barristers knew the limits. There was no storm, but the symptoms that preceded trouble. The voice sank lower but gained in intensity. Never was it then disobeyed.

Courtesy to women was so natural to Mr. Higinbotham and went so far with him that some thought he attached too much weight to the evidence of a female witness, indeed that he was soft to the sex. Here is counsel's opinion :—

I thought so formerly, but I had once to appear before him in Chambers on behalf of a very charming client who had some property but would not pay her debts. The case was heard in his own room, and he was courtesy itself. He stood when she entered. I think she dropped her handkerchief, and he left his seat to pick it up. Nothing could be gentler than his manner, and I was congratulating myself on an easy victory : but when the facts were heard, came the decision that my client must pay or spend six months in prison.

The Chief Justice in the colony of Victoria receives in salary £500 a year more than the Puisne judges. So strongly did Mr. Higinbotham hold the doctrine that the Chief was only *primus inter pares*, necessary as a chairman, and representative of the Bench, and to make official arrangements, but with no other authority, that he regularly set apart the extra £500 as if that sum was not part of his private income. With it he used to entertain the members of the profession at one of the Melbourne hotels. At the beginning of each legal year he gave a series of four dinners, to one of which he invited all the judges—County Court as well as Supreme Court—all the chief officers of the Court, and before amalgamation all the barristers, and an equal number of solicitors. After amalgamation all the lawyers were of necessity placed on a single list, but it was then impossible to invite them all every year. All who were privileged to be present on these occasions testify that the Chief was one of the best and kindest of hosts, that all judicial stiffness thawed, and the full geniality of the man came out. They testify further that the dinners served the purpose which the host desired, and brought men together in a friendly way. It is even said that feuds, perhaps more than one or two, were healed at these dinners.

The case of Ah Toy forms a sort of link between Higinbotham, C. J., and Higinbotham the practical politician. It was a law case famous at the time, involving political issues. As it was not ultimately decided on the main questions raised, the case is not important from a lawyer's point of view, but the judgment of the Chief Justice was so typical that some account of *Toy* v. *Musgrove* must be given here.

On April 27th, 1888, a British ship named the *Afghan* arrived in the Port of Melbourne, having on board some 268 Chinese immigrants, amongst the number being one Chun Teeong Toy. Having regard to the provisions of certain Acts which were then in force, and had been passed by the Victorian Legislature with the view of restricting the immigration of Chinese, this number was 254 in excess of what the *Afghan* could lawfully bring into the port. Previously to the arrival of the ship, Mr. Musgrove, the collector of customs, received instructions from the Commissioner of Trade and Customs, the responsible Minister of the Crown for Victoria, in whose department lay the administration of the laws relating to immigration, that no Chinese, other than such as were British subjects, should be allowed to enter Victoria. Mr. Musgrove acted in accordance with his instructions, and Chun Teeong Toy was one of those who were not permitted to land. In order to test the legality of this exclusion of himself and of his fellow-countrymen, Chun Teeong Toy proceeded to bring an action in the Supreme Court of Victoria, alleging that he had been wrongfully prevented from landing, and claiming damages from Mr. Musgrove. To this claim Mr. Musgrove's first defence was a denial of the jurisdiction of the Court to entertain the action, asserting that his acts were, as being acts of State, ratified and approved by the responsible Minister, and by Her Majesty's Government of Victoria. The second defence was that the acts complained of were lawful, having been done by virtue of the power or prerogative of the Crown of England to exclude aliens; that this power as to Victoria was vested in the Governor of Victoria, to be exercised by him by and through Her Majesty's responsible Ministers for Victoria; and that this power had been so exercised. This latter defence it will be observed involved the consideration of the question whether the colony of Victoria has or has not what is known as responsible government. At the outset the parties agreed that the result of the action should be determined by the decision of the Full Court on the argument of the questions of law raised by the pleadings, subject to either party's right to appeal to the Privy Council. A strong Bar was retained by each side, Mr. (now Sir Henry) Wrixon, who at that time held the office of Attorney-General, being the leading counsel for the defendant. And on account of the special importance of the questions to be decided, the case was heard by all six judges of the Supreme Court. At the conclusion of elaborate arguments, which had lasted several days, the judges reserved their decision, and after the lapse of some weeks delivered their considered judgments. All were agreed that the Court had jurisdiction to entertain the action, and that the acts of the defendant were not acts of State. As to the second defence, however, they were divided in opinion, the majority consisting of Mr. Justice Williams, Mr. Justice Holroyd, Mr. Justice à Beckett, and Mr. Justice Wrenfordsley being in favour of the plaintiff, while the Chief Justice and Mr. Justice Kerferd decided in favour of the defendant.

The Chief Justice in his judgment held that the right to exclude aliens is a continuing prerogative of the Crown of

England, and that a power equivalent to this prerogative has been vested by law in the representative of the Crown in Victoria, and can be exercised by the representative of the Crown, upon the advice of his responsible Ministers. The argument upon this part of the case, he said "raises for the first time in this Court, constitutional questions of supreme importance. We are called upon for the purpose of adjudicating upon the rights of the parties in this case to ascertain and determine what is the origin and source of the constitutional rights of self-government belonging by law to the people of Victoria, and, if such rights exist, what is the extent and what are the limits assigned to them by law." The subject he dealt with at length, and while doing so said, with reference to his predecessor, Sir William Foster Stawell :—

In this place, and by the members of the profession of the law, it is not, and I hope it never will be, forgotten, that the foremost, *longo intervallo*, of the pioneers of Victorian legislation, foremost in capacity, in public spirit, and in unselfish devotion to exacting duties and to unremitting and stupendous labours, was he who afterwards as Chief Justice of this Court administered for twenty-nine years the general body of Victorian laws, most of which he had himself designed, prepared, and carried into legislative effect. The fact that Mr. Stawell drafted the Constitution Bill and carried it through the Legislative Council is a fact of which I feel that I am at liberty to take cognisance, and it is a fact which imposes on me, and on every judge who may with me allow himself to notice it, a special duty to seek diligently until we find that of which the name of its author guarantees the existence, namely, a rational and consistent meaning and purpose in the whole and in all parts of the measure.

His conclusions were summed up in the following terms :—

I am of opinion, first, that the Constitution Act, as amended and limited by the Constitution Statute, is the only source and origin of the constitutional rights of self-government of the people of Victoria : secondly, that a constitution, or complete system of government, as well as a constitution of the Houses of Legislature, was the design present to the minds of the framers of the Constitution Act, and that that design has found adequate, though obscure, legal expression in that act ; thirdly, that the two bodies created by the Constitution Act, the Government and the Parliament of Victoria, have been invested with co-ordinate and interrelated, but distinct functions, and are designed on the model of the Government and the Parliament of Great Britain to aid each other in establishing and maintaining plenary rights of self-government, in internal affairs for the people of Victoria ; fourthly, that the Executive Government of Victoria, consisting of the Ministers of the Crown, are responsible to the Parliament of Victoria for the exercise of all the powers vested by the Constitution Act in the Governor as the representative of the Crown in Victoria, and that they, and they alone, have the right to influence, guide, and control him in the exercise of his constitutional powers created by the Constitution Act; fifthly, that the Executive Government of Victoria possesses and exercises necessary functions under and by virtue of the Constitution Act, similar to, and co-extensive, as regards the internal affairs of Victoria, with the functions possessed and exercised by the Imperial Government with regard to the internal affairs of Great Britain. Sixthly, that the Executive Government of Victoria, in the execution of the statutory powers of the Governor expressed and implied and in the exercise of its own functions, has a legal right and duty, subject to the approval of Parliament, and so far as may be consistent with the statute law and the provisions of treaties binding the Crown, the Government, and the Legislature of Victoria, to do all acts and to make all provisions that can be necessary and that are in its opinion necessary or expedient for the reasonable and proper administration of law, and the conduct of public affairs, and for the security, safety, or welfare of the people of Victoria.

From the decision of the Full Court the defendant appealed to the Privy Council, before whom Sir Horace Davey, Q.C., and Mr. Wrixon argued the case on his behalf. The judgment of the Privy Council was delivered by the Lord Chancellor, and was to the effect that no cause of action was disclosed by the plaintiff, and that the decision of the Full Court should be reversed. As the judgment was based upon the construction of the Victorian Statutes, regulating the admission of Chinese emigrants into the colony, it became unnecessary to give a decision upon the other branches of the case; and the Lord Chancellor therefore declined to express any opinion as to what rights the Executive Government of Victoria has, under the constitution conferred upon it, derived from the Crown. Thus the constitutional questions argued before the Full Court remain undecided.

CHAPTER XXV

THOMAS HIGINBOTHAM

Death of brother Thomas at Brighton— Extracts from Minutes of Institute of Civil Engineers, from the Argus, from the Gippsland Times.

LESS than two months after the acceptance by George Higinbotham of a seat on the Bench, he suffered his greatest domestic loss in the death of his brother Thomas, the engineer-in-chief of the Victorian Railways. Throughout this book very little is said, or ought to be said, of Mr. Higinbotham's home life, but allusion has been made in an earlier chapter to the beautiful friendship that existed between him and his brother. For nearly twenty-three years they had lived together in unbroken affection. The elder brother was the later of the two to emigrate, and arrived in the colony towards the end of 1857. The two brothers lived together for about three years in the small house at Emerald Hill, but towards the end of 1860 they determined to move to Brighton; and there, upon the shore of Port Phillip, a house was erected, which became one of the most charming homes in the colony. The house was built in villa fashion, with a single floor and a broad verandah running round three sides. A lawn with openings through tea-tree scrub separated the house from the beach, and a beautiful avenue of trees connected it with the road, by the side of which there was a large and pleasant garden. The planning of the building and the laying-out of the grounds were chiefly in the hands of the engineer brother. On such a subject not much must be said here, but I cannot but bear my testimony that it was a peaceful, a happy, and a beautiful home.

The death of Mr. Thomas Higinbotham was painfully

sudden. One Sunday morning, the 5th of September, 1880, he was found dead in his bed. An examination after death was made and an inquest held, when the jury in accordance with medical evidence, found the cause of death "effusion of serum in the cavities of the brain and heart." So sudden a death gave a great shock to the whole community. It was equally sudden to his relatives, for though on the previous day he had complained of not feeling well, especially of feeling chilly, there was no reason to think it was anything more than a passing ailment. Certain words which Mr. Thomas Higinbotham had used a few days previously to a friend were remembered after his death, and a new signification given to them. "I think I now see the end of the furrow I have been ploughing so long." But there was no reason to believe that he had any presentiment of death. He meant that circumstances would compel him to resign his office. Nearly three years before, Mr. Higinbotham, together with many officials of the highest rank in the colony, had been dismissed from office by the Berry Ministry on "Black Wednesday" (January 8th, 1878). When the Service Ministry came into power (May, 1880), one of its earliest acts was to reinstate Mr. Higinbotham as engineer-in-chief, and the reinstatement gave general satisfaction throughout the colony. But the Service Ministry of that year was very short lived The new ministry did not disturb Mr. Higinbotham in office, and it was said had no intention to interfere with him, but the reappointment by the Government of a subordinate officer in the department, of whom Mr. Higinbotham had serious reason to disapprove, troubled him sorely during the last few days of his life, and he had made up his mind to resign.

It has been previously stated that his brother wrote the brief memoir published in the *Minutes of Proceedings of the Institute of Civil Engineers*. The earlier part of the memoir is given at the place where Mr. Thomas Higinbotham is first introduced to the reader.[1] The remainder of it is given here :—

He continued to hold the office of engineer-in-chief until the month of January, 1878, when, as a result of the conflict which then took

---

[1] Page 40.

place between the two Houses of the Legislature, and the political excitement which followed thereon, he, together with county court judges, police magistrates, and other officers of high rank in the public service, were all removed from their offices. His services were sought for during the two succeeding years by the governments of the adjoining Australasian colonies of South Australia, Tasmania, and New Zealand. In March, 1880, he consented, at the request of the Premier, the Hon. James Service, to resume the position of engineer-in-chief of Victorian Railways; and he continued to hold that office until his death, which happened suddenly on the 5th of September in the same year. In 1874 Mr. Higinbotham was commissioned by the Government of Victoria to visit Europe and America, for the purpose of studying the railway systems of the principal countries of the world, and of acquainting himself with the latest improvements, whether in construction or in management, that might be found in any of them. He devoted himself zealously to the fulfilment of this mission, and the results of his enquiries, which extended over a period of a year and a half, were embodied in an exhaustive report, which was laid before Parliament.

The railways of Victoria were, at the beginning of the year 1880, 1,182 miles in length. The bulk of these lines were designed and constructed under the superintendence of Mr. Higinbotham, and they are thoroughly sound and substantial in their general character. With the exception of the trunk lines from Melbourne to Sandhurst, from Footscray to Williamstown and to Geelong, and from Geelong to Ballarat, which were designed and partly constructed before Mr. Higinbotham became engineer-in-chief, the average cost per mile of the Victorian railways has been £7,212. The uniform gauge of all the railway lines in Victoria is 5 feet 3 inches. Uniformity of gauge has not been adhered to in the adjacent colonies of New South Wales, South Australia, and Tasmania; and in Queensland, where the gauge is uniform, it is only 3 feet 6 inches. The Government of Victoria, some years ago, proposed that a narrower gauge than 5 feet 3 inches should be adopted for the new and cheaper lines which were then about to be constructed. To this proposal, which was powerfully supported by the newspaper press, Mr. Higinbotham felt it to be his duty to offer the most uncompromising opposition; his official remonstrances, and his evidence given at the bar of the Legislative Council, had the immediate effect of delaying the carrying-out of the proposal: and ultimately, after the lapse of a parliamentary recess, Mr. Higinbotham had the satisfaction of finding the Government and the whole community converted to his views on a question which he regarded as of vital importance.

As the permanent head for nearly twenty years of a large department, and chiefly responsible for the prudent and economical expenditure of many millions of money borrowed on public credit for the construction of railways, Mr. Higinbotham earned and generally obtained, in a more than usual degree, the trust and confidence of the Government of Victoria. He was sensitive in regard to his rights and public obligations as a member of the profession of civil engineers, and he never shrank from what he believed to be the duty of clearly expressing and recording his professional opinion, however inconvenient or unpalatable, upon any matter coming within the scope of his official functions as the professional adviser of the Government. But in the administration of a public department he never forgot the duty of submission to the advisers of the Crown under whom he served; and it was his constant endeavour in practice to observe the duty which he conceived that he owed to his profession, and to himself as a member of a profession, as well as that which his official superiors were entitled to claim from him. As an administrator he was strict and vigilant, and at the same time just, and amongst the very many to whom his personal qualities endeared him, there were few who regretted his death more sincerely and deeply than those who served the Crown under him and with him in the public service of Victoria.

In Chapter V. I have called this " restrained " biography. George Higinbotham felt that his brother was too much a part of himself for him to praise his personal qualities. As to these it may be allowed, however, to utter a word of comment and to quote the testimony of others. The two brothers were alike in many of the elements of their minds. They were alike in a personal courtesy which seemed to link them to an earlier world, in an unselfish generosity, in a strong sense of public duty, and in a keen appreciation of the point of honour. *Par nobile fratrum.* This is what the *Argus* said :—

The State has lost a public servant of a type which was always rare, and which may all too soon become unknown among us. . . . Throughout the colony his name became synonymous with integrity. It was felt by all that in him we had an officer who was absolutely incorruptible. His presence tended of itself to keep pure a department in which collusion is always possible ; but, as we all know, his honesty went much further than a mere faithfulness in money matters. He was prized because he always endeavoured to serve his country rather than to please the politicians who flit across the scene. . . .

" No purer son
Troy ever bred.   More jealous none
Of sacred right."

The following is taken from a country paper (*The Gippsland Times*).

Without question in Victoria he was the highest product of English engineering training. Natural ability, elaborate preparation, infinite skill, severe and constant labour produced a result which left him here without a rival. . . . His personal merits are to be traced in the stubborn independence and sterling honesty of his character throughout an evil time, of which our wish is alas! unavailing that he had lived to see the end— when to be just and upright are insufficient securities for the welfare and honour—even the life—of the most valued servants of the State.

Thomas Higinbotham left by will all his property to his brother George, with remainder to the latter's children. To this bequest he attached not a condition, but a request that the family name should be changed to "Vernier." George Higinbotham, however, felt that his own name was too well known in the colony for him to change it.

CHAPTER XXVI

Change from advocacy to judgment-seat—Australian Health Society—
Permissive Bill Association—Victorian Alliance—Queen's Fund
Speech in Town Hall—Presidency of Centennial Exhibition—
Withdrawal from the position—A question of precedence—Contribution to the Strike Fund.

THE last period of Mr. Higinbotham's life, from the time that he took his seat upon the Bench to his death on the last day of 1892, was twelve and a half years. A judge's life is very busy, but it does not furnish much to the biographer. Most judges testify that the change from advocacy to the judgment-seat is a great relief. At first the work seems lighter, but this feeling soon passes, for the judge's work is regular, unintermittent, and sometimes heavy, and it was but for a short time that the sense of relief brought by the change lasted in Mr. Higinbotham's case.

In this last period there fall the later developments of the Colonial Office question connected with the Prerogative of Mercy, the attempt to convince Lord Knutsford, and the position of Acting-Governor. But in other matters Mr. Higinbotham did not often appear before the public or on the platform. Many wished for more frequent appearances. Now and then he would take the chair at the annual meeting of a public charity. He was for twelve years one of the vice-presidents of the Melbourne Benevolent Asylum, but he had not time to do any committee work in connection with such matters. For ten years he was President of the Australian Health Society, and was much interested in its attempts to instruct the public in sanitary matters. "His presence at the quarterly meetings of the society," writes a friend of the cause, "seemed to exercise a magnetic power over those present, throwing brightness over the proceedings." By a speech at a largely attended meeting[1] in the Melbourne Town Hall, Mr. Justice Higinbotham took a small part in establishing the Working Men's College : but he took a more active part in the attempt to establish a Working Men's Club in Melbourne.   Not only was a handsome subscription ready -that was always ready—but he spoke at a Town Hall meeting, September 17th, 1883, and he accepted the position of president of the committee, more to show his sympathy with the cause and the workers in it, than because of any special knowledge in the matter.   Apathy on the part of the working men, and perhaps a dislike in certain quarters to some of the movers in the matter, prevented its success.   The Chief Justice was present at a meeting in 1887, when the project was abandoned and the committee dissolved.   One deliverance on education and one on religion roused public attention.   The former was at the Church Congress towards the end of 1882. The lecture on science and religion, delivered in the Scots Church in the middle of 1883, which led to the secession of the minister of that church from Presbyterianism, is described elsewhere.[2]

Mr. Higinbotham's strong belief that a community had the right, if it could secure the power, to determine the conditions of its own existence made him, when he turned his thoughts to the suppression of drunkenness, an advocate of what is known as Local Option.   As the foremost of its advocates, he became, about 1871, President of the Permissive Bill Association, which sought to secure restrictive legislation in regard to the liquor traffic.   He was not at that time a teetotaler, but he recognised some inconsistency in not being, and later, though he was never pledged, he was a practical teetotaler for twenty years.   Ultimately the Permissive Bill Association passed out of existence without having secured its object, though not without having done much work in the education of public opinion.   In 1881, when the Victorian Alliance was founded, Mr. Higinbotham was invited to become its President; but in the meantime he had been removed from the sphere of active politics by his elevation

<hr>

[1] June 26th, 1882.   [2] Page 323.

to the Bench. This he evidently regarded as a bar to his acceptance of office in the Alliance, although his approval of its aim was evident in many ways, including liberal and regular donations continued to his death. The following is the copy of his letter declining the offer of the presidency :—

Brighton, 11th July, 1881.

Dear Sir,—I have to acknowledge the receipt of your letter of 6th July, conveying to me the invitation of the Executive Committee of the Victorian Alliance for the Suppression of the Traffic in Intoxicating Liquors, to accept the position of president of the Alliance. I thank the Committee for the honour which they have proposed to confer on me, and I have given the subject the full and anxious consideration which its importance appears to me to demand. I cannot help thinking that upon the choice of its leading Executive Officer, whether he be called president or by any other title, will largely depend the failure or success of the new association. It has been formed, as I learn, on the model, and its policy will be that of the " United Kingdom Alliance." If this be so, its specific distinguishing object will be to obtain legislative sanction *for the indisputable principle that the community has the right to determine for itself whether it is expedient that intoxicating liquor shall or shall not be sold.* Sympathising, as I warmly do, with your society in this object, I firmly believe that it is an object which you cannot hope to attain unless you are led by a man who will not only devote himself, like the noble president of the " United Kingdom Alliance," Sir Wilfrid Lawson, to bringing forward a Local Option Bill, session after session, in his place in Parliament, but will also, like him, foster and stimulate public opinion throughout the colony during the Parliamentary recess, and give it in every electoral district a definite political aim and purpose. In the present depressed condition of political thought and feeling in Victoria, such feeling in a good cause may be attended with more than ordinary difficulty, but it is not on that account, in my opinion, less essential to success. When I had the honour to hold the office of president of the Permissive Bill Association, I had occasion to learn how powerless a member of Parliament is, even when he introduces a good and generally approved measure, which is opposed by powerful interests, unless he is supported by organised public opinion out of doors. I should be reluctant again to accept a similar position if I had not the ability to use the means which experience has taught me are essential to success, and which a person who undertakes the responsible position of president ought not to depute to others ; but this I cannot now do, and I therefore beg leave respectfully, and with renewed thanks, to decline the esteemed invitation.

I have the honour to be,
Dear Sir,
Your faithful servant,
Geo. Higinbotham.

The phrase in the above letter, now printed in italic, has been selected as the motto of the *Alliance Record*, the organ of the party that advocates local option.

The events in which the Chief Justice took a part that are left to be described are the establishment of the Queen's Fund, the Presidency of the Centennial Exhibition, and the contribution to the Maritime Strike Fund in 1890.

The Queen's Fund is the Victorian memorial of Her Majesty's Jubilee of 1887. On the 19th of May a meeting was held in the Town Hall, Melbourne, at which the fund was established. The Governor presided, and the Chief Justice proposed the first resolution in the following speech, which marks equally his personal loyalty and his high sense of the value of women's work in charity :—

"I believe it is an all but universal desire of the people of Victoria to commemorate in some form or other the advent of the fiftieth or Jubilee year of Her Majesty's reign. It is an event unique in our history. No female monarch has ever sat on the Throne of England for so long a period. I think it can be no matter for surprise that there has been considerable doubt, and not a little difference of opinion, as to the manner in which the event so new and so noteworthy can be most fitly celebrated. This large meeting has been convened at the instance and invitation of Lady Loch, to consider a scheme proposed by her for the celebration of the Queen's Jubilee. It has been Lady Loch's desire—and I am rejoiced to see that her wishes have been so largely responded to—that this should be a meeting chiefly composed of women and girls of Victoria. You will be asked to consider Lady Loch's proposal, and if you approve of it you will be invited and urged to exercise your great and just influence in order to carry that scheme into effect in such a way that it shall be attended with durable and beneficial consequences. I feel honoured in being invited to introduce this scheme to the notice of this meeting. I believe that every one of us would have been rejoiced beyond measure if we could have heard this scheme explained and commended to your notice from the lips of that good and gracious woman, whose kind and loyal heart and sagacious intelligence have devised this scheme ; but that could not be, and it is gratifying to me to think that the scheme is so simple and so felicitous, that, as soon as you have heard it

and understood it, you will have no difficulty or delay in
giving it your entire and hearty acceptance. Now this idea,
as it has been finally approved of by Lady Loch, I understand to be this. It is not designed to add one more to the
list of our, perhaps, already too numerous public charities.
It is not designed to establish an institution which would
have to appeal year by year for its support to public and
private benevolence. It is proposed to create a fund which
shall be called the Queen's Fund, in commemoration of this
event, this great event of Her Majesty's reign. That fund
it is proposed to create by collections, which are to be
instituted throughout the whole of Victoria, and which are
to be obtained chiefly it is hoped by the voluntary agency and
co-operation of the women of Victoria. Of course, subscriptions and donations will be thankfully received from men
also, and, indeed, we must expect that it will be from men
and not from women that the subscriptions and donations
will come in, but Lady Loch looks to women as the principal
agents for obtaining subscriptions and donations from men.
When this fund shall be collected, and I hope and expect
that it will amount to very large proportions, it will be
invested, and the income of the fund, and the income only,
will be devoted to the purposes of the fund. That income
will be managed also chiefly—I wish I could say exclusively—
by the women of Victoria, women who may be assisted by
the advice and experience of men, but who will be invited to
give a fair discriminating intelligence and sympathetic care
and attention in the selection of objects for relief. And it
is proposed that the assistance of women in all parts of
Victoria shall be enlisted in the work of distribution as well
as in the work of collection, and either by means of the
existing ladies' benevolent societies, or by other and further
associations in the country districts, that the faithful and
effective management of this fund will be secured so as to
represent the intelligence and sympathy of women in all parts
of the colony; and lastly and chiefly, this fund it is proposed
shall be devoted solely and exclusively to the aid and
assistance of women who need its aid. We desire to celebrate a memorable event in a woman's reign. It is Lady
Loch's belief that that can be most fitly done, and the wishes
of our Queen may be most fitly carried out, by instituting a

fund which shall be exclusively devoted to the relief of the
necessities and wants of her sex. Of course, this comprehensive description of the object of the fund will include
every kind and form of woman's need. It will include not
merely or alone cases in which women are deprived of the aid
and support of husbands, brothers, and sons by accident or
otherwise; it will not be confined alone to the assistance of
persons who labour with their hands; it will be extended to
every class of women; it will be extended to all forms of
womanly need. The gentlemen who have been engaged in
preparing and making the arrangements for this meeting have
made an addition to Lady Loch's scheme. It is proposed
that the committee of management of the income arising
from this fund shall be presided over in the first instance, and
we hope for a long time to come, by the wife of the representative of Her Majesty. Now that is the scheme, and it
seems to me—if I may venture to say so—a scheme
eminently felicitous and exceeding simple. It embraces a
considerable number of the objects of other schemes which
have been proposed on this occasion. I think it is a scheme
that will not provoke a single enmity or a single jealousy. I
think it will combine many sympathies, and I cannot conceive
any more proper form of commemoration, or one that will
better and more fittingly express the feelings of this
community in which this proposal has originated. I believe
that the feeling—although, unhappily, it cannot be universal—
in this community, and in all other British communities over
the face of the world, is at this time almost unanimous, and
that feeling is one of great attachment and loving gratitude
to our Sovereign the Queen. I use the word gratitude,
although I am sensible that it may be open to misapprehension
—I speak my own opinion—when I say that the very best
and most just ground for the feeling which exists in this
community and elsewhere at present is this—that as British
subjects we owe gratitude to the Queen of Great Britain. I
do not know that we often enough consider this view of the
position of a person placed as Her Majesty is at the head
of affairs, but it seems to me that a person in her position,
whether that person may be an autocrat or a sovereign of a
constitutional system of government, or the head of a
republic, is in a position in which he or she (as the case may

be) is able to confer or withhold countless benefits to her subjects. If we consider in how many ways the interests of the people are affected by the want of high qualities in the head of the state, if we consider how the administration of the affairs of a nation may be impeded, how its political and social and industrial progress may be obstructed by the exercise of arbitrary will, the display of personal feeling, the want of adequate knowledge of the wants and interests of the people, I think, then, we should be in a better position to estimate duly the possession of high qualities and the submission to duty of the head of the state as well as the obedience to the supreme law which ought to govern the sovereign, while it does govern all her subjects. At this moment, ladies and gentlemen, the world presents the spectacle of the peace of the civilised world and the lives of millions of men dependent on the will of an individual—on the will of one man. How greatly then we should estimate, how highly we should value the possession at the head of our country of a woman who, from the first time she assumed the sovereignty of this country, has acknowledged in her own personal conduct the supremacy of the law and the obligations of duty. From the time when Queen Victoria in the early part of her reign submitted without a murmur to the dismissal of the friends of her girlhood—the ladies of her bedchamber—on the authority of her lawful adviser, from that time down to the present she has invariably recognised that the affairs of the country were not to be influenced by her individual will, by her personal friendships, or by her personal feelings of any kind. She has shown at all times, and in all events of her reign, that she recognises that the interests of the people, and the views of her subjects, as expressed through their representatives, were to govern her conduct and were to influence her life. I have the honour to address an assemblage, composed largely of women. Will you allow me to say that I think that you, as women, owe a special and great debt of additional gratitude to our Queen. Queen Victoria has at all times, as His Excellency has pointed out, shown by innumerable private acts, and also in her public conduct, a sincere and warm sympathy for her sex. Queen Victoria, I think, appears to know, better perhaps than many know, that the position of women at this period of the world is one which may be advanced, which may be helped forward, but, which, at all events, must at this time be protected, and must be protected and advanced mainly by means of women themselves. I don't think we ought to regret that the age of chivalry with all its foolery is past; but I don't think that any of us would say—would that we could— that the age of true honour for women, of true respect and reverence for women, has yet fully come, but we may say that, so far as Queen Victoria has been able to do, she has benefited and advanced the position of women, and increased the respect for them among men. By her ability in administration,—as His Excellency has, no doubt from his intimate personal knowledge, told you—by her great capacity at the head of the State, she has always succeeded in commanding the respect of her successive Ministers, and through them has gained the confidence of all her Parliaments. In her Court she has always maintained a high standard of purity and honour. And we know that on more than one occasion, possibly on one occasion mistakenly, but at all and many times earnestly, and with a force of regal will which has lent power to her act, she has interfered to protect and vindicate the offended honour of her sex. I think, for these things, the gratitude of every true woman of her subjects is justly due, and if this be so, can you take a course which is better calculated to express that feeling of gratitude and affection to the Queen; can you take a course which will convey to her a more gratifying proof—I will not say of your loyalty, but of your affections—than by co-operating in that which has been a work of her reign and an object of her life? Can you do better than on this occasion accept the suggestion of Lady Loch, and institute a fund which will for all time confer a benefit upon those of the Queen's sisters, who under it will receive the help and assistance which you will be able now to create?"

In the Queen's Fund which was thus established the Chief Justice always took the warmest interest. He became one of the trustees, and the last letters that he ever wrote were upon its business. Those who know best can speak most strongly of the great good that has been done to women in distress by the six years' operations of the Victorian Queen's Fund. The revenue is small, but the wisdom of the good women who manage it has made the small revenue of great use.

To celebrate the Centennial year of Australian history, 1888, the year which Tennyson called " the century's three strong eights," the Victorian Government decided to hold an International Exhibition in Melbourne. To carry out this project, early in 1887 an Executive Commission was appointed, and afterwards a much larger body of Commissioners. The Presidency of the smaller body, carrying with it that of the larger, was offered to the Chief Justice. He hesitated to accept the position, not feeling attracted by it, nor specially suited for its work or its ceremonial. Whilst he was thus hesitating, two Ministers, neither of whom would be displeased to be reckoned a disciple, undertook to persuade him. The line that they followed was to work upon his known feeling with respect to wealth. The Government did not wish the President to be distinguished for wealth or landed estates, because this Centennial Exhibition was not to be simply a show of material products. The strong desire of its designers was to make it also intellectual, to use it as a means of education in the fine arts, to connect with it conferences on social questions, and to invite to Victoria men prominent in the world of art and letters, indeed to attempt something such as was later attempted at Chicago. The distance and the time required to travel over the intervening miles of ocean interfered with this part of the project, but the Exhibition of 1888 is looked back upon as almost forming an epoch in the mental history of many Australians, especially in painting and in music. There was a loan collection of pictures far finer than had ever been in Australia before ; and it is allowed by almost all that Mr. Cowen's concerts were an education worth the large expenditure upon them.

Persuaded by the arguments employed the Chief Justice accepted the post, and entered upon the work with his well-known vigour and conscientious thoroughness. As President, he attended the opening of the Adelaide Jubilee Exhibition on Jubilee Day, he entertained two Chinese Commissioners who visited Melbourne, and he took his part in the ceremonials of January, 1888, in Sydney. As it was in Sydney that Governor Phillip had hoisted the British flag one hundred years before, it was proper that the rejoicings of the year should begin there. It may be mentioned that this was the only visit that Mr. Higinbotham ever paid to the beautiful shores of Port Jackson.

Ceremonial, however, was not the only business of the president : there was plenty of work to do. The commissioners were charmed with the suavity and dignity with which the Chief Justice presided over their deliberations, and testified to the thoroughness with which he attended to their business ; but some of them thought it was too dignified and too slow. Most of them business men, they wanted to make faster progress, and to be more free from the restraint of formalities. The executive commission was divided into several committees, but the president wished each committee to report each week to the executive and to receive instructions from it. The reading of these reports took time, and the meetings became very long. Moreover the president felt it to be his duty as far as possible to exercise a personal supervision over all the business transacted in the Exhibition office. Had Mr. Higinbotham been willing to be an "Ornamental president," taking the chair at meetings and nothing more, the commissioners would have been delighted. But a mere ornamental figure-head he could not be. It was contrary to his whole nature, his ideas of right and wrong. When it was urged that some one must always be present, armed with authority, able to direct workmen and to settle matters in dispute, the Chief Justice was prepared to obtain leave of absence from his judicial work and undertake the duty himself : but it was pointed out that he lacked the necessary business training, and his offer was not accepted. A business man was appointed executive vice-president. To this the Chief Justice had no objection, provided that he would report everything to the weekly meetings of the executive commission, and receive either its instructions or its ratification. This, the executive vice-president contended was not practicable. The details of the controversy are perhaps hardly worth preserving. Ultimately, rather than be responsible for expenditure that he could not control, to the great regret of the whole community as well as of the commissioners themselves, the Chief Justice resigned.

It should be added further that in the original scheme the expense was carefully kept down. The building had been erected for the Exhibition of 1880 ; and the Government had intended that, whilst all extravagance was repressed, a charge should be made for floor space so that the cost should be paid by exhibitors. The Chief Secretary, after obtaining estimates from those who were experienced in such matters, announced to Parliament that a sum of £25,000 would suffice for the Centennial Exhibition. The Exhibition cost ten times that amount ; but it must be remembered the original plan was thrown to the winds, because the commissioners thought it beneath the dignity of the Colony to charge exhibitors for space.

With respect to the opening ceremony there was an unfortunate difficulty. The table of precedence in colonial life is perhaps not very accurately laid down, and the Colony has hitherto gone on without a Herald's College. The Chief Justice has always been looked upon as ranking the next to the Governor, but in England the Speaker of the House of Commons is regarded as the first commoner in the land. The Speaker of the Legislative Assembly claimed a similar precedence in the colony ; and the commissioners decided to give him a place in the procession superior to that of the Chief Justice. His Excellency the Governor advised the Chief Justice to protest, and as his protest was unheeded, the latter stayed away from the opening ceremony altogether. For himself he was the last man in the world to claim precedence or to care a button about it, but he was always jealous for his office. A daily paper of the next morning gracefully commented on " Achilles sulking in his tent." There was not an atom of sulk in the composition of the man. It should be added that the Governor at his official dinner assigned to the Chief Justice a place in accordance with the former practice.

To the period immediately after the opening of the Centennial Exhibition the following interesting excerpt belongs. It is an extract from a speech made in September, 1888, by one of the leaders of the A.N.A. (Australian Natives Association).

We natives are not ungrateful and not forgetful. Let me give point to this statement by saying that if at this present moment the native-born in Victoria were called upon to elect one man to the highest position in the State, I feel assured that His Honour George Higinbotham would be their chosen man without a rival.

In 1890 the second of the great Australian strikes took place. It was the maritime strike that began with the officers of the intercolonial steamers, whose demands were certainly just. The men joined the officers, and their cause was taken up by the Trades Hall. The gas-stokers joined in the strike, and there was a stupid attempt to leave Melbourne in darkness. The closing of the ranks on the side of labour was met by a similar closing on the side of capital. An Employers' Union was formed. The Trades Hall Council requested a conference, but the Employers' Union, not thinking that any advantage would come from such a conference, declined. Then the following letter was written :—

LAW COURTS.

The Chief Justice presents his compliments to the President of the Trades Hall Council, and requests that he will be so good as to place the amount of the enclosed cheque of £50 to the credit of the strike fund. While the United Trades are awaiting compliance with their reasonable request for a conference with the employers, the Chief Justice will continue for the present to forward a weekly contribution of £10 to the same object.

No act of the Chief Justice during the latter part of his life created anything like the storm that was caused by this act. It was no doubt due to his intense sympathy with the cause of labour. In the letter emphasis is to be placed upon the word "reasonable." It seemed to him that the request for a conference was reasonable, and that the employers in refusing such a conference were overbearing the men by the weight of their wealth. In such a conflict no one who knew him could doubt for a moment on which side his sympathy would lie. He had deliberately accepted Trades Unionism, and rejoiced heartily in the prosperity of the working classes in Australia, which he rightly or wrongly attributed to Trades Unionism. He looked upon a strike as the natural weapon of the Trades Union, a weapon often more hurtful to the wielder. The fag end of a chapter is not the place to discuss so grave a question, but the strike is a part of the war organisation of labour not of the future peace organisation, to which, it may be through serious adversity, labour is surely tending. That a strike may sometimes be successful is shown by the famous Dockers' Strike. To the Australian fund that played so important a part therein both the Chief Justice and the present writer helped to subscribe the first hundred pounds.

In the case of the Melbourne maritime strike it must be confessed that the "gracious gift" (so it was called) was quite ineffectual. The conference was never granted, and the wits used to declare that the weekly subscription should go on indefinitely. Those however who received it were satisfied when the whole strike was at an end and the fund was closed, —a period of some fifteen weeks. The gift had an effect of which the giver never dreamt in attaching to him still more closely the admiring love of the working men. By others the act was violently condemned. Many especially condemned the use of the title of his office. As a private individual, they said, he had a right to show sympathy, no right as Chief Justice. It was even thought that he and other judges might have been asked to arbitrate. How could he, if he had taken a side? To this the natural answer is that he could not separate himself from his office, that he wished to give the greatest force to his expression of sympathy, and that he had not taken a side upon the main points at issue, merely on the question whether a conference should be conceded.

The following correspondence may fitly close this chapter. Only the name of the correspondent need be withheld.

October 1st, 1890.

DEAR SIR,

I will not apologise for addressing you, as the respect I hold towards you as an intellectual man and leader of thought demands sincerity, knowing you to be ever ready to help those who "see through glass darkly."

I am a young man of twenty-seven years of age, and since I have been able to think on the great problems of life, have always looked upon you as my High Priest Intellectual of the Southern Hemisphere. I therefore now most respectfully request you to explain your action in supplying the Trades Hall with funds, knowing you to be the last man in the world to take said action without good cause and sound reasons.

To which His Honour made reply :—

October 4th, 1890.

I trust that you will not deem me guilty of discourtesy or of culpable disregard of what might be under other circumstances an appeal of imperative force, when I inform you that if my action does not sufficiently explain itself, I have cogent reasons for declining to furnish at present fuller or more minute explanation than that with which you are already acquainted.

CHAPTER XXVII

CONSOLIDATION

(By Mr. Donald Mackinnon.)

Importance of Mr. Higinbotham's Consolidation Work — His orderly mind — First Consolidation of Statutes in 1864 and 1865, when he was Attorney-General—Former condition of the law—Qualities required in consolidating—Rules laid down—Patient labour of Attorney-General—Speech of February 4th, 1864—How to keep up Consolidation—A suggestion—Dr. Hearn's Code—Evidence of the Chief Justice—Second Consolidation of 1890, begun by the Chief Justice in 1888—The labour of it—The sole reward—Value of the work.

PERHAPS no part of Mr. Higinbotham's work establishes his claim to the grateful remembrance of his countrymen more thoroughly than that which was devoted to the simplification and improvement of our laws. To have twice successfully undertaken, in the midst of pressing occupations, the consolidation of the statute law of a country like Victoria, places those who enjoy its benefits under no small obligation. Professing lawyers have too often been found in the other camp; experience has taught men to expect legal reforms rather from bookish theorists or not wholly disinterested autocrats than from those who live by the law. Yet the motives which prompted the Consolidations of 1864 and 1890, and supported the immediate adoption of Dr. Hearn's General Code of 1885, are not difficult to discover. Mr. Higinbotham had an uncommonly orderly mind; confusion and doubt were extremely distasteful to him. As appears from the evidence he gave before the committee which considered the General Code, he contemplated a possible codification of all human knowledge. The thought that law should be the monopolised knowledge of a privileged class was repugnant to him; that Mr. (afterwards Sir) Robert Molesworth and Mr. Adamson should be the only two men in the community who knew anything about the criminal law, was, in his view, little less than a public scandal. "Law not understood," to use his own words, "naturally has no place in the intelligent judgment and the affections of the people. Neither can law be supreme in a community that does not cherish a loyal attachment to the law." In addition he felt an intense loyalty to the law, and especially towards the statute law, inasmuch as it was the deliberate expression of the national will. His own feelings were exactly expressed, when, quoting the words of the famous Hooker before Parliament one memorable day in 1890, he said, "Law is the mother of peace and joy. All things on earth do her homage; the very least as feeling her care, the greatest as not exempted from her powers."

The consolidation of 1864-5 began in 1863. Mr. Higinbotham was then Attorney-General in the McCulloch Ministry. It is admitted that he not only designed the scheme of consolidation, but that he also superintended its execution. Consolidation, as distinguished from codification, is the reduction into a systematic form of the whole of the statute law relating to a given subject; its true effect is to combine in a consecutive form the provisions scattered about the statute book, to avoid repetitions, and remove inconsistencies. In order to rightly estimate the character of the work undertaken in this instance, it is necessary to understand in a general way the condition of our Acts of Parliament at that time. It is undisputed that the structure, arrangement, and method of publication of the statutes were open to the most serious objection. Partly through social conditions, in which men's minds were occupied more with material matters of personal progress than with the advantages of legal reform; partly through the accidents of the first settlement, the laws of those days were constructed on makeshift principles, or were inherited merely, or were adopted without much thought. They suggest the conclusion that they were passed only for immediate requirements, so true is it that the laws of a nation generally fit its life. The statutes, as the Attorney-

General complained, were based habitually on English legislation, and provisions of English law, applicable only to a condition of affairs existing in England, had been introduced here without even an attempt at rude adaptation to the wholly unsuitable conditions of Victoria. The result in many cases was almost grotesque. There were in force, for example, enactments with regard to copyhold, a form of tenure never known in this country. Instances of this might be multiplied indefinitely. Even among what may be called the indigenous acts, and those which were more perfectly acclimatised, slipshod draftsmanship was only too frequent. Amendment was patched on to amendment until even professional persons were puzzled to say what was law and what was not. Nor was the form in which this confused medley of errors, anachronisms, and legislative misfits, was available for the public a subject of congratulation. The two volumes of Adamson's edition and six or seven sessional volumes, which constituted the books of the law, were inadequately indexed: lawyers were fully taxed to discover the whereabouts of any enactment, and, as has been already observed, only two men in Victoria had a passable acquaintance with the criminal law. It was out of this chaos that Mr. Higinbotham proposed to evolve order.

Consolidation is not a work which calls for any special exercise of genius. Neither exact legal knowledge nor exceptional skill in drafting is required for it. To group the various provisions in a natural sequence, to eliminate all useless or obsolete matter, above all things to omit nothing— this is the chief end of the consolidator. It is a tedious and laborious rather than an original undertaking. In Victoria, in 1863, the statute law was not very voluminous; compared with the English statute law of even date, with its 18,000 acts set out in one hundred volumes, it was insignificant. It was computed that there were in all some 370 to 400 acts that required consolidation. Under the circumstances, there is no doubt the Attorney-General adopted the most suitable instrument for executing his scheme. Law commissions in England had been a failure, or at best but a qualified success. In thirty years, so it was stated at the time, three of them had cost £50,000, and the only result was an index to the statutes and a criminal bill. Besides, with a commission it was almost impossible to obtain either unity in design or uniformity in execution. The idea of a commission was accordingly abandoned, and the Attorney-General proceeded on his task with the assistance of a small number of draftsmen, among them Dr. Hearn and Mr. Travers Adamson, whose Criminal Law and Practice Act was the most successful piece of work in the consolidation.

The draftsmen each worked upon different bills. They were limited in their operations by strict instructions. As to substance they were told to construct consolidating bills and nothing else. As to form and arrangement they had a freer hand. "Alterations in the form and language of sections of existing acts were allowable, wherever such appeared absolutely necessary; but wherever the terms of a colonial act were the same as those of an English act no change in the form or language was to be made." The only substantial alterations permitted were those which might be deemed upon consultation with a law officer to be urgently required, and not to be calculated to cause differences of opinion, and those which consisted in introducing recent amending English legislation, where the corresponding English principal act was already in force in Victoria. Finally, all alterations had to be printed with the rules for the information of Parliament.

The draftsmen had most of their bills prepared by the beginning of 1864. Their method of working appears to have been to prepare each bill in strict compliance with instructions, and then to revise them in detail with the Attorney-General. At any rate it is sufficiently evident that the latter went conscientiously through every line of the bills, and satisfied himself that they were at once complete and, humanly speaking, accurate. The labour involved in this minute examination would have been considerable to a man of ample leisure; for one who had engrossing public duties to attend to it must have been little short of overwhelming. No one less endowed with the gift of marvellous patience would have carried it to a successful issue.

The first batch of bills, some twenty, was introduced into Parliament on the 4th February, 1864, when Mr. Higinbotham explained his scheme in an interesting speech. He explained that he held himself responsible for the substantial accuracy of the bills; in return he asked Parliament to pass them without a discussion of details. "As a member of the House he was not willing to accept at the hand of any Government a bill or bills which altered the law in any material respect, unless he had an opportunity of considering and discussing the measures." But he gave his word that there were no conscious alterations of substance, and Parliament, by accepting a large mass of law upon his personal covenant, proved that representative government is not incompatible with codification, and undoubtedly made the way of the future codifier easier. The Consolidating Acts were passed during 1864 and 1865. There was some discussion upon general principles; the details were generally accepted as correct; few amendments were made, and, as twenty-five years' history has shown, wisely so. This consolidation did not profess to be more than an attempt to place the statute law upon a more intelligible footing. "The value of the acts," as Mr. Ireland pointed out, "consisted in having brought together a number of scattered acts, and thus formed the basis for future amendments." No one saw this more clearly than Mr. Higinbotham. He did not claim for his arrangement of the acts that it was an orderly or scientific one. It was a rough classification; but it would form the basis of a more scientific classification which he hoped to see at some future time.

A matter which was agitated in debate during the passage of the bills deserves a passing mention here. Assuming that the statute law is once consolidated, how is it to be kept in that condition? Amendments were to a large extent responsible for the existing confusion; how were they to be prevented from causing similar mischief in the future? It was a strong part of the Attorney-General's argument that over-indulgence in amendments had been productive, not only of confusion, but of heavy expense to the country. He produced a return which showed that a Local Government Bill had cost in the first instance, for drafting and printing, £151; and that the printing of amendments had cost £694. The learned consolidator's solution of this practical difficulty appears to the present writer the weakest part of his scheme. Shortly his proposal was that the Consolidating Acts should be kept in permanent type; that every one who desired to introduce an amending bill should obtain leave to do so; that upon a bill becoming law it should be embodied in the Consolidating Act, and that the whole should be reprinted again. At the same time Parliament should set its face strenuously against amendments. But the expense of printing a large act for the sake of a trifling alteration cannot fail to be an enormous expense; and Mr. Higinbotham abandoned the idea in favour of the plan of periodical re-consolidation which obtains in some American States, and Parliament in 1889 solemnly adopted this alternative. Nevertheless, one may be permitted to doubt the advantages of too frequent consolidation; certainly, intervals of five, or even ten, years seem very short. It is admittedly impossible to avoid amendments between consolidations; however much Parliament may set its face against them, amendments are inevitable. At every consolidation the numbering of sections must be altered, and a new edition of the statutes must be prepared. It is humbly submitted that a better result might be obtained at infinitely less expense by having a re-consolidation and new edition of the statutes every twenty years. With each sessional volume there should be published, by authority, a carefully prepared table showing the effect of the year's amendments, and indicating minutely where they take effect on page or in line of the standard edition of the statutes. The preparation of such a table would be a pure vacation exercise for the Parliamentary draftsman. And in order to make the table effective, every public officer, clerk of courts, or librarian, having custody of a copy of the existing edition, should be directed by his department to carry out the directions in his copy in such a way that any one using it would understand it.

During the decade between 1878 and 1888, the subject of codification was in the air. Mr. Higinbotham's views upon this subject were what we should have expected. The doctrine that the rules which govern human conduct should be intelligible, if it applies to the statute law, applies with increased force to the law which is supposed to reside in the judicial breast and is extracted with much hesitation and doubt even by highly trained minds from the myriad cases in the law reports. Indeed it is evident that he regarded consolidation as a necessary forerunner of a complete codification. "Consolidation," as he observed before the select committee on Dr.

Hearn's Code, "had always been regarded as a necessary step
to codification, and only as a step to codification, and it was
with that view that the Government of the day (1864) brought
in consolidating bills." His ideas upon codification and the
best means of attaining it, appear very fully in his evidence
before the Committee on the General Code of 1885, already
referred to. He there pointed out that what we wanted were
forms in which the common law rules and principles are
clearly and authoritatively expressed, and that we have to
search for them in authorities more or less applicable to the
circumstances of individual cases. He also repeated again his
belief in the effectiveness of a single mind which should
design the scheme, exercise supreme command over the whole
work, and be solely responsible to Parliament for the accuracy
of the result. The Draft Code itself did not entirely commend itself to him. Criticising it from the standpoint of the
scientific jurist, and with a full acquaintance with the writings
of Austin and Bentham, he considered that its classification
was to some extent illogical, and that it involved a violent
and needless departure from the divisions of the law familiar
to lawyers for generations ; but he was prepared, somewhat
heroically as it seems, to support its immediate adoption : for
the form could be re-cast and any errors in substance could be
rapidly amended. It is now pretty generally agreed, even
among enthusiasts in codification, that a complete code cannot be made to order with any prospect of permanency : if the
common law is to be codified at all it must be done piece-
meal. For various reasons the Draft Code was, in the end,
allowed to drop.

After an interval of nearly a quarter of a century the
statute law was again ripe for consolidation. The consolidation of 1890 appears to have originated in a suggestion contained in an annual report of the Judges of the Supreme
Court dated June, 1887, and repeated in the report of 1888.
Their honours there gave their opinion that the time had come
for a new consolidation, and that quinquennial reconsolidation
and republication of the statutes was to be desired. Accordingly, towards the end of 1888, the Chief Justice with the
approval of Mr. Wrixon, the then Attorney-General, undertook
the work. The scheme was a larger one than that of 1864-5.
Like its predecessor it combined a consolidation with an edition

of the statutes. But not only had Acts of Parliament greatly
multiplied, but the number of judicial decisions upon legislative
enactments had in the interval vastly increased. As a set-
off against this, however, two excellent editions of the statutes
published by authority had made their appearance since the
edition that appeared after the first consolidation. These
with their careful arrangement and reliable cross-references
made comparatively light work of the construction of the new
scheme. The plan of consolidation was settled by the Chief
Justice himself, probably during the summer vacation of
1888-9. A month later he handed a printed arrangement
of the existing acts, grouped as he wished them to be consolidated, to two members of the Junior Bar who were to assist
him. In the case of important bills he personally settled the
collocation and sequence of sections. The sections were then
fitted into their places by the draftsmen, and the resulting
bills were submitted to him, all necessary alterations in
language being noted for consideration and discussed. He
then went carefully through the bills, clause by clause, to
satisfy himself that no section of the existing act was re-
pealed without being re-enacted. Any points that had been
noted by him in interpreting the acts, either at the Bar or
upon the Bench, were examined; all notes upon decisions were
revised and corrected. The expenditure of energy upon this
self-imposed task of revision is capable of being measured in
a meagre way by the time spent upon it. From the 1st of
March to the 1st November, 1889, he worked upon these bills
daily from four o'clock, when the Court rose, until eight and
often till ten at night, at which hour he went home to dinner.
All Saturday, not being a Court day, and every day during
the fortnight vacation in winter, was occupied in the same
way. Throughout those eight months, he faithfully performed
his judicial functions, and he must have averaged ten hours
brain work per diem.

By October, 1889, the bills were almost all prepared. On
the 8th of that month 106 of them were read for a first time
in the Legislative Assembly, and were referred to a joint
committee of the two Houses. This committee, after taking
evidence, reported that it was too late to proceed with them
that session: but it adopted the principal of decennial consolidation, and expressed a wish that certain amendments

should be made in the bills. Accordingly they stood over till the next year. Their preparation, nevertheless, was not impeded. The last session's provisions were incorporated, opinions and criticisms were invited from persons administrating the various acts, and notes on decisions were corrected and added to. The bills were re-introduced in the succeeding July, and unanimously passed both Houses, without even the slight amendment that was asked for in 1864, and came into force —with one or two exceptions—on the 1st of August, 1890. Nor did the Chief Justice's labours cease upon their passage : for he supervised and directed the compilation of the consequent seven-volume edition of the statutes. The first four volumes of this edition were published in 1890. The fifth volume, which contained an index of the Consolidating Acts, was published in 1891. The sixth volume contained a collection of private and local acts, and was published in the beginning of 1892 ; and the seventh, which contained Acts of the Federal Council and a collection of Imperial Acts applicable to Victoria, was completed before the end of the same year, but was not available for the public until a few weeks after the Chief Justice's death.

On the 16th of December, 1890, Mr. Higinbotham was publicly thanked by Parliament for his services in connection with the common law. There is reason to believe that he regarded this unaccustomed honour as the highest reward a free country can confer upon her citizens, and that he cherished it accordingly. That the compliment was a fitting one none can doubt. To have patronised two consolidations, to have borne the same nominal relationship to them that Justinian and Napoleon had to the Codes constructed respectively by Tribonian and Portalis, would have entitled him to thanks, but to have sacrificed time, comfort, and health upon the laborious drudgery of the work, placed every person in the community under a serious personal obligation to him. The speech which he made thanking Parliament for the honour done him is redolent with loyalty to the law. He urged the necessity for further efforts at amending the form of our laws ; and he gratefully acknowledged his indebtedness to all who had helped him in his labours. In this connection it may be stated that the performances of the Government printing office in printing and issuing a large volume of matter in a short time before Parliament are probably without a parallel in the annals of printing.

In estimating the value of Mr. Higinbotham's contributions towards the simplification of the law, perhaps our best course is to consider what would have been the present condition of the statute laws had they not been consolidated in 1861 and 1890. It is not too much to assume that if he had not undertaken this tedious task, it would never have been performed. There are few communities of which it can be said that their statutes are more intelligible than our own. To his untiring zeal and marvellous patience is entirely due this evident public benefit. It is indeed doubtful if Parliament would have met so large a demand upon its confidence upon any other guarantee than his. Thus our legislature has become familiar with the practice of accepting a vast measure without insisting upon an examination of details, and upon the bare assurance of its author that it involves no interference with the existing law. This assuredly is a long way towards codification. Finally, all present indications encourage the expectation that a simpler and better statement of our law is not far distant. More scientific study of law, the increasing number of scientific jurists, the abundance and excellence of legal treatises, and the recent enactment of such measures as the Bills of Exchange Act, the Sale of Goods Act, and the Partnership Act, justify the hope that the common law will ere long be more or less completely codified. In Victoria this desirable consummation has undoubtedly been brought nearer by the shining example of the enormous, but disinterested and successful, labours of the late Chief Justice.

CHAPTER XXVIII

A DAY IN DECEMBER, 1890

Thanks of Parliament— Resolution of the Legislative Council—Speeches
in the Legislative Assembly—The Speaker's Address—The Chief
Justice's reply—Bound volumes of statutes—Blow delivered on
same day— History of the New Rules—Feeling against them—
They are annulled— Report of the Judges.

FOR this great work of consolidation the Chief Justice
would accept neither fee nor reward. The thanks of both
Houses of Parliament were accorded to him, and that was
enough. He received them on December 16th, 1890.
The following was the resolution passed by the Legislative
Council :—

That this Council records its high sense and appreciation of the
valuable services rendered to the people of this colony by His Honour
the Chief Justice, George Higinbotham, Esquire, in undertaking and
successfully carrying out the great work of consolidating the statute
law of the colony.

And this was presented to him by the President with all due
formality. But the presentation in the Legislative Assembly
was perhaps more interesting, as the scene of his former
struggles and triumphs.

The following is taken from the " Votes and Proceedings "
of the Legislative Assembly, Tuesday, 16th December, 1890 :—

Vote of Thanks to HIS HONOUR CHIEF JUSTICE HIGINBOTHAM.

The Order of the Day for His Honour the Chief Justice to attend the
House having been read—
The Serjeant-at-Arms announced that His Honour Chief Justice Higin-
botham was now in attendance.

And Mr. Speaker having directed that His Honour be admitted, and a
chair having been set for His Honour on the left hand of the Bar,
towards the middle of the House, he came in, making his
obeisances, the whole House rising upon his entrance within the
Bar ; and Mr. Speaker having requested His Honour to be seated,
he sat down ; the Serjeant standing on his right hand with the
Mace grounded.

And Honourable Members having resumed their seats, Mr. Speaker
said—

MR. CHIEF JUSTICE,—

I have the honour to-day of addressing you from this place on
behalf of the Legislative Assembly of Victoria, over which it is my
privilege to preside.

Nearly thirty years have now elapsed since first you took your seat
as a Member of this Honourable House. To it you have been on
several occasions re-elected, and you have sat on the Government
benches as the Chief Law Officer of the Crown. As a private Member and
as a Minister you won the respect of the House, and your splendid
talents were in the most unsparing way constantly and conscientiously
exercised in promoting legislation and administration which commended
itself to your mind as most likely to be productive of good to the entire
community.

As Attorney-General in the Session 1864-5, in addition to discharg-
ing the duties of your high office, you initiated and carried to a successful termination the great work of consolidating the statute law of
the colony, and although the labours you then performed have now
stood the test of twenty-six years' examination, the unanimous opinion
of all jurists is that the belief entertained by Parliament in passing
them was correct, and that your work had been ably and faithfully
carried out.

The rapid development of this country year by year, and other
causes usually operating in a young and prosperous community, have
led to a more frequent alteration in our laws than would be requisite
in an older country, and the lapse of nearly a quarter of a century since
the consolidation of our statutes was effected rendered highly desirable,
if not absolutely necessary, a new consolidation. It was then in
accordance with the natural fitness of things that the successful author
of the prior consolidating acts should be looked to as the one most
competent to perform the work, and it was pleasing to all to find that,
although occupying the high position of Chief Justice, the duties of
which are necessarily exacting, you were willing and indeed solicitous
to deny yourself for the general good, and undertake a task which would
occupy all your leisure and would require much knowledge, patience,
labour, and mastery of details.

The reception which your labours have met with in Parliament must
be gratifying to yourself. So great was the confidence reposed in you,
that, relying upon the faith of your statement, both Houses accepted
from you 107 Bills, and without alteration, without examination, and
without dissent, passed them through all their stages into law.

The address of thanks which we propose to give you this afternoon you, as a student of history, will, I know, highly appreciate. Our great prototype, the House of Commons, has very sparingly given it. It is the highest honour we can bestow. It is the thanks of the entire country in which you live given by the representatives of the country in their National Assembly. It is given unanimously, and by a special order our records for all time will bear witness to the fact that no dissentient is to be found throughout the entire House. It is given sincerely for an arduous work generously undertaken without expectation or desire of reward ; zealously prosecuted from a sense of duty and a love for patriotic labour ; and executed, as we hope and have every reason to believe, in a manner so correct and complete that we feel ourselves your debtors, and for your services—to us so unselfish, patriotic, and unparalleled—this House now desires to accord to you its praise.

The Clerk of the House then read the following extract from the Journals of the House of the 23rd October last :—

    "Vote of thanks to His Honour Chief Justice Higinbotham.— Mr. Gillies moved, pursuant to notice, that this House records its high sense and appreciation of the valuable services rendered to the people of this colony by His Honour the Chief Justice, George Higinbotham, Esquire, in undertaking and successfully carrying out the great work of consolidating the statute law of the colony.

    "Question—put and resolved in the affirmative.

    "Ordered—That the Clerk do enter on the Journals of the House that the foregoing resolution was carried unanimously."

Mr. Speaker said-

Mr. Chief Justice, in the name and on behalf of the Legislative Assembly of Victoria I have the honour to present you with this address of thanks.

The extract from the Journals as read by the Clerk was then handed by him to the Chief Justice.

Whereupon His Honour, who during the foregoing speech had sat, stood up and spoke as follows :—

Mr. Speaker,—

My hearty thanks are due to this Honourable House for the resolution which has been presented to me, and to you, Sir, they are also due for the kindly words of reminiscence and encomium which you were pleased to address to me, and which to me, in this place and on this spot, are peculiarly welcome. I have also to thank honourable members for the kind reception they have been pleased to give me. The distinguished mark of approval by each House of Parliament of the Consolidation Laws of 1890, conveyed to me in this form, is an abundant and the highest possible reward for the not very considerable labour which the work has entailed upon me. I cannot claim for myself the whole, or even the larger share, of the favourable notice expressed in the vote of this Honourable House, and I ask its indulgence while I briefly enumerate those whom I know to be entitled to a share of its thanks as having contributed in various degrees to the successful accomplishment of this part of the legislation of the present session of Parliament. The consolidation of the numerous acts that have been passed to amend the Constitution Act presented some peculiar difficulties, in the removal of which the aid of the Clerk of Parliaments, Mr. John Barker, and of the Clerk of the Legislative Assembly, Mr. G. H. Jenkins, freely and promptly rendered, has proved invaluable.   The permanent heads of departments of the Government, in which various Acts of Parliament are daily administered, know better than any lawyer the hidden dangers arising from slight, but it may be necessary, changes of phraseology and construction, and alteration of the order of clauses in a consolidating bill.   The assistance of those officers was solicited; it was in every case readily and cordially given, and I believe that from this cause the new legislation will be found to work with increased ease and freedom, and will, it is hoped, be free from serious defects and errors which might otherwise have escaped detection.   Advice, suggestions, and aid of the highest value have been contributed by Judges of County Courts, the Commissioner of Titles, the Master in Equity, the Prothonotary and Judges of the Supreme Court.   The learning and experience of Mr. J. Warrington Rogers, Q.C., of Mr. Joseph A. C. Helm, and of Mr. John Burslem Gregory, in relation to the subjects included in the Water Act, in the part of the Companies Act dealing with mining companies, and in the Local Government Act and the Friendly Societies Act, have given a special value to the professional services of those gentlemen in the cases of the bills I have mentioned, which were either prepared or advised upon by them.   Mr. Donald Mackinnon and Mr. Francis Hugh Mackay, junior members of the Bar of Victoria, were the draftsmen of the great majority of the consolidating bills, and I was closely associated with them during the progress of the work.   Fidelity to the high trust reposed in him is the first quality demanded of the consolidating draftsman; accuracy in reproducing the substance, and, as far as possible, the exact form of the existing statute law is the sole test and the measure of value of the consolidating draftsman's work.   I gladly avail myself of this opportune occasion and place to state that, in my opinion, the considerable degree of success which may now be affirmed with some confidence to have been attained in the Consolidating Acts of the present session, is mainly due to the loyal fidelity, the much more than average skill and exact knowledge of the statute law, and the untiring industry applied in unceasing revision which those gentlemen have brought to their heavy and somewhat tedious task.   If Honourable Members will bear in mind the innumerable sources of errors, great and small, in a work of this magnitude, I believe they will be disposed to find in the bills which have been presented to Parliament to correct defects and errors already discovered, and in the insignificant character, with one or two exceptions, of all of those defects and errors, the best possible proof of the general correctness that has been happily achieved in the scheme as a whole.   I must not omit to add that very serious mechanical difficulties have presented themselves in the way of this undertaking, and that those difficulties and the delays thereby occasioned have been overcome only by the zeal and ingenuity displayed from the beginning to the end by Mr. Brain, the Government printer, and the officers of his department.

Twenty-five years ago Parliament accepted a scheme of consolidation prepared by me when I had the honour to be a member of the Legislative Assembly and a responsible Minister of the Crown. Parliament has now again accepted a similar scheme, entrusted by Her Majesty's Government to my supervision ; and it has taken the further most important step in advance, upon the recommendation of a Joint Special Committee of both Houses, of determining that in future there shall be a decennial consolidation, re-enactment, and re-publication of the statute law of Victoria. I shall never lose the grateful memory of the confidence which Parliament has been pleased to repose in me on those two occasions. I am now emboldened by this memory to submit the suggestion to this Honourable House that Parliament in its wisdom should extend a yet larger measure of its confidence to those whose duty it will be hereafter to prepare Consolidation Bills under the authority of the Government. If Parliament should intimate its intention so to do, and the last five years of the decennial period now beginning should be employed in the preparation, under the supervision of a Joint Committee of both Houses, of bills for enactment in the year 1900, the statute law might, before that time arrives, be reduced to a system comprising not only the statutes, but also a large portion of the unwritten law connected with the subjects contained in the statutes, the whole being embodied in the form, and expressed in the simple, concise, and uniform language of a code. By this means a great advance might, it is submitted, be safely made in the direction of a complete, comprehensive code of the whole law. This Honourable House is doubtless aware of the many evils arising from the imperfect mode in which the supreme will of the Legislature is at present expressed, as well as from the total absence of any formulated expression of a large proportion of that will, except in the reported decisions of the courts of law. The Consolidation Acts which the Victorian Legislature has just enacted are themselves but a confused and unarranged medley of enactments constituting a small part only of our law, unnecessarily cumbrous in form, inexact in expression, wanting in uniformity in the use of terms, and containing provisions not always easy to be reconciled with one another. The laws which are intended to govern the actions of a free people ought not to be open to cavil or to overthrow and defeat, as now they often are, upon grounds like these. Until our law is codified, it cannot be understood by the general body of the people, and law not understood naturally has no place in the intelligent judgment or the affections of the people. Neither can law be supreme in a community that does not cherish a loyal attachment to the law. The highest commendation of a perfect system of law has been pronounced in the words :—" All things and persons are subject to it, the very least as feeling its care, the greatest as not exempted from its control." That the law of Victoria should have supreme and universal sway in Victoria, and that it should be safe-guarded by the intelligent respect and the loyal affection of the whole people, must be the desire of every Victorian legislator. As an administrator of the law, I will use the fitting opportunity which this occasion presents of thanking the Victorian Legislature, on behalf of the Judiciary, for what it has already done in the direction of reforming by simplifying the law of Victoria, and of humbly expressing the earnest hope that Parliament will see fit to persevere in that course of reform on an enlargement of the lines which have now received the deliberate sanction of Parliament.

Mr. Speaker, may I, in conclusion, venture to solicit a favour of this Honourable House? It is, that my two colleagues with whom I have been more immediately associated in the work of consolidation and I may each be allowed to be the possessor, by the gift of the Houses of Parliament, of a copy of the Consolidation Statutes when completed and issued. Such a gift would be a pleasing memorial of our work, and a record that would be always dearly prized by each of us of the approval which the two Houses of Parliament have been graciously pleased to bestow upon that work.

And then His Honour withdrew, making his obeisances in like manner as upon entering the House, and the whole House rising again whilst His Honour was re-conducted by the Serjeant to the door of the House.

Ordered—That what has now been said by Mr. Speaker in presenting the thanks of this House to His Honour Chief Justice Higinbotham, together with His Honour's answer thereto, and the proceedings upon the occasion, be printed in the Votes of this day.

PRESENTATION COPIES OF CONSOLIDATING ACTS.—Mr. Munro moved, by leave, that in compliance with the request of His Honour Chief Justice Higinbotham, copies of the Consolidating Acts be presented to His Honour the Chief Justice, to Donald Mackinnon, Esquire, and to Francis Hugh Mackay, Esquire.

Question—put and resolved in the affirmative.

The whole scene was impressive, and will long be remembered by those who were present. The bound copies of the statutes were not ready in the lifetime of the Chief Justice. In the complete edition of the statutes, seven volumes, are included regulations made under different statutes, and the bringing of these up to date took nearly two years to complete. After his death the splendidly bound volumes were presented by the President and the Speaker to his son and myself, to be conveyed to Mrs. Higinbotham. They will be treasured in the family as heirlooms.

On the very day on which Parliament paid the Chief Justice the high compliment of the thanks of the two Houses, it inflicted on him and his brother judges a blow, which, had he known of it earlier, might have made him refuse the vote of thanks. Courts of justice have the power to draw up their own rules. The rules of the Supreme Court required revision, and the Court took the opportunity of the publication of the Consolidated Statutes to revise and publish a new body of rules. There is no doubt whatever that the new rules were drawn up and presented in a most workmanlike manner. The revision had engaged a large share of the attention of the judges for more than three years. Thus they described their work in a later report: "The rules in the civil jurisdiction of the Court were redrafted, and the rules in all the jurisdictions were amended and altered as seemed to us, upon consideration of various suggestions we had willingly received from different quarters, to be proper; and the whole of the rules were arranged in a form convenient for use." The judges allow herein that they had introduced various changes. The Chief Justice was not the judge who had most to do with the work. Mr. Justice Holroyd was the draftsman, Mr. Justice Williams helping him. The Chief Justice came in next, and then the new rules were submitted to the revision of all the judges. They were signed and sealed on November 11th, 1890, and were to come into force when the Courts met after the Long Vacation on the 1st of February following.

Members of the legal profession thought that the existing rules, in the main, were working well. They further thought that the time was inconvenient, and wished for a longer interval during which lawyers might study the new rules.

On December 4th, the Bar Committee approached the judges, asking that the rules should not come into force for six months. The judges declined this request. It is believed that there was some difference of opinion on the subject, but the view that prevailed was strongly supported by the Chief Justice and Mr. Justice Webb. They held that whenever the rules were to come into force they would not be studied until it was absolutely necessary, and that it was for the judges not for the Bar to decide. As a matter of tactics, perhaps this was not a politic answer. At any rate when it was received other opposition sprang up, proceeding from solicitors and from the Chamber of Commerce. The views of the latter had been already heard, but had not been in all respects adopted. By these three bodies, the Bar, the solicitors, and the Chamber of Commerce, an appeal was made to Parliament to annul the rules. A bill, giving the Governor in Council power to annul them, was passed through both Houses in a single day, and that the very day on which the Chief Justice was thanked. The bill went further than quashing the rules, for it took from the judges the power of publishing any rules of Court when Parliament was not sitting. By this clause it would seem as if Parliament thought that the judges of the Supreme Court, the six men perhaps most trusted in the land, were capable of bringing into force during the recess of Parliament the very rules which had just been rejected. With respect to the passing of this act the most astonishing element is that the bill passed through all its stages with so little comment or debate. The explanation offered is that it was all arranged in the lobby; many members must have thought it a formal matter to be arranged by lawyers, by the Attorney-General in the Lower, and by the Solicitor-General in the Upper House. Else it was incredible that a rebuff should be administered to the Supreme Court, or, as one newspaper put it, to the Chief Justice, without a single voice being raised against the measure. At times Parliament is a talking house; at times apparently it can be silent. No one denies the power of Parliament in this matter; the only thing denied is the propriety of its action. It is believed to be without parallel in any part of the world.

The following passages are quoted from the report of the judges for the year 1891. There is little doubt that they proceeded from the pen of the Chief Justice, who felt the action of Parliament very keenly :—

"While we are unaware of the reasons which influenced Parliament to pass this act, the intention of Parliament was made plain for the guidance of the Court and the Judges by the terms of the act itself. There is no room to doubt that the Legislature has signified through the Governor in Council its disapproval of all and each of the new rules, as made by the Court and Judges, and its preference for the previously existing rules. In view of this it would be highly improper in us to re-enact any one or more of the rules thus dissented from, and under these circumstances it is impossible for us to frame new rules such as we think would in various respects be of public advantage. . . . . It is obvious that a provision of this kind may injuriously prevent the immediate application of a remedy for an evil which called for our intervention under circumstances of urgency. We believe that no precedent for this enactment can be found in British or Victorian legislation relating to Courts of Justice or other bodies invested with similar legislative powers of a subordinate kind."

CHAPTER XXIX

THE END

THOUGH rather below the middle stature and size, Mr. Higinbotham was a strong man. A powerful frame, unusually well built, abstemious habits, and a sufficiency of exercise kept him in health : but beyond all doubt he worked too hard, and during the last five years of life this over-work told on his strength. When he was Attorney-General and Parliament was sitting, he lived at his office during the middle of each week, having a bed made up on the premises. Sometimes he would leave his home on a Monday, and not return until Friday evening. There is still an old attendant at the Crown Law Office who remembers how the Attorney-General used to work until three or four in the morning ; and then, after a short sleep and a row on the river, he would be at his office-table again at ten. He was forty-two when he left office, but his hair had turned white. He was nearly sixty-three when he commenced the second consolidation, and then after a judicial day of five hours or more, he would devote another five hours to the work of consolidation, which he never permitted to trench on the judicial time. These are specimens of excessive work at an interval of twenty-one years, but all his life through he was a willing slave to work. Ordinary judicial work, such as reserved judgments, often kept him out of bed until past one o'clock. Frequently when

work was pressing he would omit to take a satisfactory
luncheon, being consoled by his favourite cigar.   It is due to
the strength of his constitution that, in spite of such labours
as these, George Higinbotham's life nearly reached the span
allotted by the Psalmist.

More than five years before the end the first symptoms appeared of the heart trouble that proved fatal;
but at first it was not very serious.   Walking quickly
brought on a palpitation, which, if he stood for a couple of
minutes, would pass away.   A doctor did not make much to
him of the symptoms, but pointed out that old age was
coming on, and that a man over sixty must take care of
himself.   At the end of 1890, however, the heart trouble
became much worse.   During the year it had been evident
to his friends and subsequently to himself, that he was over-
taxing his capacity for work.   In December it almost
seemed as if the thanks of Parliament were going dramati-
cally to close his career.   The bulk of the consolidation fell
in 1889, but the work connected with it was carried on
through the whole of the next year.   On the very same day
as the thanks came the severe mortification in connection with
the new rules of court.   And in that month of December the
Chief Justice presided at an unusually heavy and protracted
trial, connected with the Premier Permanent Building
Society.   The trial was not over on Christmas Day, and
at its close strength seemed simply gone.   Having made
arrangements to spend the vacation at Lorne, after a few
days the Chief Justice went off to that pleasant and pretty
watering place.   To reach it a long coach drive over the
hills of the Otway Forest is necessary.   His condition after
arrival excited alarm, and Dr. Dunbar Hooper, his medical
attendant, was summoned from Melbourne by telegraph.
Mr. Higinbotham was suffering from complete physical and
nervous prostration, combined with insomnia; or when sleep
came, it was full of law work with so many legal problems to
solve that it gave no refreshment.   The measures taken,
however, proved efficacious; the doctor reports that he had
an exemplary patient; and the perfect rest of the vacation
enabled the Chief Justice to resume his work.

In 1887 the Chief Justice parted with his Brighton home,
a good offer having been made to him for it.   In earlier

years, hardly any offer would have tempted him, but feeling not so strong as formerly, he preferred to live nearer his work, and as his children were beginning to scatter in the world, his desire to retain the old home was greatly diminished. The daily journey by train was becoming too much for him. He took a conveniently situated house in Murphy Sreet, South Yarra. One day in 1889 he was travelling in a tramcar, and gave up his seat to a lady ; the crowding increased so that at last not only was he standing, but a very small foothold on the step was left to him, and as the car went rapidly round a sharp curve he was flung to the ground. Though no trouble ensued at the time, there is no doubt that the shaking did him harm.

During the last two years of life the Chief Justice tried to husband his strength very carefully. His mental powers were as good as ever, his judgment as sound ; his words carefully chosen lucidly expressed his meaning ; perhaps he was a little slower in taking in a statement, and in all physical movements he was feebler. Straitly he charged his doctor to say if he was unfit for the proper discharge of his official duties, in order that he might immediately resign. The doctor urged him to walk as little as possible, and never to travel by train or tram. A hansom took him every day to his work, and fetched him in the evening from it. Walking up the smallest hill or upstairs told upon his strength. There is little doubt that his life might have been prolonged, if he would have consented to take a holiday, which the Government of the day was not only willing, but anxious that he should take. His doctor told him he needed rest, but he would not take it. He shrank from the idea of abandoning his work, if he could possibly continue it, and so he sacrificed himself to his notion of duty, and may be said to have died in harness. Each Christmas, when the work of the year was over, he seemed to be in a state closely bordering on prostration.

In September, 1890, Mr. Justice Webb died, and some of those who stood round his open grave in the Melbourne Cemetery commented upon the frail look of his colleague the Chief Justice, who in the courts on the day before St. Michaelmas Day pronounced his eulogy. The speech was most impres-

sive, especially in the part where it was pointed out that
duty had been the ruling motive of Mr. Justice Webb's life.
Some who heard it thought that the Chief Justice never
spoke better.   Rather more than a year later he was present
at the funeral of Sir James MacBain, the President of the
Legislative Council, and one who saw him was much shocked
at his fragile appearance.   The Chief remarked that the
pioneers of the colony were fast passing away, to which a hope
was expressed in reply that His Honour would long be spared.
He shook his head, and saying "Good-bye," entered his
carriage.

During the year 1892, three attacks of *angina pectoris*
came on, but they yielded to medical treatment: and when
the legal vacation began in December, 1892, the Chief
Justice seemed to be in better health and to possess greater
strength than at Christmas in either of the two preceding
years.   But the appearance was deceptive.   Though he
seemed fairly well on the Christmas Day, which fell that year
on a Sunday, and even for a day or two later, in the middle
of the week his health collapsed once more, and it was then
with his doctor's consent he decided to resign before the end
of the vacation.   The end came with great suddenness.   At
half-past one in the afternoon he was talking to his son who,
to his father's great delight, had just come down from the
country.   Some half an hour later an attack of *angina
pectoris* came on with violence.   His wife alone was with
him at the end.   The paroxysm lasted less than half an
hour, but without much to show that it was worse than
others.   It was nearly half-past two when George Higinbotham died on the last day of the year 1892.   His last
look was an upward glance, apparently of surprised and
joyful recognition.

Amongst the last scenes of his life it is as well to preserve
the following pathetic description of his last sentence, for it
deserves greater permanence than can be expected for it in
the columns of a newspaper.[1]   The last day the Chief Justice
sat was on Thursday, December 22nd, 1892 ; and the last
sentence recorded by him was on a lad named Michael Byrt,
who was released from a penalty of twenty-two months'

1 *The Herald*, January 4th, 1893.

imprisonment on sureties being entered into for his good behaviour.   The reporter continues :—

> To those in Court, the scene was an impressive one.   The Court gradually thinned after the other prisoners were taken away, and only the lad Byrt and a few of the Court officials remained.
>
> Twenty minutes must have elapsed, the delay arising through a search for the forms necessary for the lad's liberation.   With bowed head, the Chief sat calm and dignified, never evincing the slightest impatience at the unseemly delay.
>
> On the forms being filled and scanned carefully, the judge, looking gently over his spectacles, said : —
>
> " Can you write ?"
>
> " Yes, sir," said the boy.
>
> " You have been sentenced to twenty-two months' imprisonment. which will not be carried into effect if you are of good behaviour. You are a young lad. and Miss Sutherland has promised to get you employment in the country.   Go away into the country and remain away.   You have a long life before you yet. and ample time to retrieve your misbehaviour."
>
> To those in Court the scene was an affecting one.   The gentle accents of the softened voice and the kindly advice were all characteristics of the man.   The boy was affected, the habitués of the Court were silent.
>
> Then, said the associate inquiringly, "*Sine die*, your Honour?"
>
> "*Sine die !* " said the judge.
>
> " This honourable court stands adjourned *sine die*," repeated the crier —and it stands so still.

Amongst his last public utterances the two following should be included.   The public weal was ever in his mind.   Three days before his death he wrote to Sir George Verdon about the Queen's Fund, of which they were trustees :—

> I incline to think that as trustees of a public charity we ought, *ceteris paribus*, to do what we lawfully can. though in a small way, to uphold public credit at present, and that we might therefore invest the £1.600, when available, in Victorian Treasury Bonds, or Inscribed Stock, or Government Debentures.

And very shortly before. writing on the business of the Brighton Library, of which he was a trustee, and in which he always preserved his interest, he gave this admirable advice :—

> This colony is passing through a grave financial crisis.   Please inform the committee of the library, with my compliments, that it

becomes an imperative duty devolving upon them to keep their expenditure within their income ; under no circumstances should they increase their indebtedness one penny.

It may be added that a few months afterwards the financial crisis became much more grave, but the calamities of 1893, caused chiefly by Scotch and English investors hastily demanding back the money they had thrust upon Australia, George Higinbotham was mercifully spared from seeing. They would have distressed him sorely.

The Chief Justice left behind him injunctions that his funeral was to be strictly private. It would be unnecessary to say that the motive for this was simply that he had no liking for display, were it not that the injunction has been publicly ascribed to cynicism, and disappointment with public life. There really was nothing of the cynic in his nature, and though no doubt there was much in public life that he would have preferred otherwise, he was ever ready to acknowledge that his fellow citizens had treated him well, and that, in Browning's words, he had " his deserts and a little more." He disliked pomp, and though most punctilious about attending funerals, he specially disliked funeral pomp,

All that makes death a hideous show.

Telegrams came from distant places, showing that friends and admirers were prepared to take long journeys to be present. His Excellency the Governor came to town ; two of the Puisne Judges came to the street ; the Premier wrote to me that he had wavered for an hour whether to come or not to come ; but the wishes of the deceased were respected, and the funeral was strictly private.

Various public bodies, and not in Melbourne nor in Victoria alone, passed resolutions of regret, and of condolence with relatives. When Parliament met a few days later, both Houses passed such resolutions, and very interesting speeches were delivered by old friends, younger admirers, and old opponents. When the Courts assembled after the vacation, the Senior Puisne Judge (now Sir Hartley Williams), and the new Chief Justice (now Sir John Madden), spoke words of regret, of praise, and of admiration. But if it be allowable to draw distinctions, the earliest was the best. Only a few days after the death the following address was delivered in the Practice Court by the Vacation Judge (Mr. Justice Hodges) :—

"Gentlemen of the Legal Profession,—Since this Court last sat, Victoria has lost the very first of her foremost citizens, and justice has been deprived of its ablest administrator and chief ornament. Almost with the last breath of the dying year the Chief Justice breathed his last, and members of the legal profession and the Bench have lost an ideally perfect pattern in accordance with which they might endeavour to shape their lives. Every one who has practised at the Bar with the late Chief Justice will know the infinite pains he took to master all the facts of any cause entrusted to him, and the laws applicable to those facts—how careful he was in forming an opinion, and how stoutly and ably he supported the opinion which he had so carefully formed—they will remember how courageous an advocate he was, and yet how chivalrous a foe.

"They will remember that while by every word and deed he showed that he recognised and acted upon the obligation of the counsel to the client, he yet felt himself under a mightier obligation to the cause of truth, and that he never—even in the excitement of an appeal to the jury, or of an address to the Court—transgressed the limits of honest, honourable advocacy.

"Some twelve years ago the Hon. George Higinbotham was elevated to a seat on the Supreme Court Bench, and from that time to the time of his death he devoted himself to the duties of his office as Judge and Chief Justice. To the discharge of these duties he brought a strength of will and a singleness and persistency of purpose rarely equalled—never surpassed. And combined with the iron will of fixed purpose of the hard man there was the gentleness and sweetness of woman. The combination of the qualities compelled admiration and inspired affection. He brought, too, the cultured and the specially trained mind. He had made himself familiar with that "codeless myriad of precedent, that wilderness of single instances," whereof the common law is to a huge extent made up. He brought, too, an inexhaustible patience, an untiring industry, an intense earnestness, and a zeal that never flagged. Want of truth or of integrity could not be breathed in the same sentence with his name. How perfect a judge these qualities made him can be known only by those who practised before him in the seat of justice. The judicial manner, too, was perfect, for this was but the eternal manifestation of his fine and noble nature and of the judicial character of his mind. And the greatest good fortune this young country could have had is that men like him and Sir William Stawell have filled the office of Chief Justice in it.

"Britain may have greater lawyers; Britain may have greater statesmen; Britain may have craftier politicians; but Britain has no son with a stronger, gentler, firmer, more tender, nobler nature than the man who lately presided in this Court."

CHAPTER XXX

THE MAN

THE task that lies before the writer in this chapter he feels to
be the hardest part of the work he has undertaken. He
therefore asked a friend's help, and the latter replied that
"critics could no more measure" the hero of this book
"than the caterpillars can measure Mount Everest." Yet
it is certainly necessary to give some general estimate of Mr.
Higinbotham's character, and an attempt must be made.
The friend has sent the following :—

"Higinbotham stood alone : neither ancient nor modern
degeneracy reached him. Try to name his analogue, and you
feel to the full his loneliness. You think of Bayard and Sir
Philip, of Pascal and Francis Horner, but standing below none
of these, he stands beside none. . . In one respect he fell far
below many wretches whom the world calls great. I never
knew an intelligent man whose estimates of other men were
so utterly inacurate. He was a decided optimist, and his
sympathy with the unfortunate was so extreme that his
judgments of them were almost always untrustworthy. Where

the successful were concerned, he was more discerning. [One or two illustrations are given.] . . . In short, Higinbotham, no matter how often deceived, would judge of others by himself.

"Rienzi was not a more singular compound of strength and weakness, and he often reminded me of the child with the thunderbolt in private; but when the thunder rolled out in the forum or the senate, even malignant party hatred saw only the giant. Yet this Hercules was often the dupe of inferior men to whom he deferred absurdly. His extreme humility, optimism, and lamentable lack of world-wisdom, accounted for this failing from which his habitual self-respect should have saved him. Of Rienzi's vanity he had none. From responsibility he shrank instinctively, as long as conviction did not compel him to assume it; but feeling the compulsion he would have assumed the responsibility of anything. His colleagues dreaded his injudicious enthusiasm for outspoken truth, and sat on thorns often enough while he was on his legs. They revered him, I might say loved him, as they did none other. Said one, 'I never believed in the admirable Crichton until I knew him'; and another, 'If Higinbotham had lived 400 years ago, they'd have made him a saint, and we'd have been worshipping him now.' A member not given to effusive saluting, said, 'To Higinbotham I must always take off my hat.' He took the arm of an unsteady acquaintance once, but the latter said, 'No, I'm not in a fit state to walk with a gentleman, nor to touch *you*.'

"The man, the man rose high above the politician or the judge. The highest type of intelligence and integrity yet vouchsafed to Australia was greatly admired of the many, but he had also, what he valued more, the love of many. So gifted, generous, gentle, true and brave, this orb has evolved but few such men. There may in other worlds where not evil but good is dominant be many such paragons, and many Koh-i-noors, but on this planet such specimens of sweetness and light rarely read their history in a nation's eyes, though, let us hope, they occasionally blush unseen in the sequester'd vales of life. Higinbotham disapproved—I might say, despised—epitaphs; but if his place of rest is ever to be indicated by anything of the kind, it should set forth his love of sacrifice for his fellow men. It should be an improvement on the following :—

> " This lowly goal foreclosed a high career :
> Australia's best and greatest moulders here :
> His was the hero-heart, the monarch-mind :
> Honour him ever, for he loved mankind."

Even after this excellent estimate, which readers who knew him not will think exaggerated, a little more detail may not be out of place.

The preceding pages have been written in vain if the reader does not see that George Higinbotham was a man of principle. Conscientious thoroughness ran through his whole life, public and private, political and forensic. The principles were carefully thought out by himself and for his own guidance. When the path of duty was thus clearly indicated, there was never a moment's hesitation about following it : no compromise in politics, no wavering, no paltering with the right. Never had any man a stronger sense of duty. This might be thought by some to indicate a hard character ; and there was a puritan strain of sternness that ran through his nature, but it would be a complete mistake to regard Higinbotham as a hard man. His sympathy, his courtesy, his generosity—all contend against such a view.

Higinbotham's admiration for the Duke of Wellington has been mentioned earlier. In thinking of his own character lines from Tennyson's *Ode* will spring to the mind : " He never spoke against a foe." In all the bitterness of party conflict, violent as were his attacks on the party opposed to him, never a single word offensive to an individual passed his lips. Nor was this due solely to a restraint placed upon himself in public. Those who knew him best knew that even in the most private conversation he would not speak against others. This habit he carried even to an extreme, as he would be slow to condemn even the most notorious scoundrel. Once when he was walking with a friend, the latter censured a politician for certain wrong-doing. There was no doubt the deed had been done, and no doubt that it was wrong ; but Higinbotham disliked speaking evil of a man behind his back, and at once silenced his friend. With all this there was never any doubt whether he condemned wrong.

It has been shown that he maintained the dignity of his office. This official pride was perfectly consistent with an extreme simplicity of life and manner. He energetically dissented from the doctrine with which a well-known treatise on political economy opens—"Civilisation consists in the multiplication of wants." The contrary view was his—that the truly civilised man diminished his wants. He lived, therefore, in the simplest manner and with a simplicity worthy of Washington or of Cincinnatus. In the hale vigour of his manhood, he could even have accepted the life of Thoreau. Simplicity was his ideal. No one was more unassuming in his manner. A young Englishman, on the grand tour of our times, met him at my table, and must have misunderstood the words of introduction, for soon he was laying down the law to him, saying, "I am a barrister, you know, and if you knew the law," . . . "Who is that nice old gentleman?" he asked on leaving the room, and could have wished that the earth would swallow him, when he found he had been enlightening on law the Chief Justice of the colony.

The Chief's manner to young men was most delightful. No one was ever snubbed by him, and they simply worshipped him. Indeed his manners altogether seemed borrowed from an earlier world. The charm lay in the combination of perfect courtesy with simplicity. Here our chief citizen was seen leading a blind man over a crossing, and ere parting slipping something into his hand. And Landor's dignified lines recur to memory :— —

The blind man
Knew that his king was leading him in-doors,
Before he heard the voice that marshalled Greece.

Or in another place the following incident occurred, of which the description is taken from a funeral sermon preached by a minister quite unknown to him or to me :—

I was once fortunate enough to be the sole witness of an incident which reveals his character in this respect. When living some years ago in the neighbourhood of Melbourne University. I observed, from the balcony of my house, a man attempting to lead a heavy draught horse along Grattan Street. The animal refused to be led, and the man then made several ineffectual attempts to mount the refractory creature. At that moment the Chief Justice came up, and, observing the man's difficulty, immediately extended his hand—as a footstool—

assisted the man to a seat on the horse's back, and then passed on
quietly without comment. The incident lives in my memory as an
illustration of nobility of character, destitute of that petty pride
which so often cankers real greatness. Surely such an action is in
accordance with the word of Christ. "He that would be chief among
you shall be servant of all."

But the most beautiful presentation of his courtesy was
always towards women. It was quite regardless of rank or
personal attractiveness. Off would go his hat to his cook
with a gracious bow with which another might greet a duchess.
In the last year of his life a young lady had been spending
the evening at his house, and wanted a cab. It was raining,
and he started off to fetch the cab. She, knowing that his
health was weak, said, " Do let the maid go ! " " My dear young
lady," was the grave reply, " the maid also is a woman." In
tram or train he always ceded his seat to a lady, and once the
cession led, as has been pointed out, to a most unpleasant fall.

It need hardly be said that all servants and dependents
were warmly attached to him, and would do anything for him.
An old Irishman, an attendant at the Crown Law Office,
simply worships his memory. Twenty years after Mr. Higinbotham had ceased to be Attorney-General he was admitted
to the Chief Justice's chambers to see him, and left the
room in tears. It is not allowed to speak of the hallowed
intimacies of family life ; but I may be permitted to say that
children took to him readily, and that better than most men
he understood what Victor Hugo calls *l'art d'être grandpère.*

His gracious sympathetic courtesy was but the flower of a
real goodness in the nature of the man. In spite of what
the poet says about " the fruit of loyal nature and of noble
mind," good manners may consort with a bad heart. From
earliest years there is evidence to show that in this case goodness was the root. A relative remembers a conversation held
with him when he was a boy, or little more than a boy. She
was declaring that God meant His creatures to be happy here
on earth. George broke in : " No ! not happiness, goodness,"
and with so much feeling that fifty years afterwards the relative
remembered the talk. One of his college friends testifies that
they all thought it would be quite impossible for Higinbotham to do anything wrong. And so the chain of evidence
continues.

Oftentimes in the political part of Mr. Higinbotham's career, jeers were directed at his conscientiousness. His opponents, according to Hansard, said that he spoke as if he had a monopoly of the article. He certainly had much more than most men. In the later part of his political time he was persuaded to become President of a Building Society. Many working men lived in his constituency; it was advisable that they should be induced to save, and his name would help in that good cause. Thackeray speaks of the "thorns in the cushion" of an editor's chair. There were thorns enough in the cushion of this president's chair to make it most uncomfortable. He would take nothing for granted, and in consequence protracted the meetings of the committee in a way that vexed the ordinary business man; and with all this close examination of accounts, titles, and valuations the president never felt as if he had mastered the problem, but was very uneasy because of his responsibilities. An auditor tells how the president sat through the monthly examination of accounts, and asked about everything. This presidency Mr. Higinbotham resigned when he went on to the Bench, and then he breathed more freely. The members of the committee entertained a warm regard for him, and presented him with an illuminated address to express it; but business went on more rapidly under his successor. Greater conscientiousness, it should be added, would have saved many Melbourne financial institutions from the ruin that in the last few years has overwhelmed them.

The following lighter story is told of Higinbotham's conscientiousness:—

In his barrister days he was returning from an Assize town on a coach. It was on a Sunday, and rain was pouring down. At each stoppage another barrister, of more convivial turn and more elastic conscience, warmed the inner man with hot whisky and water. He would dilate upon its merits to the dripping Higinbotham, who would not break the law; and the teasing continued until at length in pity the other pointed out that having travelled a certain distance they were *bonâ-fide* travellers within the meaning of the Act, and Higinbotham, not then a teetotaler, quaffed the desirable refreshment.

All testimony goes to prove that he was absolutely

unselfish. Many will take great trouble for a friend; he would for a stranger. In his standard of public life he was even regarded as Quixotic. For instance, Members of Parliament are presented with a free pass on the railways of the colony. Unless he was travelling on public business Mr. Higinbotham would never use his pass; not that he condemned the use of the pass in others. This was part of the decision by which he would not take pay for his service in Parliament, though he voted for the bill that enabled members to be paid.

At Ballarat not long ago, the Court rose on a Saturday, just in time to make it impossible to catch the last train to Melbourne and home. The Associate asked : " Shall I send quickly, and stop the train ?" The Chief made reply : " Would they stop the train for any poor old woman, who came up late ? No! then they should not for me. My work is done, and I am not on duty now." As a matter of fact the station-master, having heard that the Chief Justice was probably coming, delayed the train unasked, for a quarter of an hour ; and when the passengers heard the reason of the delay, not one of them grumbled. But the Chief Justice remained in Ballarat until Monday.

Irishmen as a rule are not deficient in humour, and Higinbotham's apparent lack of humour was not so much innate as the result of training. Early in life he came to the conclusion that ridicule was wrong. It hurt the feelings of others, and therefore should be discouraged. A near relative once remarked that when Higinbotham heard a joke he looked all round it to see that no one was hurt before he laughed. When subjected to that treatment humour evaporates. He could certainly enjoy a good story, but this self-restraint in face of a joke greatly diminished his appreciation of the humorous in litera-ture or in conversation. Many times he has been heard to express contempt for a " joker of jokes." It is hard to condemn the sacrifice to so excellent a motive, but the atmosphere of the world would indeed be turning gray, if the good mean to abandon the gift of humour. Why should the Devil have all the good tunes, or all the good jokes?

But Higinbotham's unselfish thought for others is most shown in an extraordinary generosity in all his dealings with money-matters. He was the most liberal of subscribers to public objects. If he was a member of a committee and there was a deficit, he would make up the deficit. At one time the vestry at Emerald Hill, at another the Brighton Public Library, had their accounts balanced in this pleasant manner. Many churches, the very whereabouts of which he had been puzzled to discover, were helped with a generous subscription; nor did he discriminate and give to churches only with the views of which he was in sympathy. He thought that all did good, and he helped all who asked. In his early years in the colony, and when he was not at all well off himself, a clergyman meeting him told him a story, how his wife on the previous evening had taken all the money that she had in the world (£22) in her pocket to a missionary meeting, where her pocket had been picked. In telling the story he had no thought of suggesting help. That evening the sum of £22 reached him "from Thomas and George Higin-botham." His charity—to use that word in its most ordinary sense—his almsgiving was unbounded. He once told me that he knew no other rule than "give to him that asketh thee"; and I urged him not to publish his doctrine, for if it were once known, not even the longest purse could stand the demands that would be at once made upon it. As a matter of fact he gave most liberally, and was often deceived. While he had chambers at 73, Chancery Lane, his giving led to a continued stream of very undesirable persons up the staircase, so that a general grand remonstrance from all the barristers in the building was prepared, and he had to put a stop to this part of his benevolence, but he did it most unwillingly. For years he was the prey to the begging letter-writer, answering generally with a cheque by return of post. One mother and daughter, in circumstances absolutely unknown to him, almost lived upon his bounty. The younger lady married, and even Mr. Higinbotham thought the line had been overstepped, when he received an application from her to provide her with a *trousseau*! In all this he let his kindness of heart bear sway over his reason. He knew that he ought to make inquiries, but he was far too busy to inquire himself. When, however, the Charity Organisation Society of Melbourne was established, his reason recognised the soundness of its principles, and he used the society for the purpose of inquiry. When the secretary was able to recommend a case as one in which money could be given without mischief, His Honour was ready to give liberally. In the distressful winter of 1892 he placed in my hands a sum of £10 a week to meet the cases of want, and he continued this for many weeks. In this as in all his charity he pursued the good old doctrine of not letting the right hand know what the left was doing. To the frequent appeals in the papers he would contribute anonymously. Many have written to tell me of his kindness to them, but not a tithe is known. One misstatement, however, it may be as well to correct. It is not true that in his garden at Brighton he erected a shed for tramps.

It is venturing on more delicate ground to pass from the analysis of character to that of motive, and to discuss his religion. Deep religious feeling was the mainspring of George Higinbotham's life, but as with most deep things there was but little sign of it on the surface. Many came to think that he was alienated from religion, because he was no longer at one with orthodoxy. His was a religious nature, but the character of his creed was of the simplest, and may be expressed in a single line, the first line of the Apostles' Creed, "I believe in God the Father Almighty." On the one side, it is certain, he had renounced what may be called the Creed of Christendom; on the other he was just as far from accepting the modern creedless creed of agnosticism. "You call yourself an agnostic," he once said to a young friend, in a manner so kind that it disarmed the criticism of all sting, "then let me tell you you possess the most uncomfortable of creeds." Speaking on education to the Church of England Congress in 1882, he said :—"I do not myself share the self-mutilating creed of the agnostic. It is not a new, and I believe that it must necessarily be only a transient, phase of human thought." He did not later approach more closely to the agnostics than when he uttered these sentences.

But as far as Christianity was concerned he with countless others had loosed from old moorings. He desired that religious education should be given in schools, but the religion that he would have had taught to children was an undogmatic Christianity, or if that be impossible, our common Christianity taught in an undogmatic spirit. Christian teachers deny that such a thing is possible: they would not have it, they would not strive after it. They tore his scheme to pieces, and some of them would have torn him too.

Not long before his death Mr. Higinbotham was commenting to a friend on the comfort he derived from the hymn that begins with the words "Abide with me." "Man," he said, "is a poor helpless mortal. God is his Almighty Father, his only refuge."

The most distinctive statement of Mr. Higinbotham's religion is to be found in the lecture on "Science and Religion," delivered on the 1st of August, 1883, and afterwards published.[1] It was an appeal to laymen amongst whom "there is a certain kind of freemasonry upon these burning questions of religious thought," with whom the influence of the pulpit has declined. To what is this waning due? To the influence of modern science and its revelations. Science is not opposed to the religion of Christ, but the Christian religion as now taught is not identical with the religion of Christ. The churches at present have conflicting systems of belief contained in hostile creeds, articles, confessions, and standards of faith. It is the duty of the laity to demand that compulsory subscription to these creeds be abandoned. Laymen must cast out from their own minds and from the Christian churches the spectres of old and now discredited fallacies.

They must simplify their faith in order to make it more real; and thus he concluded :—

For my part, I believe—and this, my deep conviction, is the last result of my reflections, which I shall "whisper" to you, my brother laymen, to-night—that it were the part of highest wisdom for you and for me, and for all thinkers everywhere, in this day of rising floods and beating wind, to withdraw resolutely and with all speed from all the lower standpoints of thought that are now no longer tenable, and to meet on the high central platform of thought—the rock of all ages, whereon every human mind may, if it will, build for itself a secure and indestructible abode—God, "the living Will that shall endure when all that seems shall suffer shock "—God, revealed to the intellect in every minute movement of matter, and in all the phenomena of this vast universe—God, revealed anew to the intellect, and also to the responsive human heart, as the Father, the Friend, the Guide,

---

[1] Samuel Mullen, Collins Street, Melbourne.

and the Support of our race, and of every member of it, in the simple but profound philosophy, and also in the sublimest life, of Jesus of Nazareth, the Light of the World.

People who like to affix names or labels to a statement of faith, will at once say that this is what in earlier years was called Arianism, in the last century Deism, in the present day Unitarianism. At the opening of a new Unitarian church in Melbourne, in July, 1887, the Chief Justice, whose maternal grandfather was Unitarian, delivered an address, in which he described the Unitarian Church as alone of all the Christian churches preserving in modern civilization the idea of the unity of God,—it alone carrying the lighted torch by which, according to its belief, the dark steps of humanity require to be guided.

Unfortunately to many minds the name of Unitarian connotes a type of religion which they regard as unchristian. It is impossible to regard as unchristian so reverent a follower of Christ as was George Higinbotham. He followed, not Christ's followers, but Christ himself ; not Christian teaching, but Christ's own teaching. In his absolute negation of self, he was a most Christ-like man. No one ever acted more on the words of the Lord Jesus, "It is more blessed to give than to receive." Fearless of consequences, he followed Truth wherever she led him.

"He was a Christian theist," writes one friend. "If Unitarian, then a Christian Unitarian," says another. "If he did not believe in the deity of Jesus, he believed in His divinity." A touching little story is told of a friend who called upon Mr. Higinbotham, angry with a neighbour who had offended him, and anxious to have the law of him. Higinbotham dissuaded his visitor on prudential and worldly grounds. At length he turned, and putting his arm in his friend's, said : "What would the Master have done ?" But with this reverent discipleship it was not inconsistent to war against the jarring Christianity of the churches.

The following estimate of his religious views is taken from an English paper to which it was contributed by one who knew him well :—

"Not recognised as among the orthodox !"—Chief Justice Higinbotham little cared for that. His was a mind that followed the straight line of conviction in spite of party or personal considerations. His conduct was based upon sincere religiousness. "His life," says one who knew him intimately, "was the outcome of a fervent, devout, reverent belief in and love of the religion of Jesus Christ, and this, not only as distinguished from but opposed to the so-called Christianity of Ecclesiasticism." "To his emancipation from the toils and trammels of an Ecclesiastical Christianity," continues the same correspondent, "may largely be attributed the development of his whole nature, intellectual, moral and spiritual, as it showed itself practically in his private life as well as in his public career. Each of these was in beautiful harmony with, and confirmation of the other." Another close observer of his life writes: "He was a true servant of God. Everything he did was done in the love and fear of God. He gave himself for his fellow men ; he spent himself and his substance in their service, never thinking of himself for one moment. People of all kinds came to him for assistance and advice, and did not go empty away." The ideal which he cherished long before emigrating to Victoria was that "it is the privilege of human life to do as much good as ever you can, and then—to die." His religious views were of the type illustrated in the writings of Dr. Channing and Dr. James Martineau, for the latter of whom he cherished an ever-growing esteem and veneration. He fully recognised that before the spread of such views can be largely effected much must be abolished in modern Christianity.

A remark to the following effect was made by another paper : " A century and a half ago his childlike faith would have sent him to the stake ; and half a century ago he would have been ostracised for his opinions." The dates assigned are certainly too modern, but there is little doubt that at an earlier period, martyrdom, and at a nearer date, social ostracism would have been Higinbotham's fate. To our own time has been reserved a toleration which is not indifference ; so that the admiration of many friends and of a far larger circle was the meed of his pure and beneficent life, and of the high principles that sprang from his genuine faith in God.

Little has been said of personal appearance, for even many words sometimes convey no picture to the mind. A single glance at the portraits reproduced in this volume will give a truer idea than carefully-constructed sentences. An extraordinary uprightness of bearing—a more than soldierly straightness—was, I remember, my own first impression of him, but it was rapidly followed by the thought of the pleasantness of his countenance. During the deadlock a paper spoke of his "wolfish cruelty," because his side would not yield its position in the contest, which was hurting others.

That evening Higinbotham was sitting on the Treasury Bench, gazing placidly upwards, when a reporter of that paper, looking down from the gallery, commented on the sweetness of his face, and ironically remarked, " Doesn't he look like a wolf ? "   Some years later a doctor told me that Higinbotham had called at his house, but not finding him in had gone away without leaving his name.   He asked the maid to describe his visitor, and she burst out : " Oh ! sir, he had the face of an angel."

The following remark was uttered nearly thirty years ago : " Mr. Higinbotham deserves no credit for being good and great ; look at his face and forehead, and you see he must be both ; *he* can't help himself, as Socrates could, and did."

All that is mortal of George Higinbotham lies buried in the Brighton Cemetery, not many paces from the broken column raised in memory of "The Poet Gordon."   Over his grave there is a simple granite cross with the text—"The memory of the just is blessed."   A few ericas are planted in the corners of the grave, and over the greater part of it mignonette runs riot.   When last I was there, the scent of this, his favourite flower, was filling the air, and I thought of the lines

Only the actions of the just
Smell sweet and blossom in the dust.

INDEX

INDEX